MW01286134

# LUKE IRONTREE & THE LAST VAMPIRE WAR

**Luke Irontree & The Last Vampire War**
Book 0 - The Centurion Immortal
Book 1 - Dark Fangs Rising - March 22, 2022
Book 2 - Dark Fangs Raging - April 19, 2022
Book 3 - Dark Fangs Descending* - May 17, 2022
Book 4 - Blood Empire Reborn* - July 12, 2022
Book 5 - Blood Empire Avenged* - August 9, 2022
Book 6 - Blood Empire Burning* - September 6, 2022
Book 7 - Blood Empire Collapsing* - October 4, 2022
Book 8 - Ancient Sword Falling* - November 29, 2022
Book 9 - Ancient Sword Unyielding* - December 27, 2022
Book 10 - Ancient Sword Shattering* - February 7, 2023

**The Luke Irontree Historical Adventures**
Rise of the Centurio Immortalis - April 5, 2022
Fall of the Centurio Immortalis* - May 31, 2022
The Moonlight Centurion* - November 1, 2022
The Highway Centurion* - January 24, 2023

*Forthcoming

# DARK FANGS RAGING

## LUKE IRONTREE & THE LAST VAMPIRE WAR

### C. THOMAS LAFOLLETTE

BROKEN WORLD PUBLISHING

DARK FANGS RAGING
C. Thomas Lafollette

A Broken World Publication
13820 NE Airport Way
Suite #K395495
Portland, OR 97251-1158
Dark Fangs Raging
Copyright © 2022 by C. Thomas Lafollette
ISBN 978-1-949410-42-6 (ebook);
ISBN 978-1-949410-43-3 (paperback)


Cover Design: Ravven
Edited by: Suzanne Lahna
Copy Editing & Proofreading: Amy Cissell

# CONTENTS

Content Warning                                    vii
Pronunciation Guide & Author's Notes                xi

Chapter 1                                             1
Chapter 2                                            11
Chapter 3                                            23
Chapter 4                                            31
Chapter 5                                            43
Chapter 6                                            51
Chapter 7                                            63
Chapter 8                                            79
Chapter 9                                            87
Chapter 10                                           95
Chapter 11                                          103
Chapter 12                                          111
Chapter 13                                          119
Chapter 14                                          125
Chapter 15                                          137
Chapter 16                                          153
Chapter 17                                          163
Chapter 18                                          179
Chapter 19                                          189
Chapter 20                                          197
Chapter 21                                          209
Chapter 22                                          223
Chapter 23                                          235
Chapter 24                                          249
Chapter 25                                          267
Chapter 26                                          283
Chapter 27                                          295
Epilogue                                            307
Leave a Review                                      315
Luke Irontree Will Return In                        317

Newsletter                                  331
Acknowledgments                             333
About the Author                            335
Also by C. Thomas Lafollette             337

# CONTENT WARNING

This book contains some gore and body horror. There is also a brief, non-specific reference to child abuse and domestic violence.

*For my Mom*
*Thanks for being supportive*

# PRONUNCIATION GUIDE &
# AUTHOR'S NOTES

**Pronunciation:** Latin names and words are mentioned throughout the book and are intended to be read with the classical Latin pronunciation. For instance, "c" is always pronounced hard, like a "k." "U" is always a short "oo" sound. "V" typically sounds like a "w." There are plenty of resources on the internet if you wish to learn more about Classical Latin pronunciation.

- Lucius – Loo-kih-oos
- Silvanius – Sihl-wahn-ih-oos
- Ferrata – Fehr-rah-tah
- Cassius – Cahs-sih-oos
- Jung-sook — Yoong-sook

**Latin Words:** Latin words are used for effect and to add to the "flavor" of the story, not to reflect Latin grammar/declensions/conjugations.

**Anachronisms:** It's nearly impossible to write historical settings without some anachronisms, especially when you're writing scenes set nearly 2,000 years in the past. Those used are done so intentionally for the purpose of story telling and to convey sentiments that would be recognizable to people then and now. Also, there are vampires.

# ONE

LUKE REACHED up from the backseat of Pablo's pickup and patted Delilah on the shoulder. "It's time."

"Remind me why Pablo can't drop us at the front door?" Delilah folded her arms across her chest, looking mildly disgruntled.

Pablo shook his head. "I'm not particularly interested in having my pickup and its license plate recorded by any nosy bouncers or security cameras. We're trying to keep this anti-vamp operation of ours under wraps. They don't need to know Clark Kent is really Pablo Sandoval."

"He's right," Luke agreed.

"Yeah, but it's raining, and I don't want to walk through it," Delilah replied, her tone laden with annoyance and just a hint of a pout.

"It's just a good Oregon drizzle. You'll dry off before you get your drink," Luke replied.

"I better not have to wait that long for a drink," Delilah mumbled.

Delilah and Luke popped out of their respective passenger side doors and strode down the block and around the corner leading to the hottest new club in town—Red Velvet Room. They set a pace and bold stride that would have looked cool and dangerous in slow motion. A gust of wind caught the corner of Delilah's dark red leather three-quarter trench coat and flipped the bottom portion out.

Their cool quickly ended as they queued up with the rest of people waiting to get into the club. Eschewing his normal plain black hoodie, Luke's hooded jacket was stylish and simple. He coupled it with expensive shoes and designer jeans, hoping the combo would ensure Luke's entrance—that and a $100 bill he planned to palm to the beefy guy at the door. Delilah, with a few more months of growth on her teeny weenie afro, wore her trench and tall soled, heavy boots and looked like a stylish hero in a 1970s Blaxploitation film. Luke ran his fingers through his slightly curly hair, his hand coming back damp but smelling nicely of product.

"Don't mess with your hair. You need to look good to get in. The damp is good on the curls, though." Delilah inspected his hair to ensure everything, waves cresting like whitecaps in a rough sea, remained in order. "OK, you didn't mess anything up."

"Thanks." Luke smirked at her.

"And you're sure everything is set up?" Delilah asked.

Luke nodded. "Yes. We're good. You ready with the soundtrack?"

"Yeah, although I don't see why you asked. They have a DJ, don't they?"

"They do, but you've got better taste…most likely. Besides, when the action goes down, I'm guessing the DJ is going to be MIA when it comes to spinning." He added the "most likely" to goad her a bit. Delilah always insisted that her taste was impeccable, and certainly better than Pablo's and Luke's.

When they got to the front, the musclebound guy gave their IDs a once over then collected their door fee—and Luke's gratuity—and sent them inside. They made for the empty table near the DJ booth which was situated under one of the speakers dangling from the ceiling, allowing the sound to project over their spot without being louder than they wanted.

"I'll get the drinks," Delilah said, casting a glance toward the bar. "He's serving the women first."

"Good idea. I don't want to give him an opportunity to give me too much of a look over if Cassius has nosed around my description. I'll take a pilsner." Luke tucked into the booth so he could watch the room.

The bartender gave off strong vampire vibes that pinged Luke's vampy senses and made his fingers itch to pull the gladius that wasn't currently on his person. Returning a few minutes later with a couple beers, Delilah set them down and slid into the other side of the booth. The bartender's gaze had flicked to Delilah a couple times as he'd watched her cross the floor. Luke hoped he was admiring the tall Black woman's curves and not eying them suspiciously.

Delilah, ostensibly watching the dancing, surveyed the area, getting a feel for the space and obstacles. Luke had shown her pictures he'd taken when the club was empty, but seeing 2D images was different from being in the room. She'd said she wanted to familiarize herself with the layout and fix any danger points in her mind, especially with the dark setting and the flashing lights of a club full of dancers.

"Where's the other exit?" she asked. "In case we get cut off from the main one?"

"Past the bathrooms. It leads out to the delivery entrance. The door's locked right now, but I'll unlock it before we get ready to kick off the party."

"You still have the keys?" Delilah asked, brows furrowed.

"I paid a lot of money to play janitor so I could get in when they were closed. How do you think I got those pictures?" Luke forced his glance away from the bartender. He couldn't help it. His mind wanted him to focus on the only vampire threat in the room.

"Luke. Quit staring at the bartender," Delilah hissed when his gaze swung back toward the bar. "You're going to draw attention."

"Sorry. He's the only vamp here, and being in his presence is like nails on a chalkboard." He shifted in the booth so he could focus on something else.

Delilah rewarded Luke with a smile. "Any chance your old pal Cassius will show up?"

Luke shrugged. "I don't know. He's not really the reason we're here."

Delilah sighed and slumped into the booth. "I know, it's just…"

"I understand. We both owe him a lot of pain, and when the time's right, we'll deliver it without hesitation."

"It's just… I'm tired of waiting." Delilah drew back the curtain in her eyes she hid the pain behind.

Luke empathized with her. "I know. I really do. I'll do everything in my power to help you take him out, but tonight's not the night. We're just not ready yet."

Delilah clenched her jaw and nodded curtly. She'd agreed with this assessment before, but it clearly galled her. Luke wasn't sure how Delilah's father had been involved with vampires. She'd refused to share any details other than she'd walked in on Cassius committing the deed. When she'd attacked him, he'd ripped out a bunch of her locs, necessitating the big chop and the short afro she now sported. Luke hoped Cassius didn't show up tonight, afraid Delilah would forget their mission and jeopardize their lives.

He still had trust issues, even though he considered both Delilah and Pablo to be friends. He'd lived and hunted by himself for decades before they forced their way into his life. Though he was glad to have their help, he had a lot of his own issues to work through. Forcing his eyes off the bartender again, he got up and went to the bathroom. When he returned, he shifted the conversation to non-business topics while they waited until it was Luke's turn to chastise Delilah.

"You're going to put a crick in your neck periscoping around like that. Also, you're drawing attention." Luke indicated the bar with his eyes. He wasn't sure if the vamp bartender was eyeing her because he was attracted to her, or if she'd genuinely caught his attention with her nervous surveillance of the club.

Delilah took in a deep breath and let it out slowly, forcibly relaxing her shoulders. Slumping in her seat, she tried to put on a more casual pose. "Sorry."

"No worries. There's no guarantee he'll be here tonight. Owners don't always show up, and he's not the reason for tonight's visit. And if he does, it'll probably be under heavy escort. When we go after him, I want to control the engagement so it ends in our favor."

He gave Delilah an understanding smile. "I know it's hard but be patient. He's not going anywhere. He's too entrenched in his and his masters' plans. They've put a lot of work into this city. Somehow, the vampires are involved with the disappearance of the mayor. Why else would he be working for the city commissioner? He'll go down, and we'll be the ones to do it. I promise."

He tried to pour all his confidence and affection for Delilah into his gaze. She met his eyes, then nodded, relaxing visibly. She settled into her seat and began bobbing her head along to the rhythm of the DJ's song selection and beats.

"I'm surprised you actually approve of the DJ."

Delilah shrugged. "He's not bad."

"Better than you?" Luke raised an eyebrow and the corner of his mouth in a smirk.

Delilah rolled her eyes at him. "As if. Another round?"

Luke checked his phone to see what time it was. "Yeah, we should be good for another." Delilah started getting up when Luke halted her. "Never mind, I see a server coming around."

He paid for their drinks with cash, then waited until she was gone before resuming their conversation.

"When do you want to start this party?" Delilah asked.

"When there are enough guests of honor to make it worth our while. They probably won't be out until late."

"Why are we here so early then?"

Luke shrugged. "I wanted to make sure we got in. Plus I wanted to ensure we controlled the timing from start to finish. We choose when we engage, not just where. We're here to make a statement to the vampires. We need to make some noise. The bigger the crowd at the club, the more effect this mission will have."

"Are you sure this is a good idea? Just the two of us?" Delilah looked nervous as she leaned across the table.

He swept his eyes around them quickly to ensure no one was close enough to overhear. "That's all we'll need for this. We're not here to clear it out, just to make it harder for Cassius and his ilk to hunt. He needs to know he can't hide from me, even if it's in plain sight. We make a mess for him, then clear out. This place gets a bad reputation, and the fangers have to figure out a new way to get easy prey. It's what I've been doing by myself, so two people is more than enough."

Delilah nodded, though it seemed less than enthusiastic. Over the couple of hours they'd been hanging out, the club had filled up with rich twenty and thirty-somethings from the Pearl District eager to be seen and the crowd from the 'burbs eager to say they got into the Red Velvet Room. It was a potent cocktail of affluence and gullibility.

As the floor filled, the lights dimmed, replaced with red mood lighting that matched the bar's name. When the affluent and expendable reached a critical mass, more vampires joined them, targeting the former for longer term parasitism and exploiting the latter for a quick snack. Luke, his body vibrating with the tension of being so near too many vampires, was ready to move.

"OK, it's about time. You have the play list ready?"

"Yeah." She pulled out an old MP3 player they'd picked up in a thrift shop. Jamaal, the North Portland Pack's head of tech, had formatted it to ensure it wasn't traceable. "I put the songs you requested in with the rest of the play list. There's some old school stuff in that list. You've got interesting taste. Where'd that come from?"

"I had cable in the '80s and '90s and watched a lot of MTV, especially 'Yo, MTV Raps.' The internet didn't really exist at the time, so I went to a lot of matinées. Pop culture kept me distracted, especially Black pop culture—Friday, Boyz n the Hood, House Party, stuff like that. I didn't really have any friends to speak of, and I was sliding into isolation more and more. Exploring this new entertainment kept me going outside the door to do more than just look for vampires." He shrugged, giving a clinical assessment of his more recent past. "Plus I had to do what I could to blend in when I went hunting where the youth of the day gathered. Had to look the part."

Delilah raised an eyebrow skeptically. "Did it actually work? Did you blend in? I mean..." She held up her hand and gestured toward him.

Luke shook his head, chuckling. "Yes and no. I didn't really blend in well with the kids. I looked like someone's dad or a narc."

Delilah let loose a loud laugh before tamping it down to avoid attracting attention.

"But at least I was on the scene when a fanger showed up."

Delilah looked delighted at the thought of Luke trying to blend in as an '80s hip-hop enthusiast. "Please tell me you have photos of you in an old school Adidas tracksuit?"

Luke winked at her. "Maybe sometime I'll show them to you, if you're nice to me."

Delilah rolled her eyes and stuck her tongue out at him.

"It's time to put on my dancing shoes." Luke shifted to get out of the booth.

"Dancing shoes?"

"Yeah. I'm going to dance."

Delilah snorted but tried to wipe the smirk off her face when she saw Luke's serious face. "You're going to dance? You? Pardon me, but you don't seem the type."

"You'll see..." He gave her a knowing smile.

"This ought to be good."

He headed to the back of the club toward the restroom. He slid behind a large potted plant and watched for an opportune moment before darting into the back hallway that led to the supply closet and the office. He fished a set of keys out of his pocket, opened the supply closet, stepped in among the brooms and mops, and shut the door behind him. Flipping a mop bucket over, he stood on it, moved the panel from the false ceiling out of the way, and pulled out the large duffel bag he'd planted when he was undercover as the janitor.

His next stop was the manager's office. He grabbed the gladius and unsheathed it in case someone was in the office watching the cameras. A different key unlocked that door. The office was empty. Either he was lucky, they were overconfident, or they just used the camera to corroborate anything they needed later, relying on security on the floor and at the door to maintain order. Stepping in, he pulled the door shut behind him and locked the door.

He flipped on the security monitor—a nature documentary played from the media device he'd spliced in. He chuckled as the screen panned across a central American jungle. When the vampires checked the security footage, all they'd find on their recording was a nice show about vampire bats. He hoped they watched it all the way through. He'd added an homage video of the Beastie Boys "Sabotage," although he doubted the fangers would find it as funny as Luke did.

He stripped off his shoes, jacket, and the button down under it and folded them into a neat pile. Opening the duffel, he pulled out his armor padding and drew it on over his undershirt. Next, he wrapped a thin black scarf around his neck to prevent his armor chafing and help cover the shine of steel.

He slipped into the armor and cinched the leather thong tight. He'd already set up the tactical bandoleer in place before they'd packed the armor. All he had to do was sheath the sword and the wooden rudis.

Both sword blades were partially visible in the semi-open scabbards Luke used to ensure quick draws over the shoulder didn't catch. The one set for his right hand was made of a steel alloy with some silver in it and was covered in crisp engravings, the visible side displaying a rising sun with flickering flames lashing out and down the blade. Its handle was made from dark wood at the pommel and an oval-shaped guard with a bone hilt. The other weapon—the rudis—was a wooden sword shaped like a gladius. The dark brown and intermixed golden tones of Persian ironwood glowed in the dim light of the office, and the silver inlay shimmered when it moved, catching bits of light. A steel-silver alloy rim formed the cutting edge, making it just as deadly, if slightly more fragile looking, as the steel gladius in the other scabbard.

Shaking out the wrinkles in the button-down shirt specially tailored to fit over his armor and swords, he slipped it on and added the custom hooded sport coat, arranging the hood to cover the pommels of the swords. He looked bulky; the armor gave him the physique of a linebacker.

He pulled out the last thing in the duffel, a backpack, and put his pile of clothes in along with the duffel bag after he'd collapsed it down. He didn't want to leave any evidence, plus he liked the clothes he'd added to his wardrobe with Delilah's help. He checked his appearance in the floor-length mirror to ensure he'd pass muster on the dance floor, then looked at the clock hanging above the mirror.

It was time. He closed his eyes briefly and took a deep, calming breath. Just a few more minutes until the waiting would end and he could get to the action. Exhaling slowly, he opened his eyes, grabbed the backpack, and headed back to the dance floor.

# TWO

PEEKING out the door to the back hallway, Luke ensured the path was clear for him to duck back into the bar. When no one was looking in his direction, he strode out confidently. If anyone asked, he could feign being lost on the way to the restrooms. He needn't have worried. People were too interested in their drinks, dancing, and potential hookups to notice one guy not in the right place. He navigated the tightly packed dance floor, his backpack held by the small handle at the top so it dangled unobtrusively near the floor, and found Delilah holding down their booth. He slid his backpack under their table and nodded to Delilah. She unzipped the front pocket of the backpack and pulled out a few sharp, pointed wooden stakes. Keeping her motion hidden, she stashed them inside her coat in one of the pockets contained within.

Delilah grabbed the MP3 player and stood up. Luke posted up in front of the DJ booth, partially blocking the view as Delilah approached the DJ. Luke, leaning casually against the book, stood so he could keep an eye on the DJ while also watching the rest of the club.

"Can I help you with something?" the DJ asked.

"Nice set tonight."

"Thanks." The DJ looked Delilah up and down, a smile growing on his face.

Delilah shifted nervously on her feet. "This is quite the club. A great place to look for a meal."

"I guess…" The DJ didn't seem to know what Delilah was getting at.

"What can you tell me about the people who run this place?"

The DJ's eyes darted around a bit, his jaw clenching slightly and a note of terror filtering into his eyes.

"Nothing much. They pay their employees on time."

"Do you know who, or I guess I should say what, runs this club? The manager? The owner?"

"I'm not sure what you're getting at…"

Delilah opened the right side of her coat, the side facing the dance floor, so only the DJ could see what was inside. She reached over and pulled the stake partially out of its pocket, displaying it to the DJ.

Delilah leaned a little closer to the DJ. "Look. You're a pretty fair DJ. You know who's signing your paychecks and what they are. I can see it in your eyes. I'm going to give you a free piece of advice. Get the fuck out of here. Do it quietly. Do it casually. Live to spin another day."

He nodded lightly but quickly, almost giving a small shiver. His eyes scanned around rapidly as his body tried to shrink in on itself, his breathing shallow and irregular. He finally settled on a course of action which calmed his body a bit.

"OK. I just spin here. I don't want any of *their* trouble. Um, can I take my laptop? It's got everything in it. It's my livelihood."

"Sure." Delilah released the stake and lapel, letting her coat fall back into place. She pulled the MP3 player out of her pocket and thrust it toward him. "Tie this into the house's soundboard first and transition over to the first track."

The DJ nodded, plugging Delilah's MP3 player in. As his song reached its zenith, he patched in the MP3 player seamlessly before he began taking down his laptop and getting ready to leave. The

Beastie Boys' "Paul Revere" spilled out into the club, exciting the mostly white crowd.

As he tried to slide past Delilah, she grabbed his upper arm. "No cops, understand?" She gave it a firm squeeze to emphasize her point and gestured toward Luke with her head. "Or my friend and I will look you up later."

He nodded.

"Remember, fly casual, got it?"

He nodded again. Delilah let go of his arm and turned to the booth to make sure she could handle the soundboard.

The bartender slid up next to the DJ. "We having a problem here, Freddie?"

"No problem. Just need to grab a bathroom break and my friend here is going to handle a few songs," the DJ said with a bright smile.

Luke admired the terrified man who could think on his feet even through his fear.

The bartender looked Delilah over, his eyes gleaming as he gave her a lascivious once over. Nodding, he headed back to the bar.

"Quick thinking," Delilah said. "Head out the back door by the restroom. It's unlocked."

The DJ nodded, then walked out a bit quicker than would explicitly be considered casual but would work for someone with a full bladder. Luke caught Delilah's eye and raised both of his eyebrows while tilting his head. She held up her index finger asking for a minute. She was searching for something in the MP3 player. A wicked grin spread across her face. She must have found what she was looking for. She looked up and nodded to Luke.

Luke turned toward the dance floor then made his way into the crowd. He could feel the vampires surrounding him, but only had the vaguest of ideas who they might be. He wanted to take a few turns around the dance floor so he could mingle and put faces to fangs. He wasn't busting out any of his fancy moves; he just wanted to bop across the floor and blend in. A few of the vampires stopped as he passed by, sniffing the air as someone with strange blood wandered by. He kept moving so they couldn't home in on who had that blood pumping through their veins. The dance floor was crowded and churning enough that it would be hard to figure out who it was—the proverbial needle in the hemoglobin haystack.

Delilah, satisfied that her playlist was under control, pulled out a pair of leather gloves and put them on. She grabbed the MP3 player and wiped it and the soundboard down, removing her fingerprints, before heading out to the dance floor to do an inspection pass of her own. From where Luke watched, it looked like she was adjusting knobs on the sound board. The booth around the corner hid much of what she was doing from mid chest down.

Luke could sense the presence of vampires, pinpointing them within the vibrating crowd. It was one of his powers, one of the tools Mithras had given him to aid him in his mission. Somehow, Delilah could sense vampires as well, although not as precisely as Luke. However, considering she was a normal human, she shouldn't be able to sense them at all.

Neither Luke nor Delilah knew how, they'd discussed it, but for whatever reason, she could, so they used it to their advantage. Together they danced through the crowd, splitting up to cover more ground, mentally marking the faces of the vamps they needed to remember, although when the action went down, they'd be first in line for a staking, trying to protect their territory and punish the violators of its sanctity.

Luke was about to find Delilah and kick off the stab-o-rama when Full Force's "Ain't My Type of Hype" started playing. Luke looked around for Delilah, finding her dancing her way toward him, a grin and a question on her face. Luke chuckled and shook his head before making eye contact and nodding once. She pointed to herself using both thumbs and mouthed "Kid" before extending both index fingers toward Luke and mouthing "Play." Luke smiled and nodded.

Luke stepped into a clear space and began the set of dance moves from the House Party dance off scene, his knees popping up as he grooved side to side and crossing his arms across his chest, issuing his challenge to Delilah. She responded by matching his moves, then throwing in some extra spice to her steps before crossing her feet and spinning and stretching her leg back to kick.

Soon, the crowd caught on to what was happening and formed a circle around Luke and Delilah as they exchanged dance moves. They did their best to replicate the moves as best as they could in the tight space until the crowd opened up for them, modifying the parts that required two people and going back and forth. The crowd was clapping and cheering as Luke and Delilah exchanged dance moves until they were about to hit the infamous kick step exchange.

Delilah danced toward Luke and asked, "Join you for the kick step?"

Luke's smile was her answer. They stepped back across from each other and danced toward each other, kicking their sides of their right shoes together once, dancing back and then toward each other, then locked their ankles and hopped around each other ending on the opposite sides. They danced back and forward again, tapping the side of their shoes together, spinning and tapping the soles of their feet together. Luke was having a blast. It'd been a lot of years since he'd done this, let alone with someone who knew the moves as well as Delilah. They completed the foot tapping sequence and like in the movie, spun out, and started dancing with the crowd that had gathered around.

Delilah, without breaking out of her groove, grabbed her coat back from the stranger who'd held it during their performance. She used a spin move to put the coat back on, the bottom of the trench flaring out as she twirled. When she stopped, she faced Luke with a challenge in her eyes as she grabbed the lapel of her coat and feigned opening it a bit.

A wicked grin split Luke's face as he nodded.

Still dancing, she reached inside her coat, crisscrossing her arms across her body, and pulled out a stake in each hand. She kept them flat against her wrists and forearms, using her arm to hide them against her body. Luke, deciding to leave it all on the dance floor, busted into the sprinkler, much to the delight of the crowd they'd just wowed with their performance. Luke's right arm was making the circuit as the sprinkler arm when he switched to his left arm into the extended position. As he continued spraying the crowd with his cheesy dance move, he slid his right hand down into his hood, gripping the hilt of his steel gladius. He made eye contact with Delilah and gave her the barest of nods as he drew his sword.

Once the blade cleared its scabbard, he lunged forward, stabbing the point deep into the chest of a young vampire who'd been watching the dance off. The vamp dissolved into a pile of dark red goo, splattering the people who'd been standing around her. Luke used the Roger Rabbit dance to back away from the mess on the floor as Delilah spun toward one vampire, staking it quickly in the chest before spinning and staking another one with her other stake. Both joined their former friend in a pile of viscous sludge on the dance floor.

The shock of the sudden assault stunned the onlookers until someone finally pieced together what had happened and started screaming. More people joined in as the crowd backed away from the violence, some shoving their way toward the exit.

Leaping into action, the vampires began crowd control, glamouring people and taking any cell phones from people trying to record. In a matter of moments, the fangers cleared the room so they could deal with the intruders.

Luke, grinning at their audaciousness, kept up his dancing, rotated his sword to a reverse grip, and switched into the running man. A vampire used the chaos of the evacuation and darted through the crowd, aiming a punch at Luke's stomach. The vamp's fist plowed into Luke's stomach, the steel plating wrapped around Luke's torso stopping it. He was knocked back and released a small exhalation of air. Even wearing armor, the vampire's punch packed some force. Hissing, the vamp staggered back a step, clutching his fist. He'd probably broken several bones. Given time and the blood of some victims, he'd heal quickly. His type did.

Luke stepped forward, dragging the blade across the vampire's throat. Reversing his rotation, he swept the vampire's legs, knocking it to the ground. Luke plunged his sword into the vampire's heart, giving it its final death and adding to the growing pile of goo. So far, it appeared that Luke and Delilah had only killed younger vampires, as evident by the liquid nature of their remains. Old ones tended to turn to dry matter in chunks or dust. Senior vampires, more powerful than younger ones, preferred sending in their expendable foot soldiers instead of risking their own vastly extended lives.

Delilah was currently engaged with two vampires, keeping them at bay with her stakes. They were trying to be more patient and create a distraction so one or the other could take advantage and remove her out of the fight. She attacked, causing the nearest vampire to rotate its back toward Luke. Taking the invitation, Luke ended the fanger. Relieved of one opponent, Delilah followed suit and finished hers. Together, they moved to a fresh spot on the dance floor.

Most of the random patrons had fled by this point, although Luke could detect a few humans still milling about, thralls most likely. If they were out with their masters, they were most likely of the voluntary variety, hoping for an eventual slice of immortality. One interceded for their masters and pulled a sizable knife on Delilah.

"You got this one?" Luke asked.

"Please." Delilah spared enough of a glance toward Luke to show him an annoyed expression. She parried the knife aside and delivered a punch to the woman's throat before kicking her back into the crowd. The only casualty, besides the thrall's windpipe, was one of Delilah's stakes which had stuck around the knife's blade when it had blocked the cutting edge. Taking advantage of the distraction the thrall had provided, a vamp lunged at Delilah's unarmed side. She'd anticipated the attack and waited until the last moment before starting her counter. Fully committed, the vampire practically impaled itself on her other stake, which she'd positioned with perfect timing.

The vampire disintegrated, creating a cloud of dust that covered Delilah. Coughing, she backed away. Luke slid up closer to her to provide any protection she might need as she tried to clear her lungs and stop coughing. Delilah wiped the dust off her face and tried patting it off her coat but was failing in the Herculean task. Her coughing finally subsiding, she nodded at Luke, indicating she was good to go.

Luke stepped away, surprised the vampires hadn't used the

distraction of a coughing opponent to attack. Instead, they'd spread out in a crescent, effectively building a wall of undead flesh between Luke and Delilah and the main exit. All the while, DJ Delilah's mix of hip hop and club beats thumped over the speakers. Taking advantage of a spare moment and a soundtrack, Luke busted out the pendulum.

"Bruh, what are you doing?" Delilah asked.

"It's a dance club. I'm dancing."

"Is that what you call it? Those moves are dustier than the vamp I'm wearing."

Ignoring Delilah's jibe, he shifted into the cabbage patch, resurrecting the old school dance moves he'd meticulously taught himself back when they were still fresh. While he kept grooving, a small cadre of vampires standing behind their main line were having a conference, periodically glancing toward Luke and Delilah. Some of the front-line vampires had produced weapons, although most hadn't expected to fight for their lives when they'd come out to dance and find new victims. Luke wasn't sure why they hadn't tried swarming them yet, other than the fact that Luke and Delilah had already downed over half a dozen vamps. Plus, everyone there had fresh memories of the carnage Luke had committed only a few months ago. They probably didn't want to be next in line to die.

Most of the weapons were small knives—switchblades and butterfly knives. One vamp had even produced a stun gun. Luke had no idea what a taser would do against his armor. It blocked physical attacks, but the steel over sweat soaked padding and undershirt might arc over his entire torso, his hoodie allowing the prongs, if it was a distance taser, to stick and pump its electricity into his body.

"Heads up. One of them has a stun gun," Luke warned Delilah.

Delilah acknowledged him, grunting while planting a stake in a vampire that had gotten too close. The vampire twisted as it dissolved on itself, tangling Delilah's stake in its suddenly extra loose clothing. "Fuck, that was my last one."

Stepping in front of Delilah to keep anyone from lunging at her, Luke reached over his shoulder and pulled his rudis, handing it to her.

"Thanks." Delilah stepped out from behind him.

"Can you hold the line?"

"Yeah." She oriented herself so that she faced the largest portion of the vamp line, keeping an eye on the entire frontage.

Knowing she was ready and covering his back, Luke feinted toward his left. The line shifted to adjust, a few tangled up with each other. Luke lunged to the side, delivering a vicious slash to the neck of the vamp, removing his head, the taser clattering to the floor. He danced back. Delilah shifted to the side to make room.

"What are they waiting for?" Delilah asked.

"No idea. Not sure I like it."

Delilah narrowed her eyes as she looked over the line of vampires. "Well, I hope they get on with it soon."

Luke scanned the room. "I'm more concerned about police obfuscating our exit."

"Yeah, I'm not interested in three hots and a cot."

"Me neither." Luke hadn't heard any sirens yet, which also surprised him. His supernaturally enhanced hearing would give him plenty of notice. "If we don't see some activity soon —"

"The door!" Delilah pointed with the rudis.

The door leading into the club opened, and vampires streamed in. They flared out, adding to the bulwark between Luke and Delilah and the exit. The last man through the door was well-dressed, wearing an overcoat with the collar turned up against the rain and cold outside and a patch cap. The combination of cap and collar obscured his face until he shucked his coat, handing it to one of the vamps standing nearby and looked up toward Luke.

"Well, well, well. Lucius. What am I going to do with you?"

Luke rolled his eyes and shook his head. Something slammed into him, knocking him forward. Delilah had lunged toward Cassius. Recovering instantly, he wrapped his left arm around Delilah's waist as she tried to tear away from his hold and attack Cassius. He lifted her off her feet, barely keeping her contained. He backed up and put some distance between them and the fangers.

"My evening just got more amusing. Your little friend appears distraught."

Luke grunted in response, trying to keep Delilah from getting away and biting off more trouble than either of them could chew. He didn't like the current odds. Keeping his voice low, he addressed Delilah, "Control. This isn't the time. There are too many."

Either she was too engrossed in her rage or was choosing to ignore Luke. "You killed my father!"

"It's possible. I've probably killed lots of fathers. What makes yours memorable?"

The flippant answer incensed Delilah further. She surged forward, nearly breaking Luke's grip. He added his other arm, wrapping it around her carefully to avoid cutting her with his sword.

Luke pleaded with her. "Dee, please." He hoped the nickname her friend used would get through to her.

Cassius narrowed his eyes slightly. "I recognize you. You had more hair then, before I ripped it out. So you're Oyelakin's brat. I see you managed to track me down. I'm almost impressed."

"You keep his name out of your mouth," Delilah yelled.

A warm drop splashed on Luke's hand, followed by more. Delilah's rage was ebbing, or at least its physical manifestation. She finally settled down and stopped fighting, tears falling down her cheeks.

"What am I going to do with you two? You've come to my place of business and killed my associates, yet again. I should tear you to pieces, but that's so messy." He nodded toward one of his goons who grabbed a couple of vampires and went to the back hall, returning a few moments later with cleaning supplies. "I'm not ready to deal with you yet. Besides, I have a business to run and profits to sink my teeth into."

Something distracted him briefly. He reached into his pocket and pulled out a cell phone. Checking it, he typed in something with his thumbs, his fingers moving like lightning, fueled by his vampiric speed. Hand moving back toward his pocket, he perked up, arching an ear back toward the exit. A few seconds later, the sounds of sirens drifted over the rainy night sky.

Cassius grinned. "Ah, Good. We've delayed them enough. That's our cue to leave. Let's leave them to the police, shall we? I'm sure they'd love a hand to match all the fingerprints they've collected over the years."

The crew cleaning the floors had finished and were removing the evidence to the back hallway. Delilah, sensing she was about to lose her opportunity to avenge herself on the creature that had murdered her father, tensed, lightly straining against Luke's still firm grasp around her middle.

"Not now. It's escape time," Luke hissed between clenched teeth.

"But..."

"I know. I really do, but it's just not going to happen right now."

She nodded curtly and stopped pushing against his arm. He didn't slacken his grip though; he wasn't interested in engaging in a fight this lopsided.

"Until we meet again, Lucius..." Cassius put his coat back on, then turned and walked out the door, his team of bodyguards following suit. The wall of vampires held their position, allowing their boss to make his exit. After a few more moments, they edged backwards toward the door. Avoiding jamming at the door, they exited in an orderly fashion, tearing away at breakneck sprints as soon as they'd cleared the door and reached the sidewalk outside.

# THREE

LUKE CHECKED that Delilah's beanie with its fake beard was in place, then made sure the exit was actually clear. The disguise, paired with large sunglasses, would do well enough to obscure their faces if any neighborhood security cameras captured their escape, though he doubted any of them would be working with vampires owning a business so close. They'd likely make sure the anything pointed in the area of their night club had been disabled after a convenient glamour augmented conversation with whoever maintained them.

"Ready?"

Delilah nodded. Together pushed the doors open, turned right, and broke into a sprint toward their extraction point.

At the end of the block, he turned the corner when pain exploded across his back and brutally shoved him to the ground. A moment later, he heard the boom of a high caliber gun. He skidded on the sidewalk, the concrete scraping skin off his bare palms. His face burned above his left eye where his brow had landed against the ground and skidded with him.

Delilah slid to a stop and ran back to Luke. "Luke, are you OK? Get up! We got to go…"

Luke could barely make out what she was saying through the fog of shock. "Ger...gerway fro me." He tried to shove her away from him.

Understanding dawned. She grabbed Luke's arm and yanked him up and into a stoop leading to a door in the brick wall they were standing next to. Luke feebly assisted her, his legs tripping him as much as shoving his body after her.

"What happened?"

"Gun. Sniper." Luke's head was clearing a bit.

"Oh, shit!" She began frantically checking Luke for bullet holes and blood. "I...I don't see any holes or blood. Did you trip?"

"Armor, I think..."

"It's bulletproof?" She sounded astonished.

"Magic. Like the swords." He was having trouble forming complete sentences.

They huddled close to each other, trying to squeeze the bulk of two tall people, one of whom was wearing heavy armor, into the alcove so nothing was in the open. Delilah reached into her coat, pulled out her cell phone, and made a call.

"Change of plans. Pick us up..." She looked around to get her bearings. "Just east of Stumptown. Leave the tailgate down."

She put the phone back. "Hang on, Luke. Pablo is on his way. Can you move quick enough to get to his truck?"

"Yeah. My head's clearing a bit. It hit the concrete pretty hard."

Delilah snorted. "Your hard head probably did more damage to the sidewalk than the other way around."

He weakly held up his hand and pulled his fingers and thumb in, leaving the middle finger up. The sound of wheels screeching as someone took the corner too fast were followed by tires screaming against the pavement as a large vehicle locked up its brakes, sending the smell of burnt rubber into the air.

"That's Pablo. We're going into the bed." She squatted and helped Luke up, lifting under his arms. He stood but wobbled some. "You sure you're going to make it?"

"My body can handle it. Except for some dinged up knees, my legs are fine. Listen, when we go out, you stay on my right side so my armor is between you and wherever that sniper is. Keep your head down, let me cover your body as best as we can. I have some modicum of protection."

"Ready?" Delilah asked.

"Yeah, let's go."

Delilah snaked an arm under his shoulder, around his upper back, and helped him dart out and across the sidewalk. They ducked behind a car just as its rear window exploded into shards followed by another boom.

The passenger side window of Pablo's truck rolled down, and Pablo yelled out, "Don't get my truck shot. Hurry up!"

Delilah made eye contact with Luke. They nodded at each other and jumped into the bed of Pablo's black Toyota Tacoma, grabbing the safety harnesses they'd rigged in the back. Delilah slammed the butt of her fist on the floor of the bed and yelled, "Go!"

Pablo mashed the pedal on the pickup, sending it lurching forward.

Delilah and Luke clung on desperately, trying to avoid being thrown out the back. They heard the distant boom of the sniper rifle. It didn't appear to have hit anything on the truck, at least that they could see or feel. Pablo screeched around another corner and away from the line of fire of the hidden sniper. He slowed down, balancing escape against drawing the attention of any cops. He was decidedly more on the side of escape than subtlety. But with each passing block and turn, the scales tipped toward blending in.

Luke, judging it to be safe, let go of the harness and crawled to the tailgate. He grabbed the edge of it and pulled back. It tipped up a bit.

Apparently, he felt weaker than he thought. "Delilah, need some help."

Delilah scooted down next to him and grabbed onto the tailgate. "On the count of three. One. Two. Three!"

Together they pulled back, Luke grunting in pain. The tailgate slammed home. Luke slid to the left and grabbed the latch of the canopy door. Delilah took the right one. Together, they pulled it down and rotated the latches enough to lock it.

Luke grinned weakly. "It's illegal to ride in the bed of a pickup truck in Oregon."

Delilah looked at him, one eyebrow quirked up and a smirk across her face. Now that they were on the move and the truck was closed up, the tension of the situation broke. She started to laugh. "Of all the illegal shit we did tonight, that was the thing that was going to undo us?"

He started chuckling too before wincing. "Oh, that hurts. I hope I didn't break a rib."

Delilah crawled back to the head of the truck bed and propped herself up in a partially sitting position. "I thought the armor stopped the bullet?"

"I think it did. But it didn't eat up the force. I still got punched hard. That level of force will do a lot of damage to a body, even with armor. You remember the punishment my body took last winter on the pedestrian bridge…"

Delilah nodded. "Yeah. You took an epic beat down."

"Took a couple broken ribs out of that too." Luke reached up and straightened the beard beanie so it was no longer askew after he'd landed on it.

"Come sit up here. It'll be more comfortable."

"I think I'll just lie flat for now." He groaned as he tried to move.

Delilah scooted around so she was propped up against the side of the bed and canopy. "At least scoot up a bit and rest your head on my leg. It'll be more comfortable than against the hard truck bed."

Luke complied, using his feet to shove himself toward Delilah. Once he got close enough, he lifted himself on his elbows and relaxed onto Delilah's lap. "Thanks, Delilah."

He looked up at her, making eye contact as she looked down at his face. "Where'd you learn the House Party dance moves? You're too young."

"My dad taught me when I was growing up. After Mom died, he wanted to make sure I was in touch with my culture, so we watched a lot of Black movies and listened to Black music. We'd have dance parties in the living room and learn all the moves…"

The last thing Luke saw before he dozed off to the soothing sound of her voice was Delilah smiling softly down at him.

PABLO OPENED the canopy and dropped the tailgate. "Wakey, wakey, eggs and bakey! Well, isn't that precious."

The jolt and clang of the tailgate flopping down dragged Luke up from the depths of his concussion-addled unconsciousness. Delilah had fallen asleep sometime during Pablo's long evasion route. She rubbed the sleep out of her eyes. She looked down at Luke whose head was still resting in her lap. "He's still out. He took a hit to the head and might have a concussion. I'm not sure."

"Well, Doc is here watching the kid. Also thought it would be a good idea to have medical attention on hand if we needed it, and Luke always seems to need it."

Delilah, cradling Luke's head, scooted out from under him and gently set his head down. He tossed and turn a bit, mumbling some words in a language neither Pablo nor Delilah had ever heard. Delilah reached down and gently shook his arm.

"Luke, we're here. Wake up."

His eyes fluttered open. "Wuh...where?"

"We're home, buddy. At least your home," Pablo added.

Luke extended a hand to Delilah, who gripped his forearm and helped him to a sitting potion. Luke gathered his legs under him and got onto his knees before settling onto his hands and crawling out. He propped himself up against the lowered tailgate. Delilah joined him on the ground. The sun was creeping up in the east, adding a gentle gray to the dark of the night.

"Pablo, get under his other arm. You know the drill," Delilah said.

The two of them propped Luke up on their shoulders and walked him toward the door.

The door popped open as they approached it, a curvy blonde woman of medium height holding it open.

"How bad is it?" Doctor Maggie Rabinowitz asked, a Polish accent coloring her voice.

"Unknown. He took a shot in the back somewhere from a sniper. I don't think it penetrated his armor, but he hit the ground hard. Maybe a concussion. Maybe some broken ribs." Delilah moved out from under Luke's arm so he could get through the door.

Maggie smiled and shook her head. "He does manage to find new and exciting ways to injure himself, doesn't he?"

"That's my pal!" Pablo added, smirking at Luke.

Luke held up his hand, giving the doctor a weak thumbs up.

"Into the kitchen," the doctor ordered.

As they passed through the entry hall into the living room, Luke spotted his ward Gwendolyn sleeping on the couch.

Following Luke's gaze, Maggie filled him in. "She was worried about you, so we watched a movie, and she fell asleep. When I tried to move her, she'd stir, so I just let her sleep."

Luke nodded before regretting the motion. Pablo and Delilah propped Luke up against the counter and began stripping him of his gear. Delilah fetched the armor stand Luke kept upstairs. With jacket, shirt, swords, and armor removed, they guided him into a kitchen chair.

"Is my armor damaged?" Luke asked, trying to twist around to look at it. He groaned in pain.

"Sit straight, dude." Pablo held up the armor for Luke to inspect. "Doesn't look like it. It's a good thing you have divine friends and magic armor." Pablo set it on the armor stand Delilah had set up.

Luke squinted at the spot where he thought he'd been hit but didn't see so much as a scratch. "I'm lucky it hit one of the bands and not one of the many weak points."

"I'm more concerned about your health. Shirt and padding off," Maggie commanded.

Luke raised his arms and Pablo peeled the padding and under-shirt off, tossing them aside. A massive, ugly, purple bruise spread across Luke's back with the epicenter just below his right shoulder blade. Luke winced as Maggie probed around trying to detect any broken ribs.

"I don't feel anything obviously broken. Might have gotten lucky with just some hairline fractures. That shoulder's going to be pretty useless until it heals." She eyed the various scars splashed across Luke's torso. Evidence of slashes and stabs and what looked like an arrow wound. "That's quite the collection of scars you've got there."

A light, sleepy voice came from the doorway to the living room. "Are you OK, Luke?"

Luke turned his head to address Gwen. "I think so, little one. Doc?"

"You'll live. We'll get you down to the clinic soon and get an x-ray to be on the safe side. You don't want a punctured lung," Maggie said.

"I'm OK. Why don't you go crawl into your bed. Take Alfred with you."

Gwen nodded, picked up the giant orange tabby, and headed to the back of the house.

Maggie looked at Pablo and Delilah. "Pablo, get me some water and a washcloth. Delilah, my kit is by the couch. Can you grab it for me?"

Pablo complied, handing the doctor a bowl of water and a clean red dishrag. She dabbed Luke's forehead, cleaning the road rash from his fall. Delilah returned and opened the kit, spreading it on the table within easy reach for Maggie. She grabbed a small set of forceps and pulled a few small pieces of debris from Luke's head wound. Satisfied it was clean, she smeared antibacterial ointment on it and covered it with a bandage.

Maggie repeated the process on his hands. "Anywhere else I need to look?"

"Those knees don't look too good, Doc," Pablo supplied.

Luke looked down at his knees, seeing the torn jeans and the bloody flesh under, and sighed.

"Better drop your pants," Maggie said.

Luke extended a hand to Pablo, who helped him stand. He unbuttoned his pants, dropped the zipper, and pushed his pants down, careful to make sure his underwear stayed firmly in place. Not bothering to bend over and take them all the way off, he left them around his ankles, then sat back down.

Maggie had Pablo get another bowl of water and another clean cloth. Carefully dabbing so as not to drive in the debris, she cleaned the torn-up skin on his knees, then picked out pebbles, shards of glass, and a few unidentified pieces. She covered his knees with large bandages and stood up.

"Anything else?" Maggie asked

Luke lifted his arms and looked down at his nearly nude body. "I'm not hiding any wounds in my underpants, so I think that's it, Doc." Luke said, using the informal mode of address he'd picked up from Pablo. Maggie didn't seem to mind.

She nodded. "Well, if there's nothing else, I'm going to head home. Get some rest. When you wake up, call me and we'll get those ribs x-rayed. Bring Gwen with you; she's due for a checkup. Plus, I want to get a blood draw and check her hormone levels, see how the puberty blockers are working."

Luke caught her hand before she could leave. Looking into her eyes, he said, "Thank you for everything, Doc. Thanks for staying with the kid. I'll give you a call to get us both down to the clinic."

Maggie smiled softly. "Oh, no problem. I'm glad she trusts me enough to let me watch her. She's come a long way from the skittish kid afraid of her own kind."

"She's still wary of most werewolves, except for you, Sam, and Pablo," Delilah said.

"It's a start, at least. I'll see you all later." She squeezed Luke's hand and released it.

"Good night, Maggie. Well, good morning, I guess," added Delilah.

"Get some rest, you three. And Luke…"

"Yeah?"

"Don't overdo it until you heal. Hairline fractures can still break, and I don't feel like treating you for a punctured lung."

# FOUR

SINCE IT WAS ALREADY morning of the day after their vampire venture, they decided to keep it mellow. Delilah crashed in Luke's guest room. Luke got what sleep he could with the discomfort of a massively bruised back and cracked ribs, and Pablo went home.

Two days after their night club raid, they met up at the Howling Moon Brewery for lunch and to rehash events. Gwen joined them in the back booth they always requisitioned when they wanted to talk privately. After the holidays, Pablo had added some improvements including some soundproof backing and had the speakers and acoustic tiles in the ceiling adjusted so the booth let almost no sound out of its confines unless someone was standing directly next to the table.

"Hi, Gwen. It's good to see you. It's been a while." The server handed out the menus.

Gwen gave a small wave. "Hi, Pam. Not since the camp."

"You doing OK?"

Gwen ducked her head shyly and nodded. "Yeah."

"That's good." Pam addressed the rest of the table. "Can I get drinks started while you look over the lunch menu? There's a real nice lamb stew with soda bread special today." She took their drink orders and disappeared.

"So, how's the ribcage doing?" Pablo asked.

"Pretty colorful. Hurts like hell, but I've had worse."

"You're lucky to be alive, buddy," Pablo said.

Luke nodded gingerly. "Yeah, I guess my armor's better than I thought. I know it'll take an arrow or heavy javelin. Hell, it's turned musket balls in the past, even some small arms fire, but I've never tried it against a high caliber rifle."

"How do you know it was a high caliber shot?" Pablo tipped his head to side and looked curious.

"It takes a lot of force to knock me down, especially at the distance that shot was fired."

"You've never tested your armor against a rifle?" Pablo asked.

"I generally try to avoid being shot. Too many chances and not enough of my body covered in armor."

"No, I mean you've never taken it out to a shooting range and shot it yourself?" Pablo asked.

Luke shook his head. "No. What if it didn't work? It's infused with magic like my swords, but what if it's not strong enough with even that? Then my magical anti-vampire armor would have a hole in it, and an uncomfortable one at that."

"Can't you just repair it?" Delilah asked.

"I've never had to replace the steel bands, not since I was given my life's purpose. I've replaced leather and rivets, but the steel has been impregnable and inviolate for almost two thousand years. Same with all the armor I was wearing that day. I'm honestly surprised the force didn't pop a few rivets. That shot hit hard." Luke winced at the memory before continuing. "And that brings me back to a discussion we had last winter that we never really finished. We need to get you both ballistic vests."

Pablo looked like he was about to scoff, but Luke interrupted him. "Even you, wolf boy." Luke adopted Delilah's nickname for Pablo to emphasize the point. "Either we can get you two or see about a custom job where the shoulder and side straps stretch. I know you'll be able to heal from most things, but why take the chance? You can kill a werewolf if you deal enough damage to them. A shot to the heart with a big ass bullet might be enough."

Pablo nodded, accepting his friend's reasoning.

"We'll need to get both of your measurements. In the meantime, the one I got you," he said, looking at Delilah, "will have to do for now. I know it's too tight around the chest, but having it fit a lot better after it's been hallowed out by a sniper is not the option we're going with."

Delilah's eyes narrowed as she frowned. "Luke, I can't afford something like that."

"It wouldn't be the first time I've provided gear for my soldiers. It used to be common practice. It's done. There'll be no arguments about this. The dynamics have changed, and we need to adapt."

Silence reigned over the table after Luke's pronouncement as they sipped their drinks.

"Speaking of dynamics changing, why the hell did we hear sirens but not see any cops? We were in a lot longer than we wanted to be, but no cops showed up. Not even when the gun went off and we were dodging bullets." Delilah looked pointedly at Luke and Pablo.

"Yeah, very curious. Very curious indeed," Luke said.

"I mean, it's not the first time we've had hints the vampires are getting inside help from the local authorities. I mean, your old friend coming out with that city commissioner—who is also the police commissioner—wasn't coincidence," Pablo said.

"Do you think Cassius is controlling the commissioner?" Delilah asked.

She looked nervous and slightly scared, but it was tempered by an edge of anger. Finding out that Cassius was involved in the city government, especially with the commissioner who oversaw the Portland Police Bureau, had shaken her resolve. It was one thing to settle a grudge against Cassius, but another entirely to chase down someone who might have access to the power of one of the US's major cities and a police department with a long history of racial abuse and violence directed against Portland's small Black population.

Luke gave half a shrug. "It's possible. I don't know the commissioner at all, only his reputation. He's always seemed weak and servile, the kind of mind that easily capitulates to whatever the Police Association wants. The kind that would easily be overwhelmed by a vampire, and for all Cassius's faults, he's an old, powerful vampire."

"I can check with Holly. She's intimately involved in the criminal justice system here. I'm sure she's had encounters with the commissioner. She's certainly had enough issues with the local police." Pablo slid his empty glass to the center of the table.

Luke raised his eyebrow and quirked his head to the side.

Seeing his curiosity, Pablo elaborated. "She does a lot of pro bono work for people who the police have been overzealous with, people who deserve to have their rights protected by more than an overworked court-appointed defense attorney who's more likely to help the prosecution than their client. She's made a few enemies downtown. You've both met her. You don't fuck with Holly, especially if she thinks you've violated another person's rights. She believes in protecting those who need it, and she carries that over to her legal practice."

"I know she's been asking around. It might be worth relaying our suspicions. Maybe she can ferret out some information we don't have access to," Luke said.

"You know it, dude. I'll mention it next time we meet. Although from what she's told me lately, the police and city hall are keeping their lips shut tight with the mayor's abduction still unsolved."

Luke furrowed his brows and squinted as an idea came to him. "If they don't find the mayor, they'll have to hold a special election to fill his seat. Holly would be a great candidate. I'd certainly back her financially." He'd looked into the city's charter after the mayor had been kidnapped from his house during his Christmas dinner.

"That's not actually a bad idea," Delilah said.

"Don't sound too surprised. I have good ideas now and then."

"It isn't a bad idea. I'll speak with Sam about it. For obvious reasons, she'd be a prime ally. Plus no one knows Holly better; she'll be able to give us an honest assessment of how Holly might react. It's not something to take lightly. It would be a lot of work for her, and she'd have to give up her practice. On the other hand, she'd really be able to make a difference in the community. I wouldn't put it past her to have thought about running for office." Pablo nodded, appearing to like the idea.

"Plus it aligns with her desire to keep her territory and pack safe. If the vamps are infiltrating the city government and the police, that will be very dangerous and make life uncomfortable for the pack since you've stood against Cassius and his master's plans," Luke said. He sighed at the new complications the vampires were adding, his anxiety increasing. He'd dealt with vampires infiltrating various governments in the past, but never a modern police force. As if vampires weren't terrifying enough. He looked over at Gwen. "Let's keep this idea under our hats for now."

"I don't have a hat," she replied.

"You have a beanie. Let's keep this under our beanies, OK?"

Gwen nodded. "OK. I understand."

"She's a smart kid and has seen a lot already for one so young. You're part of the team. Aren't you, honey?" Delilah smiled at her.

"Yup! Team old guys and Delilah!" Gwen smirked at Pablo and Luke.

"Ha!" Delilah pointed at Luke. "Told you she was smart."

"Everyone's always ganging up on us old guys, Pablo." Luke shook his head.

"Speak for yourself. Compared to you I'm a veritable spring chicken!"

"Et tu, Pable? Et tu?"

Pablo, Delilah, and Gwen all snickered at Luke.

Pablo grinned playfull. "I'm going to start wearing a toga and making you all call me Pablus."

"Wait, beanies?" A giant grin cracked Delilah's face. "Holy shit! I forgot in the chaos after the club, but talk of beanies reminded me. Apparently, our boy Luke used to be a b-boy!"

"What now? Come again?" Pablo looked like his brain had stopped computing.

Delilah grinned, her eyes sparkling with mischief. "A full-on '80s break dancing b-boy with some real moves—dusty moves—but real."

Pablo turned to his pal, his eyebrows raised as he tried to hide a grin. "B-boy, huh?"

Luke nodded.

"Tracksuit and all?"

"Yup."

Pablo turned back to Delilah. "Did he do any back spins or bust out the worm?"

"Those are kind of hard to do in chest armor," Luke said. He picked up his cell phone and checked the time, diverting the conversation. "Since we have plenty of daylight, I want to go back downtown and get an idea where that shot could have come from."

"I'm not sure it's a good idea if you and I are seen around the club again, especially not this soon. I know it's broad daylight, but they have thralls, and you're not in any kind of shape to be fighting on the streets of Portland." Delilah picked up her phone. "Sam, you free? You are? Good. We have a mission, should you choose to accept it..." Delilah summarized what they needed. "You do? Good. We'll pick you up in ten minutes. This message will self-destruct in five...four...three...two...one...boom." She hung up. "Problem solved. We'll drop off Sam around the corner, and she can play tourist and get some photos. Then we can safely look at them later."

"That sounds good. After we drop her off, we can head up to the Pearl District and pick up some more clothes for the kid, then meet her at Deschutes for beers and appetizers," Luke replied.

AFTER SAM FINISHED her recon mission and Luke had sprung for drinks and appetizers for her, Pablo, Delilah, and Gwen at Deschutes Brewery, they piled into Pablo's truck and headed back to North Portland. Once they were settled at Luke's house, he handed out beers while Gwen served up the pizza they'd picked up on the way. Around bites of pizza, Sam filled them in on her mission.

"Did anyone seem suspicious?" Luke asked.

Sam shook her head. "Nah, I had my camera and was taking

pictures. I looked like a Japanese tourist. They had a bouncer type posted up outside the club's entrance."

Luke raised an eyebrow. "Oh?"

"Yeah. He tried to look like a person just standing in the door well looking at his phone, but he kept his eyes more focused on the people passing by than on Candy Crush."

Delilah furrowed her brows. "Candy Crush?"

"He had his volume turned up way loud. I think he was trying too hard to be inconspicuous. When I started snapping pictures, he popped out and asked what I was doing. I explained in detail in Japanese, but he didn't seem to understand, so he eventually returned to his doorway."

"Did he keep an eye on you?" Luke asked.

"Yeah. But after I got what I wanted, I walked another block and took some more pictures. Then back over to that donut place that always has the lines and took more photos. He quit watching after that. Just another tourist."

When they finished their pizza, Sam gave Luke the memory card from her camera. He set up his laptop in the living room and tied it into the large high-definition TV before handing the wireless mouse to Sam.

"Alright, show us what you got."

Sam loaded up the first picture.

"This is our guard." Sam pointed to the burly looking white man in jeans and a leather coat. He had his phone out in front of him as he leaned against the wall.

"Is that?" Delilah asked.

"Yup, the bouncer from the night we were there," Luke replied. "Definitely keeping an eye on the place for the boss."

Sam changed to a new photo. "I managed to get a series from the shooting spot before the guard started eyeing me. Based on what you told me before you dropped me off, I think this photo captures where the shooter might have shot from."

Everyone leaned in toward the screen, as if that would zoom them in.

"That's a pretty big arc and a lot of windows and rooftops." Sam gestured toward the large section on the right side of the screen. "Let's see if we can narrow it down. Where exactly were you shot?"

Luke stood and lifted his shirt, showing her the massive bruise with the epicenter near the bottom of his right shoulder blade.

Sam grimaced. "You could have just told me." Sam faced the screen. "In this photo, I'm taking the shot from right about here, looking in this direction. Do you think you can orient yourself in the position you were in when the bullet struck?"

Luke turned around and backed up to the screen. He stood at an angle, back not parallel to the screen. He stepped forward and peeked over his shoulder. "I think here. I had just rounded the corner but was angled toward the curb when I got hit and knocked to the ground. It pretty much drove me straight down."

"OK, that narrows it down." Sam chuckled. "Literally."

She walked around Luke as everyone else watched them, Pablo and Delilah drinking their beers, Gwen sipping from a can of sparkling water. Sam would stop periodically, touch Luke's back and look back and forth between the screen and him. After a few minutes, she hunched over the laptop, moving the mouse around. The image on the screen zoomed in as she cropped off the sides. When she was satisfied, she turned to face her audience.

"OK, based on the information we have, as best as I can figure, the visible section of the photo should be about right. Your shooter was somewhere in that arc. Now, if we had a range, we could narrow it down further."

"Well, it was pretty far, I think…" Luke said.

"You don't sound too confident." Pablo quirked up one eyebrow.

"Well, I got hit pretty hard and my head bounced off the sidewalk, but it sounded like a short delay between the hit and the report. So, I'd say it was pretty far away."

"Like elite sniper making an amazing shot far away? Or closer in?" Sam asked.

"Hmmmm. Closer."

"OK, we should eliminate the closer buildings, then." Sam started cropping out the lower part of the photo, removing the nearest buildings.

"Let's stop here. Can you maximize the image?" Luke asked.

Sam blew up the remaining image, filling the screen from top to bottom, but leaving large areas of unfilled screen on the left and right sides of the image. With each magnification, the image grew slightly blurrier.

Sam pointed to the screen. "Could it be that big building to the right? It's got a direct line and a lot of options."

Luke considered it, stroking his bearded chin. "Mmmmm. I think it's too close."

"OK, that narrows it down even more. That's one of Portland's taller buildings, so it blocks out a lot of buildings behind it. We should look to the left." Sam centered the image to the left of the building they'd eliminated.

"We've got two options. That building under construction or the one on the left side of the screen," Luke said.

"Are there even floors at the upper levels? It looks like mostly girders on the top third." Delilah stood and walked around the coffee table, getting closer to the TV.

"It's hard to tell from this angle, and I'm not sure zooming in will yield anything better." Sam tried magnifying it more, but they'd reached the limits of this image's quality. The whole thing pixilated and blurred the more she tried to focus on the upper levels of the building under construction. She returned the photo to the previous setting, going back to the crisper image. "Yeah, not happening."

"Looks like we need to make a trip downtown and check out that building," Pablo said.

Luke looked over at his friend. "Yup, and we'll want to check out the other building as well."

"Guys, I don't want to puncture your enthusiasm, but 'check it out' seems like a dangerous option. I know you said that wasn't a world class shot, but it was still impressive," Sam said.

"Sam's got a point," Delilah agreed. "How long did they have that sniper stationed up there waiting for us? Could they have responded that quickly when the fighting broke out? I'm starting to think we didn't discover their new operation, but that they set it up to lure us in. And predictably, we responded. Probably why they didn't make it more difficult for us."

"Yeah, leave you for the sniper or the cops. Cassius gets others to do the dirty work and keeps his hands clean." Pablo sat up straighter.

"They had that sniper spot picked out. It wasn't a spur-of-the-moment decision. If the three of us go wandering in there and that sniper is still there, or other highly trained vamps or thralls, I'm not sure an ill-fitting bulletproof vest is going to be enough to save my bacon. And I'm not eager to put my fragile human body on the line for a dumb plan."

"So, 'wing it' is off the table?" Pablo asked.

Sam and Delilah looked at each other, exchanging eye rolls and nods. Both spoke at once, "Yes."

"They're probably right, Pablo. Can you see if Jamaal can get us floor plans of those buildings? He did pretty good on the Wapato plans last winter," Luke said.

"I'll ask him."

"OK, let's pause the next stage of the investigation until we get some blueprints. Besides, if you're unwilling to go in underpowered, I'm unwilling to go in with a bad arm and a concussion. We need to find a vamp or two to fix me up. Until I get my rudis into a vampire and drain it, I'm not going to be up to this level of action. For now, we avoid downtown and anywhere in the shadow of either of those two buildings. I'll see if I can map it out."

"That could be a lot of territory out of bounds, especially downtown where they like to hunt," Pablo said.

"How far can a sniper shoot?" Delilah asked.

"I'm not sure these days," Luke replied.

"Um, according to this…" Gwen halted, looking worried at interrupting the adults.

"Go ahead, little one," Luke said. "You can always jump in when you have something to say."

Gwen looked back at her cell phone. "Um, well, it says the record is just over two miles. The other long ones are around…a mile and a half. Most are around a mile."

"Thank you. Can you send me that article?" Luke asked.

"Sure, it's just Wikipedia," Gwen replied.

Luke smiled at Gwen. "OK, thanks to Gwen, I know to keep the radius about a mile, but we'll have a lot of buildings blocking shooting lanes, so we should be OK. But back to east Portland might be a better option right now. We can snag a few medicinal vampires for me while we wait for Jamaal to turn around those blueprints. Maybe we'll stumble into something interesting to disrupt while we're at it. Sound good?"

Looking around the room, they all nodded.

"Mind if I join you?" Sam asked.

"Not at all. You're great in a fight. We'd love to have you on board," Luke replied. "I suppose we should grab your measurements for a vest while we're at it." Luke disappeared into a back room and came back out with cloth measuring tape and a note pad.

# FIVE

THE NEXT DAY, Luke and Gwen walked to the pack's house. It wasn't too far away, and they'd caught a break in the usually rainy spring weather. It was one of those glorious sunny weeks that always makes Portlanders forget there were still several more months of rain before the usual July fifth start to summer in Western Oregon.

Gwen was quieter than usual. Being around werewolves who weren't the handful she'd accepted into her life always made her nervous. Luke reached out and squeezed her shoulder reassuringly.

"Maggie cleared out the pack for our visit today, so it'll just be her. She wants you to feel comfortable."

"Oh, OK." Gwen appeared to relax some, although not all the way.

Luke wasn't sure he'd seen her completely relaxed. The kid still had a long way to go in her recovery.

Maggie, sitting on the porch of the pack house, got up, her face brightening when she saw Luke and Gwen. "Hi, Luke. Hi, Gwen. It's good to see you both. Everything is all clear in the house. I've got fresh coffee for you Luke and mint tea for Gwen."

She led them inside. On a coffee table in the sitting area, Maggie had set up a tray with the coffee and tea as well as a few cookies.

"Can I have a cookie, please?" Gwen asked.

Maggie smiled. "Of course, that's why I baked them. Chocolate chip since it's your favorites. And Luke's too, I believe. Go ahead and relax. We have the house for a while."

"Luke, can I watch TV?" Gwen asked.

"If it's OK with Doc…"

"Go ahead. Don't forget to take a cookie or two with you," Maggie replied.

Gwen grabbed several cookies and her mug of tea before heading into the other room to turn on the TV.

When Gwen was out of the room, Maggie smiled at Luke. "You can call me Maggie if you'd like."

"Would you prefer that I stop using 'Doc'?" Luke asked.

"I would."

Luke nodded. "OK, Maggie."

While Gwen was in the other room, Maggie and Luke chatted amiably. Since Luke had become more integrated into the pack's life after last fall's events and becoming Gwen's ward, he'd seen a lot more of Maggie. She liked to check in on Gwen to see how the kid was doing and how well Luke was adjusting to the radical change in his life.

Physically, Gwen was thriving, eating constantly, putting on weight, growing. She also seemed to be improving mentally, at least a little. Stability was still a concept she wasn't used to. It would take a long time to heal the wounds the years of homelessness and a bad home life before that had caused. Luke wasn't sure how he'd help her, his own emotional wounds so plentiful and open, but he kept plugging along.

Luke enjoyed Maggie's presence. She was calming and kind; it almost seemed like she was checking in on Luke as much as Gwendolyn. It was fair to say Luke was growing to like Maggie and looked forward to the times when he'd see her. She was becoming a friend. It was still weird to Luke to think he had friends, and fierce ones at that.

Seeing Luke's cup was empty, Maggie offered a refill from the carafe. "Another cup?"

"I'd like that. Although we should probably get the x-rays out of the way."

"This isn't a hospital; I'll let you bring it down to the exam room," Maggie replied, smiling at Luke. Standing, she beckoned for Luke to follow.

"Gwen," Luke called, raising his voice. "We're headed downstairs to get my chest x-rayed if you need anything."

"K," she called back from the other room.

Following Maggie downstairs, they wound their way through the maze of hallways under the pack house until they arrived at a back room Luke hadn't seen before.

"We keep the x-ray here. It's good to have it handy since wolves heal so quickly. A broken bone can set improperly necessitating rebreaking it," Maggie explained, opening the door. "There's a robe there if you'd prefer. Strip down to your underwear, please."

Luke peeled his t-shirt off one-armed and grimaced as he awkwardly slid the shirt down his right arm, trying to keep it stable. Maggie winced. Next, he removed his jeans until he was standing in the middle of the room in his underwear and socks.

"Against the wall there," Maggie directed, pointing out where she wanted Luke. Satisfied, she walked over and pulled the x-ray into place, then walked over and pushed a button.

"Don't I need some lead to block...my vitals?" Luke gestured around his waist and head.

Maggie raised an eyebrow questioningly. "I'm not sure this low level of radiation will do much to you, especially how you heal."

Luke nodded. Maggie was one of the few members of the pack who knew how Luke's magic worked, how he healed and regenerated by stealing the life force from vampires.

"You're probably right. If it does any damage, it'll heal right up with the next vampire I find."

"Speaking of which, when are you going to get this taken care off?"

"I think we're heading out tonight," Luke replied.

"Good. I need you to turn. Can you lift your arm?" Maggie asked.

Luke tried but grunted.

"Here, let me help." Maggie walked over and gently took Luke's arm and hand. "OK, I'll lift it. Try to relax as best as you can. You can hang onto this rope to make it easier. When I tell you to, I want you to turn so your back is to me so I can get your side and your back."

Luke hissed as Maggie gently extended his arm up. He gripped the handle dangling from the end of the rope. "This good, Maggie?"

"Yes. I'll hurry." She positioned the x-ray again, walked to the button, then walked back. "OK, turn around."

Luke turned his back to her, allowing her to readjust the x-ray. She hit the button, then moved the x-ray out of the way.

"OK, Luke. I'm going to help you lower your arm. Then I'll wrap up your chest. I want to keep you stable until you can heal yourself."

"Thanks." Luke walked over to his jeans and awkwardly pulled them up.

Maggie took out a bandage and began working it around Luke's chest. In such close proximity, Luke could smell the pleasant, light citrusy scent of Maggie's perfume. Feeling around to check the wrap, Maggie declared Luke was done. She picked up his t-shirt and helped him slide it on over his bad arm, pulling it down into place.

"One last thing," Maggie said, grabbing an arm sling. "I'd like you to wear this."

Luke opened his mouth, ready to protest the sling.

Maggie held up a hand to forestall him. "Even when you go out. I've cut the straps and added Velcro. If you really need this arm, you can extend it, and the Velcro will pop. It's strong enough to hold your arm, but not strong enough to impede you if you need it."

"Thanks, Maggie. That's good thinking. I promise I'll keep it on. Sam is joining us tonight, so I'll have extra help."

"How's the head?"

"Still having some dizziness and occasional blurriness in my vision."

Maggie pulled out a small flashlight and checked Luke's eyes. "It's not the worst concussion, but..." She looked like she was struggling to come up with the next question. "Does that heal too? Brain injuries?"

"Always has before. It can make things dicey until I find a vampire, but it's usually one of the first things that clears up when I do." Luke shrugged with his good shoulder.

"That's good. I'm glad you have plenty of help for tonight," Maggie replied.

Judging from the tone of her voice, she seemed genuinely concerned about his safety and glad he wouldn't be out alone.

"We all good, Maggie?"

"You are. I did want to talk to you about Gwen before I see her. How is she doing?"

"OK, I think. She spends most of her time with her nose in a book or with my cat. She watches cartoons a lot. But I think she's sleeping better. She's actually sleeping in the bed. It's been a while since I found her huddled in the corner."

Maggie smiled softly. "That's some improvement. How are you two getting along?"

"Good. It's...weird having someone in the house, but I think we're getting along well enough. She doesn't talk a lot. She doesn't seem to be as jumpy as she was when she first moved in. Either that, or I'm getting used to her mannerisms."

"Yeah, after her life so far, she's probably got a hyperactive fight-or-flight response. I guess that ties into what I wanted to talk to you about. I'd like to suggest to her that she see a therapist so she can start working through some of her trauma," Maggie said.

Luke rubbed his jaw, thinking. "That's probably a good idea. Would her therapist be able to show me how to..." He searched for the words he wanted. "To do better for her? I just don't know what I'm doing."

Maggie reached out and touched Luke's arm, rubbing her hand up and down. "You're doing pretty good so far. She clearly likes you. You might think about finding a common hobby or activity you can do together. But yes, the therapist can provide you with tools to help you guide her."

"You're the doctor, Maggie. I'm all for doing whatever to help her out."

"Excellent. I have a list of pack therapists here." She pulled a list out of her pocket and handed it to Luke. "The first two on the list are probably the best matches for her needs and personality, but you may have to try a few to get a good fit. Don't feel like you need to stick it out with one just because that was your initial choice."

"Makes sense," Luke replied.

"Have you thought about enrolling her in school?"

Luke shook his head lightly. "Not really. It never crossed my mind. Do werewolf children go to public schools? I guess I never really thought about it."

Maggie tipped her head from side to side. "It varies pack to pack. Holly likes to have pack kids enrolled, so they're better integrated with the larger populace."

"Can we enroll her now? Isn't the school year over in a few months?"

"It's probably best to wait until the new school year. Plus, we'll need to get her education up to level. She's a smart kid, so that shouldn't be too difficult. You said she's reading a lot. What's she reading?"

"Whatever I have she's interested in, I guess. I haven't tracked it. Um... I don't have any kid's books, so she's reading adult books. So her reading skills are probably solid."

"That's good. How are you with math?" Maggie asked.

Luke laughed. "I've never been to school, certainly not in either of the last two centuries. All my numbers were practical application. I learned how to keep the books for my father's business. How to calculate distances to fire a ballista... How to allocate supplies for a legion on the march... How to plot a course at sea... Not really what they're teaching to kids these days."

Maggie, smiling and chuckling, shook her head. "Well, when you break those down, that's basically the kind of math they teach kids. Some of what's required to do all those is fairly advanced. They've just started teaching those things without the...uh...practical, real world...war applications. I'll reach out to Sam. She'll be able to arrange a tutor. But I'm sure you'll be able to convert your knowledge over to figure out how to do the basics with Gwen so you can help her if she needs it."

"Yeah, I guess that's true."

"You're doing great, Luke. Are you going to be able to get her to appointments with your schedule?"

"Yeah. If I schedule her for the afternoons, I can still get some sleep and head out at night. Pablo and Delilah will understand if we have to reschedule any daytime stuff," Luke replied.

Maggie smiled warmly at Luke, squeezing his uninjured shoulder. "Let's go get Gwen."

DELILAH, Pablo, and Sam gathered at Luke's house that evening to prep for their excursion out to find Luke some medicinal vampires. Delilah, grumbling, disappeared into the guest room to put on the bulletproof vest.

"I hope the new ones come soon. This shit is uncomfortable. I bought a good high impact sports bra, but this vest is just not the right size," she said, reemerging from the back.

Luke shrugged apologetically. "I'm sorry about that, Delilah. I had to guess. It was a hurried purchase."

Pointing at Sam and Pablo, Delilah asked, "Why don't they have vests?"

"We don't have any, for one thing. We'll have to rely on their wolfy healing if things take a turn. Now, I'm going to need some help into my gear." Luke took off the arm sling and set it aside.

He had everything still out from the night they'd come back from the club, using his upstairs kit to clean it. Pablo helped him into his padded vest and armor, tying it shut. After putting on his tactical harness, Luke had to decide how to attach his swords since his right arm was out of commission for now.

Delilah stared at Luke's armor. "Your armor didn't need repairs or even get a dent?"

Luke shrugged. "Nope. I guess it's more powerful than I thought.

Too bad I don't have a divinely enchanted track suit. It would be a lot more comfortable."

"Plus, you'd look cool for any unscheduled dance offs." Pablo grinned. "Can you fight left-handed?"

"Yup. Nearly as well as with my right. So," he said, looking at the swords in their snap on sheaths. "Let's put the gladius for a left-hand top draw, and I guess the rudis on the right hand for a top as well. I may have to have one of you help me out when it comes time."

Satisfied, they finished it off by helping him into his standard oversized black zip hoodie. It was identical to all the ones he wore lately. After having so many hoodies ruined during last fall's events, he'd followed through on his threat to buy them in bulk, pulling a new one from the box when the old one was trashed. Pablo helped Luke get his arm situated in the sling.

"How you feeling, buddy?" Pablo asked.

"This isn't the most comfortable I've been, but I'm used to it. I'll be happy when I get these ribs taken care of. Fortunately, Maggie has me wrapped up tight. If you guys keep me out of trouble, we should be good," Luke replied.

Sam raised her hand. "Is that what you two do?" she asked Delilah and Pablo. "Keep Luke out of trouble?"

Pablo and Delilah exchanged looks and nodded. Delilah spoke up first. "Yup, seems like it. Welcome to the team, Sam. It'll be nice to have someone new to split the load with."

Pablo grinned broadly, waggling his eyebrows smugly at Sam. "Split? She can handle all the keeping Luke out of trouble. Earn her stripes. Gotta haze the rookie."

Sam stuck her tongue out at Pablo then promptly turned her back on him and spoke to Delilah. "Pablo's job?"

Smiling ear to ear, Delilah nodded. "Pablo's job."

Luke patted Pablo on the back. "Sorry, buddy. Looks like the dynamics have shifted a bit." Luke chuckled as Pablo pouted.

# SIX

"ARE you sure this is the right neighborhood?" Luke asked.

"Pretty sure. Based on the scout teams we've had out, there have been a lot of scent pings in the area. Too many to be coincidence. At least I hope..." Pablo replied.

Based on an idea Pablo and Luke had come up with prior to the Wapato raid, they'd sent out small teams of werewolves at night to comb popular bar districts around Portland to see if they could detect specific nests or areas being worked heavily. According to the data points they'd mapped, somewhere within a series of blocks in southeast Portland between Belmont and Hawthorne, there was a vampire nest, or at least chances of stumbling on a vamp out hunting. It was a better plan than last fall when they primarily relied on walking around until Luke's vampy senses went off.

"So... You just drive around and hope to stumble on a vampire? That's your whole plan?" Sam asked, sounding incredulous.

"Pretty much," Luke replied.

"I mean, we're sending out scouts to get better odds. That's an improvement," Pablo chimed in, defending Luke.

"Guys. There has to be a better way to do this." Sam shook her head.

"Well, Delilah used to wait in bars until she could pick up a vampire..." Luke offered feebly.

"You keep my name out of your mouth. As you told me so pointedly when we first met, I was an amateur."

Luke inhaled sharply as shame washed over him. "I'm... I'm so sorry." Putting his head in his hands, he shook it. "I keep failing at my duty. I'm not equipped for this anymore. The world has changed too much while I hid in my house."

Sam patted his knee. "I'm sorry."

"You're not wrong, Sam," Luke replied. "I used to be a leader of soldiers. I commanded the most feared legion in the empire. I've outlived empires. I survived the trenches in Belgium and France..."

"Luke, buddy, we'll figure this out. You don't have to go it alone. You have resources, that means more than bodies. That also means brains." Pablo stopped, sniffing at the vents pulling in air from outside. Rolling down the window further, he popped his nose out to grab a few more breaths of air. "I think there's one around. Smells fresh-ish."

"Ish?" Delilah asked.

"Like one passed through sometime in the last couple hours maybe? Cut me some slack. I'm not a trained bloodhound. I've been living in cities for a long time. Haven't needed to hunt for a meal in a while. Whup. It's gone. Let me circle the block and see if we can get a bead on it."

Luke put away his self-pity now that the hunt was imminent. He tried to pick up the vibrations that let him know his age-old enemy was near. When they'd rounded the block, Luke felt it.

"They're near and still here," Luke said.

As they cruised down the quiet residential street, Luke felt the presence get closer. Out of the shadows, a figure emerged, walking down the street casually, hands in pockets. They could be anyone out for any reason, except Luke knew what the reason was.

"OK, Pablo. Turn at the next block and park a ways back. We'll drop off Delilah and Sam to follow him. You and I will circle back and park a few blocks ahead of where he might be going. Ladies, we'll meet you in the middle."

Delilah and Sam jumped out of Pablo's truck, shutting the doors before jogging back to the corner and turning to get the vamp back in their sights. Pablo took off quickly and grabbed the next turn that'd take them parallel and ahead of the fanger. Pablo pulled far enough forward that the chances of seeing the brake lights from the other corner would be non-existent. Once parked, Pablo jumped out and helped Luke down out of the cab.

Luke sighed. "I hate this."

"I know, dude. But you have to learn to get by with a little help from your friends. Let's start out slow; let your body warm up a little."

They set off at a brisk walk instead of a run. Rounding the corner, they checked to see if they could spot their suspected vampire. Unfortunately, the street was empty. Pablo reached into his pocket and pulled out his phone.

"Sam says he went into a house. They sent the address. She and Delilah are hiding on the corner out of sight."

"Which corner?"

Pablo texted and waited for an answer back. "Taylor and 31st."

Luke looked up at the street signs above him. "Salmon and 33rd. OK. Let them know we'll contact them when we're at Taylor and 32nd."

"Got it...and confirmed. Ready?"

Luke grimaced, trying to stand straight. "As I'll ever be..."

Luke started at a light jog, just above a fast walk. He rotated his left shoulder and extended and contracted his elbow as he went, getting his sword arm warmed up. Pablo quickly caught up. By the time they reached their corner, Luke was winded. Leaning against a post to catch his breath and try to take some pressure off his ribs, Luke shook his head, his jaw clenching, brow furrowed.

"You OK, buddy?"

Luke shook his head.

"You hurting bad?"

Luke nodded. He took several deep and steadying breaths, trying to breathe his way through the pain.

"I had Doc give me a couple pain killers for you, since you won't ask for them. It's just some heavy-duty ibuprofen. Gel caps. They'll kick in fast."

Luke snagged them out of Pablo's hands, swallowing them dry. Pablo pulled his phone out to check in with Delilah and Sam.

"OK. No one has left. They can see two people sitting on the porch drinking, but they're too alert. So guards. What do you think, Luke?"

"We might have stumbled on a nest."

"You want to call it off? Try again tomorrow? Or check another neighborhood?"

Luke thought about it for a moment. "No, there're four of us. The house's confines will neutralize any numerical superiority they might have. And if I can get one of the guys at the door, I can get juiced up."

"Alright, boss. How do you want to do it? We can't all four rush the porch, and you can't rush at all."

"How's our approach looking?"

Pablo stepped out slightly so he could check out the sidewalk down toward the address Sam had sent. "Lots of trees and bushes. We can get pretty close without being seen."

"Good. No wind..." Luke looked up. "And now a drizzle."

"Too bad you can't use your hood..." Pablo pulled up the hood on his jacket.

Luke scratched his nose with his middle finger.

"Got an itchy nose, bud?"

"Something like that. But this is good, too. Rain will pull particles out of the air. Should help hide our scent."

"Plus, with our pack scouts roaming around, they're probably used to werewolf scent passing through."

"OK, Pablo. Grab my rudis. Here's how we play it..."

PABLO AND LUKE strolled down the street, trying to look like two people just walking down the block. Once the house came into sight, they saw Delilah and Sam standing on the porch, chatting up the two guys who were ostensibly keeping guard on the door. One of the vamps said something, and both Sam and Delilah laughed, Sam selling it better than Delilah, who was having trouble making her chuckle sound sincere. One of the guys handed Delilah and Sam beers from the cooler next to him on the porch.

Luke's senses tightened, his pain receding—although not disappearing—into the background. The sound of loud music underscored the conversation on the porch. A moment later, he heard the hiss of the tabs cracking the seal on the can, letting its $CO_2$ escape, followed by the crunch of the tab pushing in the aluminum lid. Sam turned her head slightly and gave Delilah a nearly imperceptible nod. One of the guys cracked another joke. Playing their part, both women started laughing. Delilah who'd had the can to her lips a moment before spit beer and started coughing. She turned, hunching over the railing of the porch, coughing. One of the vampires stepped forward to check on her.

As she coughed, her hand slid into her coat and gripped a stake. The vamp's hand lowered to her shoulder—Luke's vision sliding into slow motion. With a cushion of air separating his hand and her shoulder, she spun hard, punching him in the chest with the heel of her left hand. The vamp stumbled backwards into the side of the house. The last thing his shocked eyes saw was Delilah plunging a stake into his heart, sending him splashing onto the deck in a messy goo.

The other vampire, shocked and slow to react, took a step toward Delilah. Seizing the moment—and his arm—Sam turned and spun him into the wall with a loud thump. She followed it with a nose-shattering punch. As the black sludge the vampire called blood dribbled down his face, he dribbled down the wall, dazed. As soon as he hit the ground, Delilah and Sam dragged him to the back corner of the porch, which was shrouded by two large shrubs, providing some privacy.

Not waiting for Luke, Pablo sprinted ahead, leaping up the stairs. Luke tried to jog but quit after a couple steps. The weight of the armor may have been a mistake before getting healed. At least the wrappings Maggie had applied kept his chest stable. Huffing and puffing, he gingerly climbed the three steps up to the porch. His rudis stood straight up in the vampire's chest.

Pablo pointed to the rudis. "Just like you said."

"Thank you. Can you help me down?" Luke asked.

Pablo took his good arm and helped him kneel over the stabbed but not dissolving vampire. Grimacing and grunting in pain, Luke placed his hands around the hilt of the rudis and lowered his forehead to the pommel button on the end of the pommel. He recited the incantation that activated the rudis, sending a glow of white light down the silver filigree of the wood blade down into the vampire and back up again into the pommel button and ultimately, Luke.

Taking a deep breath, he stood stiffly but without help. He attempted some torso movement to assess his condition.

"How you feeling?" Sam asked.

"Better, I think. The pain isn't quite as intense. I feel brittle, but better. I'll probably need at least another vampire before I'm all the way up to snuff." The burning pain in his ribs lessened to a dull throb and his focus felt sharper, though he wasn't sure if that was the concussion healing some or just the presence of vampires.

"Too bad we gooed the other one," Pablo said.

"It was the safer plan," Luke countered. "There will be more inside. I can feel them."

Luke reached down and pulled the rudis from the corpse, allowing it to decompose into a second puddle of vampire sludge.

"So...question," Sam said. "Why didn't it dissolve after your thing?"

"My thing? Oh... The rudis," he held it up for emphasis, "acts like an interrupter. It effectively breaks the circuit. Renders a vamp inert, allowing me to do my 'thing' safely. Then when I remove it, the natural process of vampire death continues. If they dissolved as soon as I put the wood through their heart, I couldn't get any juice. The gladius, however, starts the death process as soon as it enters."

"Interesting," Sam said.

Pablo and Delilah were searching through the pockets of vampires trying to find keys.

"Yuck. We should have checked the other one before Luke finished him up," Delilah complained.

"Got 'em," Pablo called. He stood up and tried different keys in the lock until one slid in and turned, the sound of music from inside covering the noise. "OK, everyone get your weapons ready."

Delilah slid her machete out of the backpack she was carrying and strapped it to her thigh. She handed Sam a wakizashi. Sam slid the Japanese short sword and its wooden scabbard under the belt of her jeans. Luke flipped the rudis around and handed it to Pablo before drawing his gladius with his left hand, keeping his right arm safely in the sling.

"Here Pablo. If we get a chance, stick another one for me. But let's be safe, so choose the kill over subduing one. Y'all ready?" Luke looked around, collecting a nod from each of his companions. Luke gave Pablo the signal to go.

Before Pablo could open the door, someone yanked it open from inside.

"Quit playing with the… What the fuck?" the vamp said, eyes going wide.

Sam, thinking quicker than the others, grabbed the fanger's arm and yanked him out the door. The vamp tumbled over Pablo, falling flat on his face. Bring her short sword down, she lopped the vampire's head off, spraying vamp blood on Pablo and the porch.

Delilah, after her momentary freeze, scooped up the head and moved it into the shadows behind the hedges surrounding the porch. Between them, Sam and Pablo moved the body into the shadows cast along the back of the porch.

"Will that do, Luke?" She extended a hand to help Pablo up.

"Yup." He turned to Pablo. "My rudis, sir?"

"Blech," Pablo said, wiping the vamp's blood off his face and hands.

"Here." Delilah grabbed the rudis. Instead of handing it to Luke, she stabbed it through the vampire's chest and stepped away. "Need help down?"

"Nah, I think I can get it on my own." Luke propped himself on rail and lowered himself carefully to repeat the process, all the sore spots in his body loudly reminding him of their existence.

The team fanned out, guarding him while he finished the ritual. He stood a little quicker than before and slid the sling off, rotating his right arm a bit.

"Back to one hundred?" Delilah asked.

"Not quite. I don't get the full charge out of a beheaded one."

"My apologies," Sam said.

"No worries. He surprised us there. We needed him down, and I got some juice. Win-win. Let's get inside." He pointed to the open door. "Not too much talk. The music will cover most of the sound and they'll assume it's just house mates unless we do something too noisy. I'm still sensing a lot of vamps."

They stepped into the house, pulling the keys from the lock on the way in. Pablo locked the door once they were all in.

"Can either of you get any idea about scents?" Luke asked the werewolves.

"Too many, dude. I'm kind of overwhelmed. Plus there's some other scents mingled in adding to the chaos. Sam?" He pointed to the smears of vampire sludge spotting his skin and clothes.

"Same."

Luke nodded and headed into the kitchen. He pulled open the pantry closet and peeked in. It just looked like any other home pantry—shelves with dried goods and canned food. It was hard to tell where the other vampires were. There were enough that his senses were jumbling them together.

"Alright, let's head upstairs. We can clean it out and then we won't have to worry about anyone coming downstairs," Luke whispered. "Delilah, Sam, you lead the way. Pablo, you bring up the rear. No need to be sneaky, really. They know there are others in the house, so just act natural."

They headed toward the staircase in the living room. With weapons drawn, they headed upstairs, keeping a solid gap between each other in case they needed room to fight. When they reached the top of the stairs, Luke swapped his gladius for his rudis, leaving

Pablo to guard against intrusions. He signaled for Sam and Delilah to start with the first room on the right.

Sam took the doorknob and turned it slowly, trying to keep noise to a minimum. When she cracked the door, they were assailed with the sounds of sex. Sam clamped her lips shut against the mirth Luke could see on her face. She peeked in, then held up two fingers to indicate the number of occupants before pointing out which wall the bed was on. Sam slowly pushed the door open enough that she and Delilah could slip through, stopping it before it was noticeable. Sliding through the door silently, Sam disappeared, Delilah following.

A moment later, Luke heard the sound of a head being removed and a brief scream followed by the crunch of fist meeting face. Luke walked into the room and shut the door without letting it latch. On the bed, a decapitated body was slumped over the back of a live woman, the leaking neck covering her in the vampire's gore. Sam grabbed the vampire's arm and pulled its corpse off the woman. She was human. That's why she'd been knocked out instead of executed.

Luke peeled her eyelids back to check her eyes. Standing, he found Delilah next to him.

Delilah leaned in and whispered into his ear, "Do we tie her up?"

Luke thought about it for a moment, then shook his head. He pantomimed sleep. By the time she awoke, they would have the upstairs cleaned out. While Luke and Delilah had their brief exchange, Sam was checking the closet. Giving the thumbs up for all clear, Luke quickly stabbed the vampire's corpse with his rudis and sucked its energy into his body. Finished, Luke pointed toward the door. They slid back out of the room and closed the door quietly behind them, the drone of music filling the house covering any incidental noises.

They repeated the procedure in the rest of the rooms, clearing each one, Luke taking what juice he could as they went. Luke was feeling nearly himself and reclaimed his gladius from Pablo. Stashing the arm sling in Delilah's backpack, he rotated his right arm, enjoying the feel of being nearly whole and mostly functional.

Luke wasn't sure how many might be in the bigger room, but he was prepared for more than the twos and threes they'd encountered so far. Sam, hand on the doorknob, waited for Luke's signal. Delilah, a stake in one hand and her machete in the other, stood behind Sam. Luke nodded and Sam quietly opened the door and slid in. Delilah followed, then Luke.

Except for the door zone, the entire floor was covered in mattresses. Whipping his head around as he heard chains clanking, his eyes jumped open when a vampire in a vinyl suit with a full mask strained against massive restraints. They'd been spotted, although he couldn't really alert anyone since the mouth hole of the mask was filled with a red ball gag. The muffled noises he was making were ignored by the handful of people on the other side of the room who were too engrossed in their sex. The wall behind the vampire was starting to bow as the bound vampire strained to free himself.

Luke pointed toward the people and vampires in the far corner. Delilah and Sam flared out, stepping carefully on the springy mattresses. Luke headed toward a vampire that'd backed up toward the wall. Once Luke stepped within range, the vamp surged forward. Adjusting his aim, Luke let the vampire impale itself on the rudis. Behind him, the sounds of screams and the splatter of blades hitting body pulled him around. Leaving his rudis in the vamp's chest, he cautiously walked back to the door just as someone made a break for it, squeezing past Delilah and Sam. As they approached, Luke punched out, catching them in the temple and sending the human flopping onto a mattress, Luke's supernatural strength rendering them unconscious. Once the last vampire went down, they were left in the room with the human Luke had knocked out, the heart stabbed vamp in vinyl, and a large pool of goo soaking into the mattresses.

Wobbling her way to the closet, Delilah checked to make sure it was unoccupied.

"Empty here," Delilah said.

"This was an interesting upstairs," Sam commented. "Vamps just having a good old time. Only two humans. Not sure if that's good or bad."

"At least we were able to spare them," Delilah replied.

Luke popped the door open to check on Pablo who gave him the all clear. Leaving the door open so Pablo could hear, he checked in on everyone to make sure there weren't any incidental injuries.

"OK. I'm going to take care of this last vamp, then we'll head downstairs and see if we can find the rest," Luke said as he walked toward the vamp dangling from the wall.

Standing over the vamp, Luke shook his head. Kneeling, he shoved the vampire back and held it in place with his left arm so the rudis was at a better angle. He wrapped his right fist around the hilt, placed his forehead against the pommel, and activated the rudis, sucking the vampire dry. Without the body to fill the suit, it fell into a pile on the ground, dust drifting from the few openings.

"Must have been an old one," Sam commented. "How you feeling?"

He twisted his torso, enjoying the lack of pain in his ribs. "After him? Pretty good. I think I'm back to 100%. Let's go see what's downstairs."

This wasn't Luke's first encounter with vampires and their hobbies. By the standards of some of the things he'd seen, this all seemed fairly tame. He'd need to check in with the gang to see how they were handling it. At least he felt good after draining so many vampires.

# SEVEN

PABLO SNUCK DOWNSTAIRS, first peeking into the living room, then the part of the kitchen he could see through the threshold leading from the kitchen. He signaled the rest of the team all was clear. Luke and Sam swung through the living room and into the large dining room while Pablo and Delilah headed into the kitchen. When they'd cleared the dining room, they walked into the kitchen to find Pablo with his head in the fridge.

"Anything good?" Luke asked.

"Want a beer? I could use one after our entrance and the little display upstairs. Looks like some various local crafts and some... home brew? I'll try the white ale." Pablo replied, holding a brown bottle with a homemade label.

He took a bottle out of the fridge and popped the top on the bottle opener hanging from the wall. Taking a big swig, his eyes bulged, his cheeks puffing out, as he set the bottle down on the counter. He looked around for a sink, but Luke was blocking it. Turning his head away from everyone, he sprayed the beer out onto the cabinets, blowing a red mist into the air.

Delilah picked up the bottle and handed it to Luke. "I don't think this is beer."

Luke looked at the white paper label affixed to the bottle then poured it into the sink. The dark red viscous liquid contrasted with the white of the sink as it ran slowly toward the drain. Pablo shoved Luke out of the way and vomited into the sink. Everyone backed away from him.

Luke held up the bottle. "It says 'White Male' not 'White Ale.'" Seeing Sam's puzzled face, he clarified, "Blood."

He opened the fridge and began searching through the hand-labeled brown bottles, handing a couple to Delilah and Sam so they could check them out as well.

"Black female, Indian male, white female, Hispanic female, African male…" As Luke clinked the bottles around, reading labels, the team got a picture of what was in the bottles.

Sam was staring at the bottle she held. "It also lists their emotional state and if they were sober or not, including the drug they were on if they weren't. It's warped as fuck, but I didn't think human blood had terroir."

Delilah and Sam looked profoundly troubled, staring at the bottles of blood in their hands with revulsion, and Pablo was dry heaving in the sink.

"Not just humans," Luke said.

He pulled a couple bottles from the back of the fridge and held them up. "Werewolf male, Werewolf female."

Pablo turned on the water and washed the sink clean before filling his mouth, rinsing, and spitting several times. "I'm never going to get that taste out of my mouth."

Sam took out her cell phone and snapped pictures of the were-wolf blood bottles. Pablo was searching through the cabinets for something to eat. Finding some tortilla chips, he shoved a handful in his mouth.

"Stale," he said around a mouthful of crumbs.

"Find any gallon freezer bags?" Sam asked.

Pablo shook his head, shoving another handful of chips in his mouth. Delilah started opening cabinets and drawers, finding a box of freezer bags in a lower cabinet. Sam pulled some hand towels out of one of the drawers she was searching through. Taking the bottles from Luke, she wrapped them in towels, then stuffed one in the bag Delilah held open. Delilah squeezed the air out and sealed the bag, putting them inside another plastic baggy. She took off the backpack and stuffed the bottles in the front pocket furthest from her back.

"We'll want to take those to Maggie and Holly," Sam said.

"Yeah, let's just hope they don't break. I don't fancy having glass and blood running down my back." Delilah slid the backpack up her arm and ran her other arm through the other strap.

"Shh," Pablo said, holding up his hand.

It took Luke a moment to home in on what Pablo heard—the sound of creaky stairs, stairs that didn't sound like the ones that lead up to the second floor.

"Where?" Luke whispered.

"Pantry?" Pablo replied, not seeming altogether sure.

Pablo tiptoed toward the door and flattened his back against the wall next to the hinges so that when the door opened, he'd be hidden. Everyone else headed toward the nearest door to either the living room or the dining room. Luke hid by the threshold leading into the dining room while Sam and Delilah were hidden somewhere in the living room section. A loud squeak followed by a solid bang of wood on wood preceded the pantry door opening.

"What the fuck?" the pantry vampire said in a vaguely German accent. "Why can't these assholes clean up after themselves?"

He slammed the pantry door. That was Luke's signal to pop around the corner. Pablo tried to tackle the intruder. However, what neither of them anticipated was the vampire catching Pablo's arm and flipping him over the vampire's back directly into Luke. He was sure the last part was purely a lucky coincidence for the vampire, but it still took out both men with ease.

It served as the perfect distraction for Delilah and Sam, who slid out from their hiding space. Approaching on silent feet, Delilah raked her machete across the back of the vampire's left leg, severing his hamstring. Sam caught him as he fell, taking his head off with a beautiful upward swing of her blade.

Sam shook her head at Luke and Pablo, who were still tangled up in each other's limbs on the floor. "Just lying around while the women do the work... Tsk, tsk, tsk."

Delilah chuckled, enjoying Luke and Pablo's embarrassment.

"Do we have to let her join the team?" Pablo asked.

"I think so," Luke replied. "She's been pretty handy so far."

Looking down at the headless corpse, Delilah asked, "You want to get rid of him here?"

"No, let's drag him into the dining room and stash him under the table. I don't want a giant slick of goo right here if we have to get out of here fast. Who knows if that's the only entrance." He pulled out his rudis and handed it to Delilah.

Opening her coat and pointing to the stakes, she said, "I've got stakes."

"Save them for later, we might need them."

Delilah nodded and took the rudis. Pablo dragged the body into the dining room, leaving a trail of vampire gore on the floor. Sam picked up the head and followed him. Opening the closet, Luke pulled out a mop with a disposable cloth head and a spray bottle on it. Giving the vampire blood streaks a good spray down, he did a cursory cleaning job and set the mop aside.

"All good?" Luke asked Sam and Pablo as they came back into the kitchen.

"All good. He's currently seeping into the rug under the table."

"So, secret door in the pantry?" Pablo asked.

"Looks like it," Luke replied.

Luke nodded and picked up his gladius from the counter. Opening the pantry door, he stepped in, pulling the string hanging from the ceiling to turn on the dangling light bulb. Luke shuffled through items on the shelf, pulling out some, lifting others, trying to find the switch to the secret door. Once he finished with the shelves, he started feeling around the wall. It wasn't until he ran his fingers up along the door frame leading to the kitchen that his fingers pushed in a small panel revealing a switch.

Poking his head out the door, Luke said, "I think I found it. Y'all ready?"

Sam, Delilah, and Pablo stood near the pantry, weapons ready as they waited for Luke to trigger the secret door. Luke pushed the button and heard a slight buzz of an electric lock being released. Turning, he pushed gently until he had enough exposed edge to safely grab the door to guide it slowly. Ensuring the path ahead was clear, Luke stood on the platform of the stairs that led down into a concrete bunker-like structure. Sam slid through and stood sentinel on a stair a few steps down.

Luke nodded at Pablo and Delilah then closed the secret door, locking them on the other side so they could open the door again if he couldn't find the corresponding switch on this side. Carefully feeling his away around the door frame and the rails around the platform and stairs, he eventually found a slight depression on the back underside of one of the rails. He pushed it and heard the electric buzz of the lock opening. Now they could get out again.

He pulled the door open by the handle that was conveniently placed on the back side. He made sure everyone knew exactly where the button was in case they had to get out in a hurry so the lead person wouldn't jam them up on the stairs.

One at a time, they tiptoed down the stairs, staying near the edge of the steps and trying to avoid any squeaky stairs. When they gathered at the small staging area at the bottom, the only option they found was a single door. At a signal from Luke, Pablo stripped his clothes off and stashed them in Delilah's backpack. When he'd finished putting on his werewolf suit, they readied to bust into the room.

Even after all the vampires they'd killed upstairs, Luke could still feel more than he was comfortable with nearby. Thus far, things had gone suspiciously easy. He took a steadying breath, readying for the plunge.

Luke, finally healed enough for full action and the only one in heavy armor, was going in first. Gripping the doorknob, he gave it a jiggle to see if it was locked. Turning it all the way, he made one last check with his team to see if they were ready when the door was yanked out of his hand.

"Either in or out, but quit rattling... Who the fuck are you?"

someone asked, standing with the other side of the doorknob in their hand.

Seeing the weapons and the werewolf, he tried to slam the door shut. Adrenaline pumping, Luke launched into action and shoved his body in the way of the door. He struck out with his gladius, awkwardly slicing across the arm of the vampire and causing the vampire to let go of the door and stumble backwards, tripping over someone. Freed up, Luke shoved the door open and cleared the way for the rest of his team. They burst through and disassembled the few vampires hanging around, leaving alone any humans who didn't challenge them.

In the tight confines, Luke had expected more from the vampires other than sluggish, poorly coordinated attacks. "Y'all OK?"

Pablo yipped, pointing to a shallow set of bleeding claw marks across his chest, though it looked like they were nearly healed. Sam and Delilah shook their heads when Luke checked in with them.

The room was a small square with a couple couches and coffee tables and two doors, the other on the opposite wall from the door they'd just come through. One of the coffee tables was littered with syringes, needles, bent spoons, and lighters as well as a few lengths of rubber tubing. A couple people were huddled in the corner, terrified of the intruders, including the massive werewolf. One person was passed out on the couch, his shirt sleeve rolled up, a needle stuck in his arm. Sam walked over to the couch, squatted, and checked the pulse of the man.

"He alive?" Delilah asked.

"Yeah, just stoned out of his gourd. Holy shit..." Sam reached up and tipped his head up. "This is Fred Bealer. He's the city commissioner that came out with Cassius last winter to announce the mayor's abduction. I guess that answers the question of how close he is to Cassius."

Luke whistled in surprise. "That's not good. It's interesting, but not good at all."

"Well, we may be one step closer to knowing who's helping the fangers navigate the city apparatus. We should pull the needle out of his arm before something bad happens," Delilah said.

"No, leave the needle," Sam said, a firm note of command in her voice.

Sam fished her phone out of her pocket and got a good picture of Bealer's face, before tipping his head back onto the couch cushions. Stepping back, she got a full body shot of him, complete with the needle stuck in his arm.

"Holly will want to see these. They might be very useful. And sending... Good, didn't want them lost on the phone if something happened." Satisfied that she had enough photos, Sam carefully pulled the needle from the unconscious man's arm.

"What next?" Delilah asked.

Luke looked over to the two humans hiding in the corner. "Hey, did you come in this door?" He pointed to the door they'd just busted in through.

One of them shook their head and pointed to the other door.

Luke stared coldly at them, hoping they were sober enough to understand. "OK. Stay down here for twenty minutes. Things are going to keep getting messy. Understand? I don't want you under-foot. Then you need to help him get out of here. We'll have cleared the way by then. If you get in our way or sound any alarms, we'll leave your corpses. Got it?"

The terrified expression on their face told him they understood.

"One of you, toss me your phone," Luke added.

Catching the phone, Luke slid the screen up to reveal the timer. He set it for twenty minutes and placed it on the coffee table. He checked to see if his friends were ready. Turning back to the scared humans, he reiterated the plan. "I set the timer for twenty minutes. Don't leave before then. Take what you want, I don't care. Just don't forget to take him with you."

They nodded vigorously. Pablo tapped Luke's shoulder and pointed toward the door, then to his ear. After a moment, Luke heard someone turning the doorknob. Pablo jogged over to the door and stood next to it, back flattened against the wall. Luke stood in front of the door, weapons drawn. Delilah and Sam flanked him to either side.

When the door busted open, Luke stabbed out, catching the

intruder in the heart. The vamp dissolved into goo, some of it splattering on Luke's clothes. Jumping over the puddle, Luke charged into the other room. While the vamps in the first room had been sluggish and easy to put down, the vampires in the second room were not. Seeing their friend eliminated, they bellowed in rage and sprang at the Luke. Jacked up, the vampires moved faster than normal, swiping erratically at him, punctuating their attacks feral growls. Luke had trouble pressing them away from the door to allow his friends in to back him up. Spinning, he shoved one of the charging vamps through the door for the others to take care of, lessening his own burden.

Out of the way of the door, he backed up carefully, bringing the raging vamps with him. Fearing he was about to run out of space, Luke stopped his retreat and returned the fangers' aggression. He was relieved to see Pablo burst through the door and start tearing into the vampires crowded around, using his werewolf bulk to shred vampires. Luke was able to dispatch a couple with stabs to the heart.

Once Delilah and Sam engaged, the tide turned in favor of the hunters. When the last of the vampires was put down, Luke and his friends were breathing heavily, foreheads glistening with sweat except for Pablo who panted lightly. Although Sam was relatively new to the team, only having been out with them a time or two since the battle on the St. Johns Bridge, her skills as a fighter were proving to be a welcome addition. With the vampires down, Delilah was shepherding a few agitated humans away from her friends and either of the exits. Their eyes focused on the machete she was using to point out her commands which earned their quick compliance.

"Looks like this is the uppers room," Sam said, pointing with her short sword to the table with little mirrors and lines of coke cut onto them. "Are vampires dealing to earn money?"

"Not quite. They're probably not even charging much. Drugs don't affect them unless they consume it via blood. You saw the bottles upstairs." Luke pointed toward the humans in the corner. "These are juice boxes flavored with their vice of choice."

"You learn something new every day..." Sam replied.

Luke didn't think she looked too happy about this newfound

knowledge. Leaving Delilah and Pablo to guard both exits, Luke joined Delilah.

"You got them under control?" Luke asked Delilah.

"I think so. They're a bit more amped up than the three from the previous room."

"Coke will do that." He handed his gladius to Delilah and turned to the three people pacing in the corner. "OK. I need you to stay down here for twenty minutes. If you get in our way, you'll get hurt. I'm going to need one of you to toss me their phone."

Their eyes kept going back and forth between his swords and Delilah's machete, nervously fidgeting.

"Let's not make me wait..." Luke said.

A man reached into his pocket and tossed Luke his phone. Luke set the timer for seventeen minutes, figuring that was close to what the other people had left, and tossed the phone back.

"You wait to go upstairs until that alarm goes off. Besides..." Luke pointed toward the table. "There's plenty to keep you occupied. I guarantee no one here will be left to make you pay for it, financially or with your life. Understand? And take the three idiots in the other room out with you in case they've nodded off."

While they seemed wary, they all looked happily at the table full of white lines and little filled baggies. They nodded.

Luke turned to his crew. "We're all good. Now let's see where these stairs go. Pablo, follow me. Delilah, guard our retreat. Let's be careful, there are more toothy bastards upstairs."

Delilah perked up, narrowing her eyes. "I thought we cleared out the upstairs already."

One of the cokeheads diffidently raised a hand. "Those stairs lead to a different house."

Luke's eyebrows shot up. "OK." He collected acknowledgements from the team to ensure they were ready.

Sheathing his rudis, Luke took his gladius back from Delilah and headed up the stairs. At the top, he halted and checked that everyone was in position. Taking a deep breath, he gripped the knob and turned it, finding it unlocked. Luke shoved it open and charged through, gladius in the lead as he emerged in a completely different house. He caught a group of vampires standing around in a circle drinking blood from bottles like those they'd seen in the other house. Luke shoved the closest vampire toward the others, hoping to trip them up, then took the head of one off with a backhand slash. He rammed his chest into the headless corpse, sending it toward another vampire.

The aggressiveness of his attack coupled with its unexpectedness allowed Luke to take about half of the group of nine down before his friends had cleared the door. Luke continued herding the vamps away from the door so it would be clear. Wading into the middle of the last four, he shoved one back toward Pablo who'd just come through the door. Luke took the arm off one fanger, then a head from another, before finishing the last with a stab through the heart. Pablo, catching the vampire by the head as he fell, twisted and ripped the head off, tossing it aside.

Sam sauntered through the carnage, avoiding the piles of goo to keep her shoes clean. "You boys are so messy. Just leaving bodies and parts all over the place." She shook her head.

Luke, taking the hint, walked around and stabbed the vampire corpses with his gladius to send them on their final journey.

"Delilah, come here," Sam said, looking at a rip in Delilah's sleeve. "That sting?"

"Now that you've pointed it out it does." Delilah twisted her neck to look at it.

"It's not too bad." Sam found a drawer with dishtowels in and grabbed one. She wrapped it around Delilah's upper arm. "That'll hold you."

"Shit. I hope I don't need stitches," Delilah replied.

While Luke disposed of the corpses and Delilah watched Luke's back, Sam and Pablo swept the rest of the first floor. When everyone was satisfied, they met at the stairs leading up. So far, the layout looked like the house they'd started in. Peeking out the front window, they appeared to be in the house next door.

Luke let go of the curtain and turned around. "I'll need someone to stand guard down here in case someone comes in the front door. If the humans from downstairs come up, let them through."

"I'll hold things down here," Delilah volunteered. "After the upstairs from the other house, not sure I'm ready for a repeat. Besides, I'm starting to drag ass and I don't want to mess up."

Luke nodded and waved everyone forward. Fatigue was settling in even after all the vamps he'd drained. He'd need some more rest to fully recover after his injuries. Pablo took the lead up the stairs, silent on his padded werewolf feet.

This time, their entrance into the house hadn't gone unnoticed. Before they could get to the top of the stairs, they were greeted with angry vampires in various stages of dress. Backing down the stairs, Delilah joined them as Pablo leapt out of the way, letting the vampires fly down the stairs.

As claws screeched across his armor, Luke silently mourned the loss of another hoodie.

"Fuck!" Delilah yelled and fell back, a vampire moving toward her.

Luke shoved his shoulder into the vamp, pinning it against the wall. Sam jumped in and assisted, hacking into the fanger's arm. As the vamp tried to push away, Luke let off the pressure and finished the vamp off as it stumbled back. While they'd handled that one, Delilah had recovered and was helping Pablo deal with the last two vampires. Between the four of them, they splattered the last vampires.

As soon as he cleared his gladius from the dissolving body of the vamp, he whirled toward Delilah. "What happened? Are you OK?"

"Yeah. Stupid asshole hit me in my arm." She turned her already wounded arm toward him, showing a dishtowel now stained red with blood. "It was only a glancing blow. Still hurts like hell though."

He heaved a sigh of relief. "I don't feel any more vampires. Sam, Pablo, can you sweep the upstairs please?"

A minute later, Sam ushered down three humans who'd pulled on some clothes and shoved them out the front door. Delilah had yelled downstairs that it was clear and sent the six people from the basement after the three from upstairs. Bealer dangled limply between two of the cokeheads as they dragged him out, the commissioner draped over their shoulders.

Sam sheathed her short sword. "I'm going to run across to the other house and make sure that woman gets out."

Luke nodded. "Hurry."

Pablo yipped and waved Delilah over. She took her backpack off and opened it, pulling out Pablo's clothes. She and Luke turned to give him a moment of privacy for his shift back to human. Half a minute later, Pablo coughed. "They made us work a bit there at the end."

At the sound of doors slamming next door, Pablo poked his head out the door. "Looks like Sam cleared the other side. We all good here?"

"My head count is good. Should be all clear, boss," Pablo called back.

"Good. Pablo mind getting the house numbers?"

"What are we doing?" Delilah asked, sticking her head into the kitchen.

"Just taking care of the evidence and leaving a message for Cassius." Luke was looking around the kitchen stove. "Perfect. Can you check to see if that phone has a dial tone?" Luke pointed at the phone hanging from the wall next to Delilah.

She picked it up with a dishtowel, put it to her ear, and nodded, before hanging it back on the receiver.

"Good. Call 911 and report a fire for this address."

Delilah looked confused by the request but picked up the phone and called in the fire. Luke jogged into the living room, found a magazine on an end table, and returned to the kitchen. Pulling the stove away from the wall and ducking behind it, he whistled as he unscrewed the gas hose from the back of the stove. The scent of natural gas spread through the kitchen. Grabbing the magazine, he stuffed it into the toaster on the other side of the kitchen and made sure it was firmly in place before running out of the kitchen.

"Now might be a good time for us to mosey on out of here in an orderly manner." Luke stuffed his hands into his pocket and strolled toward the door.

Delilah and Pablo followed him out the front door and turned left. Sam was waiting for them on the lawn and jogged over to join them. As soon as they cleared the front yard, they sprinted down the block, hung a right, and continued running until they reached Pablo's truck. They were several blocks away before they heard the sirens of the fire trucks and another block before an explosion rocked the night, sending up a large fireball into the sky.

Luke nodded his head, making a satisfied sound. "Huh. I guess it worked. I've always wanted to try that."

"Um, I hope no one else's house catches on fire..." Delilah said.

"Yeah. Didn't think of that. Shit." Luke shook himself at himself. He should have thought of that. The adrenaline of the last fight faded, leaving him feeling slightly empty. He should have felt a little better after a relatively successful mission, but he was left tired and worried about what and who he'd seen in the basement.

**THEY REMAINED** silent until Pablo's pickup merged into traffic on I-5.

It was Sam who broke the silence. "Did you pick up that magazine trick from the Jason Bourne movies?"

"Yup," Luke replied.

"Versus question!" Pablo cried out excitedly. "Who would win in a fight, Luke or Jason Bourne?"

That launched a debate as Delilah, Pablo, and Same gave their opinions, setting conditions on the engagement. Luke largely kept quiet, smiling at his friends' silliness, occasionally asking for clarification or making a point designed to egg them on.

Once they arrived at the Howling Moon, Pablo fetched the first aid kit and cleaned up the wound for Delilah. "Looks pretty shallow. I don't think you'll need stitches, but you probably should call Doc in the morning and have her check it out." He smeared antibacterial ointment over the shallow claw scratch before placing a large bandage over it.

Once Delilah's wound was dressed and Pablo poured beers for everyone, they returned to their earlier debate. No one seemed to be satisfied with the various solutions as they went round and around, continuing their spirited debate over beers.

After a couple drinks with Pablo, Luke, and Delilah, Sam took off, leaving the ongoing argument before it had reached a conclusion. She promised to fill in Holly about the evening's happenings. After letting Sam out the locked door, Pablo returned to the table with another round, this time Kenton Brown Ales, as he called them. Pablo had brewed it especially for Luke who had a hankering for a classic English Brown Ale. Having spent a large amount of time in England and Ireland over the last couple centuries, he wanted a nostalgia beer to remind of his time in the pubs of northern England.

"As promised, Luke. Your English-style Brown ale. Freshly tapped as of a few minutes ago." Pablo set the tray down and passed the glasses around before taking his seat.

Luke lifted his pint and held it in the air. "Delilah, Pablo, just wanted to say thanks for all your help tonight. You did great. I didn't feel like I needed to exert myself before I was healed. You made the healing process easy. And even with the addition of Sam to the team, you kept everything clean and smooth. Cheers!"

They raised their glasses and tapped them together with Luke's. Taking sips, they all went back for deeper drinks.

"So?" Pablo asked.

"Oh, buddy, you nailed it. Lightly roasted, balanced, and not too heavy. That really takes me back," Luke said, smiling dreamily.

"Thanks, Luke. That really means a lot coming from such a well-seasoned beer drinker as you."

Luke sniffed and chose to ignore Pablo's age joke. "So, I think I know the answer already, but do we make it official official? Sam's on the team?"

"It'll be nice to have another non-dude around when we're out hunting," Delilah said.

"You can't find many better people than Sam. She'll be an asset."

"Yeah. That was sharp getting pics of that commissioner. Cold, but sharp," Delilah added.

Pablo took a drink and set his glass back down. "Sam can be ruthless, especially when it concerns Holly or the pack. Don't get me wrong, Sam is one of the sweetest, funniest people I know, but she will fucking ruin you without hesitation if need be. You can't have a better ally, or a worse enemy."

"And she knows her business with that blade. Excellent technique on her decapitations. It's official; Sam is in." Luke raised his glass, noticing he'd nearly drained it. "Pablo, this goes down easy."

"Want another?" Pablo asked.

Luke nodded.

"How about you, Delilah?"

"Might as well if you're headed that way."

When Pablo returned, they raised glasses again to celebrate the addition of Sam to the squad and then enjoyed more beers than they should have, celebrating a successful operation after their last hadn't gone off so well. Eventually, Delilah headed home with Luke to crash in the guest room she used whenever she needed.

# EIGHT

LUKE SHUFFLED out of his bedroom toward the kitchen and a cup of coffee. Feeling a bit fuzzy after last night's celebratory drinks, Luke managed to fill the French press with grounds and hot water without making a mess, feeling it was a supreme injustice that making coffee required being uncaffeinated when one needed it most. Leaning up against the counter and sipping the first luxuriant sips, Luke finally noticed Alfred sitting rigidly outside his office door. Usually the giant orange tabby would be winding his way around Luke's legs, hoping for the morning's first scritches.

"What's up, buddy?"

Alfred replied with a terse "mrao."

"Is Gwen in the office? You know she's allowed in there." Gwen, still recovering from the traumas of homelessness and being captured, spent most of her time in the office with her nose in one of Luke's books.

"Mrao." Alfie turned and pawed at the door.

"Oh, is that it? Did she leave you out here and that's why you're all bent out of shape? Let me pour the rest of this coffee in a carafe and we'll go say good morning to your kid."

Luke topped off his cup and filled the carafe, then headed into the office. Gwen wasn't there. Another short mrao from Alfred caused him to turn around. "Uh oh." The secret passageway to his basement lair was wide open, the last volume of his Hornung edition of Edward Gibbon's "Decline and Fall of the Roman Empire" nearly tipping off its spot on the shelf, leaving the door's mechanism engaged. Luke walked through the passage and down the spiral metal staircase that led down into the smaller first room. He kept his worktable where he cleaned and maintained his armor and swords in the first room. Halfway down the stairs, he could hear the telltale sound of a record that had finished playing and was on the final loop that swished around and kept the needle in its lock groove.

As he stepped off the last step, he saw that the door to his training facility was ajar. Setting the carafe down on a Danish mid-century end table that sat between two chairs of the same style, he lifted the needle off the record and turned the power to the console off. She'd been listening to side one of Funkadelic's "Maggot Brain." Without the record drawing his attention, he heard wood thwacking on wood coming from the other room. He thought he could hear a voice as well.

Stepping through the threshold, he leaned against the doorjamb, letting the scene unfold before him. An undersized and overly skinny girl was dancing around one of his wooden practice dummies with a long, wooden practice sword in her hand. Periodically, she'd dart in and strike the dummy several times, all the while making lightsaber sounds.

"*Brooooooow.*" *thwack, thwack* "Luke, I am your father..." *thwack, thwack* "No, that's not true! *Broooow*. Search your feelings, Luke, you know it to be true..." *thwack, thwack, thwack* "No! That's not true! That's impossible!" *thwack, thwack, thwack, thwack* "*Broooooow.*" As she spun around for another pass at the dummy, she finally spotted Luke blocking the exit from the training room. She dropped the wooden training sword and tried to hide behind the tall, wooden practice dummy, but while she was small for her age, she wasn't that small.

Gwen was still quite skittish and easily startled. Several months of quiet and calm living in Luke's house couldn't erase the nearly two years of homelessness or the home that had driven her to the streets in the first place. Luke didn't want to scare her any further. He cast his voice loud enough for her to hear it but kept the tone as calm and light as he could.

"It's OK, Gwen. I promise I'm not angry. I'll be in the other room when you're ready to come out." He turned around and set his coffee cup near the carafe. That accomplished, he sat in the chair furthest from the door and the stairs up and out of his hidden basement lair. If she decided she'd rather escape upstairs, he wasn't going to make her feel trapped. After a few minutes, he heard the release of a deep breath before Gwen stepped through the door and sat down in the chair, pulling her legs up under her. She looked down at the ground, keeping her hands folded in her lap.

"First, let me reiterate, I'm not angry. How did you find the door mechanism?"

"I don't know. I was just looking for something to read..."

Luke's eyebrows rose. "Gibbon's 'Decline and Fall of the Roman Empire'?"

"I don't know. I guess it's got a cool spine. There aren't a lot of choices."

"Choices? There're hundreds of books upstairs."

"Not that I want to read," Gwen mumbled.

Luke stood up, slid the record Gwen had been listening to back in its sleeve and put it back on the shelf. "Do you like Funkadelic?"

"I don't know. I've never heard of them before. I guess it was alright."

Luke heard a meow from the stairs. Looking over, he saw Alfred poking his head around the stairs to see what was going on.

"Did you rat me out?" Gwen asked the cat.

Alfred meowed at her and came all the way downstairs. Unashamed at telling on her, he jumped in her lap and started purring.

"You know what happens to snitches, don't you?" She scratched behind his ears and around his collar. "Snitches get scritches."

Smiling to himself, Luke flipped through his records before

selecting Beirut's "Gulag Orkestar" and placing it on the turntable, setting the volume to a setting loud enough to hear but not so loud it would interfere with conversation. Refilling his coffee cup, he sat down. "Why'd you pick it?"

"I don't know. I guess it had a cool picture on the cover." Gwen took in a deep breath, steeling herself before looking Luke in the eyes. "Everything here is old guy stuff. Your books are old guys books. Your records are old guy records. It's just..." She trailed off.

"It's just there's nothing here that's specifically for you. I'm sorry. I guess I never thought about it. I've not really interacted with a lot of children, and certainly not had one in my home." Luke ran his hand through his messy hair. "I can get some things for you. What kind of books do you like?"

"Um. I don't know." Her cheeks flushed light red as she turned her eyes back to the Persian rug in the center of the floor.

Luke understood. It'd been two years since she had access to anything like books or music of her own choosing, and who knows what she was allowed in her home with an abusive father. Plus, Luke figured kid's tastes change a lot between nine and twelve years old. "I'll stop by the library when I go out and get some books for you. I'm sure a librarian can help me find something a person your age will like. Also, I'll set up your own Spotify account so you can find music you'll like."

"That would be nice," replied Gwen.

"Once the pack gets you some new paperwork, we can get you a library card, and then you can check out whatever you want."

"OK. I'd like that." The glum expression on her face lessened as she pulled back her shoulders some, growing a bit in size as she slightly extracted herself from the small ball she'd made of her body to take up less space.

They sat awkwardly for a bit as the music played. Luke wasn't sure how to bond with her. She lived in his space, but largely kept to herself and rarely spoke unless someone else started the conversation. She tried to take up as little space as possible while trying to stay unnoticed—defensive tactics from a bad childhood and life on the streets. The people Luke had spent most of his nineteen hundred plus year life around had been warriors, fighters, and soldiers. A young girl was a bewildering experience.

Thinking about what Maggie had suggested the other day at Gwen's checkup, he took in a deep breath, settled on a course of action, then let the breath out slowly. For now, he'd have to fall back on what he knew. She was scrappy and had a bit of fight in her when the occasion demanded it.

"Would you like to learn how to fight? To defend yourself?"

She raised her head and made timid eye contact. "Yes?"

"If you're not interested, you don't have to agree to make me happy. I just thought, well, being a werewolf and well... You were playing with my training sword..."

"No, I mean, yes. I'd like to learn." She smiled slightly, a look of excitement in her eyes.

Luke smiled back at her. "OK, we'll start after breakfast. I'm hungry."

"Me too!" That was the most excitement he'd heard from her since they'd met.

AFTER BREAKFAST, Luke had changed into his workout clothes and was directing Gwen through light warm-up exercises. They'd have to add workout clothes to the shopping list for Gwen. Once he was satisfied, he walked over to the wall covered in weapons racks and took down a pair of short swords.

"I think we'll start you on short swords."

"Why not on a samurai sword?" She gestured to the bamboo practice katana she'd been using.

"Katanas are cool, but you're a bit on the short side."

"But wouldn't I want a longer sword, then?"

Luke turned around and grabbed two bamboo katanas off the racks, handing one to Gwen. "Follow me." He led her to the center of the fighting mat, setting the short swords down just outside the ring marking the boundary of the fighting circle. "OK, hold the sword in both hands and extend your arms, pointing the sword straight forward. When I tell you to, walk straight toward me and poke me with the tip of the sword."

Luke set himself, sword lowered at his side. "OK."

Gwen walked forward, stopping with the tip of the wooden sword poking into Luke's chest.

"OK, now reset."

She walked back and started again. This time, Luke raised his bamboo katana and held it in front of him just as she walked within range. She stopped with the tip of Luke's sword stopping her with her sword well over a foot away from Luke. Next, he had her stand inside his reach and asked her to try to stab him or get a good slash in with the bamboo katana. Its length made it nearly impossible for her to make any kind of real contact with him.

"You're quite a bit shorter than me, so with equal length weapons, I have a reach advantage over you. And even if you do get inside my reach, a longer weapon becomes an encumbrance. I'm not sure what size you'll be when you grow up all the way, but right now, we'll have to train you to account for your size. In your case, short swords and polearms are going to be the order of the day."

"How's a short sword going to work? Aren't I going to be extra short with one of those?"

"The key to a short sword against a tall opponent is to get inside your opponent's reach. As a shorter person with a short weapon, you can neutralize your opponent's reach by being fast and getting in close, inside of their weapon and where they can do damage."

Gwen nodded, accepting Luke's reasoning. "OK."

She walked to the edge of the ring, set her bamboo katana down, and picked up the short swords, handing one to Luke in exchange for his katana. She set it outside the ring and returned to the center. Standing opposite Luke, she held the short sword in her left hand. She set her body with her left shoulder facing him and her right arm extended behind her with her hand in the air above her head.

Luke chuckled as she contorted her body into a passable imitation of the fencing en garde position. "I'm not teaching you fencing; I'm teaching you fighting. You'll want that other hand for punching or blocking or holding another weapon. It won't do you any good up there."

Gwen blushed slightly and relaxed her body back into a normal standing position. Luke approached her, corrected her grip, and showed her the position she needed to set her body in to begin with. He demonstrated the basic forms and motions. Once she had the basics, he had her connect them in various sequences, calling out the combos he wanted her to perform.

"Slow down. Go for accuracy. Speed will come with time."

She slowed down, going for precision. Walking around her, Luke corrected forms where needed but was pleased with Gwen's ability to listen to and apply the information Luke gave her. If she kept up like this, she'd make an exceptional pupil.

"Alright, little one, that's enough for today. You've done a good job."

Gwen was covered in sweat, but one of the first genuine smiles Luke had seen spread across her face. She pulled her shoulders back, raising her head a bit higher. The lesson and the praise built a bit of confidence in the reticent child. She picked up the bamboo swords and placed them back on the racks with her short sword. Luke filled a couple glasses with water from the sink, then walked into the small antechamber and sat. Gwen followed him in, picking up Alfred from the chair where he was curled up in a ball and quietly snoring, and resettled him in her lap. Accepting the glass from Luke, she chugged her water and set the empty glass on the side table.

"Do you think you want to keep learning how to fight?" Luke asked.

Gwen nodded eagerly. "Yes, please. I liked that."

"Good. If you don't mind, I'll ask Sam to join us. She's an expert with a naginata..." Seeing the look of confusion on Gwen's face, he elaborated, "It's a Japanese spear. Basically, a stick with a sword blade at the end."

"Sam can fight?"

Luke chuckled, remembering the battle last fall on the St. Johns Bridge; Sam had carved up vampires with ease. Although Gwen had been present, she'd been stationed in the middle of the caravan where she'd be safe and far from the fighting.

"Oh, yeah. She can fight."

# NINE

"I CAN'T BELIEVE I finally talked you into getting this old hot rod fixed up! You'll love the results. Jorge does fantastic work. He does all the special work on any pack cars, or really anything special we need fabricated," Pablo said.

"I'm trusting you with my beast, Pablo. Your nephew better not fuck it up."

Pablo dismissed Luke's concern with a wave of his hand. "Don't worry; he's a genius. You left all your gear in here?" Pablo pointed to the totes usually kept his gear in.

Luke shook his head, pursing his lips. "No, I need my stuff. I bought cheap knock offs off the internet. They'll do for sizing purposes. I know you trust Jorge, but can his employees be trusted?"

"Of course, most of them are pack or hand-selected. His human employees all know about us and fall under the protection of the pack. We've helped some of them get paperwork for themselves or their families. We take care of our own very well. They're loyal."

Luke nodded. He trusted Pablo explicitly. He'd extend his trust to Pablo's nephew and crew. "Did you brief your nephew?"

"Yeah. He's only got pack employees in today to handle the other work. He thought it best to keep it to those who are already aware of your circumstances."

Luke gave Pablo a closed-mouth smile. "I appreciate it. It's still taking a lot of adjustment to go from being entirely on my own to having people not only knowing about me but being willing to aid my cause. I really do appreciate it."

"That's what friends are for, buddy."

They wound their way through the streets of North Portland toward Jorge's shop on North Fessenden. Delilah followed in Pablo's pickup so she could take them back home when they were done. They parked outside of Fessenden Custom Car and Repair.

"This is it. Listen, do you trust me?" Pablo asked.

"Of course."

"Good," Pablo punctuated it with a single finger gun. "I know what we need for this beast of yours. I'll line it out for Jorge. You can jump in if you think you need to, OK?"

"I'll play it your way." Luke opened the car door and headed toward the shop.

"Hey, Jorge," a man shouted toward the building. "Your uncle is here with some people."

A tall, handsome younger brown man with a ponytail falling down his back walked out of the large garage doors and opened his arms. "Tio Pablo! It's good to see you."

Pablo hugged his tall nephew, patting his back. He let go of his nephew and gestured toward Luke and Delilah. "Jorge, these are my friends Luke and Delilah. Luke, Delilah, this is my nephew Jorge."

"It's always a pleasure meeting my tio's friends." He shook Luke's hand before kissing Delilah's hand. "Especially one as beautiful as you." He winked at before letting her hand go.

"Knock it off, knucklehead," Pablo admonished. Addressing Luke and Delilah, he added, "He likes to play the Latin lover bit with women."

"Play? What you talking about? I AM the Latin lover."

"Uncle Tony would beg to differ with you."

"Tony's not a Latino... Oh, you mean you? Don't you need to be taller?" He quirked an eyebrow up, trying to keep a straight face before breaking out in laughter. As he bent over a bit, Pablo got him in a headlock and ruffled up his hair.

Pablo let go of his nephew. "He's a good kid; he just thinks he's funny. And from what I hear, it's been a while since you had a date of any kind."

"Hey, I'm funny, and I do alright..."

"Ha, Pablo's got you there, Jorge! The Mojave's had shorter dry spells..." Several of Jorge's employees laughed along.

"I'm waiting for the right lady." Jorge winked at Delilah.

Delilah rolled her eyes, setting Luke and Pablo to laughing along, happy not to be on the receiving end of her eye roll.

Pablo put his arm around his nephew's shoulder. "Today's just not going your way. But I think we have something that might turn it around."

"Sure, pull it into the lot." He looked around and then pointed to an empty space with plenty of room along all four sides. "Put it there, then you can fill me in on the job."

Luke got back into his Volvo and parked where he was directed.

"Luke, pop the hood?" Jorge asked. When the hood clunked open slightly, Jorge opened it all the way and stuck his head in to see what he was working with.

"So, Luke, Tio Pablo said he's got some ideas. You OK with that?" Jorge asked.

"Listen to the man," Luke replied.

Jorge nodded and looked at his uncle for guidance.

"We need to add a lot more power. The stock engine isn't meeting our needs. It could use better handling as well. Shocks, struts, suspension, the works." Pablo turned to Luke. "Keys please?"

Luke tossed his keys to Pablo, who caught them in midair, then walked around to the back hatch. He opened it and gestured for Jorge to join him. He pulled the lid off Luke's substitute equipment.

"This is the other piece of the puzzle. We need a storage solution for this stuff, so it's not just sitting in a tub in the back of his car, open to the world. Try to keep it as light and as well-concealed as possible. We want the car to look like it's just got an empty trunk...

space...wagon. Shit, Luke, what do you call the space behind the back seat in a station wagon?"

Luke shrugged. "Hell if I know."

"Anyways, something easy to open. Maybe like a tray or rack that rolls out? I don't know. You're the engineer. Engineer something." Pablo gestured vaguely to the rear of the Volvo.

"OK, I've got some ideas. When you told me what you were bringing in, I found structural diagrams from this vintage of Volvo. I'll rig up some ideas in the computer and send you a rendering for your approval. Do you want any cosmetic upgrades? New paint? Fix any of these dents?"

Luke shook his head. "The dents, sure. But let's keep the paint as is. I want this thing to look like any other old Volvo on the streets of Portland. It's my camouflage, if you will."

"Speaking of dents, if you can slowly start acquiring body parts for this color and model and stashing them, that might be a good idea. We might need to freshen up the appearance without losing the vintage look. You know, in case we pick up any unique dents that might help others identify the car." Pablo winked.

"Just to make sure we're clear, you're looking for an ugly hot rod that handles like a sports car and has secret compartments?" Jorge asked.

"Hey, my car's not ugly," Luke protested.

Raising his hands placatingly, Jorge mollified Luke. "Not ugly, vintage urban camouflaged."

"That's better." Luke smiled at Jorge.

"I can't turn this into a sports car; it doesn't have the right bones. But I like the challenge you've presented. So, as long as I keep it looking the same on the outside, including the visible interior, I can change whatever I need to hit your parameters?"

Luke thought about it for a moment. "Yes."

"What's my budget?"

Pablo looked at Luke, an eyebrow quirked up.

"Whatever it takes to get the job done right," Luke stated.

Jorge folded his arms over his chest. "It could get really expensive..."

"I'd rather spend the money and get exactly what we're looking for than cut corners and not have the performance we need down the road."

"Understood. You paying direct?"

Pablo chimed in, "Use the special funds accounts. You know the ones. Nothing too big at once."

Jorge grinned ear to ear. "OK."

"Luke, you can wire the pack the money when we're done and you're satisfied. I'll put you in touch with the pack accountant, and you can figure out how to bounce it around to keep things clean from any prying eyes."

Delilah was staring at her two friends, her jaw hanging open and shock written across her face. "That sounds kind of shady..."

Luke shrugged. "When you live this long, you have to get creative when moving money and assets around to ensure the government doesn't come looking for you. The digital age has made things a lot harder."

Delilah shook her head and wandered off, mumbling to herself.

"What's her problem?" Jorge asked.

"I sometimes forget how young she is, and how she's not that far from the law-abiding upbringing she had," Luke said.

Jorge looked confused.

"She's still pretty new to our world," Pablo replied.

Jorge chuckled. "That I can understand. It was a pretty big shock when you broke it to me."

"Once the shock wore off, you took to it like a duck to water." Pablo patted his nephew on the shoulder.

"What? The fangs and furry thing or the shady stuff you do to keep it all quiet?"

Pablo laughed. "You adapted to both pretty well."

"The shady shit was easy. I was up to all kinds of shady stuff before you pulled me and mama out of Guadalajara. Nowhere near the level of what you guys are up to, that's for sure. The fur thing took a bit to adjust the old brain."

"When do you think you'll have it done?" Luke asked.

Jorge shrugged. "I'm not sure. This is going to take a lot of work.

I'll have to manufacture a lot of stuff and hunt down the right parts. I'll keep Tio Pablo up to date."

"Fair enough." Luke shook hands with Jorge.

"You hear about the grand opening, Jorge?" Pablo asked.

"Hell yeah. You know I wouldn't miss it for the world. Got an official date yet?" Jorge replied.

"We're getting close. Still waiting on some final permits. Should be anytime in the next few days. I'll let you know. Oh, Tony mentioned doing a dinner with your mom Sunday. Tell her to call Tony. He's got a new mole recipe he wants her to taste."

"Sure thing, but you know she won't be able to just let Tony make everything. She'll insist on bringing a bunch of food over too." Jorge smirked, shaking his head.

"I'll invite reinforcements." Pablo looked over at Luke and Delilah, who'd wandered back over after collecting herself. "You all free Sunday for a Mexican feast? Jorge's mama and Tony will put you in a food coma you won't want to come out of."

Luke nodded enthusiastically. "You know I'll be over."

"Delilah?" Pablo asked.

"Yeah, I'm not working Sunday."

"Excellent! Jorge, hug your mom for me. We'll see you Sunday."

"Love to Tio Tony. It was nice meeting you both." Jorge said to Delilah and Luke.

Delilah gave Jorge a quick look over before climbing in the truck. "Pablo, you mind if I bring a friend Sunday?"

"Not at all! The more the merrier!"

"Good. I think Clarvetta might like your nephew."

Pablo laughed as he put the key in the ignition. "Oh, that'll be hilarious. He'll want to play Mr. Latin Lover but not in front of his mama. That's probably a good idea, though. He's a good kid, but he's kind of shy around women, so he overcompensates with that silly persona. When he's himself, he's perfectly charming and funny. Maybe with his mom there, he won't act the jackass and scare off a nice date."

"How old is he? He doesn't really look like a kid," Delilah said.

"Twenty-eight. I just think of him as a kid. I pulled him out of a dicey situation back in Mexico when he was about fourteen. He got involved with some bad types after his dad died. So, I moved him and his mother up here and set them up under the protection of the pack. Once he got used to his new life, the boy found brains he never knew he had. The pack paid to send him to engineering school. Once he got his degree, he found a custom hot rod garage to apprentice in. After a few years, he came to us asking if we'd set him up with his own shop. So we did. Now he does all the work for the pack. He's happy as a clam doing what he loves and taking care of his mama, and we get a trustworthy shop to take our vehicles to." Pablo looked over at Luke. "Your car's in good hands. He's going to turn that thing into a one-of-a-kind vampire slaying mobile. He's geeked to work on this one. He loves challenges. I can see it in his eyes."

Luke smiled. "I'm excited to see what he does. Mind taking me up to the car rental spot? Need to get my temporary wheels."

"Are you sure? We can let you use the pack's spare car."

"Nah. Let's not let anyone trace it back to pack. The rental will do."

"Sure thing."

# TEN

LUKE, having slept late, enjoyed a leisurely breakfast while scrolling on his phone. He was interrupted when his phone vibrated. Looking down at the screen, he furrowed his brows and pursed his lips. The number calling, one he didn't know, started with +32—the international area code for Belgium. He hit the pickup button.

"Hello?"

"Mr. Irontree?" the caller asked.

"Speaking."

"Ah, good. This is Pieter van den Bergh."

Luke grinned. "Ah, Mr. van den Bergh. It's a pleasure to hear from you."

"Likewise, Mr. Irontree, although I can't guarantee it will stay a pleasure."

"That sounds ominous…"

"Troubled times are often such. I'm calling to alert you to potentially disturbing news," Pieter replied.

"I'm listening."

"To keep things short, let me say that I've recently gained control of the port in Rotterdam. With it came some startling discoveries about what's been shipping through."

C. THOMAS LAFOLLETTE

"You're being fairly circumspect. Usually you've been a much plainer speaker," Luke replied.

"When delicate matters are before me, I prefer to err on the side of caution. Let's just say, your age-old enemy is up to some new tricks."

"Yeah, I'm beginning to suspect that." Picking up on Pieter van den Bergh's caution, Luke kept his answers vague as well. "Are the issues on your end or mine?"

"We are but a waypoint, but the ultimate destination is your city. I'm uncomfortable going into more detail over the phone. I'm sending one of my most trusted factors to you. He'll bring all the details. We'll keep him updated via secure methods if the situation changes or new information becomes available."

"I appreciate it."

"It's the least we can do to repay our debt to you."

"I thought we already settled on the payment. By the way, how is that going?" Luke asked.

Pieter chuckled. "Quite well. It's been a while since I picked up a brush. It feels good to put paint to canvas. But that's hardly a fitting payment for all you've done for me and my family. And even if you consider our debt repaid once you receive the painting, how about the debt of friendship?"

Luke smiled to himself. "That is a debt I'll happily extend both ways. When can we expect your factor to arrive?"

"He'll be arriving on tomorrow's direct from Amsterdam. I'm sure you're familiar."

"I most certainly am. I'll pick him up from the airport. Who should I look for?" Luke asked.

"I'll be sending my boy," Pieter replied.

"Jan? It'll be good to see him again."

"No, the other one — Pieter."

"Ah, I'll take good care of him while he's in Portland. It'll be nice to have met the whole family. Is there anything else you need to relay?"

"No, Pieter will have all the information available when he lands. I'll let him know you'll be meeting him at the airport."

"Good. I'll pick him up just after security. It's good to chat with you again, even if it's only about business," Luke said.

"You as well, Mr. Irontree. Until next time."

"WHO ARE we picking up at the airport?" Pablo asked from the driver's seat of his Toyota Tacoma.

"Pieter van den Bergh. f," Luke answered from the back seat.

"Who?" Delilah asked.

"He's one of the sons of the Antwerp packleader," Luke replied. "Well, I guess all of Belgium now."

Delilah shook her head and looked toward Pablo for clarification.

"You've got as much information as I do. I don't know many of the non-American packs. Holly might, but I focus mostly on our own pack and help her with the neighboring packs."

Luke frowned, narrowing his eyes. "I never told you how I helped the Flanders Pack last spring?"

"Must have slipped your mind. You're five thousand years old, after all," quipped Pablo.

"Ha. Ha." Luke shook his head. "It was before the three of us met, and if you'll recall, we had a fairly full fall. Anyway, I was vacationing in Belgium —"

"Visiting the old boyhood stomping grounds?" Delilah interrupted.

"Something like that. I like to return periodically. I've accumulated quite a bit of property throughout the centuries in Belgium, Netherlands, Germany, and France. I like to check in on it periodically. That's neither here nor there. I was relaxing at a café in Antwerp when a gentleman interrupted my solitude and struck up a conversation. He secretly slipped a cell phone in my jacket pocket before he left. Turns out he was the son of the Flanders packleader —"

"The guy we're picking up at the airport?" Pablo jumped in.

"No, his brother Jan. Anyway, he messaged me later about a

mission I was uniquely suited for. He sent me a meeting place, and I showed up," Luke replied.

"Just like that?" Delilah asked.

"Yeah. I was curious who knew who I was. I don't exactly broadcast my identity. He introduced me to his father, Pieter van den Bergh the Elder—the packleader of Flanders, or rather at that time, the whole north of Belgium, the Flemish speaking portion. The new leader of the vampire nest in Liege had kidnapped his wife and daughter. The vamps controlled the south of Belgium and wanted to expand into the north. They offered to exchange his wife and child for the pack's territory."

"I bet that didn't go down well. I'm surprised they brought an outsider into that situation. Packs tend to take such slights very personally," Pablo said.

"Well, the vampires threatened to kill his wife and kid if the pack moved against them, and he took the threat seriously. I'm still not sure how the pack knew about me or how to find me, but they did. He indicated my existence was known among some of the European packs. I accepted the mission and freed his family. Although if they hadn't taken his kid, I'm sure his wife could have probably dealt with the vamps by herself. She was not a happy werewolf when the silver cuffs came off. You would have been impressed with the way she tore those vampires apart, Pablo. It was intense."

Pablo chuckled softly.

Luke continued, "We ended up killing 'The Mistress,' as she was called, one of her lieutenants, and most of her henchmen. Once their leaders fell, and the other lieutenant beat feet, the rest ran away. When I returned to Antwerp with his family, I learned who he really was."

"He wasn't the packleader?" Delilah asked.

"Oh, he was. I guess I should be more specific. I figured out who he was originally..."

Delilah was turned in her seat, an eager expression on her face. Pablo's head was cocked a bit to the side, splitting off as much attention to Luke as he could while keeping an eye on the road. Luke, feeling a bit ornery, let them hang longer than necessary.

"Bruh…" Delilah prompted him.

"I'd actually met him before, during his first life about four hundred and fifty years earlier."

"Of course you did," Pablo commented.

"I'd been going by the name of Luyc de Jaeghere at the time and I'd sought him out to buy a painting or two when he was known as Pieter Bruegel the Elder."

"You're shitting me," Delilah said. "The Flemish Master? And we're picking up his son, Pieter Bruegel the Younger, at the airport?"

Luke shook his head. "Not messing with you even a little. And yes, we're picking up 'the Younger' at the airport."

A giant grin was plastered across Delilah's face. "I get to meet one of the Flemish Masters? How fucking cool is that! I guess there's at least a few advantages to knowing old guys like you two."

"Let's pretend some of us don't have degrees in art history and fill in the Pablo. What's a Flemish Master?" Pablo asked.

"I only have a minor in art history," Delilah corrected. "The great painters of the sixteenth and seventeenth centuries who were in the Dutch-speaking part of Europe, basically the Netherlands and northern Belgium, were known as the Flemish Masters. A lot of them operated out of Antwerp. People like Rembrandt, Van Dyck, Van Eyck, and Rubens. And the Bruegels — Pieter the Elder, Pieter the Younger, and Jan."

"I'd met all of them before. Pieter the Younger was only a boy when I first met his father. On second thought, Jan hadn't been born yet. The Elder still remembered me when we met for a second time last year. He liked the joke in the name I was using at the time of our first meeting."

"What joke?" Pablo asked.

"Luyc de Jaeghere. De Jaeghere was a common name at the time. It's the Dutch version of 'Hunter.' So, Luke the Hunter."

"Ah, that is mildly amusing."

Delilah softly punched Pablo in the shoulder. Turning back toward Luke, she added, "That's so cool! Did you meet Pieter as well? Adult Pieter, I mean."

Luke shook his head. "No, just his father and brother. After I returned his family, Pieter the Elder ordered Jan and his brother to lead the rest of the pack into the south of Belgium to claim the territory the vampires had occupied. After that, I cut my trip short and headed back to Portland. Usually vampires are a little more subtle and work to stay hidden so they avoid the detection of humans and werewolves alike. And if you leave werewolves alone, they tend to ignore you. But with the vampires moving so aggressively against the werewolves of Belgium, it kind of kicked off some dread about what might be coming. I was right."

"Right about what?" Pablo asked.

"You were there—vampires." They were all silent as thoughts of what they'd faced last fall on the streets of Portland and in Wapato jail. The rest of the ride to the airport passed quietly.

"Are we picking him up at the curb?" Pablo asked.

"No, park in the garage. We'll meet him just outside security," Luke replied.

Pablo pulled into the parking garage and picked a spot. Luke grabbed a small sign with "Mr. van den Bergh" written on it and the three walked into the airport to meet Pieter Bruegel the Younger.

PABLO, Luke, and Delilah stood to the side as people filed out of the secured section of the airport after clearing customs. Luke held up the sign with Pieter's current surname. Eventually, a man with grayish blond hair and a long nose jutting out from his face emerged, pulling a roller carry-on behind him. Seeing the sign with his name on it, his expression brightened, and he changed directions toward Luke and his friends. Pieter wore a white button-down shirt tucked into gray trousers with a faint check pattern. He had a matching jacket slung over his shoulder.

"Ah, you must be Mr. Irontree." He set his roller bag on its legs and extended a hand to Luke.

Luke shook his hand. "And you must be Mr. van den Bergh…the Younger."

"Please, call me Pieter."

"Luke works for me." He turned toward Pablo and Delilah. "These are my friends Delilah Johnson and Pablo Sandoval. Pablo is the second of the North Portland pack."

"It is a pleasure to meet you both." Pieter shook Delilah's hand first, then Pablo's.

"Do you have any checked luggage?" Luke asked.

"Yes, a couple pieces."

Luke waved everyone after him as he turned to walk toward the baggage claim area. After they'd secured Pieter's luggage, they got into Pablo's truck allowing their guest to have shotgun while Luke and Delilah took the back seat.

"How was the plane ride, Mr. Brueg... I mean Mr. van den Bergh?" Delilah asked with a bit of a stammer.

Pieter turned and gave Luke a questioning look. Luke shrugged in response.

"It would appear our Delilah the art history student is a bit star struck," Pablo teased.

"It was pleasant enough. The non-stop from Amsterdam to Portland makes for a relatively easy crossing, especially in first class. And please, call me Pieter."

"How goes the consolidation in the south?" Luke asked.

"Are we free to discuss such things..." Pieter moved his hand, indicating Pablo and Delilah.

Luke nodded. "Yeah. They're up to snuff on the vampiric front."

Pieter gave a half smile. "Quite well. Removing The Mistress and her nest threw her entire network into disarray. Guillaume Geefs isn't the leader or tactician his Mistress was. You also killed quite a few of her other lieutenants. Most of Wallonia's vampires were in attendance at the festival. The few that escaped are spending more time fighting for position than defending their territory. The infighting is allowing us to sweep the south clean. We even get a few 'anonymous' tips from vampires to set us on their rivals."

"Ha!" Luke snorted and shook his head. "I'm glad it's working out for you."

"Thank you. My father is quite pleased."

"I don't know about you, but I could do with some lunch. How about you, Pieter?" Luke asked.

"Absolutely. Even in first class, airline food leaves much to be desired."

Luke reached over the seat and squeezed Pablo's shoulder. "Pablo, to the pub."

"Yes, sir!" he replied.

# ELEVEN

LUKE, Delilah, Pablo, and Pieter sat around the table at the back booth of the Howling Moon enjoying some pleasant chitchat after finishing their meals. The bar had cleared out after the lunch rush, leaving them and only a couple other people in the pub.

When they'd finished lunch, Pablo ordered coffee and another round of beers for everyone at the table.

After the incident at the Wapato Jail, Luke had offered to move as many people as possible from Hazelnut Grove into the apartment building he'd dedicated to helping the homeless victims of the vampires. Max had been put in charge of managing the building and he'd offered rooms to Pam and Jim, with whom he'd run the camp. Needing a few people to work the lunch shifts after Pablo had increased his opening hours to lunchtime, Pam had quickly worked her way up to front end manager. After delivering the coffees and beers, she left them alone to continue their conversation.

"You have a lovely bar, Pablo, and the beer is most excellent." Pieter raised his glass toward Pablo and took a sip.

"Thanks." Pablo smiled at the compliment.

"If you're feeling up to it, we can move the conversation toward business matters. Or if you're too tired, we can reconvene tomorrow after you've had a good night's rest. It's been a long day of travel and time changes for you," Luke offered.

"Thank you, but I can manage for a bit longer. Lunch and beers have gone a long way toward reviving my energy."

"Can we put a pin in this for a minute or two?" Pablo asked. "I need to make a quick call."

"Sure, Pablo." Luke scooted out, letting Pablo slide by.

Pablo returned after a minute and sat down at the end of the table. "I had Pam lock the doors and put up a 'Closed for Cleaning, Reopening at 5pm' sign."

"Is she pack?" Pieter asked.

"No, but she knows what we are and is one hundred percent trustworthy."

Pieter nodded his understanding.

"So, Pieter, your father said you'd be bringing some important information. What do you have for me?" Luke asked.

"Straight to the point. I like it. We've recently merged with the South Netherlands Pack." Seeing Luke's upturned eyebrow and inquisitive expression, Pieter added, "One of my nephews had been dating the daughter of the South Netherlands's packleader, and they recently married. Our families decided it would be best to merge the packs to secure our combined territories more effectively. With that decision came control of Rotterdam and its port."

"Congratulations! With both Antwerp and Rotterdam under your sway, that's a lot of shipping under your control." Luke nodded appreciatively.

"Thank you. When father and our team combed through their books, we found discrepancies with certain containers."

"Intentional discrepancies?"

"No, the South Netherlands packleader had put a less detail-oriented nephew in charge. On the surface, all the containers looked fine, but when our accountants dug deeper, they saw troubling signs, or rather a lack of signs."

"What do you mean?" Delilah asked.

"At first glance, all the shipping containers looked above board— proper paperwork filed by seemingly legitimate companies. But when we poured sunshine on them… That's the proper idiom, right?" Pieter asked.

"Close enough. Exposed them to daylight might be closer," Luke said.

"Well, much like vampires, once exposed to daylight, these companies vanished into dust."

"Interesting, but what does that have to do with us?" Pablo asked. "I'm sure there's all kinds of illegal shit that gets shipped out of ports all over the world."

"True. And some of it is even shipped by various packs. However, by courtesy, the other European packs do not ship those containers through our ports. None of these containers had any of the marks of the packs, nor did they look like the more mundane commerce of organized crime," Pieter replied.

Luke could tell Pablo was getting annoyed. He was used to being more direct both as the second of a pack and an American. Luke reached under the table and patted Pablo's leg to let him know he understood and to be patient.

"Do you know where the containers originated?" Luke asked.

"No. Unfortunately, they led to dead ends once we dug far enough through their transit history. But we do know where they're going. Once they get into our ports, they're tracked very carefully, and unless they're changing ships out in the middle of the ocean, they're making it to their assigned ports. We've checked the landing records on those that have reached port and they're landing where they're supposed to be."

"But who knows where they go after that, right?" Delilah interjected. "And we don't know what's inside these shipping containers."

"Well, that we do know." Pieter reached down into his carry-on bag and pulled out a laptop. "Let's hope the battery still has some charge on it." He hit the power button, and the screen blinked on. "Ah, good." He turned to address Delilah. "We were fortunate enough to catch one container still in port. I recorded this video as my team opened the doors."

He turned the computer so everyone could see the screen before reaching down and hitting play. On both sides of the screen, they could see the end of automatic rifles and the hands holding them. A uniformed woman walked into the center of the screen with a circular grinder and began cutting through the shanks on the many padlocks keeping the doors secure. Once the locks had all fallen to the ground, she handed the grinder to someone off camera, waved everyone else back, and beckoned over another person. The woman and a man in a similar uniform grabbed the handles of the door, lifted them out of their cradles, and pushed them forward, rotating the bars to unlatch the doors. Finally, they heaved and opened the doors, keeping the doors between them and whatever was inside the container.

"Fuck..." Pablo whispered.

A series of flashlights illuminated the inside of the container. Huddling in the back, away from the sunlight pouring through the doors, stood at least a dozen vampires. One or two of the braver ones tried darting out at their captors but gave up once their skin started smoking in the sun. A few appeared to be trying to get into some crates or cases. Once the lid came up on one of them, someone issued the order to fire and the automatic rifles sprayed high powered ordnance into the bodies inside the container. Although ordinary bullets can't kill a vampire, if enough damage is done it will incapacitate them. When the movement inside the container stopped, the perspective backed up, showing a crane lowering a giant lifting magnet onto the top of the container just over the entrance. Once it'd made its connection, it lifted and pointed the opening into the air, aiming it toward the sun. Smoke and shrieks poured out of the container in equal measure until both ceased.

Once the container was lowered, they advanced into the interior. The inside was covered in a mix of goo from younger vampires and dusty ashes from older vampires. While Pieter held the camera, someone opened the lid on the first container. It contained a variety of high-powered automatic and semi-automatic weapons. Another one contained body armor. The last was maybe the most troubling. Inside, they found a selection of sniper rifles.

His body leaning in toward the screen, Pablo let out a low whistle. "That's some heavy-duty stuff..."

"Yeah, we thought so too," Pieter replied. He stopped the video.

"That was a pretty neat trick with the crane." Delilah reached down for her pint.

Pieter smiled at her. "Thank you. It seemed like the easiest way to deal with the situation."

"What was the destination of this container?" Luke asked.

Pieter replied, "Portland, Oregon, United States."

LUKE LOOKED around the table at his friends, gauging their expressions as the news sank in.

"And was this the only container bound for Portland?" Luke asked.

"No."

"Fuck." Luke shook his head.

"Yeah, that about sums it up, Luke," Pablo added.

Delilah slumped into her seat, her brows squeezed together in a pensive expression.

"Vampires are bad enough on their own. But that kind of weaponry is going to change things significantly. How many containers in total?" Luke asked.

"Let me see..." Pieter reached into the bag and pulled out a file folder, setting it on the table he pulled out a pack of stapled papers. Running his finger down the page and moving his lips as he counted silently, he flipped through the short stack of papers. "Twenty-seven that we've identified."

"That's not good," Delilah said quietly.

"What's that list?" Pablo asked.

"It's all the containers that couldn't be properly traced to their origin," Pieter replied.

"How long is it?"

"There are about one hundred and thirty containers on the list with about fifty different destinations."

"So Portland got about one-fifth of the containers?" Delilah asked.

"Yes."

"Why?"

Pieter nodded toward Luke. "That's why."

Pablo chuckled. "Looks like you're managing to win friends and influence people. Eh, buddy?"

Luke took in the information as Pieter and his friends went over it, trying to compartmentalize the rush of anxiety and fear for the safety of his friends. This went far beyond chasing down a few roving fangers. Although this was innovative, he'd dealt with vampire surprises all his life. Looking around the table, he wondered who would survive this or if he'd be able to save them at all. He finally broke his silence. "How many have landed, and how many have yet to land?"

"Five have already landed, leaving twenty-two still on the water."

"Could they be landing in Portland and getting shipped elsewhere?" Delilah asked.

"It's possible, but unlikely. Portland's port can't handle the largest of the super freighters. The 'Willa-met-teh' River isn't deep enough to accommodate them. Usually if you're shipping to Portland, it's for Portland."

"It's pronounced 'Will-AM-mit,'" Luke corrected.

"Sorry," Pieter replied.

"No matter, just giving you a heads up before you talk with the locals so they don't make fun of you."

Pablo, tapping his fingers on the table, asked, "How many ships are we talking about?"

"I'm not sure what you're asking…"

"Are the remaining twenty-two containers coming in ones and twos, or are they more concentrated on just a few ships?" Pablo asked.

"Ah, I see." Pieter looked down and sorted through his paperwork. "It appears the first couple containers came in one to a ship, probably to test the route and ensure the local vampires could handle their end of the equation."

Seeing the confused looks on Pablo's and Delilah's faces, Pieter clarified, "You know, ensuring the proper authorities are under control and customs agents are properly glamoured to allow the containers to pass through without inspection but getting the proper OK so they continue looking legitimate. Those appear to have landed late last summer or early fall. The following three arrived on one ship in January of this year. I can understand why they might want to send in elite teams to track down The Hunter, but nearly thirty containers seem too many."

"Well, we kind of fucked up their operations last fall, pretty significantly." Pablo's mouth split into a feral grin he shared with Delilah.

Pieter looked confused, so Luke ran him through what had happened after Luke had helped free Pieter's stepmother and half-sister.

"You've been quite busy over the last year, haven't you, Mr. Iron-tree?" Pieter covered his mouth with his hand as he yawned deeply.

"Jet lag catching up with you?" asked Luke.

"Ja." He yawned again.

"One last question before we let you get some rest. How long before the next containers land?"

Pieter flipped to the third page and ran his finger over one of the highlighted sections, stopping over a series of number that were too small for the rest of the table to read. "It should land in about two or three days. That's why my father put me on a plane for Portland as soon as we figured out what was going on."

Luke nodded and smiled. "I appreciate it. Do you have a hotel arranged? We can probably find you a room for an evening or two."

"Actually," Pablo interrupted. "The call I made was to Holly." He addressed Pieter. "Pieter, we have a pack guest house we maintain for visiting dignitaries from other packs. It's quite nice. As the second of the North Portland Pack, I'd like to officially offer you guest status and the use of our guest house."

"That's most gracious. On behalf of the Flanders Pack, I accept your offer."

"Excellent! I can take you there now so you can get settled. Luke, you want a ride home?"

"No, thanks. I'll walk. The weather's not too bad."

"Delilah?" Pablo asked.

"No, I'm about to go on for the dinner shift."

"In that case, when you're ready to go, we'll head back out to my truck and get you settled in. We can meet tomorrow to discuss the containers coming in. Sound good?"

Luke and Delilah nodded at Pablo.

"Sleep well, Pieter. We'll talk more tomorrow." Turning to Pablo and Delilah, Luke said, "See you two later," before turning and walking out the door.

# TWELVE

LUKE WAS ABOUT to walk out the door when he got a text from Pablo. *If you haven't left yet, can you stop and pick up some coffee beans? Please.*

Luke replied, *Just leaving. I'll stop by my coffee shop and pick some up. Text drink requests, and I'll bring them over too.*

He'd planned on stopping by his favorite coffee shop anyways. He jumped in the rental car he was using while his Volvo was getting upgraded by Pablo's nephew. He liked the newness of the rental but missed his old beast. They'd logged a lot of miles and hours together.

When he got out of the rental, a text with Pablo's and what he guessed was Pieter's order were waiting for him. Delilah must not be there yet. It didn't matter; he knew Delilah's first choice order. The door tinkled as it clipped the bell dangling just above it, announcing his presence. Luke must have caught the shop at a bit of a lull. There were a few people seated around tables, but no one in line. He walked up to the counter and waited. A woman's voice drifted from the curtain-covered door leading to the back room at the end of the counter.

"I'll be out in a moment!" A half-minute later, a short white woman with lightly curly brunette hair peeking out from under a knit beanie walked out and greeted Luke with a sparkling smile.

Luke's lips cracked into a smile. The woman, who appeared to be in her early thirties, was his favorite coffee shop employee.

"I haven't seen you for a few days! Can I get the usual going for you?" she asked.

"Yeah, been a bit busy lately. Yes, the usual. Also, I'm going to need a sixteen-ounce mocha, a twelve-ounce quad shot Americano, and a twelve-ounce latté to go with it. I'll need some pastries and a pound of the house roast as well."

"Meeting with friends, eh?" She winked at him. "I'll get the pastries first, then the coffees so they're still hot when you arrive."

Luke pointed out the pastries he wanted. After she'd boxed them up and handed them to Luke, she set about making his coffee drinks. Setting an unused espresso shot aside, she took out a sharpie and wrote a "3" on the cup of the last drink.

"This one is your triple shot Americano. 'Q' for the quad. 'M' for the mocha. The unmarked one is the latté." She put all four drinks inside a cardboard cup carrier, pushed them toward Luke, then began entering everything into the register. "That'll be $63, please."

Luke handed her four twenty-dollar bills. "Keep the change."

"Thanks! See you next time." She turned to address the next customer who'd gotten in line while she was working on Luke's larger order.

Luke stacked the coffee carrier on top of the pastry box and headed out the door. The last thing he heard was the barista offering to add the free, unused shot to the new customer's drink. Luke juggled the coffees and pastries, finally getting the car door open and his breakfast goods situated. He was about to get in the driver's seat when the barista popped out of the coffee shop.

"Oh, I'm glad I caught you. You forgot your beans." She handed him the brown coffee bean bag.

Luke grinned at her. "Wow, thanks! That was the main thing they asked me to get."

"No problem. Happy to keep your friends happy with you." She bounced on the balls of her feet with her hands behind her back, smiling up at Luke. "Well, um. I better head back in."

She was just about through the door when Luke's brain clicked into gear. "Thank you, again. I really do appreciate it."

She turned and smiled back at him and gave him a little wave.

Luke, with a smile on his face that didn't seem to want to go away, dropped his keys on the ground as he tried to get in the car before realizing he'd already unlocked it. Gathering himself, he put in the address Pablo had given him for the pack's guest house.

Delilah arrived a moment before Luke and had helped him carry in everything. "You look awful chipper this morning."

Luke wasn't paying attention. "Um, what?"

"You. You look chipper, more chipper than I usually see you anyways."

"Am I not usually chipper?" Luke asked.

Delilah chuckled. "No, I'd not consider you the most avuncular of individuals."

Luke shrugged. "Fair enough. Yeah, just having a good morning."

"Good. I like seeing you with a smile on your face."

Pablo was waiting for them in the open doorway. "Welcome to the pack's guest house! Pieter's inside."

Luke handed out the coffees while Delilah found a plate for the pastries. The basics handled, they pulled out chairs and arranged themselves around the dining room table. Luke took a drink of his triple shot Americano and reached for a lemon poppyseed scone while Pablo and Delilah made idle conversation with Pieter. Once they'd worked through a pastry each, Pieter, dressed down in a T-shirt and designer jeans, got out his laptop.

"I've keyed in the GPS code for the freighter in question." A map of the northwest and the Pacific Ocean popped up on the screen. He zoomed in. "As you can see, the freighter has just entered the mouth of Columbia River..." He zoomed in again. "...just outside Astoria."

"Will it stop at Astoria?" asked Delilah.

Pieter shook his head. "No. Now that it's through the Columbia

Bar, it'll head upriver and dock in Portland. Pablo, does your pack have any access to the ports?"

"No. That's not what we're about. I'll have Holly check with the other local packs."

"Your pack isn't the only one in town?" Pieter asked.

"Nah. There are a couple other packs in the Portland area, and a few others in Oregon. Holly coordinates with the packleaders, but we're all independent."

"Huh. All werewolves in Belgium belong to our pack. I guess you could call the various groups spread around Belgium sub-packs, but they all report to father."

Pablo shrugged. "Different strokes for different folks, I guess."

"Back to the containers. All five are on this freighter?" Luke asked.

"Yes."

"Do you know how long before it docks?"

Pieter shook his head. "Not yet. I called home this morning. The pack is getting the details from the shipping company. The ship will have an official registered dock time by now."

"What are we going to do?" asked Delilah.

"I'm not sure yet," Luke replied. He looked back at Pieter. "Is the freighter controlled by vampires?"

"I don't think so. It could be, but we've found no evidence to indicate they're doing anything other than catching a ride."

"Hmmm." Luke rubbed his chin. "Let's wait until they're unloaded. I don't suppose you have any truck drivers in the pack, do you, Pablo?"

"Not currently. I'll check the records and see if anyone's got any history with trucks."

"OK. In the meantime, I'm going to need a CDL." Seeing Delilah's confusion, he added, "A commercial driver's license. Pieter, I'll need documents that'll release the containers to us."

"Wait, you know how to drive a semi-truck?" Delilah asked, her eyebrows raised skeptically.

"Yeah. Did it for several years in the '70s. It was a good way to travel around and hunt vampires. Plus, I got to see a lot of the country. It's hard work, truck driving, but I still think of that old Peterbilt fondly from time to time."

Pablo nodded at his friend appreciatively. "You're a never-ending wonder. Never would have figured you for a steel-belted, gear-jamming, rig jockey."

Delilah snickered behind her hand. Pieter looked as confused as Luke felt at Delilah's laughter.

"I'm not getting the joke. What's so funny?" Pieter asked.

"Don't you get The Simpsons in Belgium?" Delilah asked.

Pieter shook his head.

"Neither of you have seen the episode where Bart and Homer are truck drivers?" Pablo looked scandalized and huffed his annoyance.

"I thought it was funny," Delilah said placatingly.

Pieter, a serious expression on his face, looked at Luke. "You have very weird friends."

Luke grinned and looked Pablo and Delilah. "Yeah, but they're the best kind of friends."

"Right back at you, dude." Pablo winked at Luke.

"I don't know if we need you to drive the truck in. We can simply pay a company to pick them up, assuming we have a safe place to take them. I wouldn't want to open the containers in the middle of the city with a bunch of pissed off vampires inside." Pieter folded his hands in front of him.

"Yeah, especially not with vampires who have heavy weaponry," added Pablo.

"Where can we take several shipping containers and open them safely? I can't imagine Holly would let you take them up to the farm." Delilah looked worried.

"You imagine correctly. I'll talk to some people and see what we can come up with," Pablo said.

Luke sat up straight, decisions made. "I'll contact some trucking companies who are licensed to pick up at ports. Pablo, you get us a place to unload them, and Pieter, get us the paperwork we need to pick them up."

"You still want that CDL?" Pablo asked.

"Yeah. Even if we don't need it for this mission, it'll be handy to have in the future," Luke replied.

"What about personnel?" Pablo leaned in toward Luke.

"What do you mean?" Luke asked.

"We'll need to bring in some extra people. The four of us shouldn't be doing this unaided."

"We can handle it. We've got Sam, and I'm sure if I ask politely, Pieter will join us." Luke was puzzled why Pablo would want to risk more people than were already involved. "I don't want to bring in anyone else. This is too dangerous."

Pablo folded his arms across his chest. "Dude, we've been through this. We've been helping you for months now. The pack showed up for Wapato. We're letting you train hunter and sweeper groups."

"Yeah. And we got lucky at Wapato with only a few injuries. I don't want to press our luck now that the vamps are turning up the temperature. Sweeping the streets for scent evidence of vampires is pretty low risk," Luke replied.

Delilah, frowning at Luke, waved her hand to interrupt. "This goes back to the conversation we had with Sam. You need more than just yourself and a few other people. You're going to have to get that through your head eventually. You keep bragging about leading armies. You have recruits ready to sign up and help you. Lead."

Luke felt like Delilah had slapped him. He looked from face to face. Pablo looked sympathetic but had nodded along in agreement when Delilah spoke. Delilah was angry and frustrated. Pieter looked uncomfortable with the sudden tension from the virtual strangers.

"Pablo?" Luke looked for a lifeline, even though he knew what Pablo was going to say.

"She's right, dude. I'm here. Holly has committed the pack to helping. You just need to ask."

Luke wanted to argue. He opened his mouth as if to speak only to close it again. Finally, he ran his hand through his hair then nodded. "OK, Pablo. Get us a team together. And if anyone has a gun, tell them to bring it."

"What about me?" Delilah asked.

"Get ready to kill some vampires," Luke said.

"That, I can do," Delilah replied.

"I hope this doesn't interfere with my plans for the grand opening," Pablo replied.

"It shouldn't," Luke said, adding, "Everything we have to do is standard workday oriented. Your karaoke bar can open as planned."

"Good." Pablo turned to Pieter. "If you're feeling up to it, I'm having a grand opening for a karaoke lounge I'm adding to the brewpub. You're more than welcome to come."

Pieter looked skeptical. "I'll see how I'm doing on jet lag, but thanks for the invitation. I'll keep it in mind."

# THIRTEEN

LUKE, yawning and reaching for his coffee, waited until the last of his hired trucks started up, then pulled in line behind them. Pick up had gone entirely too smoothly, something that set his teeth on edge. Things hadn't been going smoothly for him in ages, everything seemed to have a hitch in it. The paperwork Pieter obtained for them and the ID the pack had created got him through the enhanced security at the port of Portland.

With the five modular containers loaded on the back of their five empty chassis, Luke kept waiting for something to go wrong. When it didn't, he let Pablo, Delilah, and Sam know they were on the road and it was time to get the teams prepped. They'd arranged to use a large fenced-in lot with an empty building the pack had bought but hadn't put to use yet. Even though the spring sky was gray, he'd hoped the weak daylight was enough to function as an extra ally when they opened the containers.

Once they got onto city streets, Luke focused on his driving so he didn't stall out his rented semi-truck. He'd been a truck driver for quite a while in the '70s, but it wasn't exactly like riding a bike. He'd had a little trouble at first keeping the engine running. Pablo and Delilah had a great time laughing at his rustiness.

When the caravan arrived at the pack's empty property, it was Luke's first time seeing it. Based on the loading dock, the large lot looked like it'd held some sort of warehouse at one point, but most of the pavement had given way to gravel and weeds. Whatever it had been, it was a mostly empty lot now and ideal for what they had in mind. Pack members posing as the crew removed the containers from the chassis one by one until only Luke's remained. Once his was on the ground, he parked out of the way, giving the signal to close the gate so they'd have privacy. Pieter, turning off the crane they'd used to move the containers, climbed out and met up with Luke near the back of the first trailer.

"Pablo, getting any signs of life?" Luke called to Pablo who had an ear to the side of a container.

"Not a peep."

"That's odd. When we opened the container in Rotterdam, there was a lot of activity." Pieter walked over to a different container and put his ear to the side, shaking his head after a few moments.

"What about you, dude? You picking anything up?" Pablo asked Luke.

Luke shook his head. "And that's what's worrying me."

Several of the werewolves exchanged nervous glances.

"OK, let's cut the bolts on that container," Luke said, pointing to the last one on his right.

Every one of Luke's trained hunters who owned a rifle or handgun were enlisted for today's activities. Shooting a vampire wasn't the most efficient thing, but it would be better than nothing and provide distraction while the others moved in with stakes. It would also come in handy if they got in a firefight with any of the vampires inside the containers. Once the last shank was cut, the werewolves took hold of the handles.

Luke drew his swords as someone with a large flashlight stepped beside him and flicked the beam on. Luke nodded to the door openers. They picked up the handles and pushed them around to unlatch the bars that kept the container doors firmly closed. The two wolves pulled back on the doors, letting out a loud squeak from the hinges.

When the light flashed in, illuminating the forty-foot container, the team tensed, gun barrels aimed down the length of the container.

Luke squinted but only saw shadows and reflections, nothing that moved. "Guns down."

When the guns' safeties were engaged and their barrels pointed toward the ground, Luke strode forward and looked down the entrance of the container. Nothing but a few crates with their lids off.

"Anything there, dude?" Pablo called.

"No, just a few crates. I'm going in."

"Sure there are no secret compartments?" Delilah asked.

"Not that I can see, but I'll be careful," Luke said as he talked into the container.

Swords at the ready, Luke stepped foot inside the container. When he got to the end, he found several empty storage crates and some weird plastic bags on the ground. Luke picked one up and turned around. Under the light of the sun, he inspected the empty blood bag.

Holding it out to Pablo and Delilah, he cursed. "Well, shit. At least we know what they were eating en route."

Pieter walked over to the container and picked up the cut locks, inspected them, then tossed them back on the ground.

"What's our next move, Luke?" Delilah asked.

"I guess we open the rest. We'll stick to one at time just to be safe." Luke shook his head. He was happy they didn't have to subject raw recruits to vampires but disappointed and annoyed, probably closer to angry, that the vampires had pulled one over on him again. Exhaling his frustration in a sigh, he gathered everyone to open the next container.

After each one, the mystery grew. All were empty except for a bit of detritus. It was possible someone could have gotten to the containers quicker than they had once they were offloaded if they had someone on the inside at the port. They could have unloaded the containers right there, with a bit of privacy.

"This didn't go down the way we wanted it to," Pablo said, scratching his head.

Luke pursed his lips and shook his head. "No, it did not. Pieter, what are your thoughts? You're the shipping expert here."

"I don't know. I don't think they can keep enough cold blood in these containers for trips that long. I guess if they've got the customs office under control, they could be off loading them immediately."

"Yeah, I haven't been able to figure out the victuals side of things either," Luke said.

"Hey, Pieter," Delilah interjected. "Do they make refrigerated containers?"

"Yes. Yes, they do."

"I bet you could store a lot of blood in one of those. If they have people under their control all over the place, they could just as easily gain control of a crew member or sneak a vamp on board. They could unlock the containers and they'd have access to the refrigerated container. Did you check the origins of any of the refrigerated containers?"

"Shit. I didn't even think of it. Why would they ship vamps in the cold? I should have been more thorough," Pieter said, chastising himself. "I'll be able to check when I get back to my laptop."

Pablo elbowed Delilah playfully. "I can't believe neither of the old geezers thought about refrigeration. I guess when you were born thousands of years before it was invented..."

Delilah shook her head at Pablo. "Oh hush, you. You're only making fun of them because with Pieter here, you're no longer the second oldest. You're pre-refrigeration yourself, Grandpa Pablo."

Luke pointed at Pablo. "Ha! You earned that one." He looked at Delilah, Pablo, and Pieter, and rubbed his chin. "Alright. We've at least got some new information we can add to the equation. Let's get these containers returned to the port. When we're done, I'll need one of you to meet me at the truck rental spot. Pieter, while we're doing that, can you track down those refrigerated containers? Check for any other anomalies while you're at it."

"Anything else, boss?" Pablo folded his arms, giving Luke a saucy look.

"Yeah. Everyone think of our next move on how the fuck we stop these containers. Oh, and see if Jamaal has those plans yet."

"I'll check with him." Pablo's face lit up, adding, "Permits came through on the lounge. Doing the grand opening on Friday! I hope to see you all there."

"Wouldn't miss it, buddy," Luke said, patting Pablo on the shoulder.

Delilah nodded her agreement.

Looking around at the empty containers, Luke shook his head and grunted with disgust. "Guess we better get these containers back to the port." He turned then stopped. "Everyone meet at the Howling Moon when we're done. I'm buying lunch."

The werewolves let up a cheer. No one had been hurt, and the pack had participated in a mission to protect their community, even if they didn't get the vampires. The mild success called for a bit of celebration.

After cleaning out the containers and bagging what debris there was inside for later inspection, they loaded up the containers and took them back one by one since Luke's rig was the only one left after the hired drivers had left.

# FOURTEEN

LUKE SAT NEXT to Delilah in the karaoke lounge Pablo had installed in the basement of the Howling Moon. It was opening night, and they'd showed up to support their friend's newest venture and the pack's newest addition to its business community. People drinking beers, wine, and cocktails filled the seats and cushioned benches. Low knee-high tables were scattered about the room allowing people a place to set their drinks. Luke recognized a few people from the assault on Wapato last fall and from various pack events he'd been invited too. He'd assumed the crowd would be mostly pack tonight, but there were still quite a few people he didn't recognize.

Sam set three beers on the table in front of Luke and Delilah. "Hi, gang! Your glasses looked empty, so I picked up a round at the bar."

Luke smiled his thanks and made room for her as she sat next to Delilah. While Sam and Delilah chatted, Luke looked around the room. His mind wouldn't shut off, and he was having trouble relaxing. A small underground room was a dangerous place if vampires happened. He was tugged away from eyeing the room by Sam. She reached across Delilah and grabbed a handful of Luke's shirt, pulling him toward her face.

"Quit prowling for trouble."

"I'm not prowling. I'm sitting perfectly still," he said seriously.

"Your eyes are. Turn the hunter off for the night. Enjoy some relaxation with your friends. You're no good to anyone so wound up." Sam looked him deep in the eyes.

Luke sighed and nodded. "You're right. I'm still getting used to having more in my life than just vampires to kill."

Sam's face split into a grin. "Good! And I better see you putting in a song at some point tonight."

Luke blushed, getting nervous. He'd never done karaoke before but wanted to give it a try with his friends.

"Hello, hello? Ah, it's on." Pablo pulled the microphone out of its stand and addressed the crowd. "Welcome to the Howling Moon's karaoke lounge grand opening."

Pablo reached behind him and pulled a piece of cloth that was hiding something on the wall. A couple of low wattage track lights flicked on and illuminated the sign. The wall behind Pablo had a wolf's head inside a full moon, just like the sign on the Lombard Avenue side of the building that guided customers into the brewpub. The only addition was a winding line that ended in a microphone just above the open and howling mouth of the wolf.

"Welcome to the Howling Room!"

Everyone in the room clapped and cheered.

Once the crowd calmed down, Pablo continued, "OK, a few ground rules... Number one, no heckling. Tease your friends when they get back, but no heckling while they're singing. It may be some-one's first time, and we want this to always be a welcoming environ-ment. Number two, a couple songs will be off the list—Bohemian Rhapsody. You're not Saint Freddie Mercury, hallowed be his name; let's save that one for head banging in our AMC Pacers. Second song, no Werewolves of London..."

The werewolves in the crowd booed. The other half of the crowd looked confused; it wasn't a particularly popular karaoke song, and certainly wasn't overdone or offensive.

"I kid! I kid! Just a little joke, but only once per night. Other than that, you can cuss if it's in the lyrics, just don't use slurs if they're in the lyrics. For example, if you're doing some hip-hop, skip right over those n-bombs if you're not Black. That's it! The Howling Moon has always been a warm, inclusive, and welcoming environment and that's what we want the Howling Room to be, too. Cheer on the singers and let's have fun! Now it's time to introduce everyone to tonight's KJ! Tony, get your sexy ass up here."

Tony, dapper as always, strode out of the crowd, stopping briefly to give Pablo a hug and a kiss before settling behind the KJ booth. He leaned down and spoke into the microphone extending up from the sound board, "You can find our song list at howlingroom.com. Just come tell me what you want to play and we'll put you on the list."

A display screen turned on to the side of Tony. At the top of the list was Pablo's name. Tony continued, "You sing in the order you put in your songs. Duets count as your turn. New singers are at the bottom of the list. After a certain point, we'll cycle back to the front even if we're getting new singers to reward the people who were here early. If we don't have a song, we'll try to acquire it for you for later, so have a backup ready. You ready, dear?"

"No fair, Pablo only gets to go first because he's sleeping with the KJ!" someone shouted from the audience. People laughed.

"That and he owns the place," replied someone else Luke didn't recognize.

Pablo nodded. The opening strains of Guns N' Roses' "Paradise City" filling the room as people cheered.

Luke, Sam, and Delilah watched their friend as he belted out Paradise City. What Pablo lacked in vocal finesse, he made up for in showmanship, even doing a passable imitation of Axl Rose's snake dance. The crowd, excited to be a part of a new place, was enjoying the performance. Some sang along while others cheered as Pablo danced around. A few people had already turned in new songs, and the list on the screen was growing. When Pablo finished, the crowd cheered enthusiastically as he made his way to an open seat next to Luke.

"Nice job, Pablo." Delilah reached across and patted him on the knee. Sam and Luke nodded their agreement.

Pablo grinned. "Thanks, and thanks for coming out tonight. It means a lot to me to have my friends here."

"I wouldn't miss it for anything in the world," Luke said.

"You going to sing anything tonight?"

"I don't know, Pablo..."

"Yes, yes, he is," chimed in Delilah.

Luke sighed, slightly exasperated at being put on the spot even if he did want to try out karaoke. "I guess I don't really have a choice."

Sam smiled warmly at Luke. "You'll do great. We'll all cheer extra loud for you."

Luke nodded, then stood up and strode to the KJ booth and gave his song to Tony. When he returned, he sat with his friends and watched the parade of singers while talking about unimportant topics that end up being the most important things when you're building friendships. For the first time in a long time, Luke felt like he indeed had friends. The warm feeling it brought also felt weird, rusty, out of use, like it had been in a scrap yard somewhere. Pablo, and then Delilah and Sam, had knocked off the corrosion and applied the care needed to revive the old feeling for Luke. And for the first time in recent memory, he felt a bit less hollow.

"Let's welcome our next singer. Luke, you're up," Tony called.

Luke's stomach dropped and was quickly replaced a swarm of overactive butterflies, or flame drunk moths, or angry wasps. His crew cheered him up to the stage, and although their enthusiasm and loyalty heartened him, he'd much rather be facing a horde of hungry vampires than a crowd of people he had to entertain for a few minutes with a song he'd only sung in the basement while reading lyrics on his phone screen.

Tony looked over at Luke, covering his mic on the soundboard with his hand. "Ready to go?"

Luke nodded, swallowing to try to get some moisture into his suddenly dry mouth. The first notes of Roxy Music's "Mother of Pearl" sounded loudly through the room. Where were the lyrics? Why did he have to pick a song with such a long instrumental opening? Was he supposed to dance? Other people had filled space with some light dancing. Why'd he have to pick such a long song? He could have gone with the Ramones. Their songs barely topped out at two minutes.

Finally, the words appeared on the screen, counting him in. With his eyes focused on the monitor, he shut the rest of the room out and started singing tentatively. But as he sank into the lyrics and remembered his days singing marching songs, his voice strengthened. The lyrics were more rhythmic and didn't require a huge singing range. Soon he settled in comfortably, feeling like he was doing a passable job for his first time at the mic. By the time the last lyrics passed over the screen, he was even having a good time. When the last note died down, he took a deep breath and let it out explosively. He handed the mic back to Tony.

Tony patted him on the shoulder. "Good job, Luke."

His nerves returning, he nodded and smiled, turning back to face the room.

Luke walked back to his seat to a chorus of friendly cheers and claps. His cheeks warmed as he kept his eyes on the floor, the attention feeling simultaneously nice and disconcerting. Once he sat down, he accepted the praise of his friends with more embarrassment. He was so focused on his own awkwardness that he didn't notice the new person sitting at the end of the bench near Sam. Staring at the floor, he noticed the nice sneakers and shapely bare calves before working his way up to her royal blue dress. Usually her hair was up in a ponytail when she worked behind the counter at the coffee shop. Tonight, it was cascading down and over her shoulders, the relaxed curls creating a well-controlled wavy mass of hair. She swept her hand along the right side, placing a few errant strands behind her ear.

"Coffee shop woman!"

"Triple shot Americano, pass the extra shot along." She smiled warmly at Luke.

"Triple shot, pass the extra?" Delilah asked.

"It's his usual order," she said, addressing Delilah. "You ever seen 'You've Got Mail?'"

Delilah shook her head. Sam nodded.

"Anyways, there's this whole bit about how a coffee order says a lot about a person. It's a confident order that says he knows the right amount of caffeine and flavor for his needs. And since we only pull doubles, that leaves the fourth shot unused, so he passes it along to a customer down the line. It's a nice gesture that always brightens someone's day. It's a nice order."

Delilah nodded, her lower lip poking out as she considered the commentary on her friend. "I'm Delilah. This is Sam and Pablo. And Mr. Triple Shot is Luke."

"My name is Heather," she reached out and shook all the offered hands, lingering a bit on Luke's.

Delilah and Sam smirked at each other. He'd probably missed some important social cue they'd tease him about later.

"Do you karaoke a lot?" Heather asked.

Luke chuckled. "No, this is my first time, actually. I wanted to support my friend's new business." He put a hand on Pablo's shoulder.

"Congratulations," Heather said to Pablo.

"Thanks!" Pablo replied.

She turned her attention back to Luke. "That was really good for your first time."

The low lighting hid his blush. "Thanks."

"Is that your favorite song?"

"No, just one I figured I could sing. Are you going to put your name in?"

"Probably. I go out to karaoke periodically with my friends." She pointed toward a group of women.

After that, Luke and Heather sat awkwardly until Delilah came to his rescue. "How long have you known Luke?"

"I mean, he's been coming into the shop since it opened. Not sure if that qualifies as knowing him, but we've chatted at the register off and on over the last few years. In all that time, he may be one of the few male patrons who's never tried to get my number."

Luke shrugged. "I don't hit on people while they're working.

They're being nice to their customers, not flirting. I just always found it kind of creepy."

"Well, I'm not working now…" She let it hang there for a moment.

Delilah rolled her eyes at Luke's lack of understanding. She took pity on him. "Luke, give me your phone."

Luke handed her his phone.

"Heather, what's your number?" Delilah entered Heather's contact info in Luke's phone, then typed a message and hit send. "Here's my oblivious friend's number. You might want to text him first. He's a great guy, just a bit on the shy side."

Heather blushed and nodded at Delilah. "Thanks. I'll take your advice. Well, I should rejoin my friends. It was nice meeting you all." She stood up and waved, twinkling her fingers at them. "Luke, I'm glad to finally have a name to go with the face." She gave him a last look, then turned to rejoin her friends.

"Hey, buddy! You scored some digits." Pablo patted Luke on the pack.

Delilah pursed her lips. "I scored him some digits. You're welcome, by the way."

Luke was flummoxed. "Thank you," he stammered.

Sam snickered behind her hand before putting on her serious face. "Heather seems very nice, and she obviously likes you, Luke. Give her a call. Go out on a date. It'll do you good."

"I haven't been on a date in…" He rolled his eyes up, trying to remember what year it might have been. "…in a very long time, if you could even call it a date."

"When was the last time you had a girlfriend?" Sam asked.

"Um… In the twenties, after the Great War. Paris. I don't think we ever used the terms 'boyfriend' or 'girlfriend,' but that was the last time I spent any serious intimate time with a woman."

"The twenties?" Pablo seemed shocked. "That's almost a century ago. Was that the last time…" He tipped his head and arched his eyebrows up, leaving the air thick with innuendo.

"I mean. I've had assignations since then," Luke said, flustered.

"When was the last time?" Pablo asked.

"Pablo, don't pry," Sam sounded firm, stepping in to protect Luke who was floundering.

Luke covered his face with his hand. "I think the '70s..." Luke didn't want to look up and see the pity he assumed filled everyone's eyes.

"Pablo, that's enough. You're his best friend. You're supposed to look out for him," Sam said.

Looking up, he saw Sam glaring at Pablo, who looked shocked and ashamed. Delilah looked thoughtful.

"Luke. I'm so sorry for prying. It was none of my business, and it certainly wasn't OK to drag it out in public in front of our friends." Pablo reached out and patted Luke's knee apologetically.

Squeezing Pablo's shoulder, he smiled sadly. "It's OK, buddy. I'm not mad at you. It's just..."

"You don't have to explain," Pablo said.

Luke nodded.

"So, Paris in the twenties? That must have been something..." Sam said to break up the awkwardness, smiling at him with a wistful look on her face.

"There was a lot of wine, gin, absinthe, coke, opium..." He trailed off as his friends stared at him.

"What? We'd all just survived the horrors of the first truly modern war and were trying to bury the pain. I spent years in the muck and blood of the trenches. I still have nightmares about it, maybe more than any other horror I've ever seen." Luke's breathing was getting shallow and short, his eyes darting around.

Pablo put his arm around Luke's shoulder. "It's OK, buddy. You're with friends."

Luke tensed under the touch but relaxed when Pablo added a reassuring squeeze. Luke took a deep steadying breath.

"Why don't you go get a breath of fresh air? You're looking a bit wan," Sam suggested.

He nodded at her, gave Pablo's leg a squeeze, and then stood awkwardly and walked out. Once he got outside, he walked around the corner and darted into the doorway of the brewery's office. He ran through some breathing exercises, trying to stay in control.

After a few minutes, his heartbeat returned to normal and his chest loosened somewhat, although not completely returning to a relaxed state. A buzz from his pocket alerted him to a message.

*If you need to bail, no worries. I'm glad you made it out. If not, the next round is on me.*

He smiled at Pablo's message. Luke hadn't known a friend like him in a long time. He took one last deep breath and headed back into the pub and down the stairs to the karaoke lounge. He sat back down in between Sam and Pablo.

"Where's Delilah?"

Sam pointed to Delilah, who was sitting very close to a Latina woman with black hair and brown skin. The woman threw her head back, laughing at something humorous Delilah must have said. The woman reached her hand out and rubbed Delilah's forearm before leaning in and whispering something in her ear. It was Delilah's turn to laugh.

"That's going well," Pablo commented.

"I'd say," Sam said. Seeing Luke's confusion, she added, "I invited Delilah over to hang out with some of my pack friends. She and Rosa hit it off…"

They all stared as Delilah reached in, running her finger along Rosa's jaw before going in for the kiss. Allowing his friend the courtesy of not staring for too long, he returned his gaze to Pablo and Sam who'd also turned back to their small circle.

"Apparently they hit it off real well," Pablo said.

"I'd say so. Good for her. Rosa is a sweetheart." Sam smiled pleasantly.

"Werewolf?" Luke asked.

"Yup. She's a newer pack member, from Honduras. She's only been in Portland for a few years."

"Good for them." Pablo smiled at Sam and Luke. "I promised this guy another round on me. What you both having? I'll get the lovers' order on the way up."

"I'll take another pale ale," Luke said.

Sam held up her wineglass. "House red, please."

Pablo paused by Delilah and got hers and Rosa's orders.

Delilah looked over at Sam and Luke. She made eye contact with Luke, a questioning eyebrow lifted. Assuming she was checking on his health status after he walked out, Luke smiled softly at her and nodded that he was OK. She returned the gesture before breaking into another laugh at something Rosa whispered into her ear.

Luke looked away and saw Sam looking at him; she gave him a look, but he wasn't quite sure what it meant.

"Oh! I wanted to ask you a favor," Luke remembered.

"Sure, Luke. What can I do for you?" Sam replied.

"I've started teaching Gwen how to fight. I discovered her down in my sparring room, playing around. So I asked if she'd like to learn to fight, and she sounded enthusiastic about it." Luke shrugged. "I mean, it's something we can do together. Not sure I have much else to offer her."

Sam scooted closer to Luke. "You have plenty. She doesn't know how to express it yet, but I can see how she looks at you. You're her protector. You're the first adult that's really looked out for her in a real and substantial way. You're both suffering from a lot of trauma, I think. You'll figure it out, but I can see why this would interest you and Gwen. How can I help?"

"I think short swords and long weapons are going to be the right choice for her. She's going to have to compensate for her short stature unless she catches up to her size. I'm solid with spears. I can throw them, and I'm good with them on horseback. But it's not my strongest weapon on foot. You are a bona fide expert. I'd love it if you'd help me with her training. Plus I'd like to brush up myself."

"Of course! I'd be honored. You know I'd do anything for Gwen. She's such a little dear."

Luke smiled warmly at Sam. "Thank you. We both appreciate it. Also, since we're talking business, the team and I would like to extend an official invitation to join our little gang of slayer misfits. I know you've been coming out with us lately, but we wanted to invite you properly."

"You know I'm down. I like hanging out with you, and it's a way I can contribute to the pack." She reached over and patted his knee.

With the addition of Sam to their little team, warmth filled Luke at the reminder he had people to watch his back, and maybe more important to him, people he could trust and that he enjoyed spending time with. Since their first adventure last fall at Wapato, Sam's brand of humor had brought many a smile and laugh to Luke. She'd be welcome for far more than just her weapon expertise.

# FIFTEEN

LUKE HAD BEEN SLEEPING POORLY since they'd picked up the empty containers. The crew had been expanded for their planned excursions to sweep the two potential sniper sites. They'd gone through the building plans multiple times and briefed everyone until they could recite their objectives by rote. Between Luke and Pieter, they'd looked at it from every angle they could.

By all measures, they should be as ready as possible, but the what ifs weren't leaving Luke alone. He kept having nightmares about disasters, inconceivable things that in his dream, he felt he should have been accounted for. In his waking hours, ninja vampire monkeys would be hilarious and awesome, but in the anxiety-filled hellscape of his nightmares, they were eight feet tall demons more agile and stronger than his werewolves. He watched as friend after friend was torn apart, their body parts and blood raining down on him.

After each brutal nightmare, he'd wake in a sweat, nearly hyper-ventilating. The worst nightmares, though, weren't the ones his brain made up, but the ones it forced him to relive from his life. His platoon taking a direct hit in their trench from a German shell and vaporizing. Seeing the death camps for the first time while gathering intelligence. Raiding a vamp breeding station preying off the camps. The first half of the twentieth century had been a horror show Luke witnessed first-hand, breaking him after walking the earth for eighteen centuries. It's not to say the previous eighteen hundred years had been kind to Luke or his psyche, but World Wars I and II had taken a fragile thing and shattered it.

In the run-up to their raid on the two potential sniper nests, Luke was increasingly irritable and jumpy. The only solace seemed to be training time with Gwen. The kid had proven to be a natural—her hunger to learn fueling her skill. Rarely did he have to correct her more than once. Her hyper-vigilance came in handy as she was able to pick up the tiny signals that showed where her opponent's body was going.

The training and her extended interactions with Luke also had the double effect of improving both her humor and her hunger. Now that she was coming out of her shell, she was laughing more, although she was still a serious kid. She was also ravenous, the exercise and her metabolism fueling an increase in Luke's food budget.

As she got more comfortable in Luke's home, she started venturing out into the neighborhood on her own, going to the corner market to get a soda if she wanted to or to the park. Luke trusted her ability to stay out of trouble. She'd done it for a couple years when she was unhoused, but he insisted she always take the cellphone he'd bought her. Although that was less of a concern as she loved her phone and the world it opened up for her.

Luke, trying to unwind with a book, startled when he heard the doorbell. Throwing a coaster in the book to hold his place, he went to the door and saw Maggie standing on his porch.

"Hey, Luke. How you doing?" Maggie slid by him into the living room.

"Not bad. How about you?" He took her coat and hung it in the closet.

"About the same," she replied.

Today, her long blonde hair was braided. She wore her usual jeans and a form-fitting red sweater. Luke's gaze lingered longer than it normally might. He chalked it up to his tiredness and slow brain.

Once he stepped into the light, she caught the dark circles under his eyes, concern furrowing her brow.

"Have you been sleeping poorly?" Maggie asked.

"No, not really."

Gwen walked into the room and coughed into her hand, "Liar."

"Excuse me, missy?" Luke asked.

"Dude, you're waking up at least a few times a night, noisily." Gwen walked up and hugged Maggie. "Hi, Doctor Maggie."

"Hey, kiddo, good to see you again. What do you mean, he's waking up noisily?"

"He's having night terrors."

"I'm waking you up?" Luke was horrified.

"Hey, I'm a light sleeper," Gwen replied. While she'd been off the streets for several months, they still weren't out of her system.

"Gwen, would you mind giving us some privacy for a few minutes?" Maggie smiled, rubbing her back affectionately.

"Sure thing," Gwen said, turning back toward her room.

Luke waved Maggie to follow him into the office where they'd have some privacy. He sat in his office chair, leaving the armchair for Maggie.

"Night terrors?"

Luke sighed. "I didn't realize I was making any noise when I woke up."

Luke was coming to like and trust Maggie. Her quiet seriousness and kindness made her easy to be around. Her care and affection for Gwen meant Luke saw her a lot when he took Gwen for appointments or when he asked her to stay with the kid when he was going out for bigger missions. Gwen could take care of herself, but he could tell she got nervous when he had something bigger coming up. She was an observant kid and could easily read Luke's moods, picking up on his tension.

"How long has it been going on?"

"A few days. Since we started planning this raid." Luke looked at his hands in his lap.

"Do you have periods like this? When you're more stressed?"

Luke nodded.

"Well, hopefully after tonight, you can get back to some semblance of normal."

Luke laughed, though it sounded harsh to his ears. "Once the nightmares start, they take a while to recede again."

Maggie, her brows furrowing lightly, gave Luke a sympathetic closed-lip smile. "I know you're busy now, but when you get this settled, I want to get you in to see one of our pack doctors to talk about it."

"Yeah, that's probably a good idea, I guess." Luke sighed.

"When you're done with this, try to get some rest. I can get you a sleep aid if you'd like. But for now, about all I can offer is a hug, if you'd like one…"

Maggie seemed nervous about the offer, although Luke wasn't sure why.

"I think I'd like that."

Maggie stood as Luke did. They awkwardly stepped forward, wrapping their arms around each other. The warmth of her body against his eased the tension somewhat. He rested his chin on her shoulder, the two of them tipping their heads against each other's. She gently rubbed his back. He felt able to breathe a little deeper. Drawing in a breath, he caught a whiff of Maggie's light perfume. A slight smile spread across his face.

He didn't really want to let go. It had been a long time since he'd been hugged so warmly, but he didn't want to linger past Maggie's comfort level. Withdrawing his arms, he held Maggie at arm's length.

"Thank you. I needed that," Luke said.

"I'm glad." Maggie leaned forward and kissed him on the cheek. "Luke. Be careful tonight."

"I'll do my best."

LUKE MET the rest of the team at the pack house to touch base one last time before rolling downtown to investigate the potential sniper nests. He'd insisted on rental vans instead of using pack or personal vehicles to help keep some semblance of anonymity.

Everyone had ski masks or the silly bearded beanies, some mixing in lighter tinted sunglasses. When they hit their targets, they didn't want any way their actions could come back on them or their friends and families, either from the vampires or the cops. Although it was becoming increasingly evident that the latter were involved with the former in some manner that could prove dangerous to everyone's safety.

They'd split everyone into two teams of eight with Delilah and Luke leading one team and Pablo and Pieter leading the other. If they needed to, they could further split into squads of four. Delilah was eager to strike back at Cassius in any way possible, especially after the containers had turned out to be duds. Luke fidgeted in the front seat next to Archie, the werewolf driving the van.

He wasn't feeling like much of a leader at the moment, but when the time came, he knew he'd be ready to go into action. Periodically as they drove around the area of their target, the high rise under construction, they'd drop off someone so they didn't look suspicious when a van suddenly disgorged a bunch of people at once. When it was down to Luke and Archie, they looked for parking. The werewolf pulled into a nearby 24/7 loading zone and threw the fake permit they'd forged in the window.

Archie pulled the hand truck out of the back of the van and stacked a large crate on it. Pretending to be delivery people was good camouflage and allowed them an easy way to move their equipment to the site.

"Keys, mate." Archie tossed the keys to Luke.

Luke snagged them out of the air and locked the van. "Ready to go?"

"Aye." Archie turned and pushed the hand truck toward the construction site.

They met up with the rest of their crew in the darkest corner. Delilah already had a hole cut in the chain-link fence with some bolt cutters. She and one of the new wolves Luke hadn't yet learned the name of waited outside, looking casual. When Luke and Archie approached, they peeled the hole back and waved them through, following when Luke disappeared behind the fence.

Once everyone was inside, Luke pulled some zip ties from the crate and tossed them to a Korean woman. "Mind strapping that plastic back in place so no one gets too curious? Sorry, I don't think we've met. I'm Luke."

"I know, sir. My name's Jung-sook, sir."

Luke nodded. "Luke is fine."

"Sorry, sir. I mean Luke. It's a hard habit to break on operations," Jung-sook replied.

"Military?"

"Yes, sir. Infantry, Republic of Korea Army, 1964 to 1971," she replied.

"Well, it's good to meet you."

"I don't mean to be too forward, but I hear you're watching over the young trans werewolf?"

Luke nodded.

"Well, my partner and I would be willing to take her in if she's looking for a home with other trans wolves."

"I'll certainly keep that in mind," he replied politely.

Luke knew that was a possibility. Maggie and Holly had spoken to him about moving her to a trans family when she was more settled. It had sounded logical at the time. Now, though, it spiked his anxiety, although it could be the timing of the offer. He sighed and pushed it aside for now.

He addressed everyone else while she zip tied the plastic barrier that kept prying eyes out of the construction site. "If you haven't already, masks on. Stay alert and be careful."

Luke pulled out the few firearms they had and passed them to the people who could use them best. Luke made a note to acquire some better options. He didn't want to escalate to guns, but he'd rather have them if needed instead of the other way around.

He keyed in the radio, not sure if he'd be able to reach Pablo from this distance with so many buildings around them. "Spartacus calling the Pooch, do you copy?" Luke asked, using the handles Sam had created during the Wapato raid last fall.

"Spartacus calling the Pooch, do you copy?" he repeated.

"This is Bandit. I'm taking over the radio for the Pooch. Over," Sam replied.

"Copy. You on site yet?" Luke asked.

"Yup. About to head in."

"We're in, about to start our ascent. Check in —" he looked at his watch " —fifteen minutes."

"Copy. Out."

Delilah handed Luke a set of binoculars from the bottom of the crate, then checked to make sure it was empty. He couldn't tell who with everyone masked, but someone was wiping down the crate and hand truck with an alcohol-soaked rag to wipe any incidental fingerprints that might be on them. If all went well, they'd pack them back out again, but Luke liked to cover all eventualities.

Seven people stood around Luke, waiting for his directions. He gave the hand signal to follow him. The building was an in-process skeleton with floors and a good deal of its eventual height, but little else. They found the stairwell and started up, keeping their progress quick but careful and checking for any potential booby traps. As long as Luke didn't sense any vampires, they ignored the bottom floors that wouldn't have line-of-site of the vampires' night club and the street where Luke had been shot a couple weeks ago by the sniper. Luke also had the werewolves check for any fresh scents to see if either humans or werewolves had been through the stairwell recently, though no one

"Shit, I should have been hitting the stair master," Delilah complained. As the only full human — Luke wasn't sure if he qualified anymore — she didn't have supernatural strength and stamina but was always a trooper, keeping up with everyone else. The hard work she'd put in with her exercise regimen was paying off.

"Alright, let's take a quick breather. My quads are burning," Luke said, calling a halt at one of the landings of the stairwell. He turned his back to Delilah. "Mind grabbing me a bottle of water?"

The backpack was custom made to hold Luke's swords if necessary and fit snuggly around his armor encased chest, but that didn't make it easy to get off and on. She handed him a bottle, grabbing one for herself. While Luke slid the nozzle under his mask and sucked some water down, he scanned around checking for anything troubling like a security camera or other dangers. It was probably pointless in the dark and at this early stage of construction, but checking his environment was a multi-century habit. Plus, the vampires didn't want their activity documented, so they'd probably eliminated any cameras already.

When he was done, he handed his bottle to Delilah. She took it silently and tossed it back into his pack along with hers, zipping him up. He checked with the rest of the team. Getting a nod from them, he started up the next set of stairs. When they were five floors from the top, they went silent, switching to hand signals for communication so they wouldn't alert anyone or anything that might be lurking on the top floors.

He didn't anticipate running into the vampires; snipers rarely stayed in the same spot for days on end. But even after all these years hunting them, too many times he'd learned the hard way not to expect standard behavior from vampires. Besides, now that he held so many lives in his hands, over-caution seemed the best way to ensure they didn't come to harm on his watch.

When they neared the top constructed floor, they paused one last time to get a quick drink and rest, readying weapons. Luke pulled his swords. Delilah slid her machete out of its sheath and pulled a stake from inside her coat. The other six members of their teams had firearms, a mix of handguns, rifles, and one double barrel 12-gauge shotgun. It was a motley crew, but they were ready, several of them having served in various armed forces.

When he'd checked that everyone was paying attention, they crept up the last set of stairs on silent feet until they lined up behind the door, out of the way. Pausing for a moment, Luke still hadn't felt any vampires nearby. Counting down five with his hand, Luke yanked the door open. Delilah grabbed it and quietly placed a chunk of broken concrete to prop it open as the rest of the team came through the doors in twos, splitting left and right. Delilah brought up the rear.

Luke had his sector swept and kept an eye on the door while he waited for everyone else to report back. When the rest of the team signaled the all-clear, an upside-down fist patting the top of their heads, he relaxed and waved everyone in. Jung-sook and another wolf he didn't recognize jogged back to the door, aiming their rifles downstairs in case anyone was creeping up on them.

Delilah jogged up. "Looks like it's all clear, Luke."

"OK, let's sweep around for any evidence." He raised his voice slightly. "Keep the flashlights under control. If anyone's looking, we're going to be obvious enough. Let's not draw any more attention than we need to."

Light beams flicked on and began sweeping the floor and some of the partially built walls. While his team worked, Luke looked across the empty sky toward the apartment building where Pablo, Pieter, and the rest of their team were advancing toward the floors they suspected the sniper might have shot from. Pulling out the binoculars, he walked along the floor until he found the viewpoint to the place he was shot. Finding it, he marked it mentally so he could focus his searches there on the lower floors.

Luke keyed in his radio. "Spartacus to Bandit, progress report, over."

"Almost there. Going silent. Out." Sam sounded like she was keeping her voice down.

As he stared out into the night, a tap on his shoulder sent him jumping.

"Shit, sorry, Luke. Jumpy?" Delilah asked, backing away.

"Yeah. A bit. Sorry, Delilah."

"All clear here. Next floor?"

Luke nodded and waved everyone forward and back into the stairwell. Delilah picked up the rock and followed everyone else down to the next floor. They repeated their entrance, Luke diverting to the sector he'd marked out from the floor above, the rest of the team adjusting to his shift. As they silently fanned out to cover their adjusted sectors without a word, Luke smiled, impressed the team was flowing so naturally.

They swept that floor, then the next. Soon, they'd be too low for the angles to work and they could get out of there. Luke was busy checking the spot where he'd been shot. Still good. He stared at the spot he'd fallen and where Delilah had pulled him out of the line of fire, saving his life before the sniper could adjust to his head.

"Oh my god…" someone said behind him.

"Luke…" Delilah tapped him the shoulder, pointing toward the other team. "Look."

Flames and debris belched out the top floors of the building where his friends and comrades were searching.

"Pablo…" Luke's knees trembled, and he reached out to steady himself on a nearby girder.

"Sam! Luke, call Sam. On the radio." Delilah said frantically.

When he didn't respond, his eyes locked on the flames licking the top of the building, she punched his arm.

Luke shook himself to attention. "What?"

"Get on the damn radio. Call Sam," Delilah ordered.

Luke clicked the talk button. "Spartacus to Bandit, come in. Spartacus—"

"Luke!" someone yelled. "Come here, now!"

Luke pulled his eyes away from the building. "Delilah, keep calling."

He wasn't sure why she hadn't called herself; she was tuned in to the same channel on her FRS. Probably the same reason she'd had to hit him to get his attention. He ran toward the werewolf who'd yelled at him. When he approached, they held up their hand, pointing toward a vertical cement column. Taking out his flashlight, Luke shone it over the area where. It was a shell casing for a high-powered rifle citing on a metal box.

The werewolf reached for it.

"Don't!" Luke said, grabbing their wrist. "Cassius likes to play games." He pulled out his flashlight and moved it over the area around the shell casing. Wires painted the same gray of the concrete rose out of the box and ran up the wall. At the end of the wires, he found blocks of a light gray clay-like substance.

"Shit. C4." He took a step and thought he felt something under his foot.

"Luke. Don't move. I heard a click," Jung-sook said. She'd wandered over when Luke had been called.

Luke, trying not to shift his weight at all, turned the flashlight toward the floor. He saw the lines that marked some sort of plate. "Everyone back away from me. I think it's a pressure plate."

"What are we going to do? We can't leave you standing there all night," Archie said.

"No. I'm not sure I can stay here for too long, anyway. I'm standing in a really awkward position, but I'm afraid to move in case it triggers." Adrenaline coursed through his veins as he tried to find a solution.

"If it hasn't blown now, it might be pressure release," Jung-sook said. "We need weight. Anything we can stack around Luke's foot. Someone go grab that rock we've been using on the doors. Look for anything else you can find." Jung-sook looked around at the team. "Hurry. Or we're going to be leaving this tower in pieces."

Luke tried to force some saliva into his mouth. "Get everyone evacuated."

Delilah jogged up. "Luke, I can't get a hold of Sam." She looked him over. "Why are you standing like that?"

"I'm standing on a pressure plate and there's a bomb on the wall," Luke gritted out the words between clenched teeth.

"Jung-sook, all we can find is a bit of construction debris. Should we run downstairs bring up anything from the site?" someone said.

"Luke?" Jung-sook asked.

"I'm not sure I can hold this position much longer." His legs burned, and his body vibrated.

Jung-sook nodded. "Grab whatever you can. Grab all the junk you can find. We'll stack it around Luke's foot.

The small team burst into activity running around the floor, finding anything that looked worth stacking on the pressure plate. Soon, they had a small pile nearby.

"Luke, there's something on the wall in front of you." Delilah pointed a flashlight at a piece of paper that had blended into the wall. "I think I can reach it without getting too close to you."

"Are you sure? I find myself not being terribly curious about it." He stared at the illuminated note, his curiosity growing more intense. "Fuck. Be careful."

Delilah edged toward the wall, sweeping her flashlight over the ground and looking for any indications of disruptions to the smoothness of the concrete. Once she stopped, she stretched her arm out to its full extent and snagged the piece of paper. "Want me to read it?"

"Go for it, back away slowly and stick to where you stepped before. Then read it."

*What's the saying, my old pal? Curiosity killed the cat? I hope you feel like meowing now. So predictable after all this time. Can't help but stick your nose in where it doesn't belong. Except now your nose will be able to be in multiple places at once as will the rest of you. Love you to pieces, C.*

Delilah cursed under her breath.

"Damn. He's a real bell end, isn't he?" Archie chuckled nervously and shook his head.

Luke nodded anxiously, his head wobbling lightly.

"Luke, I think we've got everything we can find," Jung-sook said. "You ready?"

"No. But It's not like I have a choice. I'm struggling here. Let's only have one person do the stacking. Everyone else can hand them the junk," Luke replied.

Jung-sook nodded then edged forward until she knelt on the ground near Luke. After a few moments, she had a sizable pile stacked around Luke's foot. Once one side was surrounded, she moved to the other side and continued, stacking as much on the area of the plate as she could.

"That's as good as we're going to get, Luke." Jung-sook stood up and backed away.

"Everybody, get ready to go. As soon as I pull my foot up, we need to fly." Luke took several deep breaths to ready himself.

Once he counted heads and saw the team gathered around the door, he shifted his weight slightly to the back leg. "Go! Now! I'll right behind."

The wolves took off at a dead run, Delilah bringing up the rear. As soon as he saw her back disappear into the door to the stairwell, he took a last breath, then exploded into movement. The junk clattered around on the ground the plate where his food had been. He hobbled slightly from standing so awkwardly but burst into full speed, slowing only enough to make the turn into the stairwell.

He couldn't see anyone ahead of him, but he could hear their footfalls and heavy panting punctuated by an occasional curse reverberating off the concrete walls. As he turned to hit another stairwell, he could see Delilah ahead of him. He was gaining on her.

"Delilah, I'm behind you. Keep going," Luke called to her so she'd not be surprised by his presence behind her.

As Luke rounded the next turn, he saw Delilah trip and take a dive onto the landing, skidding across the rough concrete floor. He bounded down two steps at a time and leapt over her as she tried to push herself off the ground. He slammed into a wall, then turned around and helped her up. Her hands were a bloody mess, as were her knees. Although it was hard to tell with her mask if she'd hit her head, she appeared dazed.

He reached behind her, opened the backpack she had, and pulled out a small bottle of bleach. He ripped the lid off and dumped it on the concrete, spreading it around to cover the visible blood spots he could find with his flashlight. He was about to screw the lid back on when the building shook, a sound wave ripping through the air, knocking him and Delilah down. They tumbled down a couple stairs. The junk had weighed enough to buy them time but wasn't heavy enough to keep it from triggering the bomb.

Luke, recovering first, crawled over to Delilah and covered her head and upper body as a debris cloud rained down from above, chucks of concrete rolling down the stairs.

Luke shook his head, wishing he'd brought his helmet as the back of his head throbbed. He couldn't hear much except a whining noise that seemed to distort everything around him. Coughing, he tried to wave the dust out of his face, squinting.

"Delilah?" He wasn't sure if he was shouting.

Delilah wiggled under him, turning her head and saying something. He couldn't hear her through the whine.

"Ge...off...me..."

"Oh!" He moved down to a lower step.

Delilah got on all fours, shaking her own head. Out of the corner of his eye, he saw movement. Standing unsteadily, he drew his gladius and readied himself, relaxing when he saw Archie come bounding up the stairs.

Archie was speaking; Luke could see his lips moving and hear something, but it sounded like an adult from a Peanuts cartoon. Luke sheathed his sword and checked on Delilah. She was trying to stand. He reached down and helped her up as Archie waved at them to hurry.

"You OK?" Luke yelled.

Delilah shook her head again, trying to clear it and gave him a thumbs up. He slid an arm under hers and supported her as they started down the stairs. Luke felt wobbly, sure that whatever was going on with his ears had fucked up his balance as well. Delilah must have been feeling a little more steady; she shook Luke off and continued on her own, going as fast as she could while keeping a good grip on the handrail. Luke grabbed the rail as well and sped up, trying to keep his balance.

When they got to the bottom, the group was fanned out and alert, keeping an eye out for any intruders.

"Any injuries?" Luke hoped he was speaking at a low enough volume.

Again, Archie moved his lips but Luke couldn't get much from it. Shaking his head, Archie pulled out his phone and started typing. He held the screen up for Luke.

*Nothing serious with the wolves. You've got blood coming out of your ears though.*

Luke reached up and touched the skin near the entrance to his ear canal. Blood glistened on the finger of his glove.

Archie typed in a new message. *Plan?*

Luke replied verbally, "Scatter. Probably lots of people running away. Everyone go to their planned meet up points and we'll pick them up. You, me, and Delilah to the van."

*Take the cart and the crate?*

"Leave it," Luke replied.

Archie started issuing Luke's orders, the rest of the team

nodding. They moved toward the fence they'd entered through. Archie pulled out a knife and cut a slit in the heavy plastic they'd zip tied back in place earlier to conceal their entry. One by one, the team poked their heads out and darted away, heading to their designated extraction points. After the five wolves exited, Luke ushered Delilah out then followed her. Together with Archie, they stumbled toward the van looking like any other scared victim of a catastrophe.

Luke, fishing the keys out of his pocket, handed them to Archie as he passed. By the time Luke and Delilah made it to the rental, Archie had the engine fired up and was ready to pull out into the street. Luke helped Delilah into the bench seat behind the front seats and joined her, shutting the door. As soon as it latched, Archie pulled out into the street, weaving around people running away from the scene or milling about. Once he got clear, he made for the first extraction zone.

Luke's head throbbed. He reached up and carefully pulled the ear bud from his ear, cringing with pain as it stuck for a moment before sliding out. The end was caked with blood from his broken eardrums. Feeling for the throbbing on the back of his head, he drew back bloody fingers. He checked again; it didn't feel too bad, probably only a minor cut in his scalp. He looked over at Delilah. She was staring out the window with a dazed expression on her face. He could see light reflecting off some blood near her ear. He hoped it was only minor; she didn't have magical healing like he and the werewolves did.

The first wolves picked up were Jung-sook and a face Luke had trouble putting a name to. Jung-sook took shotgun in the van, turning around and holding her phone out for Luke.

*The pack has an emergency plan and meet up spot for triage and treatment. Activate it?*

Luke took the phone and typed in a message of his own. *Yes. You and Archie are in charge from here on out.*

Jung-sook nodded and turned to Archie, her lips moving. Archie nodded back. After that, Luke quit paying attention. Someone else was in charge. He tried texting Pablo, Pieter, and Sam, but heard nothing back from any of them. He hoped they'd made it out. Hoped they wouldn't be the victims of his failures as a leader. He disappeared inside his head, losing himself to the world until they reached their final stop and someone helped him out of the van and into a building he didn't recognize. They'd arrived at the pack's medical office.

# SIXTEEN

WHEN HE CLEARED THE DOOR, he saw Maggie holding back Gwen. He tried to muster a smile, but it felt more like a grimace. He settled on giving the worried looking kid a thumbs up. However long ago since the blast, he still couldn't hear anything but a whistling noise and dull, distorted noises. Maggie, with Gwen's hand in hers, stepped forward and grabbed Luke's hand, leading him to an examination room.

Luke hopped up on the table while Gwen took a chair out of the way. Maggie started talking, but Luke held up his hand to stop her, pointing to his ears.

"I can't hear you." He turned his head so an ear was pointed toward her.

Understanding dawned for Maggie. She looked around the room, took a white board off the wall, and grabbed the marker.

*Besides hearing loss, what else?*

"A cut on the back of my head. Probably some scrapes. Maybe a concussion. It's hard to tell whether the dizziness is that or the eardrums." Luke wasn't sure how loud he was talking or if he was speaking clearly, but Maggie seemed to understand.

Maggie wrote another message on the board. *How much pain?*

"Not too bad. If you're needed elsewhere, I can hold."

Maggie nodded and opened a cabinet, pulling out a large bottle. She shook out four ibuprofen and handed them to Luke. Next, she waved him forward so she could examine the cut on his head. Satisfied it wasn't a pressing issue, she gave some instructions to Gwen, reached out and patted the kid's shoulder, then left the room, setting the white board where Gwen could reach it. She picked it up and started writing.

*I'm glad you're not hurt too bad.*

"Yeah, it could have been a lot worse," Luke replied.

She cringed back.

"Too loud?" he asked.

Gwen nodded.

"Sorry. I can't hear myself and it's hard to talk. That better?"

She nodded. Luke tried to muster a smile for the kid. She looked worried about him.

*Can I do anything for you?*

He was thirsty and needed to swallow the pills. The dust from the exploding building lingered in his throat.

"I could use something to drink."

*I saw a soda machine in one of the rooms. That OK?*

"That sounds perfect. Cola or a lemon-lime would be good. No orange or grape." He fished his wallet out from under his armor, pulling out a five dollar bill and handing it to her. "Get something for yourself as well."

She nodded and headed out the door, looking back once before closing the door behind her. As soon as he had privacy, he stripped off his filthy and shredded hoodie, tossing it in a garbage can. Then he took his armor off. It took a few tries to get his fingers to untie the leather cord holding the halves together, but he pulled the thong and shucked off the armor, setting it out of the way.

Luke walked over to the sink in the exam room. He turned the faucet on and rinsed his mouth, gargling to get as much of the lingering taste of concrete out of his mouth. Finding some tissues, he blew his nose, then washed his hands. He'd just sat back down on the table when Gwen returned with two sodas.

She handed Luke the cola and had an orange soda for herself. She offered his fiver back, but he waved it off.

*They were free!*

Her enthusiasm wore away at a tiny corner of the numbness that had taken over since he'd climbed into the van and turned over the reins of the operation to Jung-sook and Archie. Luke cracked his can open and took a sip, sighing as the bubbles and flavor covered up the grimy taste in his mouth.

"Do you know if Pablo or Sam are back yet?" Luke asked.

*No. I can go check.*

"No, it's best to stay out from underfoot. Let the doctors take care of their business."

She nodded and sat down to enjoy her orange soda, pulling out her phone to read. He leaned back on the reclined table and tried to relax but failed as he waited in the noisy silence of his concussed head and broken eardrums. He tried to scroll through his phone but couldn't focus and gave up. When Maggie came back into the room, he sat up.

"Any word on the other team?" Luke asked before she could even close the door.

She grabbed the white board. *Not yet.*

Luke slumped, disappointed with the lack of news. Maggie started by checking Luke's vitals and making sure he didn't have any injuries that might have been covered by his armor. Satisfied, she moved on to his wounds. He grimaced as she gently cleaned the blood from his ears before peering in with her otoscope. She said something to Gwen. Gwen grabbed the white board and started writing.

*She said burst eardrums.*

"Yeah. I figured. Not the first time it's happened to me. Still sucks."

*She says hold still so she can cover your ears.*

Maggie covered his ears with gauze, securing the gauze patches with tape. Finished with his ears, she had Luke sit on the doctor's stool so she could clean and examine the wound on the back of his head. She'd finished putting a few stitches in his scalp when something from outside the room drew her attention.

"What is it?" Luke asked.

Gwen wrote on the board. *She said she'll check.*

Maggie poked her head out the door and turned around, saying something to Gwen.

*She says it looks like the other team is coming in. There are injuries. She has to go.*

Luke stood up and peeked out the door Maggie had left cracked when she'd dashed out to assist. Sam's face was the first he saw. Covered in soot and smudged with sweat, he barely recognized her. She looked like she'd been crying.

Pablo limped behind her, held up by Pieter and one of the Portland pack. His leg was coated in blood, although it didn't look like it was flowing anymore, thanks to his werewolf healing. The last two werewolves carried a stretcher fashioned out of a discarded pallet with an unconscious person on it. Luke looked on in horror seeing if he could find the eighth wolf he'd sent to the apartment building.

Everyone was covered in soot and debris, several had ripped clothing and signs of injuries. Luke staggered back into the exam table, his head in his hands. When he caught Gwen walking toward the door, he shook himself alert and slammed the door shut before Gwen could see what was happening outside.

He shook his head, sending stabbing pain radiating from his ears. "You don't want to see that."

She nodded and returned to her chair and started fidgeting, trying to distract herself with her phone. Luke vacillated between anger and numbness, not wanting the former to take control. He wasn't sure how long he'd sat there when Sam popped her head in. She said something Luke couldn't make out through the din of his ruined ears.

Luke held up a hand to stop her. "I can't understand anything you're saying."

Gwen said something and held up the white board. Sam took it and scrawled on it quickly.

*I'm going to take Gwen up to hang out so we can talk while I wait for*

*Maggie to come check me out.* Seeing the shock in Luke's eyes at sending Gwen out into the hall, she quickly erased the board and added, *It's clear. Everyone else is in a room, that's why I need to share this one. We don't have much space.*

Luke nodded. "Gwen, if you can, take a nap. It's late."

She nodded and followed Sam out of the exam room. He didn't have much hope she'd take a nap with everything going on. She'd worry about people she knew, and even though Luke wasn't in terrible shape, he'd caught her checking on him, her brow furrowed and her eyes anxious. He tried sitting in the chair, figuring if Maggie needed to exam Sam, she'd want the table. He slid into the chair, fidgeting while he waited.

Sam returned a few minutes later and picked up the board. *I got her set up with the TV. She's worried about you. She says you look really mad.*

"I am."

*How bad was it?*

"I'm not sure. I don't think anyone took anything serious except Delilah and me. We were quite a bit behind everyone else when the explosion went off. If my eardrums are blown—" He interrupted himself. "Am I speaking too loud?"

Sam shook her head, wincing. *Yeah. My ears blew as well. They're mostly healed now.*

"Do you want to sit?" He gestured at the exam table.

*No.* She turned around.

Her clothes were shredded on her back and butt, although her legs looked fine. He hadn't noticed it early when she'd come in. She turned back around.

*Don't feel like sitting much. I have glass in my back and ass.*

He winced.

*Yeah. It's not fun. I can feel it moving around my skin as my body tries to heal it. Hazards of being a wolf.*

Nodding, he clenched his jaw, his brows furrowing. "Did everyone make it out?"

She shook her head. The slight gesture was a punch to the gut. Luke could feel his anger shifting to rage.

*Jennifer didn't make it out. She fell. Pieter dragged me away, or I'd be dead too. When it went off, I was near a window.*

"Pablo?"

*Should heal fine, took some serious shrapnel to his leg. I think it cut his artery, but we yanked it out hoping his healing would get ahead of it. It worked.*

"What about the other wolf they were carrying in?"

*Herschel? I don't know. His leg looked bad.*

Luke was surprised when Maggie walked in, startled by her sudden appearance and the blood staining her white coat.

"Are you needed with the others?" Luke asked.

Maggie shook her head, taking the board from Sam. *I'm not a surgeon. I did what I could until they arrived. They've got it in hand now. I'll just be in the way.* She erased the board after showing him her first message and kept writing. *Pablo is OK. We got the debris out of his leg. He's healing now.*

"Delilah?"

*Bruises and scrapes. One eardrum burst, the other looks OK. She's asleep right now.*

"Hersch?"

*He's probably going to lose the leg. I think it's damaged beyond what a wolf can heal. We'll clean it up and see if his body can take care of it, but if not...*

She left it hanging. Luke crumpled in on himself a little more.

*I'm going to need help with Sam. We have to get the glass out of her back. Do you know ASL?*

Luke shook his head, chalking it up to one more failure in his life. He'd had all the time in the world, he could have dedicated some time to it.

"Whatever you need," he said.

She taught him the letters "S" and "F," so he could hand her the scalpel or the forceps. She also asked him to wipe any blood she pointed at. While Maggie got the equipment ready and washed up, she had him help Sam undress and lie down on the exam table. Sam, even maintaining her good humor with an ass and back full of glass, winked at Luke as he helped her onto the exam table.

He washed up thoroughly to his elbows and put on the gloves

Maggie had laid out for him, happy to have something to contribute that would distract him from his growing anger.

Maggie worked quickly, starting on Sam's back and working her way down, cutting the embedded pieces of glass from Sam's body. Luke handed Maggie the tools she needed when she signaled and dabbed Sam's blood when called for. He wasn't squeamish after serving in too many militaries and wars during his nearly two-thousand-year struggle against the vampires. He was just tired of seeing it, especially when it belonged to his friends and loved ones.

The task at hand kept his mind focused and distracted from worrying at everything that had gone wrong. Where the cuts were made and the debris removed, the wounds quickly closed, leaving pink lines that would likely disappear entirely thanks to her werewolf healing. When they finished, Maggie washed Sam's back and butt and sent Luke to get some spare clothes from the pack's stash in the supply closet.

Luke had questions to ask about the facility but didn't feel like making them write out the answers. After he found a vampire or two, his ears would heal, and he could ask his questions then. He wished he'd interacted with more packs over the years. He had no idea where the North Portland Pack ranked, but from everything he'd seen, it was one of the best run organizations he'd seen. It seemed like Holly and her people had a plan in place for nearly everything or were so flexible that they could adapt their facilities to fit the circumstance.

He hoped the pack's resources wouldn't break under the pressure of joining him in his cause. Every day, he thought about what a mistake it was for them to hitch their pack to his star.

Something drew Sam and Maggie's attention. What more could go wrong? Maggie stepped out to check the newest development while Sam dressed. When she was finished, she poked her head out the door. She looked pale when she turned. Reaching for the board, she started writing.

*It looks like one of the sweeper teams took some injuries. One of them looks really bad.*

Luke paced in a tight circle, spitting a stream of curses. Sam darted out of the room, reappearing a few minutes later.

*A group of vampires ambushed them. No dead, but one of them is in rough shape.*

"What else can go fucking wrong?" Luke spit out.

*Should we pull the teams off the street for the night?*

Luke thought about it for a moment. "Yes. Pull them until further notice."

Sam raised her eyebrow but pulled out her phone and sent the order. She reached out and gave his armored shoulder a pat. He did everything in his power not to shake it off in his anger. Maggie returned a minute later, fresh blood on her white lab coat. She spoke to Sam who wrote out her words on the board.

*We need this room. You two can get going. Get Gwen to bed.*

Luke nodded, picking up his shredded hoodie. Sam tossed the board onto the counter and pulled Luke out into the hall and out the way they came, then up a set of stairs. They found Gwen watching cartoons. Sam held up her cell phone, shaking it at Luke.

He reached into his pocket and pulled his out, but the screen was cracked and the phone wouldn't turn on. He must have sat on it sometime after sending the texts earlier that evening. He had no idea how much damage it had taken in his fall from the explosion. It could have started the damage there, finishing its destruction any time after. He sighed shaking his head, holding back the curses he didn't want to say in front of his ward. Sam borrowed Gwen's phone, handing it to him before texting him.

*Sorry about the phone. This will work for communication. We're only a few blocks from the rendezvous point. I'll walk you back, and you can drive home from there.*

Luke was silent, partially because he couldn't hear but mostly because of the anger roiling under the surface. Gwen, stressed and tired, held Sam's hand, but checked on Luke regularly, worry written clearly on her face. When they got back to the parked cars, Luke fished out his key. The phone vibrated as Sam sent one last message.

*Go get some sleep. Let the doctors work. We'll deal with everything once we've licked our wounds and healed. We'll be in touch.*

*I have a spare phone at home. I'll get it activated. Goodnight, Sam.*

Sam, instead of texting back, pulled Luke in for a hug. Finished with Luke, she gave Gwen a hug, telling the girl something Luke couldn't hear. He waved to Sam and opened the rental car, setting his armor in the trunk before getting behind the wheel.

He was glad he didn't live too far away. Not being able to hear was messing with his senses. It wasn't the first time he'd had his hearing blown, and the way his life went, it wouldn't be the last. Inside the house, Gwen gave Luke a fierce hug then went to her room. Luke went to his office to find his spare phone.

While he waited for the phone to get enough of a charge to turn it on, he opened his laptop and logged into the tracking software they'd been using to catalog their potential vampire sites. He wasn't sure what team had been hit tonight, so he tried to figure out which one had stopped their route in the last hour or so. Finding a likely candidate, he stared at the screen, grinding his teeth. The anger and despondency he'd been fighting to keep under wraps until he could get away from everyone roared back to the forefront.

They'd hurt him. They'd hurt his friends. They'd killed one person with two more on the edge. He needed to do something. He needed to strike back. He wanted to make the vampires bleed.

# SEVENTEEN

BEFORE HE LEFT, Luke ran down to his lair and back to his locked room in the back of his training space, grabbing a bundle he hadn't used in a while. He checked it to ensure everything was there. It looked complete. Luke always ensured his gear was put away in a ready state so he could grab it and not have to worry about function or missing pieces. While he was there, he grabbed a fresh hoodie since he'd thrown away the other. The bookcase back in place, Luke tossed the bundle into his tub.

Luke shrugged into his armor and pulled his hoodie over it, then grabbed the tub with his remaining gear and threw it in the back of the rental car, squeezing into the driver's seat and taking off. He'd left a note for Gwen. When his phone had charged up enough, he set up the map and keyed in the information on potential vamp houses near where the likely team had been ambushed. He plugged in the car charger and pulled out onto the street, following the map to vampires and the satisfaction of taking his anger out on their bodies.

He sighed. It was hard to feel like a badass in a rental sedan. At least his old beast had character. He'd have to rely on his fury to carry him. Glad of the empty late-night streets, he felt uncomfortable driving without a proper sense of hearing. When he arrived in the Grant Park neighborhood, where they suspected there might be at least one vampire nest, he slowly wove through the neighborhood, waiting for his vampire senses to go off while he looked for anything suspicious.

When he felt the first twinge of a fanger, his body went into high alert as he triangulated a location based on the strength of his feeling. Once the ping weakened, he found a parking spot and stepped out of the car. He opened the trunk, took out his helmet and the bundle, and stuffed them into a backpack. Next, he strapped his greaves onto his shins over his jeans, then pulled out the denim sleeves with an elastic band at one end. He pulled them over the greaves, zipping them on, so it looked like he just had poorly cut jeans instead of rare antiquities on his shins. It had been Sam's idea.

He thought they looked ridiculous, but they allowed him to cover up his metal shins while out in public. And right now, he needed every bit of protection he could get.

Grant Park was one of Northeast Portland's nicer neighborhoods with plenty of well-maintained and remodeled old Portland homes in varying architectural styles. His vampy senses tingled strongly as he got closer to the source. He caught a faint whiff of cigarette smoke ahead.

The narrow street was quiet this late with most of the lights off as the residents slept. When he spotted the smokers, he headed toward them. As they smoked, they watched over the neighborhood, looking for danger or prey. If he wanted to get close to them, he could ask for a cigarette from them. Vamps were arrogant and hungry enough to let him approach if he didn't look too scary. He slouched to hide his height and bulk, hoping he didn't look too intimidating because of his size or too weird with both ears covered in gauze. He should have grabbed a beanie to provide some cover.

Luke waved to the vampires, a man and a woman, drawing their attention. "Can I bum a cigarette?" he asked, hoping he'd regulated his voice properly.

The male vampire said something but also nodded, so Luke

walked forward. The woman pulled a pack out of her pocket and shook one out of the opening, offering it to Luke. He pulled it out with his left hand and put it in his lips.

"Light?"

The man pulled out a Zippo and flicked it open, summoning a flame. Luke leaned forward, inhaling and drawing the flame onto the end of the cigarette. He took a drag, then blew it out.

"Thanks!"

The woman said something, pointing to his ear.

"These?" He paused for a moment until an excuse flashed through his head. He pointed to his right ear. "I had some earrings get infected. Hurts like hell."

They both spoke. Luke just tried to look like he understood as he let his right hand drift to the back of his neck and inside his hood, feeling the pommel of his gladius. He put the cigarette between his lips and left it there. He slid his left hand back down to his waist band and gripped the handle to the wooden rudis.

They were looking at him weirdly by now since he was contorted around. Before they could do anything about it, he pulled his blades out and stabbed the woman in the chest. She dropped like a rock, taking his rudis with her. Using the momentum, he spun and took the head off the male vampire before he could react. Luke, losing his balance, tumbled into the door heavily.

He slid to the floor of the porch and kicked the slumped body of the dead female vampire onto her back so the rudis stuck straight up. He crawled over, wrapped his hands around the hilt, placed his forehead on the pommel, and spoke the incantation. Light serpentined down the silver inlay of the blade, into the chest of the vampire, then back up again, disappearing back into Luke's head.

He exhaled, a shiver running through his body. Standing up, he worked his jaw to pop his ears. They still hurt, but the pain was reasonable instead of excruciating. His balance felt a bit better as well.

He looked around the quiet neighborhood, making sure he didn't have any observers or that there weren't any cars or pedestrians coming through. Seeing nothing, he returned his attention to the other vampire, and noticed he hadn't quite taken the head all the way off. He hoped there was enough connection to give him the full juice up, but either way, even a partial would go a long way to getting him back to one hundred percent.

"Waste not, want not," Luke mumbled, able to hear himself, although it was still a garbled and muffled.

He quickly repeated the process. Finished, he stood, nudging the clothes into a pile in the corner of the porch and letting the gooey remains of the vampires drip off the edge into the bush filled beds surrounding it. He pulled his backpack off and opened it up.

Unwrapping the bundle, he pulled out two sawed-off double-barrel shotguns in holsters. He hooked the Stevens 311s on to his belt, strapping one to each thigh with a leather strap at the bottom of each holster. He'd picked them up cheap in the '70s at Sears to cut down a shotgun when he was hunting a vampire motorcycle gang. He grabbed a box of shells from the backpack and loaded all four barrels, dumping the rest of the shells in his hoodie pocket. He moved the second box of shells into the backpack's smaller pocket so it would be easier to find.

He looked down at the ridiculous pants dickies. Right now, he didn't feel like being subtle. He stripped them off quickly, shoving them in the bag. Next, he pulled out his helmet covered in ornate engravings and protective incantations and strapped it to his head. Last, he pulled on a thin pair of leather gloves. If the vampires wanted to declare open warfare, they were going to get the response of a steel-clad warrior. They'd hurt his friends and killed people who'd made the mistake of joining him.

Tonight, he could afford to be noisy and gratuitous. The cops would be downtown dealing two bombed buildings. What few cops they had to spare would be slow to respond to any reports of Luke's activities, not that they ever responded quickly with reported 911 response times near two hours according to the news. Tonight, he could indulge his desire to punish the creatures that had wounded him and hurt his friends.

He didn't bother looking for keys. He leaned back and kicked the door next to the knob with the sole of his boot. His vampire aided strength and his towering fury blasted the door open, ripping jagged chunks out of the door frame.

He stepped through the entrance, the door bouncing off his shoulder as it recoiled. A vampire stood in front of him, stunned at the sudden and violent ingress of an intruder. A glass bottle slipped out of their hand and crashed to the floor, a dark, reddish viscous substance splashing his shoes and spreading across the hardwood floor.

Before the vampire could do more than look down at the shattered bottle, Luke had his gladius through the fanger's chest and into his heart. When Luke ripped the blade out, the vampire flopped to the ground a giant splat of reddish-black goo.

To his left, Luke heard footsteps pounding down the stairs. He jogged over, both swords at the ready and hid next to the stairs with his back flat against the wall. When the first vamps cleared the corner and saw the mess on the hardwood and the busted door, they skidded to a halt.

Luke sprang to action, putting down two in quick order — removing one's head and turning the other into a pile of dust with his rudis. Before anyone could react, he'd killed or incapacitated the remaining three. One of the vampires, the one he'd only hamstrung, was crawling away. Luke lopped off his head on the way to the door. He pushed it shut and flipped the deadbolt to hold it closed so it didn't look suspicious from the street. He finished it with his gladius.

"What the fuck is going on down there?" someone yelled.

"I just killed all your pals, and I'm going to kill you next," Luke yelled back.

Luke saw a head peek down the stairs then pull back quickly. Dodging the bodies and mess he'd just made, he sprinted upstairs, screams ringing out, as people in various stages of undress pushed each other to get back into their rooms. When Luke cleared the last step, he halted.

"If you're human, lie on the floor with your hands above your head and no harm will come to you."

Luke walked to the first door, kicking it open like the front door, and peered in. Everyone was on the ground.

He shook his head. "Naughty, naughty."

He stepped forward and kicked out hard, catching the vampire's head with his greave as he tried to get up. The crunch of the vampire's skull was satisfying. He brought his gladius down and through his neck. When the next vamp tried to make a run for it, he spun around, catching him on the back and sending him tumbling into the door frame. Luke shoved the rudis through his heart, turning him into a pile of goo. He dispatched the headless vamp the same way, leaving only two partially nude humans lying on the floor on their stomachs.

He held up his finger to his mouth. "Shhhh."

He pulled the door shut behind him just in time to see several vampires trying to sneak out from the other rooms. He caught them flatfooted, beating them to the reaction, and mowed them down, leaving a trail of corpses and goo. He sorted through the last few rooms, leaving the humans alive and on the ground, slaying any fangers. Finished with the upstairs, he stalked downstairs.

Seeing no activity, he checked the closets, feeling around for anything that might open a secret door. He couldn't find anything. Luke checked his phone to see what time it was. If he wanted to hit more houses, he'd have to get moving. He slid out the back door, closing it quietly, and snuck around the house, disappearing into the darkness and back to the rental car. All told, the excursion only took less than ten minutes.

WHEN LUKE GOT BACK to his car, he looked up the next likely house. On his way, he'd heard sirens, but none heading to the house he'd just left. Tonight would probably be the only night he'd get away with this level of wanton carnage. Driving by the house, he didn't like the busier street it was on and the well-lit approach, so he moved onto the next option—a house further away in a poorer neighborhood. It suited his needs better. He doubted he'd be able to get away with another raid in a wealthier neighborhood, even with everything else going tonight.

Parked, he played it the same way, clearing out the main and second floors before looking for any underground haunts. Portland wasn't a basement heavy city, but enough of the older houses had them to make it worth his while to look, especially after they'd found the drug den complete with Commissioner Bealer.

Just as he rounded the corner of the stairs, he saw a door creak open and a head peek out. They made eye contact. The vampire's eyes went wide, seeing Luke's swords dripping with blood. They slammed the door shut.

"There's the hideout."

Being cautious, he checked the other doors, finding nothing but closets. Although like the house they'd raided that was connected to its neighbor, there could be a secret doorway leading to hidden rooms in any of them. For now, he'd check out the one place he knew there were vampires. The first house hadn't sated his appetite for bloody revenge, feeding it instead.

Luke backed up against the wall, slid the rudis back in its sheath, switched his gladius to his left hand, and grabbed the doorknob. He cracked the door and waited to see if anything happened. Hearing nothing, he pulled out his sawed-off double barrel. He slid the blade of his gladius into the crack of the door and used the tip to nudge the door open. The hinges creaked.

Slowly, Luke peered around the door frame. They'd turned the lights off. All he could see was a few stairs leading down to a small landing that turned to the left. He wished he had a grenade or at least a flash-bang he could toss down there. He looked around for a light switch, peeping around the corner and looking at the ceiling to see if maybe there was a pull string dangling from the ceiling.

He stepped back, leaning up against the wall. As he straightened up, the light flicked on. He hadn't felt the switch through his armor. Tilting his head toward the door, he thought he heard some muffled speaking and shuffling about.

Taking a deep breath, Luke turned into the door frame, pointing his shotgun down toward the landing. The upper part of the staircase was walled in. He'd be OK for the first few steps. He crept down the stairs, keeping his back to the left wall. At the corner of the turn, he quickly peeked around the edge.

The blast of a gun caused him to yank his body back, his heart racing.

"Ow, fuckhead, that was right next to my ear!" someone yelled from downstairs.

Luke aimed his shotgun around the corner and fired off a round, pulling back as two more shots rang out. He flinched at the sound, the beginning whine of tinnitus returning to his sensitive ears. Apparently, a vampire and a half wasn't quite enough. Dust from the paint and drywall puffed into the air where the shots hit the wall opposite Luke. He fired off his other shell blindly, relying on the shotgun's primary method of spray and pray.

He looked down at the gladius in his left hand, preventing him reloading the shotgun. "Shit."

He shoved the sawed-off in its holster, then sheathed the gladius. He pulled the shotgun back out, cracked open the barrel, and removed the shells from the chamber, dropping them in his pocket before reloading. He wished he'd set up his sword's sheath on his hip so it would be easier to get to. He'd have to bring an extra next time just in case. Reloaded, he pulled the other shotgun out of its holster.

"Fuck, fuck, fuck," Luke muttered to himself. A shootout around blind corners was not his favorite way to fight vampires, even with the addition of shotguns.

He took one more deep breath and stepped around the corner, firing once with the sawed-off in his right hand. Someone scrambled backward. When something metallic and shiny poked forward, he fired a round from his left hand.

He pushed against the right wall as he worked his way downstairs to give himself the best angle.

"Go! He doesn't have any more shots in that double barrel. He's probably reloading," one of the vampires yelled.

The vampire with the handgun jumped out, the pistol in his hand shaking. Luke unloaded the last shot from his right sawed-off into the chest of the vampire, knocking him back into the vampire that'd shoved him forward. Firing his last shot, he caught the second vamp in the head.

He shoved the gun in his right hand into its holster. He popped open the gun in his left hand, yanked the empties, and grabbed two more from his pocket. As soon as he locked the barrels back in place, he felt safer. The whining had returned to his ears in full force. He'd have to drain several more vampires to get them back to normal.

Risking it, he reloaded his other shotgun and slowly worked his way down the last steps. Once he saw what he was dealing with, he darted across the open door and put his back up against the narrow wall next to the door. The scent of piss and shit assailed him.

He couldn't be sure with the tinnitus, but he thought he heard voices coming from the room. He also thought he felt at least one vampire. He wasn't sure though. The two on the floor that weren't staked could be throwing off his vampy senses. It'd take more than lead buckshot to kill a vampire.

Taking another deep breath and grimacing at the smell, he jumped through the door, guns leveled at waist height, covering as much of the room as he could. He wasn't ready for the sight or the stench to intensify when he entered the room. He found half a dozen people huddled in the corner, chains attaching some of them to the wall. They cringed away from the guns as he trained them on the huddled group. Now that he was a bit closer, he could feel one live fanger.

His eyes adjusting to the dim light, he got a better look at the people huddled in the corner. The had dark hair and skin tones that ranged from pale to brown. Looking from face to face, he thought he caught one of the men trying to disguise his anger, flashing glares at Luke before returning to an overly affected cringe.

"Vampire? Vampiro?"

A woman sitting behind the one Luke suspected darted her eyes toward the potential impostor. Nodding her head to the side to point at him since his eyes were firmly fixed on Luke.

"Keys? Who has the keys to your locks?" Luke slid the shotgun in his right hand back into its holster.

The woman who'd identified the vampire pointed toward the two mostly dead vamps Luke was blocking, a manacle rattling on her wrist.

"He does. With the gun," she said with a strong Latin American accent.

Luke gestured toward the suspected vampire with one of his sawed-offs. "You. You're unchained. Go find me the keys."

The man stood up quickly, eager to be moving.

"No sudden movements. Keep it slow. Understand?" Luke said, keeping his shotgun trained on the fanger.

The vamp nodded. Luke stepped further into the room, making room to get past him to the bodies. Luke kept one gun pointed on him while he kept the other trained on the group in the corner. As the vamp passed, Luke's sense confirmed his suspicion.

"Nice and slow," Luke reminded the vamp.

The vampire rummaged through the pockets. Jingling keys alerted Luke the vamp had found what he was looking for. Luke watched him out of the corner of his eye. The vamp kept eyeing the gun on the ground on the opposite side of the shot vampire's body.

"Toss the keys into the room," Luke instructed.

The keys jangled as they hit the ground in front of Luke. Luke looked down. When he saw a blur diving for the gun out of the corner of his eye, he went into action. The people in the corner screamed.

The vampire's desperation made it clumsy. Luke dove after the vampire, ripping his gladius from its scabbard and down through the vampire's arm. His anger returning, he followed by lashing out with his foot, catching the fanger in the side of the head with his steel covered shin. The vampire tumbled away, dazed.

He shoved the sawed-off into his left holster and pulled out his rudis. He stepped over to the pile of vampire bodies and shoved it into the chest of the vampire he'd shot in the head when he was descending the stairs. It'd begun twitching some. Luke hadn't got a clean shot at its head. A few of the people squeaked at the violent action.

Luke's ears screamed at him. Shotguns in a confined space were never a good idea. As the pain rose to distracting levels, his enthusiasm for this rampage waned.

He bent over and picked up the keys, tossing them to the woman who'd helped him twice. She snatched them up and unlocked the manacles holding her before working on the others. While they worked, Luke looked around, finding the source of the stench. The vampires had provided a toilet bucket for their captives and hadn't emptied it regularly.

He looked toward the woman. She was the only one watching at him, the rest seemed too scared to lift their heads.

"OK. I'm going to get you out of here. First, I need to take care of these vampires. It's best if you don't look. Can you please turn around?" He tried speaking loudly, guessing their ears were ringing nearly as badly as his from the earlier gun fight. He holstered his other shotgun as a sign of his intentions.

She nodded and relayed the instructions in Spanish. They turned and faced the wall away from the vampires. Luke scrambled over, ensuring he was still facing the captives. He ran through the incantation as quickly as he could on all three vampires, sending them on their gooey way. He felt better than he had in a while. The whining in his ears was gone.

"We can go now. You'll need to be careful so you don't slip. Step on the clothes." He thought over the options and sighed. "Shit. You can't go free when you leave here. Any vamp that has fed on you recently will be able to track you. I can take you to a place where we can help you. We can get you out of town where the vampires won't be able to track you."

"What about our families?" the woman asked.

"They can come with you, but we have to get you to safety first, then we can find them." Luke rubbed his forehead.

"How can we trust you? How do we know you aren't worse than these...these...these monsters?" she asked.

"Well, you'll have to for now. You can go free, but you'll be hunted down by the vampires and killed to keep you from causing trouble. I can get you to safety. Look, we need to get going in case someone heard the guns and called the cops. Most of the cops are engaged elsewhere, but I don't want someone fresh on duty to come looking." Luke pulled his helmet off and stashed it in his backpack.

The woman nodded and relayed the instructions to her companions. Luke stepped back to the bottom of the stairs. When all five survivors were over the pool of vampire goo, he headed up the stairs, and they followed in a line. He motioned for them to halt as they approached the door. He opened it, checking to see if the one side was clear. He shoved it all the way open and leaped out, shotguns leveled toward the side that he hadn't checked. All clear.

"It's clear. Come on up." Luke lowered his shotguns.

The survivors cautiously left the stairwell and joined Luke in the living room. He led them to the back door. They slipped out into the night and back around the house to the front. Seeing it was clear, he pulled off his backpack and shoved the shotguns inside.

Luke turned to the woman who'd been translating. "My car is a couple blocks up. It'll be tight, but you should all fit. It's a short ride after that."

They followed him as he jogged toward his car. When he got there, everyone looked reluctant and scared. They kept looking at the woman, one asking her something in Spanish.

"They're scared," she said. "They don't want to be kidnapped again."

Shucking his backpack, he pulled out one of the shotguns. "Do you know how to use one of these?"

She nodded.

He flipped it around and held it by the barrel, offering her the stock. "Take this. You can ride up front with me. Keep the barrel on me. If I betray you, pull the trigger."

She reached out for it, wrapping her hand around the stock.

"Keep your finger off the trigger. It's loaded. The button on top is the safety. It's currently engaged."

She disengaged it and reengaged it, nodding at him. Everyone looked more confident with her having the gun. He tossed his backpack in the trunk, slamming it shut. In the distance, he heard sirens. The off-duty cops the city had no doubt activated after the bombings must finally be out on the streets.

"Everyone in! Quick." He opened his door and slid in.

The woman ran to the passenger side and jumped in. The remaining four people squeezed in as best they could, barely getting the doors closed. Luke pulled out onto the dark road and took the first turn he could away from the sound of the sirens. Trying to keep to the darkest streets, he wanted to get away without being observed with too many people in his car. Getting pulled over for a seatbelt violation would be an unfortunate way to end his rampage.

He'd wanted to get a third house in before sunup. He still hadn't worked out the rage his failures had caused. The injuries and death he'd failed to prevent. As he drove away from the scene of his last brutal retaliation, he stewed in his self-loathing, silently clenching his jaw while ignoring everyone else in the car.

When he'd determined they'd gotten far enough away from the house, he got them on track for the apartment building he'd converted into a place for the unhoused people he'd rescued from the vampire's last fall. With werewolves always on duty, it was one of the safest places to take the folks who'd been picked up by the vampires for easily exploitable meals.

He checked on the woman out of the corner of his eye. She had the gun pointed toward the center of the console—not on him, but close if she needed to act. When he pulled up to the apartment building, he parked out of the way in the shadow of a tree.

"We're here. You won't be able to take the gun in without causing alarm. I'll open the trunk, and you can toss it in. Safety on, please. Are you OK with that?"

She nodded, relaying what was happening to the people in the back. He got out of the car; she followed suit. After he opened the trunk, she carefully set the shotgun in and stepped back. Luke closed the trunk and waved for the group to follow him. Traffic clear, he crossed the street and punched in the code to the building's door, holding it for everyone.

"Excuse me, sir, what's going on?" A Black woman who'd been

sitting at the front desk stood up, looking irritated. Seeing Luke, she added, "Oh, sorry. I didn't recognize you."

"Can you ring Max, please?" Luke asked. "It's an emergency."

"I can tell." She picked up the phone behind the desk and punched in some numbers.

He thought she might be pack but wasn't sure. He waited patiently while she talked to Max.

"He'll be out shortly. He just needs to throw some pants on," the desk attendant said.

"Thanks. Can you rustle up some food and water, please? Everyone here could probably use it."

"You're not kidding. They look a little worse for wear." She eyed their necks, seeing the evidence of recent vampire feedings. "Take them into the conference room. I'll send Max in and bring some snacks."

Luke motioned the group to follow. He stepped into the building's conference room, shutting the blinds before sitting down at the head of the table. The people he'd brought with him took chairs along one side, huddling together away from Luke and whispering urgently. Despite Luke's hearing being fixed, he couldn't pick out what they were saying, nor did he really feel like trying. His mind kept pulling back to everything that had happened in the last twelve hours.

Before Luke could descend too far into his head, Max walked into the room. Max's graying brown hair was tousled into an epic case of bedhead. He'd pulled on a T-shirt and a pair of jeans, slipping his feet into some flip flops. In the several months since the incident at Wapato, he'd put on weight, filling out his underfed frame. He was looking healthier than Luke had ever seen him. The man who had looked after the houseless community at Hazelnut Grove had taken to his new job well.

"Hey, Luke. You're up early," Max said, offering to shake Luke's hand.

Luke peeled off his gloves and shook Max's hand. "More like up late."

"Who do we have here?" Max gestured toward the huddled crowd.

"Found them in a vamp nest. I couldn't turn them loose."

Max shook his head. "No, I don't reckon you could. Usual procedure?"

"Yeah. The woman..." Luke gestured across the table. "Sorry, I didn't catch a name."

"Maribel." She didn't elaborate.

"Maribel is in charge. She can relay any information to the rest of the group." Turning toward Maribel, he introduced Max. "Maribel, this is Max. He's a good person. He'll help you out. He'll also help you get in contact with any family members so you can make arrangements."

Max smiled kindly across the table at the scared people. "I speak a little Spanish, but I'd still appreciate any help you can give with your friends so everyone feels safe and understood, OK?"

Maribel nodded. The woman from the front desk came in with the promised snacks and waters, setting them down on the table before returning to her post out front.

Luke gestured toward the food. "Eat whatever you want, but please try to drink as much water as you can. You're probably dehydrated after being fed on by the vampires. You'll need to replenish."

Maribel nodded, picking up a pastry and a bottle of water. The gesture encouraged the others to dive in.

Luke made eye contact with the woman. "Maribel, I'm going to leave you with Max. We've done this before. We've helped people taken by the vampires. Please listen to him. We'll ensure you're safe until the vampire tracking wears off. When it does, we might have options for you and your families if you need them."

Maribel nodded, looking wary but calmer than he'd seen her since he'd found her and the others.

"I can take it from here, Luke." Max said. "You look beat. Go home. Get some sleep."

Luke nodded, standing up. He squeezed Max's shoulder on the way by. He made eye contact with Maribel on the way by, giving her a nod before stepping out the door.

Luke checked his watch. It was five. He wouldn't have time to hit another house under the cover of darkness. He'd gotten lucky—no serious injuries other than his ears and no cops. The two houses hadn't helped his anger. Besides being exhausted, he felt worse. He'd hoped to salve the emotional wounds of his failed mission by paying back those who'd hurt his new friends. Instead, he just felt empty and hollowed out.

# EIGHTEEN

WHEN LUKE RETURNED HOME, Gwen was sleeping on the couch. Sometime during the period when he'd left, she must have woken and not found him. He tried being quiet so as not to disturb her, but she was still a light sleeper.

"Luke?" She rubbed her eyes. "Where were you?"

"I had to take care of something. You can go back to bed now." His voice sounded monotone even to his own ear. Gwen was another person he was letting down.

"Are you OK?" Gwen asked.

"Yeah." It was a lie.

He was far from OK. Killing two nests and sucking several vampires dry to heal himself hadn't felt good or relieved the guilt of his failure.

"I'm going to head downstairs," Luke said.

He walked into his office and triggered the secret door behind the bookcase. Dropping the tub, he stripped the backpack off and set it on top. Vampire blood soaked the hoodie in places. He tossed it into a plastic bag so it wouldn't stain anything. He finally removed the bandages on his ears, sighing in relief as sound returned to normal. The last three vampires had healed his ears. He stripped down the rest of his gear, putting them on their respective racks so he could clean them. After washing his hands in the sink, he pulled out Muse's "Origins of Symmetry" album and put it on the console, wanting something aggressive and weird to distract his mind. "Space Dementia" fit the bill. If nothing else, it sounded good loud. He was glad he'd had such thick insulation installed; Gwen wouldn't be able to hear anything in her room.

One by one, he cleaned and inspected all his equipment to ensure he hadn't damaged anything in his rampage. The simple process almost worked like meditation for him—something he could do without thought that let him focus his brain away from the world around him. Pattern and repetition could be comforting, though they weren't this time. When the last item was finished and everything put away, he stared at his hands, unsure what to do with himself now.

When he returned upstairs, Gwen had gone to her room. He hoped she'd get some sleep after last night. He needed a shower. Cleaning his gear hadn't provided the distraction he'd hoped for, but perhaps the steam of a hot shower would wash away the feelings he was trying to avoid. Unfortunately, that didn't do it either.

He grabbed a bottle of whiskey and poured three fingers, then drained the glass returned to his secret lair, wanting to isolate himself so his night terrors didn't wake Gwen. He pulled out a sleeping bag and rolled it out on the rug, crawling inside and letting exhaustion and whiskey put him to sleep.

EVEN WITH THE WHISKEY, his dreams haunted him. Names and faces—some he recognized, some he didn't—assaulted him with his failures. All the innocent lives he couldn't save. All those who'd put their trust in him, who'd helped him fight vampires, who'd come to a violent end because their paths crossed his. Several times, he woke up in a cold sweat, voice raw.

When he heard footsteps on the spiral metal stairs that led down to his lair, he feigned sleep until Gwen sighed and left again. At one point, he woke up and found Alfred curled up next him. Running his hand through the giant orange tabby's soft fur felt nice, and soothed him, allowing him to fall back asleep, this time into a quieter doze.

After another nightmare woke him, he gave up and went upstairs to use the restroom, finding Gwen gone. She'd left a note saying she was going to the park. He was glad she wasn't there so he didn't have to see the disappointment in her eyes at what a miserable guardian he was. Not sure he could face her, he made a sandwich and went back downstairs.

He tried listening to records, but they only soundtracked his thoughts instead of providing emotional relief. Scrolling on his phone didn't help either; news of everything that had happened the night before filled the feed. Two massive explosions in downtown Portland made national news. The explosions had killed thirteen people and injured at least fifty people in the apartment building. Then he checked his texts, there was still no word on the body his other team had left behind or on Herschel's condition. When he saw the death tally, he sobbed, then settled into a cold numbness.

He spent the next few days staring at the wall, only getting up to change a record when he eventually noticed the static and click of it hitting the locked groove. He'd let his phone battery go dead so he wouldn't have to deal with the incoming calls from his friends. He did the bare minimum to maintain himself, making occasional trips up for the bathroom or to stuff something into his face. He had plenty of food upstairs for Gwen and had given her cash so she could buy anything she wanted. There were shops and restaurants and a few fast-food places she could easily walk to. He thought it was best she didn't see him as he was.

A couple days into his self-exile, Sam showed up. Hearing Gwen talking to someone when she activated the door down to Luke's space, he quickly moved into the training room, quietly shutting the door.

"He's down here somewhere," Gwen said. "He's been sleeping down here since he came back after going out again after... Well, you know."

"And he's left you on your own?" It was Sam.

"I guess. He comes out periodically. I have plenty of food and a place to sleep. I've had less."

Luke sighed and shook his head at himself. His peak achievement of late was to be slightly better than being unhoused.

"Luke?" Sam called. "You in there?"

Luke didn't answer, not wanting to see the disappointment in yet another set of eyes. He sat quietly against the wall, staring into the darkness of his unlit training room.

"We've been trying to get a hold of you for a while. We need to talk about what to do next."

Sam spent a few more minutes trying to coax Luke out but gave up when he didn't even respond to her.

"Gwen, do you want to stay with me for a few days? Until Luke's feeling better?" Sam asked, raising her voice slightly before continuing. "He really shouldn't be leaving you on your own like this."

"No. I should probably stay here and keep an eye on him, make sure he's OK," Gwen replied.

"You sure? You got enough food?" Sam sounded skeptical.

"Yeah, there's plenty. And Luke gave me cash for emergencies."

"OK. Well, at least let me order you something hot from a delivery service or we can go down to the Howling Moon since it's close."

"No, I should be here in case Luke needs something," Gwen replied.

"Are you sure? It's close. Luke can manage himself. He's a grown adult...most of the time."

He'd never heard that tone of annoyance and anger in Sam's voice before.

"I guess."

They left after that. Luke waited until he was sure the kid was in bed before re-emerging. When he stopped at the fridge, he found a box of food from the Howling Moon. Sam must have ordered extra for him. He stood at the counter and mechanically worked his way through the plate, Alfred rubbing up against his legs the entire time. After he set the plate in the sink, he turned around. He'd only taken a step before he returned to the sink, picking up the plate and putting it in the dishwasher so Gwen wouldn't have to deal with it in the morning.

The next day, Pablo showed up.

"Is he down here?" Pablo asked.

"Yeah. But good luck, he's not responding to anyone," Gwen replied.

"Hey, buddy, hear you're hiding out down here. Just checkin' in on you. My leg is doing much better. Pretty much all healed up."

Luke didn't respond.

"I don't know what's going on with you, but you should come out and talk with me. We can figure it out." Pablo knocked gently on the door. "Your friends are here for you, Luke. You just have to lean on us. We miss you. I miss you."

Luke couldn't bring himself to answer, to reach out to his closest friend. He just sat and stared, hating himself even more for letting down people who called themselves his friends.

Pablo sighed. "Luke, I know you blame yourself. You always do. Your friends need you. You need us."

"I don't think he's coming out," Gwen said.

"No. I'll try again later, I guess."

When Luke went up later that night, he found a plate in the fridge with some salad rolls and potstickers. He didn't see Alfred this time and guessed he was with Gwen. Even the cat would rather be with someone else. He returned to his cave and took down a bottle of whiskey to force himself into another troubled night of bad sleep.

When he finally gave up on trying to get restful sleep, he put on Funkadelic's "Maggot Brain," but instead of letting the album play through, he sat next to the record player and restarted it so he could listen to the title track over and over again. He could have tied his music app into it and just played that, but didn't, unsure why he was creating the repetitive inconvenience for himself. He loved the song and its painfully emotive guitar. The song was ten minutes of sorrow poured through reverb, distortion, and blazing guitar riffs.

When he heard his hidden door open, his ears perked up.

"He's just down there listening to the same song over and over and over," Gwen said.

Luke wasn't sure who'd showed up today to talk him out of his self-banishment. He stood up and went to hide in the other room, shutting the door behind him. This time it was Gwen who spoke.

"Luke, your friends are waiting for you upstairs. I told them to stay until you come out."

When the song proceeded to the next, Gwen turned the record player off, the music grinding to a halt.

"Luke, it's time to come out. Please? Your friends need you. They care about you."

For the first time since he'd heard about the deaths in the apartment bombing, tears returned to his eyes. He still couldn't respond. He heard a light thump on the door. The next time Gwen spoke, it sounded closer, vibrating on the door. Gwen must have put her head against it.

"Luke... Are you giving up? Are you going to abandon your friends when they need you?" Gwen sniffled, when she started speaking again, there was a tremble in her voice. "What happens when things get tough with me? Are...are you going to give up on me eventually? Are you going to...are you going to...abandon me too?"

Gwen sniffed again. Tears streamed down Luke's cheeks. He'd abandoned his friends when he was needed, when their friendship was needed, when his guidance was needed. He'd betrayed their trust. He pushed himself up. Worst of all, he'd abandoned Gwen, forcing the poorly equipped preteen to try to take care of him.

"Gwen." When he spoke, his voice was rough from disuse and unsteady from the tears still streaming down his face. "I'm coming out."

Gwen had been leaning on the door; it creaked as she pulled back. When he cracked the door, it took a moment for his eyes to adjust after being in the dark room.

Gwen looked him over. "You look terrible."

"At least I look how I feel. Gwen, I'm so sorry. I shouldn't have left you alone."

Gwen dashed the tears from her face and stepped into him, wrapping her arms around him. His arms responded, wrapping around her as his brain kicked into gear, startled by the gesture he wasn't sure he deserved. Maybe it wasn't a hug for him, but one for her. His disappearance had clearly cut her deeper than he thought it would.

Gwen sniffed. "You smell bad."

Luke gave a half-hearted, single chuckle that sounded more like a huff. "Yeah, I probably do. I'm really sorry, little one. I'm not doing well." Luke sighed. "I guess I better go face the firing squad."

**HE FOLLOWED GWEN UPSTAIRS.** Pablo, Sam, Delilah, and surprisingly, Maggie were waiting for him. Delilah still had a bandage over one ear. She looked angry, scowling at him when he appeared. He sighed. Her anger with him was righteous, as it often was. She'd put a lot of faith in him to help her get revenge on the vampire who'd killed her father, and thus far, he'd only brought failure to the endeavor.

Pablo looked sympathetic. Sam looked somewhere in the middle. Maggie's expression was inscrutable. Gwen chose to go to her room to give them all privacy.

Holding his hand up, he stopped. "I'm going to have to ask you to hold off for a few minutes on giving me my rightly deserved ass chewing. For your benefit and mine, I'm going to take a shower first."

He looked down at his clothes, realizing he was still wearing the same jeans he'd stained with vampire blood about week earlier when he'd gone on his ill-advised solo revenge sortie. He'd showered when he'd gotten home but had put on the same clothes he'd been wearing, unable to muster the mental energy to grab clean ones. Between his own sweaty mess and his abused clothing, he had to be extra pungent to his werewolf friends with their sensitive noses. Gwen must have really needed that hug to brave getting that close to him.

He made the shower quick, scrubbing thoroughly, but skipped trimming his beard. He did take time to moisturize. No sense making

Delilah angrier after she'd pounded a skin care regimen into him. Hair damp and feeling refreshed, he asked Gwen to join them and walked back into the living room in fresh clothes.

"Look, I know you're all probably interested in telling me what a piece of shit I've been, but I'm not sure any of you can top what I've been telling myself. I'm sorry. I'm sorry I've betrayed your trust with my actions. You don't have to accept my apology. I'm not putting that burden on you, but I'm offering it without reservation."

He turned to the child. "Gwen. I'm sorry. I took responsibility for you, and I owed you better. You put your faith in me, and I let you down. I promise to do better if you'll let me."

Luke ran his hand through his damp hair and tried to convey his sincerity to Gwen. When she finally broke eye contact and lowered her head, he couldn't tell if it was a nod of acknowledgment or just looking away from him. She didn't owe him an answer in the moment, and he'd let her have the time and space to decide if she still wanted to live with him.

Looking around the room, he hoped he could head off further recriminations, partially to keep his forward momentum from devolving and partially to move onto some action that could help distract him from his own thoughts.

Pablo checked in with Delilah and Sam with a quick glance, then cleared his throat. "Well, we need to figure out what the fuck to do next. Pieter has been looking through shipping manifests. Downtown is a no-go zone after the explosions. We have no new intelligence since the sweeper teams have been off the street."

Luke thought about it for a moment. "I guess we should meet with Pieter and go from there. The vampires that are here will have to wait, but we have to find a way to stop the flow."

"You up for some beers? Lunch crowd is probably thinning out about now. Got some good food specials today," Pablo replied.

"Yeah, that sounds like a good option. Meet you in thirty?"

His friends nodded and stood up. Pablo waited by the door. Sam walked by and patted him on the shoulder before heading to wait with Pablo.

Delilah popped him hard on the back of the head. "I haven't

decided if I'm going to give you the ass chewing you deserve or not, but that'll hold me for now."

Maggie looked at everyone else. "I'll be out in a moment. I need to have a private word with Luke."

They all nodded and headed outside to wait.

Maggie walked up and put her hand on his upper arm, rubbing it reassuringly.

"Luke, I just wanted to remind you of Gwen's appointment with the therapist tomorrow."

Luke picked up the phone from where he'd plugged it in to charge and checked his calendar. "Yup. It's here. We'll be there."

He held in the sigh that nearly escaped. He'd have forgotten about it likely or not seen it if he hadn't plugged his phone in after avoiding it.

"Luke?" Maggie asked.

"Yes, Maggie?"

"I'm glad you're out of the basement."

"It's not really a basement," Luke replied. "I'll show you around next time you're here, when my smelly stuff isn't lying around."

"I'd like that." She looked like she was about ready to turn toward the door but changed her mind. "Call me if you need anything. I don't live that far away. I can look after Gwen. Or if you want to talk."

"It wasn't really a medical problem."

She squeezed his arm gently. "That...that wasn't what I meant. You've got my number. If you want to talk or just...hang out, I'm only a call away."

"OK. I'll keep that in mind." Luke smiled at her. "Coming to the bar with us?"

"Sure. I could use lunch and a beer." She smiled at him, then headed to the door and outside.

When it was just him and the kid, he turned to Gwen. "Want to go to lunch with us?"

Gwen scooped up Alfred to pet him. "Won't I be in the way if you're talking plans?"

"Are you in the habit of talking to vampires and telling them our strategies?"

Gwen shook her heard. "Not really."

"Then let's go."

# NINETEEN

**WHEN GWEN AND LUKE ARRIVED,** they slid into their reserved booth in the back corner. Luke sat next to Maggie as Gwen took the other side by Delilah. Pam came and collected their drink and food orders, leaving everyone to chat while they waited for beers and lunch.

When Pam had cleared the plates and wiped the crumbs, leaving a clean table for them to work on, they scooted forward in their seats, elbows on the table. Pieter, eyeing Luke warily, pulled out his folders and laptop. While Pieter kept giving Luke odd looks, Pablo seemed to be giving Pieter the stink eye. Something had happened between them while Luke had been hiding from life. He didn't have time or the emotional bandwidth to dig into it; he was barely keeping himself afloat as is.

Luke cleared his throat by way of calling the table to attention. "So where are we at with incoming ships, Pieter?"

"Well, we missed the five containers that started the debacle..." He looked down at his folder with sheafs of paper covered in high-lighted lines. "Looks like the next scheduled one is several weeks out. But it's a big one." He pulled his laptop in front of him, looking intently at the screen as he typed rapidly. "Shit."

Everyone was leaning forward, waiting on bated breath as Pieter's typing sped picked up, his fingers striking the keys harder as his brow furrow deepened.

"Well, shit. I have an update on this one from father. We knew this freighter had the most containers on it, but as they've been digging deeper into the records, they've found more on this ship." He leaned into his computer, eyes quickly scanning over the lines back and forth. "I'm counting thirty...thirty-seven containers."

"That's...a lot," Delilah said, slumping in her seat.

Luke took a deep breath before letting it out. "That's an invasion."

"What can we do?" Sam looked deeply concerned. "Can we get to the containers quicker? Before they're emptied at the port?"

Luke pursed his lips. "I don't know if we can, not with our lack of access and Homeland Security protocols at the port."

"Can we get to it earlier? Maybe while it's on the river before it docks?" Delilah asked.

"What do you think, Luke?" Pablo asked eagerly.

"I don't know. Capturing a ship on the river is going to be risky. Noisy. Too close to cops. And their loyalty to public safety is suspect at best."

Pieter looked confused.

Luke ran his hand through his hair. "There's been evidence that the vampires have infiltrated the police and possibly the city government. We haven't been able to figure out how deeply or thoroughly, but enough so that it adds a very dangerous wild card into the equation. Portland's police are bad even on their best behavior, but as the foot soldiers of the vampires? Not good."

"And if they've infiltrated Portland's police, who's to say they don't have other police departments in their pocket, or at least some officers?" Sam added.

Luke nodded. "True. We could be seeing an army of vampire-controlled cops counter-attacking our efforts. Hell, they could be helping the vampires unload their cargo."

Delilah leaned forward, ensuring she had everyone's attention. "Well, what if we attack before they get close enough to land?"

Pablo turned to Luke. "Yeah, that could work."

"How though, logistically speaking? You got a battleship in your pocket?" Luke scoffed.

"You've seen me naked." Pablo smirked.

The women rolled their eyes. Pieter just looked confused. Gwen giggled.

Luke narrowed his eyes. "Ha. Thirty-seven or more containers. That's a lot of vampires even if some are supplies and equipment." He looked at Pieter. "What about the crew? How many? Any chances they're in cahoots with the vampires?"

"A typical cargo ship of this size, maybe twenty crew members." He lowered his head to the screen, making a couple clicks on his mouse. "Probably not in league though; the captain and at least a few of his crew are werewolves from Germany."

"Well, that doesn't discount that they're working together. Vampires and wolves have teamed up before. So, we have potentially twenty crew members, and who knows how many vampires with who knows how much ordnance. Even assuming we can get a big enough assault force, we have no way to get out to the freighter. I don't have any shipping contacts."

"Boats we might be able to provide," Sam said, making eye contact with Luke. "The Coast Pack used to be heavily involved in fishing. They still have a lot of larger boats and probably have the contacts to get more."

"Would they be willing to put them at risk for this?" Luke asked.

"Lauren and Owen will listen, and you can hire them if that helps. They really don't need the money. They're making a killing since the state legalized marijuana, but the gesture is always welcome. It would also be a boon to the coast's economy. Fishing isn't what it used to be and a lot of people would gladly rent their boats for some extra income."

Pablo looked back at Luke. "We've been digging into the background of the pack members. We've got a fair few with military experience in past lives. Between them and some of the more interested sweeper teams, we can put together a good strike force."

Luke's anxiety spiked as he looked around the table with everyone's eyes boring into him. His breaths shortened and grew shallow as he tried to keep panic from overwhelming him.

"It's too dangerous. Too many people could get hurt. I—"

Delilah sat up and slammed the heel of her fist into the table, causing a few pieces of silverware to jump and clatter. "Damn it, Luke. It's already dangerous. People are already getting hurt. If that ship lands and the vampires get onto Portland's streets with the kind of heavy firepower we think they have, we're fucked. We might as well just pack up and leave now, because the city will belong to them. You won't be safe. I won't be safe. The pack won't be safe. Every citizen of this city won't be safe."

She took a deep breath, shaking her head. "You used to be a leader of men, soldiers, warriors. Fucking lead, because if you don't step up to do it, you can add this city to the tally of those you've failed. You can add everyone at this table and all their family and friends to that tally." She turned to Sam. "How many people live in the Portland area?"

"Over two million."

Delilah turned back to Luke. "You remember Wapato. Do you want to consign those two million people to that? What about the next city after this one turns into a breeding ground for an army of those evil fuckers? You can't back out now. You've pulled us all in too deep with you. If you quit, I'm done with you."

Luke swallowed, trying to keep eye contact with the blazing glare of Delilah's anger. He looked around the table, trying to figure out what they were thinking. All his brain could process were Delilah's words ringing loud and true. Licking his lips, he took a deep breath, released it, and returned his gaze to Delilah. The silence hung heavy and potent between them. She wasn't giving him any quarter. It took a moment for him to recognize the feel of someone's hand sliding over the back of his hand, fingers wrapping around his hand and under his palm to grip it reassuringly. Finally, he broke eye contact with Delilah, hanging his head in shame.

"You're right. I got us into this. I can't quit on you all now. It seems like today is a day for me to say 'sorry' repeatedly." He sighed, lifting his gaze and giving everyone an apologetic nod. "So. Naval assault it is."

Sam cleared her throat. "Let's take a few minutes and stretch our legs. Pablo, can you lock the doors until happy hour so we have some more privacy? We really need to come up with a command center. We can't always use this bar."

"Another round to cool our throats?" Pablo asked.

"What I wouldn't give for a pintje of lager," Pieter said.

"A what?" Pablo asked.

"It's a small glass, 25cl. So about eight ounces. It's how they serve a lager or pils in Belgium. It's easy to get through before it goes warm," Luke replied, filling in Pablo on a nugget of Belgian beer culture.

Pablo nodded. "Well, I'll see what I can do."

Maggie—it had been her hand holding his, providing reassurance —let go of him, giving his leg a couple pats. "I need to get going. I have to check in on a couple patients and begin organizing supplies and medics."

"Thanks, Maggie." A faint smile tugged up at the corners of Luke's lips as a measure of warmth spread though him.

She smiled at Luke softly, holding eye contact for a moment before turning to leave. He watched her walk away, his eyes lingering after she disappeared out the door.

ONCE THEY ALL took a stretch break and cleared their heads after the tense argument, they settled into planning. Pablo and Delilah were in charge of organizing the assault teams and coordinating with Sam on enlisting the aid of the coastal pack. They also had to arrange for people to cover those who'd need time off if they worked in a pack business. Maggie, who already knew her job, was prepping medical supplies and personnel.

"How long before that freighter gets into Oregon waters?" Luke asked.

Pieter pulled out his laptop and clicked away at the keyboard.

"Looks like it's just entered the Caribbean. So, depending on how long it takes to get through the Panama Canal, we're looking at around three weeks. Once it clears the canal, it's about twelve days to the Port of Portland."

"OK, that gives us some time to get everything organized. Good, good." Luke nodded, thinking.

Luke had some ideas but wanted to work privately with Pieter on how best to handle their upcoming assault. Besides helping lead the Belgian pack, he'd enlisted in the Belgian military and gone through commando training in the '70s, making his recentish military experience a prime tool to help plan their upcoming assault.

It had been several years since Luke had planned anything this big or audacious. He didn't have a lot of time or the necessary resources, but he'd have to figure it out with what he had. Fortunately, a multitude of problems could be solved with money, of which he had more than enough.

When he got home, he sorted through his gear, more for a sense of familiarity and comfort than any need for maintenance, stumbling on the sawed-off twelve gauges he'd busted out for the first time in decades.

"Hmm, double barrels won't be terribly helpful, but..." he mumbled to himself.

He went upstairs to the office and opened his laptop, searching for gun auction sites and local gun shows.

LUKE, sitting outside Gwen's therapist's office, texted with the various members of his team, working over the plans they'd set in motion the day before at the Howling Moon. He also checked on his gun auctions and purchases, ensuring they'd arrive on time. Everything was moving fast as they stared down the barrel of a short time-line and a big mission they weren't sure they'd be able to pull off.

The therapist opened her door and poked her head out. "Mr. Irontree?"

"Yes?"

"Would you mind stepping into my office?"

He got up and followed her into the office, taking the seat next to Gwen on the couch.

"Mr. Irontree, I'd like to get Gwen on the schedule again, if you don't mind."

"Please, call me Luke. Well, the next few weeks are going to be a bit hectic…" He thought about it. Weighing what he was doing against his other responsibilities. If he needed to take a bit of time to get Gwen to her therapy appointments, someone else could stand in for him for a few hours. "You know what? I can make it happen no matter what."

They picked a date, and Luke put it in his phone's calendar.

"Gwen, it was really nice meeting you. We'll see you in a week, OK?" Dr. Schmidt said with a smile.

"OK," Gwen replied.

"Gwen, can you wait outside for a moment, please?" Luke asked. "I'd like to talk to Dr. Schmidt for a minute."

Gwen nodded and left the room, shutting the door behind her.

"Thanks for working to get her in, Doctor."

"Please, Connie works."

Luke nodded. "How is she doing, Connie?"

"Overall, not bad, all things considered. She's got a long road and a lot of work ahead of her, but that's only to be expected. Once I've had more time with her, we'll discuss treatment options to figure out the best approach to help her deal with her trauma. I want to take a moment to go over patient/doctor confidentiality and how it works in regard to her guardian."

She pulled out some informational pamphlets and handed them to Luke, discussing the law and how it affected Gwen's rights and his rights as her guardian.

"I understand. I'm not looking to violate her privacy. I would like some help making sure I'm providing a solid home for her. Um, the main reason I wanted to talk to you, though, isn't about her. I think I need to see someone myself."

"Ah, yes. Maggie mentioned you might ask. I have a couple of recommendations, but I think you should start with Dr. Hamdi.

They specialize in posttraumatic stress disorder and complex post-traumatic stress disorder in adults." She handed him a slip of paper with two names and numbers on it. "As far as helping you with Gwen, there'll be some sessions where you're in the room with us so we can work on some joint things.

"I don't want to rush you out, but I have to get ready for my next patient. It was very nice to meet you and Gwen, Luke."

"Thanks, Connie. We'll see you in a week." Luke got up and walked out the door.

Gwen, seeing Luke, stood up and walked with him out of the building and back to the rental car.

"So, do you think you'll like seeing Connie? It's OK if you don't. We can find someone else. Maggie said it can sometimes take a few therapists before you find the right one for you."

Gwen thought about it for a minute while they pulled out onto Mississippi Ave. "Yeah, I think I like her. We'll stick with her for now."

"That sounds good. If you ever change your mind, let me know. OK?"

Gwen nodded and smiled at him.

"Hungry? We can stop up at Prost and get a sausage. Then we need to go home and pack up some clothes. Sometime in the next few days, we'll be moving up to the farm to get some stuff ready for the mission."

"OK," Gwen replied. "A sausage sounds good."

# TWENTY

LUKE HAD BEEN LARGELY IGNORING the texts from Pablo and Delilah inquiring about his whereabouts. All they knew was he was preparing training sessions, beyond that, he'd simply replied they should wait and see. Well, the wait was over and it was now time to see what he'd been up to with Sam and Pieter.

When the time came, he sent out a simple text, *Alert everyone going on the mission: Meet at the farm, bring several days' change of clothing, some workout clothes & hiking boots, and all their trip kits for the boats. We'll be heading to the coast from here.*

Luke had enjoyed the secret and keeping his friends in the dark. After all the times they'd surprised him, he owed them one, at least a small innocuous one. When they finally arrived at the farm, Luke, Sam, and Pieter met them and the rest of the invitees out front.

"Sorry about the quiet. I just wanted to have this set up, and it was a lot of late nights to get it done. Why don't you get situated in your rooms and meet back here in twenty minutes? Sam's affixed your names to your room assignments."

As their people headed toward the main house, they chatted enthusiastically with each other trying to figure out if one of them had more information than anyone else. Over the next twenty minutes, they trickled back into the yard in their workout clothes, ready to see what the surprise was.

Luke looked over the people assembled before him, all werewolves except for Delilah. "Most of y'all know each other, but let's do introductions and include any military service and experience with firearms. Pieter, why don't you start."

"Hello. My name is Pieter van den Bergh, werewolf from the Flanders Pack. My most recent military service was with Belgian special forces in the 1970s, Captain Retired."

"Sam Wakamatsu, Onna-Bugeisha serving at the battle of Wakamatsu Castle against the Meiji forces. Werewolf, North Portland Pack. Knowledgeable about the basic use of handguns and rifles."

"Delilah Johnson. Human. No military service. I've used handguns before."

"You forgot kickass vampire slayer," Sam added.

Delilah nodded her appreciation at Sam. "And kickass vampire slayer."

Archie stepped forward. "Archibald Hampton, 6th Royal Tank Regiment, 1939 to 1946. Fought in North Africa, Italy, Normandy, and Germany."

"Tanker?" Luke asked, impressed. The tank battles in North Africa had been particularly brutal between the Nazis and the British, especially with Germany fielding the superior armored units against the under-equipped Brits.

"Yes, sir. Driver. Mk Is, Churchills, and Cromwells. Even had a spin in a Sherman."

"I'll have to see if we can find a tank for you to drive," Luke said, his tone deadpan. He enjoyed the looks on everyone's face. They didn't know him well enough to know if he was joking or not. And if push came to shove, he could lay his hands on a few tanks.

"Jung-sook?" Luke waved the Korean woman forward.

"Jung-sook Kim, Republic of Korea Army, infantry 1964 to 1971."

They went down the line. Most of the people had served in peace time, a few during WWII, and one in France in WWI. Only Pablo and Delilah had no military experience, but Luke wouldn't leave them out of a mission. They were the most experienced vampire fighters besides himself. Sam had advised him to go last, expanding on his experience where most had been fairly succinct with their pasts. Many of the people here hadn't really worked with Luke much if at all, and few knew more than rumors. Sam wanted him to establish his authority as a soldier, vampire hunter, and their leader.

"Luke Irontree. I joined the legions of Rome in 103 of the common era, joining the XXX Ulpia Victrix and fought in the Trajan's second Dacian War, promoted to Optio by 107. Basically, a lieutenant. Transferred at the emperor's direct request to I Adiutrix to create an elite cohort. Fought in Trajan's Parthian War. Killed my first vampire in 117 in the mountains of Armenia."

Murmurs rose as the dates Luke had mentioned sank in, people looking at their neighbors in surprise as they leaned over and whispered.

"That's enough, gang. Please give Luke your attention," Sam said, her voice raised.

Luke nodded his thanks to Sam. "After that, I was given authority under Hadrian to form my own elite legion, the I Aelia. We were referred to as "The Black Legion" because of the colors I chose. We were tasked with guarding the empire from vampires. I protected the borders of the empire until 332 when Constantine expelled me from the empire at the end of his Gothic campaign and my memory and that of the Black Legion were erased from the empire."

He paused for a moment, the memory of expulsion still brought up bitter feelings after all this time. "More recently, I served in Belgium and France with the British Expeditionary Forces from 1915 to 918 and the Special Operations Executive from 1940 to 1945, most of that spent in occupied Europe. I've fought vampires for nineteen hundred years, sometimes under a uniform and banner, but most the time by myself."

He looked from face to face, giving each person a small smile. "Some of you have been assisting me in my mission for the last few months. Others of you are new to it. But as of now, we're all one team with a common cause—protect our city and our friends and family. We're all vampire slayers now. Together, we can protect each other and come out the other side on top. Now, I'm sure you're tired of listening to me, so let's get to it."

Luke walked over to a couple long tables he'd set up near the edge of the woods. Ensuring everyone was with him and he had their attention, he pulled the cloth off the table, revealing a row of shotguns. He picked one up, and a small wave of queasiness settled in his stomach.

"This is the Winchester model 1912 trench gun edition. It'll hold six 12-gauge shells. It's outfitted with a heat shield on its twenty-inch barrel." He lifted the gun, displaying the metal shield with holes surrounding the barrel. His hand drifted up. "It also has a bayonet lug and convenient swivels for a strap for ease of carrying. And my favorite feature…"

He slid the ear protectors over his ears. Everyone picked up a set and followed suit. Luke raised the shotgun to his shoulder, took aim, pulled the trigger, then emptied the magazine. Only having pulled trigger once, he fired the trench gun by pumping the pump action — each pump firing a shell and discharging the empty from its ejection port. When the last shell dropped to the ground, Luke removed his ear protection. The team pulled theirs off as well.

"Some of you may have used these or similar weapons at various points. They put a lot of firepower into a tight space. You pull the trigger once and just pump. They worked wonders clearing trenches once we got that far." Luke shuddered at the memory, his chest tightening a little. "They also can vaporize vampires when you replace the standard shot with wood and silver. I've currently got some of the pack hand-producing special shells for us. Unfortunately, I don't have any of those on hand, so right now, we'll use standard shot for live fire practice."

"That's an ideal weapon for a tight space where noise won't be an issue," Pablo commented.

"I had the same thought myself," Luke replied. They would have been handy during his little solo adventure, but unfortunately, he didn't have any available. "I've been acquiring as many of these as possible. They've been out of production for fifty years, but they were manufactured for a long time so I've been able to get a few pretty quickly. Well, at least enough to train a few elites to lead the teams. I've also got parts coming in case they need repairs and for the future. We've set up a basic course to run you through. First, individually to get used to the conditions, then in twos. I'll want at least two people with shotguns in each group—that way one can fire while the other reloads and we can put constant fire power out if we need to."

Luke walked them through the course, complete with stand-ins roughly constructed out of a couple boards nailed to a frame and base. The walls of the gauntlet he'd created were similarly crude.

Luke gestured toward the mess of plywood and two-by-fours. "Sorry for the lack of finish on the dummies and the walls, but we had a limited amount of time."

"It'll do, mate, it'll do." Archie, the reserved Brit and WWII vet, patted him on the shoulder.

"Pieter, would you mind taking everyone to work through some basics on the guns to familiarize the more experienced shooters, then start running them through the course?" Luke suggested.

Pieter's recent service in the special forces had been put to use training his packmates back home, which made him an ideal choice to help with the crew.

"I'll take Delilah and Pablo and run them through the basics. Sound good?"

Pieter brought his hand to his forehead in a salute. "Aye, Luke." He gestured for his trainees to follow him. "Leave the shotguns for now. Let's just take a dry run through the course."

"Delilah, Pablo, select a shotgun."

Each selected one by whatever criteria they had.

"Have either of you used a shotgun before?" Luke asked.

"It's been a long time," Pablo replied, "I've been hunting with a double barrel, but that was for food, ducks and birds and rabbits."

Luke nodded. "Were you any good?"

Pablo grabbed his stomach and gave it a little shake. "Didn't go hungry. But it's been a while."

"Delilah?"

"No. I've gone to a gun range and shot handguns before, but never a shotgun."

"OK." Luke picked up a shotgun off the table. "This is the safety. In this position, it's engaged. We'll want to leave it engaged for loading practice. I've got some blank shells to practice with. Might as well be extra safe." Luke flipped the gun over and slipped a shell into the entry port. "That's where the shells go. Six is the capacity."

Delilah and Pablo began sliding shells into their shotguns. After a few, Pablo's all shot back out the entry port. Delilah laughed at his mishap just before shells plopped out of her shotgun's magazine.

"Ha! That's what you get for laughing at me."

Luke smiled at his friends. "You have to make sure the action slide catches the shell before you let go." He demonstrated the motion they needed to imitate to get the shells smoothly into the magazine and how to safely unload it. "You two work on that for a bit. I want to check on Pieter."

As Luke walked up to the entrance of the obstacle course, Pieter was walking out with his group. Luke raised his hand in greeting as Pieter changed directions to intercept him.

Luke stopped as Pieter walked up. "How's it look, Pieter?"

"It's a good approximation. It'll certainly be better than going in blind. I'll run them all through with the M12s." Pieter ran a hand through his gray-streaked blond hair.

"Good. I'm going to take Delilah and Pablo over to the range to fire some live rounds."

"Are you sure Pablo and Delilah are up to the task? Everyone else here has military training, some seeing combat," Pieter asked in Flemish Dutch.

"Oh, they've seen heavy fighting with vampires. There are no two people I'd trust at my back more than them. They've seen more vampire combat than anyone here other than me and maybe you. They're quick students and know how to work with me. They'll be fine," Luke replied in English.

Pieter gave Luke a respectful nod and rejoined his team at the shotgun table. Luke followed him over to collect Pablo and Delilah.

Bending over, he opened a large crate filled with belts lined in shotgun shells. He held one up and got everyone's attention.

"OK, people. These are just loaded with standard buckshot. I'm still having the anti-vamp shells loaded. Once we get a few to spare, we'll compare effective ranges. Just know for now, the standard shells will probably have a longer effective range, but you won't really need to be worrying about distance shots with these training conditions or on our mission. We have plenty of shells, so don't feel you need to be parsimonious. I'd rather buy more rounds and have you well trained than the other way around."

They all nodded and lined up to get their own belts. Luke pulled out two more, one each for Pablo and Delilah, and beckoned for them to follow him over to the shooting range while the others returned to the gauntlet Luke had set up. Once at the shooting range, Luke handed them their belts, and they put them on.

"OK, load up. Make sure your safety is engaged." He noticed that neither of them had brought their ear protection. "I'll go grab the earmuffs." Luke jogged over, grabbed three, and jogged back.

They turned their heads toward the gauntlet as the first shotgun blasts rent the silence of the forest. Luke flinched each time a shot rang out. Taking a moment, he tried to breathe through it and put the sound to the back of his mind.

Earmuffs secure, Pablo and Delilah took aim. Pablo's grip looked good, his past use coming back to him. Delilah, on the other hand, looked a bit nervous. Luke halted her before she could fire.

"You need the butt resting firmly against your shoulder. If you hold it away, it's going to recoil and you'll get a nasty bruise." He pulled his shotgun into his shoulder, showing her how to properly set hers. "Also, rest your finger against the trigger guard or the body of the gun. You don't want it near the trigger until you're ready to shoot. Don't worry about being fast or accurate. Just worry about holding it correct and steady. Also, safety. Always practice safe techniques."

Running through everything Luke had told her, Delilah situated the shotgun and held it like he'd showed her. Eventually, she took aim downrange and squeezed the trigger. Nothing happened.

"Safety off, and load one into the chamber."

She clicked the safety and pumped a shell into the firing chamber before squeezing off her first shot. It blasted up a puff of dirt about ten feet in front of the target. Pablo was having better luck—each shot getting closer to the target as he got used to the weight of the gun and how it shot. Delilah's next shot also thudded into the ground short of the target.

"Delilah, you're closing your eyes and letting the barrel dip."

She nodded back and corrected herself, this time hitting the bottom of the target. The next several shots shredded various edges of the paper target pinned to the poles. Pablo, now on his second load, was consistently hitting around the bullseye. Before he could start up again, Luke signaled for him to hold on. Delilah finished her last shot, and Luke caught her attention as well.

"Looks like your skills are coming back pretty quickly, Pablo. Nice shooting. Why don't you practice slam firing? On your first shot, just hold down the trigger and use the pump to fire. Go slow at first. Delilah, How you doing? Any questions?"

"I don't think so. I think I got it."

Luke smiled at them. "Just take your time and concentrate. Speed will come with familiarity."

She nodded and grabbed some more shells. Her nimble fingers made quick work of it. A few seconds later, she was blasting away at the target, this time more confidently. After a few more rounds of reloads, she said, "This is kind of fun."

"Fun?"

At the tone of his voice, she turned and recoiled a bit. He tried to control the sour expression on his face but was struggling as old feelings threatened to overwhelm him.

Luke's heart rate slid upward. "Guns are a tool that serve only one purpose—killing. The reason we're doing this is to ensure the people killed aren't our friends."

Delilah's eyes widened, and her jaw dropped slightly. She let out a low gasp.

Pablo, who'd stopped shooting, turned around to address Luke. "Lighten up a bit, dude. This is dark enough business as is. Let her find some joy where she can. It won't lessen her diligence or our task."

Luke took in a slow, deep breath, and released it. "Delilah, I'm sorry. Pablo's right. It's just..." He lifted his M12 a bit. "I've used a gun just like this and killed men. Germans who didn't want to be in that trench any more than the British I was leading—all because a Serbian revolutionary killed an Austrian Archduke. Using a shotgun in a trench is personal. It's often not a fast death. You see their eyes. When I use my swords or a knife, I can end it quick. Buck shot at range, if you don't hit the heart, brain, or an artery, it can take time for them to bleed out. It's not a pleasant thing to witness, to cause. The acrid reek of gunpowder. The stench of fetid water, blood, shit..." Luke's complexion was dipping toward the pasty, a sheen of sweat breaking out on his face. His breath raced shallowly in and out of his mouth until he couldn't speak anymore. He stumbled over to a bush, bent over, and heaved out his breakfast.

Pablo set his shotgun down on the table they'd been standing behind, jogged back to the supply crates, and opened a cooler, pulling out a bottle of water, and ran over to Luke. Delilah stared at Luke, jaw open, sympathy pouring out of her eyes as well as a few tears. Luke was still bending over, one hand on a knee, while the shotgun in his other hand rested against his other knee. Pablo rubbed Luke's back, speaking in a voice that only Luke could hear.

"You got yourself worked up a bit there, buddy. It's OK. Delilah and I are here for you." He moved his hand off Luke's back to pop the top off the water bottle. "Here, rinse out your mouth and take a little walk. I'll work with Delilah on her aim. OK?"

"OK." Luke took the bottle of water, rinsed out his mouth and spat it into the bush. He walked away from both the range and gauntlet to collect himself.

Pablo walked back to Delilah. They started speaking, thinking he couldn't hear them with the earmuffs on, except his only blocked high decibel sounds, letting regular noise in.

"Looks like our boy is still suffering from shell shock, probably untreated," Pablo said.

"Shell shock?"

"Yeah, it's what they called PTSD during World War I."

"Ah," Delilah replied.

"Let's practice some more while he collects himself."

"Is he going to be OK?" Delilah asked.

Pablo rocked his hand back and forth. "For Luke. I mean, how OK is he really? He's doing better than when we first met him, but…"

"Yeah, he seems a bit more lighthearted, but that's not a high bar for him. His eyes, if he's not paying attention to someone he's talking to, always seem so forlorn."

Pablo nodded at Delilah's assessment, a curious look on his face. "Yeah, I think we've pulled him out of the deepest pit he was in before we brightened his shores, but he's a long way from healthy. I'll speak with Doc, maybe one of the pack shrinks can help him out. I doubt a regular talk doc is up to handling the problems of two-thousand-year-old immortal vampire slayer with too much trauma in his life. A werewolf might be a better choice."

"I'm not sure he'll take that suggestion, but he always manages to surprise me."

"That he does. Shall we?" He indicated the table with their shot-guns resting on them.

They returned to loading and firing their guns, both of them quicker and more accurate as the day went on. Luke eventually rejoined them and fired off several loads himself.

They were right. Their friendship had gone a long way toward helping him. But he needed something more. When this was done, he'd call the number Gwen's therapist had given him. For now, he'd have to collect himself and get him and his friends through this complex operation. He didn't speak to them until he called a quits for an early afternoon break.

Luke sighed, placing his hand on Delilah's shoulder. "Delilah, I just want to apologize again. That was uncalled for, and I'm sorry."

"It's OK. I sometimes forget that wagon you're draggin' has a lot of baggage in it. Apology accepted."

Luke smiled at her softly, his eyes glowing warmly but sadly at her. "Thank you."

"Team hug!" Pablo gathered them both in his arms, both Delilah and Luke towering over him by a good half foot as they returned his hug. "How about a lunch break? Tony and Sam are whipping up some ramen for lunch. You're in for a treat."

"Speaking of Sam and Tony, why aren't they out here?" Delilah asked.

"They have both declined for various reasons. Sam will join us, of course, but we're working on something besides shotguns for her. Tony..." Luke said.

"Tony," Pablo supplied, "is on the pack council now. He's picking up a lot of the slack since me, Sam, and Holly have been so busy with other things. He and Jamaal will run things while the rest of the pack is out of town."

"Ah... Wait," Delilah said. "Does that mean Tony was in the military?"

"Yup. He was a very handsome flyboy during WWII. If you're nice to me, I'll show you some pictures of him with his P-51 Mustang."

Luke chuckled. Pablo's joking helped clear the fog of the earlier incident. He really did appreciate Pablo's ability to make him feel better through humor. Without Pablo's joviality and friendship, he had no idea where he'd be emotionally, but it would be without one of the best people he'd met in ages.

# TWENTY-ONE

THEY SPENT the next several days running through the course and practicing their shooting and teamwork. As Luke expected, Pablo and Delilah learned quickly and were soon coordinating well with the more experienced members of their leadership squad. Sam had joined them while Tony and a werewolf Luke didn't know managed the kitchen. Instead of a shotgun, Sam used an odd-looking bow Luke had acquired for her.

Pablo pointed at the bow the first time she'd joined them. "What kind of bow is that? I've seen Sam shoot a Japanese bamboo bow, but not a small, curvy guy like that."

"It's a horse bow—"

"A horse bow?" Pablo interrupted.

"Yeah, for horse archers. It's a recurve bow patterned off the bows that steppes archers used, like the Scythians, Sarmatians, and the Mongols. And while the yumi is an exceptional war bow, Sam and I figured a shorter, more compact bow would work better for this circumstance. She'll be able to provide silence and medium range sniping."

Sam was currently bullseyeing targets at the shooting range, getting used to the draw and action of the bow. Luke had acquired a heavier than normal draw for the bow since it would have a were-wolf's arm behind it. It would give Sam extra power and distance.

Pieter walked over and watched her for a few moments. "How far can she shoot with that antique?"

Despite seeming in a zone, Sam must have heard him. She turned, aimed toward the gauntlet, and bullseyed a dummy about two-hundred and fifty yards away before returning to her target practice.

Pieter's eyebrows shot up as his jaw dropped. "Damn."

Pablo chuckled. "That answer your question, waffleboy?"

The normally affable and easy-going Pablo had taken a dislike to Pieter since the first time they'd met. It had solidified when Luke had retreated into his basement. Luke had never seen his friend quite that snarky with anyone before; Pablo got along with everyone. Luke could see why Pieter might rub Pablo the wrong way. The Belgian had a quiet confidence that dipped a bit too far into arro-gance for Pablo's taste. His arrogance rubbed Luke and Delilah a bit raw at times as well, but they both liked the man. After several weeks of spending time together, Pablo's dislike had settled into a competitive rivalry complete with ribbing. Waffleboy was his favorite at the moment.

Luke suspected his friend was a bit jealous of Pieter's accom-plishments and his friendship with Luke. The friendly rivalry between Luke's two friends seemed to push both toward better performance. Plus, it gave someone besides Luke for Delilah to roll her eyes at, which was a bonus in Luke's book. He'd seen this sort of thing plenty of times and hoped it would settle out into friendship, but he'd accept an awkward alliance for now. Besides, eventually Pieter would fly home after this mission and rejoin his own pack.

Luke had watched everyone, sizing up skills and compatibility, and was beginning to see some very good chemistry between certain people. Those people he paired into teams and let them run the gauntlet. No matter what he changed or how difficult he made it, everyone was getting crisp and professional.

The last day, he added in the final element.

As they gathered post breakfast, the team assembled around the table Luke was standing behind. He removed the cloth covering it.

Pablo shook his head. "Dude, you can just show us without all the production."

"Allow me my small joys, Pablo," Luke replied airily.

Lined up neat as soldiers were special stakes. Each was rounded with a fire-hardened point and attached to an odd-looking dagger hilt. Luke picked up his shotgun and one of the daggers.

"I figured since we had bayonet lugs on these things, we might as well do this right." He fixed the bayonet to the end of his shotgun. "Grab one and follow me."

He walked toward the target range which had a new addition, a sand-filled bag affixed to a square frame that suspended the bag over the ground about at the height of a human's chest. He pulled down his ear protection and waited for everyone else to follow suit. He fired a full load of shells into the range. Then he pivoted and violently rammed the bayonet into the spot where a heart would be. He turned and faced everyone.

Luke lifted his ear protection from his left ear. "I thought that might be a nice option if you were in between reloads and a vamp got too close. I'll have three for each of you in case of breakage. They're not quite as sturdy as a steel bayonet."

The team attached the bayonets to the end of their guns. One by one, they stepped up to the range to fire at their targets before stabbing the dummy. A couple got in an extra poke or two. Once they all made it through, Luke had them gear up with their ammo belts and extra bayonets.

Luke stood in the entrance to the gauntlet and faced the group. "You've all done a great job. I appreciate your attention and efforts. You've really come together in a short amount of time, and you're looking damned sharp. Your hard work is going to keep everyone safe and make sure we complete this mission successfully.

"Since you've done so well, I thought we'd have some fun and add a bit of competition. Overnight, we've had a crew rearrange the gauntlet. Pieter and I will go through first while you wait here. We'll establish the time to beat. Then the rest of you will go in pair by pair and see if you can beat us. We've even got prizes."

The team cheered and shit-talked each other a bit.

"First prize, generously donated by Pablo, is a night out at the Howling Moon, all expenses paid, and a gift certificate to the Wonder Ballroom for a show. Second prize was donated by Tony. He'll come to your home and make you and your family dinner. Third prize—"

"A set of steak knives!" someone interrupted.

"Third prize was 'you're fired.' Steak knives were second place. If you're going to interrupt, at least get the joke right," Archie said.

"Thanks, Archie. Anywho, third prize is a gift certificate to Kenton Overlook Coffee Shop." Luke had stopped in, partially to pick up the gift certificate, and partly as an excuse to talk to Heather. "And, to spice it up, if anyone can beat Pieter's and my time, you'll get one story of my life from the time period of your choice."

That got people murmuring in interest. Luke's life was a mystery, even to Pablo and Delilah. He kept his life a closed book except for a few tantalizing snippets. The rest of the pack knew how old Luke was and a little about his origins in the legions of Rome, but speculation about all he'd experienced in nearly two thousand years was a hot topic for people who loved to gossip about the new supernatural associating with the pack.

"There are a few spotters making sure everyone hits their targets. There are shooting and bayonet targets. We'll run it again after dark. Five second penalty for a miss. Combined lowest scores wins. Any questions?"

Everyone shook their heads. People shuffled from foot to foot and looked around at their friends and competitors.

"You ready, Pieter?"

"Ja, boss. Let's do it." He raised his hand for a high five which Luke obliged.

They proceeded down the entrance of the gauntlet, Luke in the lead and Pieter behind, gun ready but barrel pointed safely at the ground. The first several challenges went smoothly, each nailing their targets on their turns and the exchanges and reloads going quickly without any time burned. It wasn't until near the end they encountered their first problem.

Luke had finished his round and was working another round of shells into his shotgun when Pieter called out, "Fuck, broke my bayonet."

"Got it." Luke shoved the last shell into the magazine and crept up on Pieter's right shoulder. The next couple stops were shots, which Pieter hit. The next set however featured the bayonet. Pieter fired his last round and dropped back, letting Luke jump forward and stab the bayonet target before he moved onto their final set.

Pieter loaded his shotgun double time and swapped out his bayonets just in time to catch his last round of shots. They crossed the line painted in the grass and someone yelled, "Time!"

Pieter exhaled sharply. "Thought our time was fucked there for a minute when my bayonet broke off. Thanks for picking up that one for me."

"No problem. Great job on the reload and swap. That kept us right on time. I think that'll give the others something to aim for." He patted his Belgian friend on the back. "Let's get our time."

They jogged around the gauntlet back to the start where Tony was standing with a clip board and a stopwatch.

"Two minutes and seventeen seconds is the time to beat," Tony called out. The waiting competitors clapped and whistled, a few taunting how bad they were going to beat the time.

While they'd been working their way through, Tony had filled a hat with names.

"Luke, draw a name." Tony turned and addressed the rest of the competitors, "Whoever Luke draws, goes next."

Luke reached in and drew a piece of paper. "Archie and Jung-sook."

"Archie and Jung-sook, you're up. As soon as you cross the threshold, your timer starts," Tony instructed.

Archie and Jung-sook walked toward the entrance of the gauntlet, nodded at each other, then burst across the threshold and disappeared around a corner. A few minutes later, the cry of "time" from the end of the maze prompted Tony to click his stopwatch and record the time. One by one, the rest of the teams had their names drawn so they could make their run. So far, Luke's story looked safe. The first run finished, the times were read out and ranked for all to hear.

It was time for a break before the night runs.

Luke wanted to ensure that everyone felt comfortable in both conditions. They intended to strike during the day when the vamps would be out of commission, but Luke believed in over preparation. Better to plan and train and not need it than to be caught with his pants down. Besides, the training would always be useful for later operations.

The team secured their weapons before heading into the house to relax. They chatted and joked with each other, the camaraderie built over the last several days really shining through as they saw the end of their training in sight.

Delilah was first through the door. "Oh my god, what is that smell?"

Tony, who'd headed inside when the trainees were securing their shotguns, popped his head out of the kitchen, a towel in his hands. "You're in luck tonight. Pablo's tia is making dinner. We're having a Mexican feast after your last run, and Pablo brought a couple kegs from the pub. Once you're cleaned up, there are nibbles in the dining room to tide you over until tonight."

Pieter looked skeptical.

"This is the real deal, not the pale imitation stuff you get in Europe," Luke reassured his friend.

Pablo, who'd overheard them talking, asked, "No good Mexican food in Europe?"

"Not that I've found," Luke replied. "I'm sure there has to be one restaurant somewhere, but I've yet to locate it."

Pieter nodded in agreement with Luke's assessment. "I'm genuinely excited. Is your tia a good cook?"

"Exceptional," Pablo replied. "She's been teaching Tony since I moved her and my nephew up here."

"Wouldn't he be your cousin?" Luke asked.

"Technically, he's my nephew many times removed. She'd be my niece, but since she's older than me in appearance, she prefers for me to call her 'tia.' It makes her happy. It took her a long time to get used to the werewolf thing and the gay thing."

"Ah, the werewolves' dilemma. I understand. She got used to both?" Pieter asked.

"Yeah. You've met some of the crew here. You've seen how welcoming everyone is. Once you enter the pack's protection, you're family. Especially if you're already family. She's a pushover, though. All it took was Tony asking her to teach him how to cook some authentic dishes, and she became his tia too."

Pieter nodded. "I'm continually impressed with your pack. It's honestly one of the best run ones I've seen."

Pablo smiled broadly. "Thanks. Holly will be happy to hear it. It's her creation, and she's the driving force behind it."

"I can't wait to meet your aunt and try her food. They both sound wonderful."

That sealed it for Pablo. He beamed at the compliments and the sincerity in Pieter's voice. He put his hand on Pieter's upper back and directed him toward the dining room. "If my nose isn't betraying me, you can try some of her cooking right now. I smell taco fixings. You have to try her al pastor."

Luke smiled seeing his friends finally break down the barrier that had separated them. Also, he'd had Pablo's tia's cooking before, and he was excited to dive into a few tacos. And if he knew Maria, there'd be fresh salsa and chips to go with them. His trek into the dining room was halted when Tony cut him off carrying a large stone bowl of guacamole.

"Excuse me, Luke, cutting through."

Luke grabbed a plate and dished up before joining his friends for some much-needed refreshment. He wasn't feeling chatty, but he enjoyed the give and take of those around him. The camaraderie of being part of a team on a mission warmed him, and a relaxed smile spread across his face.

The night runs went well for everyone, although Tony was keeping all the times and deductions secret. He wanted to announce everything after dinner to add to the evening's festivities.

Everyone was anxious to get to the prizes, but nobody wanted to rush through Maria and Tony's enchilada feast. Her chicken mole was particularly in demand. Beers were flowing, and people ate way more than they normally would because the food was so amazing, and there wasn't going to be strenuous activity in the morning. Luke basked in the laughter of his friends and comrades. Training together was for more than just learning about the weapons and mission; it bound them into a team. Even though most of the people at the table were pack, they hadn't worked together at a serious task before. The familiarity had made the initial camaraderie easy and pushed them in friendly competition, deepening their bond over a shared purpose judged vital to the safety and interest of the pack.

AFTER EVERYONE HAD STUFFED themselves with enchiladas, they retired to the large sitting room. Tony had handed out the prizes, Archie and Jung-sook taking first place. Now, it was time to relax. No one had bested Luke and Pieter's time, but despite that, people kept trying to talk Luke into telling them a tale of historical Luke.

As Luke walked through the sitting room, he raised his arms to gather everyone's attention. "I know you all want a story from my past, but would you settle for a tale about the origin of werewolves?"

The room was dead silent, the only sound the crackling of fire in the large fireplace along one wall.

Luke looked around, gauging interest and seeing confused and shocked looks. "Is that a story you all know?" He had no idea what lore was maintained in the packs throughout time.

He knew human history was obscured through the mists of time as things were lost or covered up. He'd figured something out of the primordial past might be lost, even among the long-lived werewolves.

Sam was the first to speak up. "You actually know the origin of the werewolves? No one knows where we come from. We kind of just thought we'd always existed."

There were several nods from around the room.

"If you'd like to hear the tale as it was told to me, I can recite it to you. It was an old tale long before I was born and told to me from one who knew its details. It's tied up in the creation of vampires; that's why it was relayed to me."

"I know I'd like to hear it," Pablo spoke up, several people agreeing with him.

"It's an ancient tale that involve gods unknown in the west and long forgotten in their own homes, although it involves the dark entity of Zoroastrianism, Ahriman, the evil counterpart to Ahura Mazda. There are still some active Zoroastrians left in the world spread out in India, Iran, and the US, though not many. I guess I'd peripherally fall into their numbers as an agent of Mithras, but that's neither here nor there."

Luke stroked his beard as he thought. "Let me see... I'm going to have to translate this on the fly—"

Sam held her hand up, signaling for Luke to hold up. "Luke, sorry to interrupt you, but let's take a quick minute to let everyone get drinks and rearrange the furniture so we can listen properly. Luke, take a chair and set it by the fire. Let's do this right."

"Need a refill buddy?" Pablo asked.

"Yeah. I'll take another beer and a glass of whiskey if you don't mind?"

Luke picked up an armchair and set it next to the fire, but not blocking it so he could look out over the room. The werewolves arranged the chairs and couches so they were all facing Luke, radiating out into the room. Satisfied with the seating, they filed into the kitchen to top up their beverages of choice.

Sam looked around the room, waiting for the last people to get seated. "OK, Luke. I think we're ready."

Luke nodded, clearing his throat. "This story involves some Indo-Iranian gods—old gods—and comes out of the northern Caucus Mountains and southern steppes of what's now Ukraine and Russia. Let's see, where to begin..."

Luke dug up the memory of the story being relayed to him—the images he was shown and the story accompanying it. As he dusted the memory off, remembering how it was given to him, it felt more immersive any virtual reality could mimic. He'd seen it alongside

Selene, the moon goddess, as if were there with her when the events happened.

"Ahriman, seeking to supplant Ahura Mazda, sought confederates in order to gain more power to destroy all that Ahura Mazda had created. Traveling to the north, to the wide-open spaces of the steppes, Ahriman came upon a lower deity named Saubarag who claimed the darkness as his dominion. Among his own pantheon he was known as a thief and a liar. He was the god of the darkness, sometimes called the 'Black Rider.' Speaking honeyed words of destruction into Saubarag's ears, Ahriman wooed him to his cause, promising to bind his destructiveness to Saubarag's darkness.

"Together, they sought to create a new race of beings to worship them, and in that worship, grow their power so they could challenge their enemies, Ahura Mazda and Tabiti, respectively. Saubarag, lord of the darkness, knew humans feared the wolf and associated it with his domain, using the fires of Tabiti to protect themselves from the wolves. Through Saubarag, Ahriman searched for the lord of wolves, Tutyr.

"Tutyr loved the wolf, the fierce hunter of the steppes, wily and cunning, fierce and loyal, strong in numbers. It saddened him that the humans feared his beloved wolf. When Saubarag approached him with an idea that would birth a new race that would bring man and wolf together, he acquiesced and offered a few of his children, the Aralezner, to use in his efforts. An Aralez was a powerful creature that could take on the form of a wolf or a large dog resembling an Armenian Gampr or a wolf. Some believed they were winged, strong in the magic of Tutyr and their pantheon, or even the oldest of gods who predated anthropomorphic deities. Though, their greatest gift was the gift of resurrection."

Luke paused to let that sink in as his friends leaned over to whisper to each other. Others stared back at Luke with wide eyes.

"Although Tutyr, having run with and as a wolf, feared not the darkness, he knew Saubarag was often not all he seemed as he used the darkness to shield his thievery and clandestine machinations. To counter the baser aspects of Saubarag, Tutyr selected the noblest of his Aralez who could resurrect wounded warriors through licking their wounds.

"Hiding their deed, Saubarag and Ahriman selected the darkest night of the month when not even the glow of the moon could shed light on the evil they planned. With their combined powers, Saubarag and Ahriman forced together the Aralezner with humans to create a new creature, a hybrid of the two, a wolf-man. The process was painful to the new creature and created a being of rage.

"The wolf-men, in their pain-addled fury, attacked a small band of wandering nomads and savaged them. Most died from the ferocity of the attack, but those who didn't became wolf-people on the first dark night of the month before the birth of the new moon. The power of Aralez's resurrection became an infection for the wounded."

The whispering turned a bit louder.

"Hey, let's keep it down, please," Pablo said over the murmuring. When the audience quieted, Pablo nodded at Luke.

"Tutyr's caution was rewarded. The Dark Rider had come to him alone, keeping his confederate a secret in order to gain Tutyr's acquiescence. But Tutyr chose his Aralez well. Within those he'd sent, he'd selected the ones with the truest spirit of his offspring with the wolves. Within most of the wolf-people, the independence and free spirit of the steppes bred true."

Luke took a sip of his whiskey, letting the burn linger. The crowd hung rapt on his story, eager eyes waiting for him to continue.

"With the rage of the forced transformation waning, some of the wolf-people looked at the destruction they'd committed and wept at the cruelty of it. They rebelled against Saubarag and fled, leaving behind those of their new kind who preferred the destruction.

"One night, on the eve of the full moon, Selene, the Greek goddess of the moon, heard the lamentations of the wolf-people as she drove her silver chariot of moonlight across the night sky. She took pity and approached them. The wolf-people begged for her protection in exchange for their worship.

"Selene heard the pleas and went to Artemis, whose domain is creatures of the wild and hunters and brought the wolf-people's offer to her. Together, they decided to accept the worship of the wolf-people. Both Artemis and Selene returned the next night, and in the light of the full moon, they accepted the wolf-people under their protection. But the goddesses were wise, and their blessing bestowed a weakness on the wolf-people."

Pablo raised his hand like he was asking a question in school. "Wait. How did they go from one set of gods to another? Aren't those pantheons from different regions?"

"That area of the world isn't that big, and people will always travel to trade and explore. Plus, the Greeks sent out colonists throughout the Mediterranean and the Black Sea. And just as the people mingled, so did their gods."

"But wouldn't they be loyal to their own gods?" Archie asked.

Luke chuckled. "No. Pagans, especially ancient pagans, were a bit more ecumenical. Since gods often had overlap in duties, it was easy for worshipers to swap names or meld them for their purposes."

"Ah," Archie said.

Luke looked around the room to see if anyone else had questions before continuing. "Selene and Artemis, in consultation, decided to make the wolf-people vulnerable to silver, a substance both goddesses favored. Artemis, goddess of the hunt, often used a bow of silver when she set aside her bow of gold. Selene's chariot was made of silver and from it she cast moonlight as she rode across the night sky.

"The wolf-people loved their new goddesses and respected the dominion of silver. In honor of the goddesses, the wolf-people would transform to wolves on the night of the full moon to worship their divine protectors."

Luke gestured around the room. "And thus, the wolf-people have prospered and mastered their wolfish magics."

Luke hadn't been keeping eye contact with his audience, staring at a point in the distance as he told the story. When he looked around, everyone's gaze was focused on him, yet they said nothing. When a log popped behind him, he jumped slightly in his chair. The chair, which had been comfortable, now made Luke squirm under the intense gaze of the room full of werewolves.

Pieter broke the silence, asking the question many were probably thinking, "Is that all true?"

Luke shrugged. "As far as I'm aware. The story wasn't told to me by someone who had an agenda with werewolves, but as a piece of the tale about the origin of vampires."

"And who told you?" Pieter asked.

"Selene. In the mountains of Armenia nineteen hundred years ago. When Mithras took me and made me into his weapon against the vampires."

Pablo looked stunned. "You knew a god?"

"Yeah, a few. How do you think I've lived this long? All my equipment was enchanted by Mithras. I was recreated by him."

The room was filled with skeptical looks. Most had grown up in a western Christian world, some in Jewish or Muslim traditions and few who'd probably grown up in Buddhism or the various faiths found across Asia. Mithras was more an artifact of history, although he made some appearances in the Vedic aspects of Brahmanism and Hinduism as well as some forms of Buddhism. To his knowledge, Luke was the last true adherent of Mithraism as he learned it from the soldiers' cult of the Roman elites and legions. Although he hadn't practiced any aspects of the faith in a while, not exactly feeling loyal to the deity who'd invested Luke with his powers and long life. There was some fine print on the contract that Mithras had failed to mention to him nearly two thousand years ago.

Most of the people in the room hadn't seen Luke fighting vampires. They hadn't witnessed his strength and speed in combat or experienced the magic of his rudis. There was a good deal of room for skepticism in a world ruled by technology and science, even if those in the room were themselves supernatural creatures.

Sam stood up. "Hey, Luke. Thanks for the story. When we have more time, I'd like to sit you down with our pack historian, if you're willing."

"I can do that."

She looked around the room, catching everyone's attention. "I hope you all realize what a rare glimpse into our own stories Luke has been generous enough to give us. We might be the first wolves in centuries to know this."

"We've never heard anything of this in our pack," Pieter said, adding the weight of his European pack to Sam. "My father is nearly five hundred years old and knows a lot of werewolf lore. I'm sure he'll be delighted to add this to his collection of knowledge."

Sam yawned. "Well, I think it's time to wrap it up for the night. Luke, any last words?"

Luke stood up. "Everyone, I just want to thank you all for putting so much hard work in. Tomorrow afternoon, the rest of our teams will arrive and we'll run them through some basic training in the gauntlet so they know the conditions. You'll be in charge of training your folks on the M12s so they can take over if needed. I'll have a schedule up tomorrow morning so you'll know when your turns on the range will be. Sleep well."

The wolves stood and filed out with a range of expressions on their face from skeptical to neutral to troubled. He didn't know if he'd challenged anyone's knowledge of the world, but he hoped they'd get something out of the tale about the spirit of werewolves and how they evolved out of darkness into the light through their own free will and determination.

The next few days would be long as they prepped the teams for the assault on the freighter. As each person walked past him, he wondered how many would come home after, and who'd meet their end fighting against the enemies of humanity and werewolfkind.

# TWENTY-TWO

LUKE AND DELILAH waited at a coffee stand while the rest of their crew stowed the gear in the fishing boats. They'd woken up well before sunrise to get down to Astoria's docks so they could load and be out on the morning tide. Delilah was practically falling asleep on her feet, a quad mocha still too hot to drink in her hands. The stand was busy filling cardboard to-go boxes full of drip coffee. As the equipment got stowed, everyone filed back and got into line to get their personal orders in and help carry the extra coffee to their assigned boats.

As Luke looked around, he saw a mix of people joking gregariously and others standing quietly, fidgeting in place. Having learned about these people as he trained them, it all seemed exaggerated — overcompensation for nerves that everyone, including Luke, were fighting. He'd seen pre-battle jitters thousands of times on thousands of faces throughout his long life. As more eyes looked toward him, flicking away just as quickly, Luke realized they were looking for something from him. Straightening from his tired slouch, he drew his shoulders back and shifted into the body language of a leader. When eyes moved to him, he made eye contact and gave a measured nod in response. After a few minutes, the group calmed some. Although the nerves were still present and evident, they felt Luke had everything under control. It was a costume he could wear for his people even if his nerves were as unsettled as theirs.

The Coast Pack had rallied every fishing and seaworthy boat they had access to into service, keeping their crews light to free up space for Luke's assault teams.

Lauren, the Coast Pack's leader, sauntered over to Luke and Delilah. "Y'all about ready? The tide waits for no one."

"Yeah, we've just about run the stand out of coffee. Gear is stowed. Everyone has their billet. Can I buy you a coffee?" Luke asked.

Lauren gave Luke a lopsided smile. "Sure thing, handsome. Make it a tall hazelnut latte."

Luke placed the order then turned back to Lauren. "I haven't seen Owen this morning."

She rolled her eyes. "He'll be meeting us later today out at sea. He's got a surprise for y'all. Plus he didn't want to draw attention on the docks. Sometimes he's got good sense."

Luke knew Lauren and Owen well enough to know the ribbing she and her brother exchanged was good-natured and their way of expressing their affection. They'd been guests at the farm several times over the last week, meeting with Luke and his command team to plan the naval assault on the vampire's freighter.

The members of the Coast Pack were a bit more rough and tumble than the North Portland Pack he'd unwittingly become involved with. The Coast Pack was made up of a mix of loggers, fishers, and hippies with a few formerly clandestine marijuana farmers mixed in for good measure. Many of them were members of the various indigenous tribes of western Oregon. Lauren and Owen were members of the Chinook Tribe. When marijuana became legal in Oregon and Washington, first medically then recreationally, the pack had shifted more resources into the cash crop, especially as logging and fishing had been in a long decline along the Pacific coast. They'd been gracious enough to find extra boats, renting them from non-pack fishers so things wouldn't be too crowded.

The journey out to meet the freighter would take a couple days.

There would already be some shift sharing of beds as is. If there was anyone who needed rescuing, it would make things even tighter on the return trip.

Luke paid for the massive order, grabbed his quad Americano and a jug of drip, and followed Lauren out to her boat.

"Really? The Minnow?" Luke stared at the rear of the boat where the name was painted across the aft.

"Don't worry, we're not going on a three-hour tour. You'll be fine!" Lauren winked at him.

"You've got a warped sense of humor."

"Don't you know it, honey. Get on the boat, or I'll leave your ass here, standing around with that dumb look on your face."

Pablo and Delilah exchanged grins as they watched the interaction, loving that Lauren always seemed to get Luke's goat.

Luke looked at his friends, ignored their mirth and gestured toward the boat. "Shall we?"

The three friends joined Lauren and her oldest son Tobias and found a seat out of the way so the experts could navigate them into the Columbia River and past the dangerous Columbia Bar.

Luke, having been on smaller boats and rougher seas, fell asleep, even after his quad shot of caffeine as the flotilla assembled in the Columbia. And while there were an impressive number of boats, more would be meeting them out at sea. Lauren wanted to use several different docks to ensure they weren't causing too big of a scene that would draw curious eyes.

He woke sometime later to the sound of Pablo heaving his guts over the side.

"Oh, that's nasty," Delilah said, moving away from Pablo to avoid any incidental spray in the breeze and choppy water.

"Apparently, our boy Pablo doesn't have sea legs?" Luke asked, opening his eyes.

"You could say that…"

"Fuck you, gu…" Pablo leaned over the side of the boat and continued retching.

When Pablo stopped for a moment and pulled his head back in, Luke raised his voice. "Don't worry, you'll settle in. Once you're able to get away from the edge, find a spot where you can keep your eyes on the horizon."

Delilah poured coffee into Luke's empty cup and brought it over to him. "How are you doing?"

"Oh, doing fine. This isn't too bad. You've not seen rough seas until you've crossed the Horn in a frigate with a busted seam spilling water into your hold in a near hurricane force wind." Luke stretched, taking the cup of coffee.

"The Horn?"

"The tip of South America, Cape Horn. I did a stint in the British navy in the nineteenth century. You'd have laughed your ass off at me the first time I crossed the eastern Mediterranean on a trireme on my way to Syria."

"Seasick?"

Luke shook his head, a smirk on his face. "It wasn't even rough seas, but yeah, thought I was gonna puke my caligae up."

"Is this guy for real?" Tobias asked his mother.

"Rumor has it, he is." Lauren said, keeping her eyes forward. "Holly believes him and trusts him, and you know that doesn't happen easily. Go get Pablo a damp cloth to wipe his face down. He'll feel better in a bit."

Tobias went below deck and fetched a damp cloth for Pablo, who'd decided he was done vomiting for the moment and was trying to get his body under control.

"Of course, that was before I got my little gift. That was when it happened, during that campaign. After that, never got seasick again. Not sure if Mithras intended that or if it's just a happy side effect." Luke sipped his coffee, ignoring that Tobias was staring at him.

"How old are you?" Tobias asked.

"Tobias, that's rude to ask. But thanks for saving me from having to do it myself," Lauren chimed in.

"Let's see... I was born in the year 86 of the common era. You can do the math."

"You're older than any werewolf I've ever heard of..." Tobias stood there, eyes agog. "You've got to be kidding."

"Not today, kid. Not today." He took another sip of coffee. "If you're going to stand there with your mouth open, why don't you get a pastry to stuff in it. Grab me one too. There's a bag tucked next to the table."

The flotilla worked its way out to open sea and away from the Oregon and Washington coast. It wasn't until mid-afternoon when the surprise Lauren promised entered their field of vision, knifing through the ocean waves from the southeast.

Luke shaded his eyes with his hand. "What is that?"

Tobias pulled out a set of binoculars and handed them to Luke.

He let out a low whistle after he brought the binoculars to his eyes and identified what was flying through the waves. "Is that a PT Boat?"

Just then, the boat found another gear, or several more, and exploded into peak speed, sending up arcs of water from each side of the bow.

"Your uncle is so juvenile sometimes." Lauren shook her head.

Tobias answered his mother with a ridiculous grin, staring at what must be his uncle's favorite toy. Owen backed off the throttle after his initial display and changed course toward the boat his sister captained, pulling alongside The Minnow and matching the much slower speed of the fishing boat.

"Uh, Luke. Are those actual torpedoes?" Delilah was next to him, watching the new boat join their fleet.

"Those look a bit too realistic for mock-ups."

Delilah shifted, crossing her arms over her chest. "And those machine guns look like the real deal, too."

"Yeah." Luke looked over at Lauren. She smirked at him and went back to minding her wheel.

Tobias tossed some rubber bumpers over the port side. When he finished, he caught a line tossed over from the PT Boat. The two boats eased toward each other until the PT Boat snugged into the rubber bumpers.

Luke shouted across to Owen, who was currently behind the wheel of his boat. "That's some fishing trawler you've got there!"

Owen's response was a single hand in the air with his middle finger rising skyward.

"Mind if I come aboard?"

"Please." Owen stepped away from the wheel, handing it over to another man.

Luke leapt up onto the side of the fishing boat and jumped across to the deck of the World War Two era torpedo boat. The men shook hands.

"Where'd you get this beast?" Luke asked.

"Argentina."

"How'd an American PT boat get to Argentina?"

"The government sold some after the war. I crewed a .50-caliber on one during the war. Got a hankering to be a captain and found one of these Higgins made boats in Argentina. I greased the right wheels..." He rubbed his thumb and forefinger together making the "cash" motion. "And voila, my own torpedo boat."

"You've done quite the job restoring it."

"Yeah. It's a constant work in progress. Lauren refers to it as my 'money pit,' but hey, we all have hobbies I guess."

"And everything works?"

"Yup. Although I've not fired off any torpedoes. They're kind of hard to come by..."

"I'll say." Luke looked over one of the torpedoes, catching a bit of Cyrillic lettering along the nose of one.

Seeing where Luke's eyes rested, Owen smirked. "I know a guy."

Luke's eyebrows rose toward his hairline. "Don't suppose you've got depth charges, too?"

Owen looked over toward the racks of barrels. "Nah, just extra diesel."

"I thought these things ran on aviation fuel."

"You know how expensive that shit is? I love those old Packard engines, but efficient they were not. I swapped them for some high-power diesel engines. We wanted to have extra diesel, so we've got some on a few different boats. I can carry the most though. The racks work well enough for the task." He pointed back to the rows of barrels that ran along the deck's edges. "I only had two torpedoes anyways."

Tobias transferred over to his uncle's boat. As Owen showed

Luke around the PT Boat, Tobias eased the throttle forward as he joined the outside of the fleet. It was still early on the first day out from port. It'd been a while since Luke had last been in this confined of space with virtual strangers. Luke already liked the gregarious Owen, but it'd still be tight quarters on the seventy-eight-foot boat. Owen introduced Luke and Delilah to the Coast Pack members they'd not met yet. Pablo took the opportunity to crawl into one of the unclaimed bunks and fell asleep.

LUKE PACED the deck of the PT Boat, mumbling angrily to himself. The freighter was late, and the sun had set. They'd have to face the vampires.

Owen scowled toward Delilah. "Tell your boy to keep it down. I'm trying to listen."

Delilah nodded at Owen before walking over to Luke and taking hold of his arm. "Luke, hush up. Owen thinks he hears something."

Luke nodded and stopped pacing and grumbling.

Owen picked up the radio mic. "Everyone, cut your running lights."

As the boat crested the wave it rode, Luke saw the lights splayed behind them blink out as the word went down the line. The PT Boat had taken the lead when the expected rendezvous with the freighter hadn't happened earlier that day. Luke had wanted to attack the freighter in the daylight and take the vampire factor out of it, at least on the deck. Now, they'd be operating in the vampire's element. Fortunately, the werewolves were equally comfortable in the dark, even if they kept mostly daytime hours passing as humans. It still didn't keep him from grumbling. They'd done nighttime drills, but there were always more chances of something going wrong with visibility restricted.

They'd spent the delay refueling the boat. Owen and Tobias drained several of the barrels into their tanks. Even though they'd changed to diesel, the three engines needed a lot of fuel, even at the low speeds they'd been using to stay back with their fleet of fishing boats. They could only go as fast as the slowest boat.

The PT Boat, now at the bottom of a trough, started up the next swell until it crested, lifting the boat above the waves. There it was. The running lights of a very large vessel shone out over the darkness of the Pacific night, shrouded in a dense layer of clouds. Luke's anxiety flattened out as it often did when the action was about to begin. He walked back to the cockpit and stood next to Owen.

"OK, everyone knows the plan. Keep the speed down to keep the noise to a minimum. Let them come to us. Out." Owen returned the mic to its clip. "Everyone to stations. Ready grapples and ladders."

Tobias popped his head above deck and jogged over to one of the .50-caliber machine gun turrets and strapped himself in, giving the turret a bit of a left right swivel to ensure it was operating. Delilah climbed into the other.

Luke grabbed a large duffel bag and opened it. Unzipping his heavy jacket and stripping it off, he set it aside. He took out his padded shirt and tossed it on, following with his scarf. Reaching into the bag, he pulled out a set of ornately carved and molded greaves. Smoothing out the denim of his skinny jeans, he strapped on the greaves. Next, he removed his lorica, which he shimmied into before using a leather strip to strap it closed.

The werewolves from the Coast Pack had never seen him gear up. They stared as he worked his way through the bag. He pulled on his tactical belt with its shoulder straps which crossed in the back. His gladius, he strapped to his left hip, the rudis so the hilt could be drawn with the left hand, just over the left shoulder. Taking out a hoodie, he slipped it on, covering his armor and the sword strapped to his back. Except for the greaves and the sword on his hip, he'd look like anyone else with a hoodie and scarf.

The boats slipped toward the massive freighter as it plowed through the water. People began flopping out bumpers on each side of their boats in case they missed their first tie up.

"Delilah, would you mind helping me get the rest of this ready? Someone else can handle the .50-cal."

Delilah crawled out of the small turret, a disappointed look on her face. "What do you need?"

"Let's get the shotguns loaded and ready. Then we'll need to load up the backpack. I brought my helmet, but I think I'll stuff it in there."

They took the shotguns out of the bag they'd stowed them in and began feeding shells into their magazines. When they'd been loaded, he pulled out his two sawed-offs and strapped one to his right leg, giving the other one to Delilah as a backup. Pablo strode over to help them. Taking the shotgun Luke used most of the time, Pablo loosened the strap so it would fit around the increased size of Luke's armored torso.

"Here, buddy, try this on. Make sure it'll fit and you can get it around." Pablo held up the strap and helped Luke slide it over his shoulder. "That'll work."

Luke practiced removing it a few times to get the motion clean with his increased bulk. The rest of the wolves who'd be going on deck prepped their guns and gear. Luke assumed these preparations were going on with the other boats as well, the North Portland Pack readying to make their next round of war on the vampires trying to invade their city.

As the freighter closed the gap between them, Owen pulled the boat around so their bows were aligned and both vessels were facing the same direction. Luke gathered his squad on the back of the boat. Making eye contact with each of them, he reached out and patted the shoulders of a few who looked like they might need the extra encouragement. He knew there would be wounds, but they were committed to the action. He was ready, his worries and fear pushed to the back of his mind where they wouldn't distract him from his job.

"OK, I'm going up the first line, and I'll hold the deck. Pablo and Ahmed will follow and get the ladder secured so the rest can follow. I'll cover you while they help the others over the top. Any questions?" No one spoke up. "OK, let's keep it quiet from here on out. I don't think they can hear us over the sound of their own engines, but let's not take chances. They're loud as fuck, so be wary of anyone sneaking around. If it's too loud, use your ear protection. That's why we got you special earplugs for your radios. The decibel levels on these things can exceed a rock concert depending on where you are."

Luke got out the grappling hook and ensured the rope hadn't tangled during its journey. Satisfied, he twirled the hook a bit, getting ready. Owen gave him a nod, signaling he was ready to do his part. Luke increased the circumference of his circles until he launched the grapple into the air and over the railing of the freighter. He pulled back until the grapple snagged on something. Luke tugged at it, putting most of his weight on it to see if it would hold well enough for him to climb.

"Don't fall in. You'll sink straight to the bottom in all that iron," Owen said.

"I can swim."

Owen's eyebrows shot up. "In all that?"

"Standard legionary training. I don't fancy doing it in this swell, but I can keep above water until someone fishes me out."

"OK…" Owen didn't seem too sure. "Once you get going, I'll back away from the side a bit so if you do fall, you won't hit the deck or get crushed in between. I don't want your corpse scratching the paint on my baby."

"Understood." Luke worked his way up the knotted rope, moving quickly for a man encumbered by heavy armor. He grunted in annoyance when a wave sent a spray up, soaking one of his calves. Just before the top, he stopped and popped his head above the deck to see if anything awaited him. Ducking and letting go with one hand, he gave the "OK" signal. He finished his climb and flopped over the top of the rail, sliding slightly on the foot the wave had soaked. He pulled his shotgun off his back and stood guard, making room for the next climbers.

Pablo was next. He shimmied up the rope, making quick work of it. Down below on the deck of the PT Boat, someone tied the end of the rope to a rope ladder and stood back. Pablo hauled the rope up. When he'd gotten it to the top, he affixed it to the rails, ensuring it was tight. He signaled down that all was ready. One by one, the squad from the PT Boat made their way up the ladder and over the rail. Delilah was last up. She had a rope tied around her belt. Once

Pablo helped her over the top, they pulled up the rope which had a large bag attached to it.

They opened it and pulled out several backpacks, including the one Luke had stashed his helmet in. They were distributed to the various members of the team so they'd have the tools they needed, including boxes of additional shotgun shells. With the large bag empty, they tossed it back over the side to land on the deck of the PT Boat.

A shot cracked on the other side of the ship, pulling Luke's attention away from their task. His mouth was half open, ready to order everyone to assist the other side, but they had their own objective. They'd have to rely on their teammates to handle their own objectives. He huffed and waved everyone to follow him toward the lane running down the middle of the ship from the bow to the superstructure.

# TWENTY-THREE

AFTER THEY PASSED the first row of containers, vampires boiled out of the darkness further down the central alley. Luke's sense of vamp went from present to oppressive as they rushed toward him and his people, who were running hard, shouting, and brandishing a variety of weapons. Luke and Delilah stepped to the front and flipped off the safeties of their shotguns. Ahead of them, the horde of vamps assembled against them looked thick enough to walk across. So many...

Luke pumped a shell into the firing chamber as the sounds of the rest of their squad following suit drifted up towards them. Off to his right, he heard a shotgun blast go off, then another. He couldn't see down the darkened gangway towards the path on the port side of the boat. His friends had engaged the enemy. He hoped he'd see them again, though against such a hateful mass, that seemed a fruitless hope.

Luke pulled his attention back to the vampires getting closer. He raised his shotgun to his shoulder, squeezed the trigger, and in quick succession pumped six shots into the crowd. As densely packed as they were, he had no fear of missing since every shot would hit something, though there were more than enough to replace the fallen.

With a bit of luck, some of the wooden or silver pellets would explode through a heart, turning the vampires into splatter debris. Delilah similarly unleashed her firepower into the crowd. They backed up several steps as the werewolves in line behind them stepped forward to take their places.

Luke and Delilah drifted to the back of their line and shoved shells into their guns so they'd be ready for their next round. Luke watched as the team did their best to hold back the oncoming tide. Those waiting their turn shuffled nervously, anxious to get to it while their eyes held fear at the numbers arrayed against them. After the people in front of them unloaded their shotguns into the vampires. Luke stepped forward and took his next round. Their incursion had held back the first rows of vampires as the groups in front of them literally vaporized, covering the fangers behind them in the spray of their companions. It sapped their enthusiasm to be first to defend their freighter. Luke started firing into the next rows.

The vampires jammed up as they crammed the narrow lane between stacks of shipping containers. The tight confines kept the engagement from tipping out of control in favor of the vampires who had numerical superiority in this fight, but eventually they'd overwhelm Luke and his small squad if he didn't get reinforcements from one of the other squads.

"Jam!" Delilah shouted.

Sparing a glance, Luke saw a smoking shell partially jammed in the ejection port. Delilah desperately tried to yank it out, but her sweat covered hands slipped over the plastic of the shell. In her escalating panic, she'd abandoned trying to unjam the mechanism using the pump to open the chamber all the way. Seeing her predicament, a vampire closed in on her raising a machete to strike her down. Forgetting the shell, she rammed the wooden stake bayonet into the vampire's chest. As he fell, he yanked the shotgun out of her hands before dissolving into sludge. The vampire next in line, seeing Delilah pulled forward and off balance, unleashed a wicked uppercut punch that knocked her backwards and off her feet.

Luke watched in slow motion as his friend went down and pumped the one shell he'd loaded into the magazine into the firing chamber, blasting the offending vampire in the chest, sending wood and silver ripping through its chest cavity. He stepped over Delilah, putting his body between hers and the horde of vampires. He yanked the pump back, expelling the spent shell. Not quite having enough time to even get a single shell loaded, he rammed the bayonet into the sternum of the vampire that'd gotten inside his reach. Holding the vampire at bay with the empty shotgun, he grabbed another shell. Shoving it into the ejection port, he rammed the pump forward and fired off the next round.

He punctuated the shot with a roar, venting his anger. At that range, the vampire's chest cavity dissolved into bone and gore splattered everyone behind him. A few of the silver and wood projectiles caught a vampire or two behind it. Luke reached down and grabbed another shell. Pump back, shell in, pump out, fire. Pump back, shell in, pump out, fire. Over and over and over again until he reached down and couldn't find another shell on his right side.

"Shit, it's happening," someone yelled behind Luke. "Pablo warned us. Get ready."

"What do we do?"

"Load your shotguns, we'll pass them up."

"Luke, right hand, drop the empty!"

Luke wasn't sure whose voice that belonged to, but he continued his advance, ramming his bayonet into the chest of the next vampire in line. Turning his head slightly, he saw a shotgun being stuck out for him to grab. He ripped the shotgun out of the guts of the vampire he'd just staked and dropped it, grabbing the offered one and pumping the first round into the chamber. He kicked out with his right foot, planting a vicious boot to the face of the vampire that had tripped in the goo of his fallen buddies. Luke would let someone behind him take care of its final death.

The wall of vampires in front of him began to shove back against their own lines, trying to escape Luke's wrath. In rapid succession, he squeezed the trigger, held it, then unloaded all his rounds into the front lines.

"Luke!"

Another shotgun was offered on his right side. He dropped his just in time to snag the new one, pumped a round into the firing chamber, and continued his death march. Out of the corner of his eye, he saw a hulking werewolf jump up and climb to the top of a shipping container. Letting their body drop, extending their arms, they yanked themself up, allowing them to grasp the top of the next container on the stack. Soon, the werewolf was at the top of the stack of containers and running down the line towards the back of the group of vampires. Reaching the point they wanted, they jumped down into the middle of the vampires near the back of their line. Whoever they were, they began shredding vampires with their claws, ripping open chests where they could or yanking off heads.

Luke fired off the last of his rounds, then pulled both swords from their scabbards and charged into the line. He didn't want a stray shot hitting his werewolf ally. While the wood would certainly sting, the silver could be lethal. Soon, any vampire that could get away used all their strength and speed to escape the efficient violence of Luke's advance and the terrible, body-rending chaos of the pissed off werewolf. Getting closer, Luke recognized the werewolf form of his friend Pablo. Of all the werewolves Luke had seen in action, none were so brutal in their treatment of vampire bodies than Pablo when he was defending his friends. He showed no mercy, allowing no opportunity for anything within his reach to escape. Turning up his own intensity, Luke laid about with his swords, ending the lives of the undead just as quickly as Pablo was. Finally, they met in the middle as the last few vampires went down or ran away. Both men were breathing heavily. Pablo bled from a series of claw marks, though none of them looked deep.

Archie, taking the brief respite, ran up with Jung-sook. He carried two shotguns. Setting one down by Luke, he pumped a shell into the chamber on the one he still held. "It's loaded Luke. We'll chase this lot down. You two catch your breath. Delilah's OK, I think."

Luke nodded at Archie and sketched a quick salute, sword still in hand. Handing his wooden rudis to Pablo, he pulled a rag out of his pocket and wiped down the steel blade of his gladius and returned it to its scabbard. He took his rudis back, picked up the shotgun, and walked back towards Delilah. A still-bayoneted vampire weakly writhed on the ground next to her.

"Pablo. Mind moving the shotgun out of my way?" Luke set down the gun he was carrying and stared down at the vampire, who stared back at Luke, hatred radiating from its eyes.

Pablo took hold of the shotgun with both clawed paws and yanked it out, giving it a good twist to add a little extra punishment to the vampire. Before the fanger could recover, Luke plunged his rudis down into its heart. He knelt over the impaled vamp; placing his forehead on the pommel, he recited the incantation that sent a white light winding down the silver inlay work of the wooden sword and into the chest of the vampire before the light wound its way back up and into the Luke. The vampire turned to goo.

He wiped down the rudis's blade on a scrap of shirt he found. Someone had propped Delilah up against the wall of the container where she'd fallen. Luke squatted down to examine her. There was swelling along the side of her face where the fist had landed. "You're going to have some serious bruising."

"Yeah. I bet. I've already got the headache to go with it. Fortunately, he just grazed my face. He caught my shoulder more."

"You're lucky he didn't break your jaw. How's the shoulder?" Luke asked. "How's the sensitive ear?"

"It hurts." She reached up and touched the ear that had blown out after the bombing. It was healing but didn't need more damage. "Earplug is still in. I don't feel too lucky. I feel like he swung an anvil at my body."

"Can you get up?"

"Yeah, let's try." She extended her good arm toward Luke. He grasped it, stood, and helped her rise to a standing position.

She leaned heavily against the container wall, her eyes closed and breathing shallower and a faster than normal.

"You going to be OK?"

"Yeah. Give me a second to finish clearing my head." She rotated her shoulder, wincing.

Luke extended his hand towards Pablo, who placed the shotgun he'd pulled from the vampire into it. Luke reached across his body and plucked some shells from the left side of his belt and loaded them into the shotgun before setting it down next to Delilah's leg. He unzipped the backpack she had on, pulled out a box of shells, and began stuffing them into his ammo belt. Pulling a second box out, he loaded the other shotgun, then worked a few into the empty spots on Delilah's ammo belt.

Delilah exhaled heavily. "OK, I think I can keep up."

"Good, we need to go see..."

A crack of a rifle followed by the yelp of a werewolf changed the sounds from distant grunts and screams punctuated by the occasional boom of a shotgun, to yelps of pain and angry wolves. Another crack and corresponding yelp rammed home the change in the situation.

"Shit. They've got someone up high with a rifle. Delilah, stay behind us. Keep up as best as you can. Let us know if you can't. I don't want you falling behind and getting picked off by a roving band, OK?"

"Got it." She let go of the wall, wobbly, but determined. She picked up the shotgun. "Let's move, but start slow."

Luke nodded, then turned around. If the shooter was on the superstructure, they could shoot down the three lanes running the length of the ship. If they were on the containers, it might limit their field of attack, but they'd be highly mobile which could grind their entire advance to a halt. The only way to move forward would be down the few rows running across the width of the ship, but to move to the next would leave one exposed as they worked down main lanes.

When he got to the first intersection, he posted up at the corner, and peeked around the corner briefly before stepping into it, shotgun leveled down the new alley. Keeping an eye down the lane, he used his head to indicate they should keep going down the row they were currently in. Once Delilah and Pablo made it across the intersection, Luke followed them.

They followed the trail of ruined clothing and vampire goo around a corner, then another until they spotted Archie and his squad crouching low while hugging the wall of the container behind them. Luke crept up to the corner of the container, opening up to the lane where his friends were pinned down. He peeked around the corner quickly. A wolf, still alive and moving, was down in the center of the lane.

"You two stay here. I'm going to chat with Archie."

Luke ran down the cross row to the port side, peeking out to see if he was clear. The wolves on this side had advanced ahead of Archie's position but had hunkered down when they heard a gunshot that wasn't one of theirs. Taking a chance the lane was clear, he darted out and ran to the row Archie was hiding in. Archie was working his way down and met him about halfway.

"Looks like we're in a spot of trouble here," Archie said, his calm British accent really selling the understatement.

"You might say that." Luke wanted to roll his eyes, but it was too dark for it to have any real effect. "How's…?"

"James. Alive for now. The shooter got his legs. Given time, he'll heal, but if the shooter puts one in his head, that might be more than his wolf can handle."

"Any idea where the shooter is?"

"Not exactly. The best I can figure is down, slightly to the right and up a couple levels. We're safe on this wall, but I'm not sure how far down until we're in range or not. All the cross walks on the upper levels are cutting down the sniper's shooting lanes, but without knowing where they are, it's hard to figure out where's safe."

A shot barked out, hitting the downed wolf in the arm, eliciting another yelp, this one more piteous than the previous which had been more tinted with rage.

"Bloody hell. Now that's just cruel." Archie shoved his fore and middle fingers in the air vaguely aimed toward the shooter.

Luke nodded in agreement. A low whistle sounded back down the alley from on high. Another shot ripped through the growing silence. Something flopped down hard on top of the stack of containers behind them. Luke raised his shotgun toward the sound. A head popped out over the edge. It was Sam, face painted dark to help her blend into the night. She crawled over the edge and let her body dangle before letting go, landing like a cat. Luke and Archie scooted down, making room for her. She zipped across the open intersection and joined them against the wall.

"Well, that was fun," Sam said. She spied the downed wolf and her face soured. "I know right where they are, but I can't get a shot off without them getting me first."

"About how far?"

"About seventy-five yards."

"Too far for a shotgun. Damn." Luke paced back and forth on the narrow corridor. "That leaves over the top off the menu. Unless..."

"Unless, what? We're not going to rely on your armor to protect you. There's too much exposed flesh, including your head. If that's a good sniper out there, that'll be enough. That's not a difficult shot at this range." Sam stared at the downed wolf in front of her. "They're probably not too far back from the edge of the superstructure to hit at this angle. If I can get a glimpse of their muzzle flare, I can put an arrow on them pretty fast."

"And we're back to my 'unless.' Delilah has my helmet in her backpack."

"Will it turn a bullet?" Sam asked.

Luke narrowed his eyes and nodded. "It should. It's got the same enchantments as the lorica."

Sam pursed her lips, raising an eyebrow. "Should? You're willing to risk everything on a 'should?'"

"At this point, we need to get to the bridge before they can call the Coast Guard, if they haven't already. Also, if they've got one sniper up there, it won't be long before they get more and start organizing a counterattack. We have to keep the initiative." Luke keyed in his radio. "Foxy Lady, this is Spartacus. I need the backpack. Give it to the Pooch to toss down this way."

"Copy," Delilah said over the radio.

"Wait until the signal," Luke added. "You'll know when. Out."

"Archie, take your shotgun and aim it up toward the top of the structure. When I say 'go,' fire. Give it a couple seconds between each round."

"I won't hit anything, not at this range," Archie replied.

"No, but hopefully he'll think we've got something a bit more long range than some 12-gauges. I just need a few moments of distraction." Luke kept his voice low, relying on the radio's microphone to carry his words so they wouldn't be overheard over the noise of the various engagements and the constant thrum of the freighter's heavy diesel engines.

Archie nodded and backed up to the corner, gun ready.

Luke peeked around the corner back toward the row where he'd left Delilah and Pablo. He saw a werewolf paw stick out from behind the container the owner was hiding behind. It gave him the "OK" signal.

"Archie, go."

Archie stuck his gun out into the open, exposing as little of himself as he could. He squeezed off his first shot one-handed, propping the butt of the gun against his arm. He pulled the shotgun back behind the container, pumped the next round into the firing chamber, and repeated his shot. While Archie provided distracting fire, Luke popped his head out to see a dark backpack floating through the air in a gentle arc toward his location. When it was in range, he snagged one of the straps and got back under cover.

Luke exhaled in relief. "Thanks, Archie. That's enough."

"Alright, mate." Archie nodded.

Luke clicked on his radio. "OK, I need a sprinter. Someone who can run and jump."

A voice Luke couldn't place called back. "I'll go."

"Good. Get a grapple and a shotgun from someone. Next, I need someone with a flare gun to get to the top of their section," Luke said.

"Copy that," answered someone else.

"When I say 'go,' stick your hand over the container and fire it toward the roof of the bridge. Don't stick your head up, just get it in the right direction. Keep the angle low."

"Understood," the wolf with the flare gun replied.

Luke looked over at Sam but left the radio button engaged. "Work your way up to just short of the top. When you're in position, let me know. When I give the signal for the flare, finish your climb and get your shot ready. Hopefully, the flare will blind the shooter and give you cover for a few seconds. At the point, I'm going to dive into the lane here. Hopefully, the flare can give you a good idea where the shooter's at and you can take them out. Sprinter, once the flare goes off, count to ten and then you're over the top. Get to the roof of the bridge as fast as you can. You might need to finish the shooter. Your job is to hold the roof until we can relieve you. Understood?"

"Yeah. I can manage that," the sprinter replied.

"Good. OK, everyone get in position." Luke opened the back-pack and pulled out his steel helmet. He'd left the crest at home. They didn't have enough space in the bag. He strapped it on, settling it snugly in place. He gave everyone another minute to ensure they were in position, then called out the checks.

"Flare?"

"In position."

"Sprinter?"

The only answer he got was a growl and a light yip. The sprinter had shifted to werewolf.

All he needed was Sam to signal she was ready. A moment later, the bird whistle she liked to use drifted down toward Luke.

Clicking the radio, he called out, "Everyone's in position. On my count. Three. Two. One. Go!"

The hiss of a flare lighting up the night sky sounded overhead, briefly illuminating the ground around them as it flew over. Luke leapt out into the central lane. Landing on his stomach, he rolled so his back was directed toward the shooter, providing a bit of protection for the werewolf who'd already taken a few rounds. He tucked his arms and legs in as best as he could and arched his head back so the neck guard on his helmet covered the gap at his neck. A shot rang out, striking the deck near his head, sending up sparks. The shooter must have taken an eye full of flare, throwing off his aim. Another shot barked out. This time, Luke felt a burning along the top of his buttocks.

"Fuck, that stings," Luke mumbled. He didn't feel the penetration of a bullet, but it must have grazed him. He tried to pull his limbs in tighter. In the distance, he heard two non-rifle rounds sound out.

Static buzzed over the radio, followed by a short yip.

"All clear," someone shouted.

Luke unwound himself and rolled onto his back. Pablo, still in wolf form, reached a giant paw down and helped his friend up. Several others were pulling the shot werewolf behind cover. The call for a medic went out. Everyone got back under cover in the alleyway they'd been hiding in earlier. Luke hobbled over to join them.

"Luke, you're bleeding from your butt," Delilah said.

Pablo chuffed his laughter, unable to laugh without his human vocal cords.

Luke groaned in annoyance. "My butt cheek, not my butt. It's just a flesh wound. It just grazed me, I think. When you say it that way, it sounds way more messed up."

She smirked at him. "I said what I said."

Sam slid down the ladder a few feet from where everyone was huddled. "Got him! Good plan, Luke. Everyone OK?"

Delilah, trying to control her laughter, chimed in, "Luke got shot in the butt."

"What?"

Luke let out an exasperated sigh. "The shot just grazed me — in the butt cheek. I did not get shot in the butt." He turned around to show her.

Sam turned to the pack member who was functioning as their medic for the mission. "Get Luke patched up first. We need to move forward." She turned to one of the other pack members. "Stay here and help James. Get him off the boat as soon as you can, then get back into position."

They both nodded. The medic looked at Luke. "Um, I'm going to need you to drop your pants."

Luke rolled his eyes and turned around. It took him a second to get to the belt buckle hidden just under the bottom edge of his armor. He pulled his pants down to his knees and leaned up against the wall of the container in front of him.

"This might sting a bit," the medic said.

Cold liquid hit the spot just above the wound and dripped in as more was flushed over the wound to clean out any incidental debris. This was followed by gentle patting.

"OK, I'm going to put some butterfly bandages to close it up, then a large pad over it. That should get you back in action." A few moments later, the medic gave him the all-clear to pull his pants up.

"No vampires to use?" Sam asked.

"We've been pretty thorough staking them. Had one a bit ago, but used it before I got shot," Luke replied.

"Oh, well. At least you're not hurt seriously. That flare probably stopped you from getting more broken ribs, or a nasty concussion if he bounced one off your helmet."

"Yeah, we got lucky, but we better not wait around much more or our friend holding the roof might bet lonely. Delilah, you good to keep going?"

She thought about it for a second. "Yeah, I'm good."

"OK, you, Sam, and Pablo are with me. Grab two more wolves. Everyone, make sure you're reloaded and have enough ammo. Delilah," he picked up his shotgun and handed it to her. "Mind making sure this is ready? I need to coordinate with Pieter."

"Spartacus to Waffleboy. Report."

"All clear back here. Just sweeping all the rows clean. Light resistance," Pieter replied.

"OK. Continue your sweep. I'm heading to objective A."

"Confirmed. Out."

"Archie, do you have enough support to continue sweeping the front half of this barge while we go over the top?" Luke asked. "We're bleeding time, and we're going to have to take some risks."

Archie looked around, assessing who he had left. He looked over at the person standing next to the medic. "Rhonda, when you're done helping James, get some more shells off the boat and meet back up with us." Turning to Luke, he said, "Yes, we'll clean them out."

Luke nodded at Archie. Taking his shotgun back from Delilah, he addressed everyone going with him. "OK, let's get topside and move out. Watch your footing. The mist is making the tops slippery. Does one of you have a grapple?"

"I have one," Ahmed said.

Luke nodded. "Alright, let's move out."

He took the broken bayonet handle and put it in the backpack Delilah was wearing, then let out the strap and slung it over his shoulder and across his back.

# TWENTY-FOUR

"ALL CLEAR." Luke pulled himself up on the container and took out his shotgun to cover his team as they pulled themselves onto the top row of containers, each of them helping the next person in line. "OK, Sam and I will take point. Ahmed, you bring up the rear. I don't want anyone sneaking up on us. Everyone else in the middle. Let's spread out a little."

Luke jogged forward, checking quickly to make sure there weren't any vamps hanging out on the walkway below. Finding the walkway clear, he leaped across the narrow gap between stacks of containers. He slipped a bit as he landed but quickly righted himself. He kept moving forward, checking the next gap to ensure it was clear. Glancing back, he saw everyone had made it across the first gap. He took a few steps back, then leapt to the next stack of containers.

As Luke got closer to the bridge, he could only make out the dim glow of the instruments and a few vague human-shaped outlines moving about. Whoever was running the bridge had turned out the cabin lights to keep things a mystery. Luke hated approaching blind but had little choice at this point. He jumped across to the next container, picking up speed before jumping to the last container and sprinting to the end so he was just under the window of the bridge, tucked away and out of sight. The rest of his team joined him.

"Grappling hook, please." Luke held out his hand. "Pablo, can you do your werewolf thing and let whoever's up there know not to shoot when we come over the top?"

Ahmed pulled the grappling hook out of his backpack and handed it to Luke. Luke stepped back, spooling out some rope. Swinging the hook around in bigger circles, he released it and gave it a tug to set it. He walked back to the rest of his team before putting all his weight on it to make sure it was truly set. With the engine noise and the groaning of the freighter and the containers, one clank would hardly be noticed.

Luke smiled. "Nice, got it on the first time. Pablo, we safe to start climbing?"

Pablo gave him a clawed thumb up.

"OK, Ahmed, you first. Keep an eye out for anyone unwanted." Luke pulled the rope around his back and grabbed it with his other hand to give Ahmed a stable rope to climb. The small man strapped the shotgun around his back and then zipped up the rope like a rocket. When he crawled over the top, he unhooked the grappling hook from the rail and wrapped it around and re-hooked it for a more secure placement. Satisfied, he leaned over the rail and gave everyone a double thumbs up. One by one, the werewolves, both in warrior werewolf form and human form, joined Ahmed on the roof of the bridge until only Luke and Delilah were left at the bottom.

Delilah leaned closer to Luke's ear. "Um, Luke. I'm not really good at climbing ropes and the hit to my shoulder is not going to help. I kind of skipped that part of gym class."

"It's only a short distance." He could see the worry on her face. "OK, no problem." He made a loop at about the height of his head before bending over and making another in a lower spot. He held up the lower loop. "Foot in here, grab the other loop, and we'll pull you up. Can you hold the rope while I go up first? I'll get to the top, then we'll pull you up."

Looking relieved, Delilah took the rope from Luke and wrapped it around her lower back like Luke had. An old pro, he was at the top lickety-split. He unhooked the grapple and handed it to Pablo before grabbing a section of the rope. Looking over the edge, Delilah gave him the thumbs up she was ready. Between Pablo's werewolf power and Luke's freshly juiced strength from the vampire earlier, they pulled her up easily.

The sound of a shotgun discharging yanked their attention to the back of platform. Luke unslung his shotgun and jogged back as more shots rang out. The wolf they'd sent over first was firing down the stairs that lead up to the roof. Luke split off towards the left side of the platform. The stairs were exposed below him. He leaned over the rail and began unloading shells into the back of the vampires trying to make it to the top. After five or six went down, the rest retreated into the interior that led to the crew quarters.

"Delilah, you take my spot here. Everyone, hold steady." Luke jogged back to the front of the roof and found the remains of the body of the vampire sniper. Sam must have put the arrow down the top of its shoulder into its heart. That's about the only way she could have killed the sniper with them laying prone. It was a hell of a shot. He picked up Sam's arrow and the rifle. Extending its strap, he threw it over his shoulder.

Rejoining his squad, he handed Sam her arrow and began issuing orders. "Ahmed, you join Delilah down at that end. Cover us while I clean off the stairs. Pablo, you're with me. Everyone else, wait at the top of the stairs until I signal you. Delilah, you and Ahmed follow them and guard the rear as we break into the cabins."

There were still a few bodies down below, a couple still moving. With a fresh stake bayonet attached to his M12, he popped around the corner, barrel leveled towards the door. When it open and a head poked out, he fired. The vamp yelped and pulled back. Luke gingerly stepped over the bodies still on the stairs, keeping the door covered. Pablo was following him, staking anyone that needed it. When Luke got close, he fired toward the door, hoping to angle at least some of the shot inside. A vampire, using its speed, yanked the door closed.

"Pablo! Get the door before they can lock it," Luke yelled.

Pablo leaped down the rest of the stairs and grabbed the wheel door handle, using his considerable werewolf strength to keep it from being turned by the vampire inside. He growled, his muscles bulging under his fur covered skin as he heaved with all his might in a tug of war. Luke watched the door as the struggle progressed, hoping Pablo's effort wouldn't be in vain, even as the gap between the door and the wall shrank.

Luke readied himself to pop through the door and sweep it clean of opposition as soon as Pablo yanked the door open. Making eye contact with his lupine friend, Luke nodded. Pablo put all his strength on pulling it open. As the seal broke on the door, shouts drifted from inside. Luke couldn't tell what they were saying, not sure if it was because there were too many speakers or too many languages. He got the gist of it; the vampires were trying to pull the door shut so they could seal it.

Luke flattened himself against the wall as another werewolf in bipedal form joined Pablo. A third stood ready, and as soon as the crack was wide enough, they stuffed their clawed hands in and pulled.

Luke raised his shotgun, taking aim at the hands and forearms he could now see. Making sure the wolfs' fingers were clear, he fired off a shot, blasting through one of the vamp's arms, leaving its disconnected hand dangling from the door wheel. Blood misted in the air as the silver and wood blasted into other vampire arms. The three wolves pulling on the door nearly fell over the railing at the sudden loss of a counterforce on the other side.

Stepping into the void, Luke unleashed the other five rounds, blasting left, center, right, center, left. He kicked a body out of his way and rammed his bayonet into the chest of a fallen vampire. Getting out of the way for whoever was following, Luke stepped out of the doorway, back against the wall, and pulled out his double barrel from its hip holster. Delilah followed him and fired off a steady barrage of shots further down the hallway, clearing a path through the vampires caught up both advancing and retreating. Luke, returning his sawed-off to its holster, hurriedly fed more shells into his shotgun. A wolf still in human form burst through the door and laid down another cover barrage before hiding behind a wall on the far side of the room.

Luke stepped back into the path and began blasting his way further down the central hall into the crew cabins. Delilah, fully reloaded, followed him.

"Can you get these doors?" Delilah asked.

The wolf in bipedal form reared back and kicked the door in for her. She stepped into the cabin, leading with her shotgun.

She poked her head out and shouted, "Clear!" before repeating the procedure with the cabin across the way.

The other wolf in human form fell in behind Luke, handing him her shotgun when he fired his last round. Working with supernatural werewolf speed, she rammed shells into the magazine, waiting for Luke to hand her another empty shotgun to refill. The resistance was literately melting in front of Luke's onslaught. The scatter gun was designed for this kind of messy work—short range with a spray pattern. Luke slowed his advance as the vampires in the rear fled back the way they'd come. Watching his step, he kept up his advance through the quickly slickening floors covered in dissolving vampire goo, the wood and silver pellets of the shotgun shells sending the vamps onto a true death.

Delilah kept calling out "clear" as she advanced behind Luke, checking inside each cabin. It wasn't until the second to last door on the right side of the corridor that her tune changed. "I found someone."

Luke shook his head hoping to clear the whine from his ears, although it was a futile gesture. Firing off guns in such tight confines had their consequences. He'd have to rely on draining a vamp to clear the shotgun induced tinnitus. "Alright. Everyone, halt here. Hold the line if anyone advances."

As soon as Luke crossed the threshold of the cabin, he was assaulted by the stench of waste. A Black man with gaunt cheeks and a pallid complexion sat in a corner, his legs and arms chained to multiple points on the wall. The manacles glinted in the dim light, the flesh around them angry and red with festering blisters. Angry breaths sizzled in and out of his mouth.

"Do you speak English?" Luke asked.

"Ja, I speak some."

"I speak German, if you prefer," Luke said in German.

"Thank you," replied the captive in the same language.

"What's your name?"

"Johann Wagner."

"Are you a member of the crew?"

"I'm the captain," Johann replied.

"Where's the rest of your crew?"

"Some are dead. I don't know about the rest."

"Are you a werewolf?"

Johann looked sharply at Luke, wariness returning to this face.

"Your wrists. Those manacles are silver, aren't they?" Luke asked.

Johann's face relaxed, his face sagging in defeat. "Yes."

"Are the rest of your crew werewolves?"

"The dead ones. When these fucking blood drinkers, these vampires, took over, they tossed all my wolves overboard into the Atlantic. They kept me alive because they needed me. They threatened the lives of the rest of my crew if I didn't cooperate. My crew follows their orders; the vampires use their magic eyes to control them."

"How did the vampires get on board?" Luke asked.

"They were hiding in containers."

"How'd they get out?"

"I found one of my crew letting one out. She was a new hire. She betrayed us." He spat in disgust.

"Probably a thrall." Luke nodded, acknowledging the betrayal the captain felt. "Do you know how many vampires there are?"

"No. I've only seen their leader and the few that captured me. They got me when I was asleep and locked me in here." Johann shifted his position, trying to get comfortable.

"How long have you been locked up?" Luke asked.

"I don't know...weeks."

"Can you move?" Luke felt for the poor captain. They both knew the responsibility of leading other people and the keen pain of failing them.

"Yeah. I think so. They've kept me fed and watered and walked, like some animal." His lip curled in a silent snarl.

"Do you know who has the keys to your lock?"

"The leader of the vampires. She's vicious. If I had the strength, I'd rip her to shreds." His face twisted in anger.

"Well at this point, I'm not sure if we've taken her out yet or not." Luke stuck his head out of the door and called out in English. "Archie. Can you grab the axe out of the fire suppression station, please?"

"Johann, I'm Luke. This is Delilah. Archie will be coming in shortly to bust you out of these chains. If we can, we'll see about getting those cuffs off you. I can offer you the protection of the North Portland Pack until this is over and you're healthy enough to figure out your plans."

"How can you speak for a pack?" Johann asked. "You're not a werewolf."

"True, but right now I'm leading everyone here, including the wolves. The pack beta is around here somewhere and will also officially extend the pack's protection. I can't speak for the Coast Pack in this matter, although I'm leading them as well for this mission, but only as it comes to this raid." Luke turned his head when motion outside the door caught his attention.

Johann nodded.

"Hey, Luke. Got the axe."

Luke stepped out of the way. "Thanks, Archie. Would you mind securing the release of our new friend? He's under our protection. His name's Johann. He speaks some English, not sure how your German is…"

"I speak a bit. I think we'll make do," Archie said.

"Delilah, let's go see if we can get onto the bridge."

Luke was just about out of the cabin when Johann called his name. "Luke, my cabin is at the base of the stairs up to the bridge. I keep a spare set of keys hidden in the compartment above my headboard. There's a false bottom. I don't think they've found the spot."

Luke nodded at Johann. Rejoining his crew at the end of the hall, Luke looked both directions. "Anything down that way?"

"No, just more empty cabins. We didn't go to the left," Ahmed replied.

"Anyone poke their head out?"

"No. I can hear some shouting, but I can't quite make out what they're saying, though."

"Thanks, I'm going to pop into that cabin below the stairs. Cover me."

Luke pumped his shotgun, loading a shell into the firing chamber. Checking the doorknob first and finding it locked, Luke solved the problem by kicking the door just to the side of the doorknob with the bottom of his foot. The door flew open and bounced back into the door frame. Someone behind him snickered. Poking the door with the barrel of his shotgun, he pushed the door open, finding the captain's cabin empty. It stank of vampire. They'd been using the room regularly. The sheets were mussed with a few drops of blood splattered on them.

Luke walked over to the bed to search for the false bottom in the compartment Johann had mentioned. Finding the edge, he lifted the lid, exposing the false compartment underneath. His fingers tripped across something that felt like a credit card. He tried to get a finger-nail under it so he could pry it away from the wall, but at the angle his arm was twisted to reach it, he couldn't make his body move that direction, not with the bulk of his armor making it more difficult. He pulled the dagger out of the sheath on his belt and used it to lift the card away from the wall. Success was the sound of plastic clacking lightly on the floor. After sheathing his dagger, he bent over and snagged a magnetic key card.

He gathered his advance team and took them back to the crew cabins corridor, speaking quietly so the vampires wouldn't be able to hear with noise of the freighter and the thick walls and doors separating them. "I'll unlock the door. I imagine they'll try to hold the wheel shut again. Pablo, can you get it open?"

The giant werewolf nodded, a feral grin spreading across his wolfy snout.

"It looks like it opens inward, so when Pablo gets the door opened, we're going to have to push our way through." He pointed to Jung-sook, still in human form and holding a shotgun. "You loaded and ready with that?"

"Yup."

"Good, you're with me. We'll go through first. Fire at anything that moves. If they're coming at us, they're hostile. Once we secure the door, we can assess. If they're any humans in there, we can sort them out if they allow us to."

Everybody nodded at him.

"Delilah, you and Ahmed will follow us in. Just make sure you don't shoot us by accident. Also, let's try to be gentle on the instruments. We might need that bridge intact. Understood?"

They gave him a round of thumbs up. Luke waved them after him. Everyone fell in line in the order they needed to be in to execute Luke's plan. Walking slowly so as not to raise an alarm that the bridge door was being approached, Luke snuck up to the door, putting his back up against the side opposite of the hinges. The vamps knew they were there, but they didn't need to know Pablo followed, doing his best to keep his claws from clacking on the metal decking. He gripped the wheel and got his body into position to give the maximum amount of torque his supernaturally strong werewolf body could give. Jung-sook took her position next to Luke. Delilah and Ahmed took up theirs a few steps back.

Luke looked around at this team, making eye contact with them one at a time. Each time he did, he got a nod back, indicating they were ready. He raised the key card to the pad and held it for a second. The red light blinked, then turned green, the sound of a lock signaling the plan was live. As soon as the lock stopped making noise, Pablo wrenched the wheel as hard as he could but only found the resistance it would normally have. When it stopped turning, reaching its terminus, Luke backed up to the door and shoved hard, adjusting his steps to swing with the door.

Someone was shouting into a radio in a language Luke wasn't familiar with. Another person, Luke got a strong vampire vibe, held an AK-47 pointed toward several humans in a corner. The barrel swung toward Luke but didn't finish its arc before Luke unloaded two shotgun shells into the vampire's chest, sending him flying into the instrument panel. Once he collided with the hard metal, he burst into a cloud of dust. The vampire shouting into the radio reached toward something on the panel Luke couldn't see. Whatever it was, the vampire's body blocked it. Luke didn't wait to find out. He pumped two more shells into its body, turning it into a matching pile of desiccated vampire dust. He turned and pointed his shotgun toward the corner, replacing the AK-47 with his Winchester M12. Jung-sook strode into the room, pointing her barrel toward the humans cowering in the corner. The rest of his squad followed them in.

"Any of you speak English?" Luke asked.

"Ja, I do," pipped up one man, his shaking hands held high above his head.

"Good. If there are any here who don't, please relay this message. I want you all to line up against the wall facing outward. Sit down. Keep your hands on your knees. If anyone moves, you will be shot. Do you understand?"

He nodded his head emphatically.

"Good. Please relay my instructions to the others."

The man spoke in rapid German. He didn't know Luke was fluent in the language, and there was no need to betray this fact. The man told his fellow crew mates Luke's instructions and what the consequences would be of violating them.

The man turned back to Luke. "I told them. Is it safe for us to move into the positions you asked us to?"

Luke nodded. "Yes, but slowly."

They shifted carefully, keeping their motions slow and deliberate until they were arranged as requested.

Luke addressed the man who spoke English. "Are you all the original crew? Translate that question, please."

The man rattled off more German. No one responded with an affirmation or rejection. Instead, they all got incredibly still, except their eyes, which all shifted toward a woman in the middle. Whether they'd done it intentionally or not, they'd identified the fox in the henhouse.

Luke pointed his shotgun at the woman. "Pablo, Jung-sook,

would you mind locking her in one of the cabins? I don't think her presence here will be useful."

Jung-sook leveled her shotgun at the woman while Pablo grabbed her by the shoulders and yanked her body into a standing position.

Luke walked up to her. "I'm assuming you speak English, thrall."

The tightening of her jaw and the narrowing of her eyes betrayed her understanding and apparent disdain for the word thrall.

"If she resists or tries to flee, shoot her."

The grin spreading across Jung-sook's face seemed to convey that she'd only be too happy to have an excuse to put a round into the vampire's pet. It convinced the thrall to go along, her face sagging in defeat. Keeping a clawed paw on one arm, Pablo marched her out of the bridge and back toward the crew cabins, Jung-sook following with her shotgun at the ready. As soon as they crossed the threshold out of the bridge, the remaining humans appeared to relax some.

Luke waited until they were well out of the way. "You don't seem nearly as surprised by my werewolf friend as I'd expect."

"We knew who and what our captain and crew mates are, were..." He collected himself. The memory of the treatment of his werewolf crew mates watered his eyes. "They were our friends and these fucking blood suckers murdered them. Then they made us do things..."

"And you're not under their control?" Luke asked.

"No...I mean, I don't think so." He sighed. "It's hard to know anymore what's real and not. I think after a while, they just decided that normal terror was enough to control us and so they stopped doing that eye thing. They had no need to fear us. They had their... thrall, is that what you called her? Anyways, their thrall kept an eye on us constantly. They outnumber us. They're stronger and faster than us. We did what we were told. We knew what would happen otherwise."

"That's understandable. How many vampires are there?"

"I don't know exactly. Dozens, maybe hundreds. They don't let us see much beyond maintaining the ship's operations or the galley."

"Have they been feeding off of you?"

The man shook his head. "No. Their leader won't let them."

"Did they bring thralls along? More than just that one?"

"Not that I've seen. I guess they could have brought bagged blood. We have refrigerated containers, too."

"OK, are you in good enough shape to show us around down below?" Luke asked. "It'd be better if we had a guide."

"Yeah. I can do that."

Luke sighed quietly in relief. The undersides of these big ships could be a maze, and he'd like to get off this ship before too much longer. "Good. Tell your crew mates we'll protect them from the vampires. Does anyone else here speak English well enough to take and relay instructions? I'm not sure if I have anyone else on my team who speaks German."

"Ja, Hilda speaks English some." He gestured toward a blond woman with short hair.

Luke addressed Hilda. "Hilda, you'll follow Delilah. She'll get you to a safe spot on the deck away from the fighting." He turned to Delilah. "Delilah, take them up to the bow. Grab a couple wolves to guard them, then head back here. Grab Pablo on the way by to help you. Also, if you see Pieter, send him my way. I think we're going to need his special prize."

"Got it." Delilah lowered her shotgun slightly and addressed Hilda, "Tell your mates to move toward the bow. And no fast movements. We wouldn't want any misunderstandings until this is all cleared up."

Hilda relayed the information. The crew stood up and filed out the door, being careful and deliberate so that no one could mistake any of the movements as hostile.

Luke looked back at the remaining human crew member. "What's your name?"

"Matthias."

"OK, Matthias. Can you draw me a map of the access points below deck and the layout of the engine compartments and their access points?"

"Yes. May I move? I need to grab some paper."

"Go ahead." Luke tracked him with his shotgun, not raising it, but keeping it at the ready in case Matthias tried anything. "Are there any guns on the bridge?"

"Ja, captain kept an old luger under the center console, about halfway back. I don't know if it's still there." He reached into a drawer slowly and pulled out a pad of paper and pen and set about drawing some maps of the information Luke had requested.

Luke bent over and checked under the dark console. He didn't see anything. Getting on his knees, he reached back until he felt the grip of a pistol. He pulled it out of the holster attached to the under-side of the console. Checking the firing chamber, Luke found it loaded and ready. He ejected the bullet and stashed the gun in his hoodie's pocket. Not wanting to leave the AK-47 for anyone to find and figuring it would be a nice addition to his growing arsenal, he picked it up and handed it to one of the human-form werewolves.

"Might as well keep it. Make sure to get it back to me when we hit shore."

She nodded and replied, sling it over her shoulder. "Got it."

LUKE WAS WRAPPING up with Matthias and the maps when someone called up into the bridge. "Luke, you better get down here!"

Luke worked his way down the stairs, werewolves and people squishing up against one side of the wall to make room for him to get through. When he got to the bottom, he found out who'd called him down.

"What's going on, Archie?" Luke asked.

"Take a peek out the door. Something doesn't look right."

He took the handle and cracked the door, inching his head out until he could see what Archie was talking about.

"Well, fuck. They've set up a nice little killing field out there..." He pulled his head back just as a shot rang out and blasted into the door, yanking it out of his hands and flinging it open. After the rela-tive calm of the bridge, his adrenaline started pumping again. "Yup."

The vampires had moved the various vehicles that had been

rolled onto the freighter and set up a wide-open space with the vehi-cles forming a fortified wall of steel and glass. If the vampires had heavy arms, as it appeared they did, they'd open fire and create a wall of bullets in the open space. It would be a massacre.

He turned toward his team and looked them over. "They've moved all the cars down there to form a killing field that starts just outside this door and runs for quite a ways down the deck. Then, it's cars turned sideways forming a barricade. They're lined with rifles and automatics. No one's going out there and living."

Luke took a deep breath, darted out, grabbed the door handle, and yanked it closed as another round of bullets flew toward where he'd just been. He fished the key card out of this pocket and used it to lock the door. He shoved on it, making sure it was firmly latched after the damage it had taken. "Alright, everyone back upstairs."

As they made it back upstairs, Jung-sook and Ahmed emerged from one of the cabins with the captain. He'd taken a few minutes to wash off the collected weeks of his own filth and put on some clean clothes. His wrists still looked nasty with red pus-filled blis-ters where the silver manacles had kept him tied down and powerless.

"Captain Johann, you're looking a bit better," Luke said.

Johann rubbed his wrists. "Ja, thanks for letting me get cleaned up, and thanks to your crew for prying the manacles off. Please, call me Johann. I'm not much of a captain if I can't keep control of my own vessel."

Luke could hear the dejection in his voice. "A massive swarm of vampires is more than you and a handful of other werewolves and humans can handle. What was your crew, fifteen? Seventeen people?"

Pieter stepped through the door leading to the stairs from the roof of the bridge along with a couple of the North Portland Pack's wolves. Luke held up his hand to stop Pieter from speaking until he was finished speaking with Johann. When Pieter acknowledged Luke, he gestured for Johann to continue.

"Twenty-one," Johann replied.

"Twenty-one, even with some of them being werewolves, isn't

enough against those odds. But right now, I need a captain's knowledge of his vessel."

Johann nodded, straightening up. "That I can provide. How can I help?"

"I can't get to the engine room through the decks below. They've got a killing field set up, and I'm not risking my team to take out a few hundred vampires with heavy firearms in a fortified position. I need to get explosives on the diesel tanks."

"You're...you're going to blow up my ship?" Johann's jaw dropped, his eyes opening wide in shock.

Luke hated to be blunt, but time was not on their side. "As you've said, it's not your ship anymore. It's theirs." He pointed toward the stairs. "And I need to make sure they don't make it to land. I don't have enough werewolves to take them all out, and they'll get someone out here who can steer this thing into port. I need your knowledge to protect Portland, both humans and werewolves."

Johann stood frozen for a few moments before he collected himself. "Right. Right. I can do that. It's going to be cramped, and we won't be able to get everyone down there this way. Also, you'll need ear protection. It's loud down there."

"Right. Ear protection we have." Luke pointed to the two werewolves who had the C-4 explosives and detonators. "Pieter and Rhonda, you're with me. Anyone got a box or two of shells I can have? Also, I need one more volunteer with a shotgun."

Jung-sook raised her hand as people rifled through backpacks, pulling out what spare shells they could find. They distributed them to Luke and Jung-sook.

"OK, Jung-sook, you bring up the rear. I'll go in first with the captain behind me. Pieter and Rhonda, you'll be in the middle. Delilah, you and Pablo get everyone onto the deck and back on their boats. I want as many people off this boat as possible, so when we're done, we can get out of here. Archie, pick a couple of people and hold the top of that stairwell. They may decide to see why we aren't trying to attack their position and come see what's up."

Archie saluted, then pointed to a couple of his packmates still in human form and toting shotguns. They disappeared back up the hall toward the stairs that led to the lower decks. Pablo and Delilah began organizing the pack and made sure everyone was loaded and ready to go. Luke pulled out his radio and gave the evacuation code to anyone listening. The other squads responded in the affirmative.

"OK, Johann. Lead the way." Luke gestured for the captain to proceed.

The captain, mustering a last reserve of strength, took them through a warren of gangways and narrow, winding paths through the inner workings of the ship until he signaled they were there.

He pointed toward the end of the room. "That door leads to the engine compartment."

"OK, you guys get the explosives planted." Luke walked down the last few stairs and over to the door. He found a huge wrench on a shelf and used it to wedge the bulkhead door locked, fitting the wrench head into the crook of the wheel and placing the other end in the corner of the door. If anyone tried to crank the wheel open, it would block them, using their motion to further lock the wrench in place.

Pieter called down to Luke, "Luke, we're done here."

Luke climbed the stairs, stopping to inspect the rows of C-4 plastic explosives wired together.

Rhonda tossed a remote at him. "Twist the dial to arm it, push the button to detonate. It's got an OK range, but with this much hull between us and the receiver, you might have to be pretty close to light it off."

Luke nodded. "Alright, let's get out of here."

They made room for Johann to get in front to lead them out. Luke brought up the rear this time. Once they got back to the main structure, they grabbed Archie and his packmates and made their way back on deck to the central walkway.

Luke clicked the talk button on his radio. "Spartacus calling Foxy Lady, we're finished up here. How's your end going?"

"Good. All the survivors are split up and on boats. We've got a few people up here keeping an eye on the ladders down, but most people are on their boats and floating away... Hold on." Delilah clicked out. A moment later, a static burst announced her return.

"You better get your ass here in a hurry. Our hosts just intercepted a message from the Coast Guard. They're a few minutes out and prepping to dock with the freighter."

"Fuck. Just what we need, the government poking their nose in our business," Luke said.

"I don't think it's the government who are in control of the boat coming in. Captain O says they've been communicating with the freighter as if they know each other," Delilah replied.

Luke sighed and shook his head. "So, the vampires have a Coast Guard vessel now…"

"Looks like it. O is moving everyone to other side of the ship so the freighter is blocking them from the Coast Guard."

"Does he have any idea what vessel is coming in?" Luke heard Delilah shouting something away from the mic as she left the button depressed.

"He says it's the cutter out of Astoria."

"Well, hell. Alright, we're moving as fast we can. We'll be coming out hot, so keep your fingers off the triggers. Out." Luke turned to the seven people following him. "Johann, we're going to need to move fast. Can you keep up?"

"Do I have a choice?"

Luke reached out and squeezed Johann's shoulder, before addressing the rest of the remaining team. "A Coast Guard cutter out of Astoria is nearly here. Owen's not sure, but it sounds like it's under the vampire control, or they're collaborating somehow. We've got to move fast. We're going down the central lane. Archie, you take your team down the right side, call out clear or not. Jung-sook, Ahmed, you're with me on the left. Pieter, you stick with Johann and make sure he can keep up."

They walked through the hall under the bridge. Archie grabbed the door and waited for Luke to give them the go ahead to open it. Luke popped out and swept the deck making sure no one was waiting for them.

"Clear! Go."

For once, things moved smoothly. Archie called out "clear," on each crossing as did Luke until they emerged onto the bow. Luke was relieved to see Pablo and Delilah waiting for him. Although the other werewolves had performed admirably, he'd grown accustomed to Pablo and Delilah's presence at his side. He almost felt naked without them.

"Pablo, you and Jung-sook help Johann down onto the fishing boat. The rest of you, with me onto Owen's boat. We may need some extra crew."

Pablo, still in wolf form, went first in case the captain fell. Jung-sook followed. Luke sent everyone else down the ladder onto the PT Boat while he kept watch. When it was finally his turn, he threw his shotgun over his shoulder and vaulted over the rail and down the ladder while several shotguns were leveled at the deck in case anyone got too close.

# TWENTY-FIVE

"TOBE, get those .30-calibers out and set up, now!" Owen shouted.

"Yes, sir."

"We're going to need to give people time to get away. Tell everyone to keep the freighter between them and that incoming cutter. Let's hide behind the freighter, use it to shield us from their radar. Then we can pop out and distract them if we have to," Luke said.

"Roger that." Owen began issuing orders on the pack's radio frequency.

As people made it down their ladders onto their boats, the boats, which had been moving alongside the freighter until they needed to extract their crew, sheared away from the freighter, taking a southerly course. Owen kept the PT Boat steady alongside of the freighter, trying to keep the freighter's bow wake from throwing them too far away and out into the open.

Luke kept scanning around. He heard some shouting from above. Looking up, he saw a head poking out from the side, peering down at the boat. Luke raised his shotgun and squeezed off a shot but missed as the vampire used its preternatural speed to pull back as soon as it saw Luke lifting his shotgun. The freighter plowed ahead on a general course to the mouth of the Columbia, no one at the helm, either running on automatic or its great bulk keeping it steady for now. Whoever was up on the deck must have alerted the cutter. They heard its klaxon calling everyone to stations.

"I think they've been alerted to our presence. Drift back. Let's see what they'll do," Luke called out.

They didn't have to wait long. Rising over the edge of the freighter and into the sky, the cutter's HH-65 helicopter lifted into the air. It swooped toward the line of retreating fishing boats.

Owen's head tracked the helicopter. "Well, shit. What do you recommend now, boss?"

Luke raised the binoculars and tracked the helicopter. He watched the side door slide open and a long, black barrel emerge from within. The sound of machine gun fire and the light of barrel flashes alerted them to the helicopter's intent.

"They just fired on those boats..." Owen sounded stunned. As a fisher on the Pacific coast, he knew of more than a few people the Coast Guard had saved, including a few of his packmates.

Luke dropped the binoculars as the fishing boat caught fire. In the light of the flames, Luke saw bodies jumping into the ocean. Owen froze.

"Delilah, take that thing down!" Luke yelled.

Delilah pulled back on the hammer, cocking the twin .50-cal brownings. She swung the unit around, took aim, and fired off a burst of rounds before adjusting and firing again. Satisfied, she fired off a longer burst, zeroing in on the Coast Guard helicopter. The .50-caliber guns vibrated the wooden PT Boat as Delilah poured rounds into the night sky until she found her target, ripping it to shreds and sending it spiraling in flames down into the waves.

"Holy fuck, you just shot down a Coast Guard helicopter..." Owen said.

Luke yanked the radio out of Owen's hand and keyed it in. "Everyone, pass out life jackets. Evasive maneuvers. That cutter is going to be going after everyone."

Owen stared, wide eyed and open-mouthed. "Shot it down..."

Luke reached out and shook Owen's shoulder. "Owen, you've got to pull it together. That wasn't the Coast Guard, at least not the ones you know. They're under the control of the vampires. They'd never fire on civilian boats like that. I need you to pilot this barge now."

"Barge?!" Owen's eyes focused on Luke, the insult pulling him out of his daze.

"Good. You can punch me when we get back to shore, but right now, I need you here. We need to distract that cutter before it fires on our friends. I want you to throttle up to about half speed and make toward the burning boat. We've got to get some life vests in the water in case they're not wearing any. Also, it'll give the cutter something to focus on."

"Yeah, yeah. Got it. Tobias, get below and pull out some life vests. Pass them around to everyone, then get a few extras." He reached down and shoved the throttle to the halfway mark.

The boat lurched forward, a thoroughbred released from its tether. Luke was nearly knocked to the ground by the sudden surge of power. He braced himself as Owen swung the boat toward the potential survivors. Tobias, staggering under the awkward load of life vests, shoved them at Luke before disappearing to grab more. Luke took them and walked to the rail.

"I see them up ahead. Slow down a bit. I don't want to hit them," Luke yelled.

Owen complied. As they got within throwing distance, Luke threw several life vests toward the cluster of people in the water as they passed. Luke spied another couple people treading water ahead. He threw a few more vests into the water as close as he could get them to the survivors. One of the fishing boats was swinging around, probably intending to rescue the people in the water.

"Owen, someone's swinging around to come after the survivors!"

Owen looked over. "Fuck, it's Lauren. Of course it is. Well, shit. We'd better keep that cutter busy because there's no way she's listening to me."

"I didn't think she would, not in a case like this. It's probably for the best, though. This water's too cold for prolonged exposure." Luke settled into the cockpit next to Owen. "Swing this beast back around. Keep her pointed toward the shore. I want to get some space on that freighter. What do you know about this cutter?"

"It's a Coast Guard cutter..."

"Is it big, old, new? Does it have one of those big deck guns?" Luke asked.

"Nah. Old. I think it can only handle about 20 knots. But it's got some .50-cals and a cannon, maybe 25mm size."

Luke pursed his lips. "Shit, that'll tear through those fishing boats. What's your armor like on this?"

Owen laughed. "Not a lot. These things were made for speed, not to take a beating."

"Well, you're faster. Let's use that speed."

Owen edged the speed up further. Despite being early spring, the Pacific Ocean was treating them kindly without a storm in the short-term forecast. The gentle seas allowed the PT Boat to maximize its big engines and design to its best affect, allowing it to nearly double the speed of the cutter, while keeping it more maneuverable than the Coast Guard ship which was nearly three times as long.

While Owen piloted the boat, Luke looked around, checking on the ship's crew. Delilah, as focused as ever, stared in the distance toward the oncoming cutter, her guns trained on it. The rest of Owen's people looked steady, save for the small signs Luke had seen thousands of times through the centuries—nervous shuffling, fingers tapping, and fidgeting, jerky neck motions as every sound or sight was tracked... Some turned back to the burning debris of the sinking ship or the downed helicopter, seeking a reminder of why they were about to open hostilities with the United States Coast Guard. They'd do their parts when the time came.

"Start edging it north," Luke said. As they rounded the blind spot the freighter provided, they saw the cutter pulling a tight circle, trying to get turned around and ahead of the freighter.

Owen's eyes narrowed. "What the hell. That doesn't make any sense. They should have kept going straight and pulled around the back of the freighter. Who's the moron who decided on that maneuver? They've spilled all their speed."

"Well, like I said, even if it's Coast Guard personnel at the helm, they're being piloted by vamps, and clearly not a vamp with a good understanding of how to pilot a ship. Bring me up on her tail, but not too close," Luke said.

Owen throttled down some and made the sweeping turn, carving a large S as he aligned his bow toward the tail of the cutter.

"Owen, this is good. Try to match her speed." Luke raised his voice some. "Delilah, put a burst along her tail, please."

She complied.

"Owen, you got a white flag we can run up?"

"Tobe, grab a pillowcase off one of the bunks." The boy ran below deck and emerged with a pillowcase and a broom. He grabbed a roll of tape and affixed the pillowcase to the broom handle before handing it to Luke.

"Delilah, another burst please," Luke called.

As the .50-caliber rounds thudded into the hull of the cutter, a spotlight swung around, finally finding the PT Boat. Luke waved the broom back and forth. Someone at the helm cut the speed. Owen matched his speed as the large boat moved forward in its lazy arc, spilling more speed. They saw shadows appear near the tail on the railing. Luke raised the binoculars to his eyes and mumbled, "Son of..."

Cassius stared back at him through his own set of binoculars.

"That PA speaker work?" Luke asked.

"Yeah, why?" Owen replied.

"Hand me the mic and switch on the PA, please."

Owen handed him the mic and then flipped the switch to the speaker.

Cassius lifted a megaphone. "Lucius? How the hell do you always find your way into my plans? And where'd you dig up that old piece of shit?"

Luke pushed the button on the mic. "Cassius..."

Before Luke could finish his sentence, Delilah opened up her twin .50-caliber machine guns. Everyone on the deck of the cutter dove for cover. Luke reached over and pulled the wheel so the PT Boat pulled to the left, taking it out of the arc of Delilah's machine guns. After a few seconds, she let off the trigger with an angry sounding grunt.

He let go of the mic button. "Damn it, Delilah. You can't kill him with that thing. We're trying to buy time," Luke hissed just loud enough for Delilah to hear. He let go of the wheel. "Sorry about that, Owen. Figured that was the quickest way to stop her."

"No, good thinking."

Cassius popped his head over the railing to see if it was safe. He rested the megaphone's rim on the edge, refusing to stand completely. "That wasn't very nice. And under a flag of truce. I thought better of you, Lucius."

"Unlike you, I don't control the minds of my companions, or in your case, underlings. Some of them have righteous beefs with you."

Cassius chuckled. "Ah, your little friend? She still mad about that thing with her father?"

Delilah let out a steady stream of curses, placing her hands on the rails around her turret and gripping them tightly to keep her hands from the temptation of the trigger. Owen looked amused at the entertainment unfolding around him.

"She's going to kill you, you know." Luke snorted at Cassius's stupidity. Taunting Delilah was never a good idea.

"She wouldn't be the first to try, but if she manages it, she'll be the first to succeed. I don't see that happening."

"Where'd you get the cutter?" Luke asked.

"Took it. Where'd you get the antique?"

"Favor from a friend."

Cassius stood, leaning on the railing with one arm as he returned the megaphone to his lips. "It suits you. An antique man wearing antique armor floating on a delicate little piece of antique plywood."

"I don't know why you're making fun of antiques when you're just as much of one."

"Yeah, but I've moved on. Picked up new hobbies. Found new paths of fulfillment. You're the one running around in a tin can, acting like an asshole. You should find a hobby or get a job. Maybe enroll in community college."

Several of the werewolves standing at the various stations

snorted.

"I hear companies are looking for truck drivers," Cassius continued.

"It's good, honest labor. Wouldn't be the first time I've done it," Luke replied. "But honest labor isn't something you and your kind are familiar with. Always the great exploiters." Luke shook his head.

"Exploit this," Cassius bit out.

Cassius was surrounded by activity as vampires began popping up, holding what looked like automatic weapons. A couple of them were attaching a much bigger machine gun to the railing.

"Owen, that's our cue to get the fuck out of here. Back around the freighter. Open fire!" Luke yelled.

Owen's other .50-cal turret opened fire as the smaller machine guns swung around to target the deck. A mix of .50-cal and .30-cal bullets zinged about the back of the cutter, sending vamps and their thralls scrambling and occasionally hitting one or two. Delilah was the only one who couldn't bring her guns to bear, so she fired up at the railings of the freighter as vampire heads popped up to watch the goings-on down below. Her anger was rewarded when she caught a couple people in her sights, their heads exploding like melons meeting a sledgehammer.

"Grow that back, you fanged assholes," Delilah shouted.

"Remind me never to cross her," Owen said.

"Smart move," Luke agreed, waiting for them to make the turn around the back of the freighter.

As the angles shifted, the gunners stopped firing one by one. Delilah, getting a chance to fire at Cassius one last time as her turret came back into the right angle, fired off a steady burst until she too lost sight of the cutter as they pulled fully behind the freighter.

They'd bought some time for their flotilla, but Luke wanted more. Even more than time, though, Luke needed to stop the pursuit entirely, or Cassius would chase them down and destroy their fishing boats.

Luke's eyes flicked toward the torpedo strapped to the deck of the PT Boat, a vicious grin spreading across his face. "I think we'll need to borrow a torpedo or two."

"You going to swim out and get them back?" Owen asked. "With all the rounds we've fired off and now my torpedoes, you're going to owe me a pretty penny."

"I'm good for it."

"Good. Don't suppose you know your way around a torpedo, do ya?"

"No. I can load and fire an eighteen-pound cannonade, if that helps." Luke shrugged.

Owen shook his head. "It doesn't."

"Last boat I was on with a torpedo tube was a confiscated German U-boat during the Great War, and I was just a passenger."

"Tobe, get your butt up here," Owen called.

Tobias left his gun station and joined his uncle in the cockpit.

"Take the wheel. We're going to make a torpedo run on that cutter. You remember what to do?"

Tobias nodded nervously. "Yes, sir."

"Good. I want you to swing out more to the southeast. We need more distance when we come around the freighter and make our run, OK?" Owen didn't wait for the answer. He was already heading toward the port torpedo strapped to the front third of the boat. As he leaned out over the torpedo, the wind picked up the hair of his long ponytail, streaming it out behind him. "OK, take her on a northeasterly heading now."

"Yes, sir." Tobias banked the fast-moving torpedo boat to the left and adjusted his course to meet his uncle's orders.

The cutter had finally made its turn and was coming around, trying to resume its pursuit of the fishing boats.

Luke shouted over the noise of the engine and hull slapping over the waves, "Forward guns, short bursts along the rails and super-structure! Let's remind them of their mortality."

The twin .50-cal turrets opened up, as did the .30-cal on the nose stand. They swept the deck, working in short, controlled bursts. Delilah focused on the superstructure, probably hoping to put a half inch bullet or twenty into Cassius. Even if she couldn't kill him, she could hurt him. Despite her anger, she still followed orders and kept her bursts short and strategically aimed.

Owen relayed hand signals to Tobias, directing him to adjust their course to the left or right so he could line up his shot. Judging the distance right, he armed the torpedo and yanked the release, letting the torpedo flop into the water where it took off in a sizzling line toward the cutter.

"Bring 'er around to the port side, Tobe," Owen shouted as he walked toward the cockpit. "Put us back behind that freighter."

The gunners kept up their short bursts just to be cautious. Everyone else stood, watching the line in the water work its way toward the bright white cutter with its orange diagonal stripe. Luke raised the binoculars he'd been using and watched the deck of the cutter. Finally, a few people standing near the rail noticed the torpedo speeding toward their hull. They waved and shouted frantically, pointing toward the water, but it was too late. The boat tried swinging away from the torpedo but ended up providing a better target.

The torpedo exploded into the side of the cutter, sending up a column of water and smoke. The explosion reverberated over the vessel, sending shivers over its frame as if a giant placed a fist around each side of it and shook it before placing it back in the water. They watched the cutter list to the side as it took on water until Tobias yanked the wheel hard, knocking several people off balance. The clack of small arms fire alerted them to a new danger. The gunners on the port side of Owen's boat began working the decks of the freighter, trying to keep the vampires from getting easy shots at the PT Boat and its crew and passengers. Tobias edged the throttle up and started arcing away from the freighter.

"Swing us back around! We're moving out of range. Swing us around the tail," Luke called, frantically reaching into his pocket to grab the detonation remote.

Tobias looked at Owen, "Uncle?"

"Listen to him, Tobe."

Luke fished the detonator out of the pocket of his hoodie. He rotated the switch, arming it. The light switched from red to green, indicating it was armed. He held his breath and depressed the button. Nothing. He waited a few more seconds and gave it another push. Still nothing.

"Tobe, give us a bit of a zig zag. Let's not make it easy on them," Owen ordered.

The gunners were alert, waiting to fire if needed. Luke was getting concerned about the remaining ammo. They'd been shooting a lot. They were practically on top of the freighter when Luke's button-pushing got a result. The muffled sounds of deep thumps rocked the freighter. What they hadn't expected was what happened next. The superstructure vaporized into a huge plume of flames as the diesel ignited, exploding in the tanks. The shock wave knocked several people over and shoved the PT Boat sideways, rocking it hard to its port side.

"Shit, give me the wheel, Tobe." Owen slid behind the wheel and brought it around hard, so they turned away from the flaming freighter. "Uh, how many billions of dollars have you just sent to the bottom of the Pacific?"

"A fair few, I'd imagine," Luke replied, half-distracted watching vampires jump into the water to avoid the growing conflagration on the deck of the freighter. The ship still appeared to be coasting forward and hadn't started listing. "How do you feel about one more torpedo run? There are still several hundred vampires on that ship. We didn't kill as many as we needed to."

"Fuck it, why not?" Owen appeared to be trying to rationalize the wanton destruction he'd just participated in. "Might as well make a thorough job of it..."

Luke pointed toward the rear of the freighter. "Let's see if we can put it on the back corner. If we damage the roll-on ramp, that might help flood it a little quicker."

"Hey, Luke. Will vampires survive underwater?" Delilah asked.

"I don't know. They're not terribly buoyant. Plus cadaver, be it ambulatory or not, is a favorite food for a lot of things in the ocean. Even if they survived, it's a long walk to shore through miles of things that'll look at them as free food. How deep is the Pacific here, Owen?"

"This far out, about a mile and half or so. We're past the continental slope," Owen replied.

"I don't know if that depth will crush a vampire, but I don't imagine anything going into the water will be coming up anytime soon."

Delilah had a wicked grin on her face. "Good." She sat back in her turret and watched the vampires fall into the ocean trying to avoid the flames of the freighter.

Owen got the PT Boat into position for its torpedo run. Before he handed the wheel over to his nephew, he throttled down to about ten knots. "We don't need to evade fire at this point. Might as well not waste my last torpedo trying to be fancy."

He went to the one remaining torpedo and repeated the process from earlier, giving Tobias hand signals to help him align their shot. Satisfied, he yanked the lever that released the torpedo into the water. "Tobe, throttle it back to zero. I want to watch this one."

Owen pulled out his own set of binoculars and watched the white snake flying through the water toward the rear of the freighter. Everyone stood to get the best angle and waited on bated breath, counting the seconds of what felt like an ever-expanding clock. Finally, the torpedo hit home, plunging into the back of the freighter. The sound rocked them back as water and smoke spouted into the air. Drops, riding the shockwaves, sprinkled them. The sides of the hull rippled out from the explosion, sending the freighter forward and bucking the back nearly out of the water. The long ramp the freighter used to load or off-load all the trucks and cars below decks quivered and groaned. The stress of metal bending and breaking was followed by the ramp slowly falling to one side, dragging into the water, and pulling the back of the freighter down. They could see the turbulence of the water rushing into the back of the ship, filling the lower levels.

"And you got all the humans and werewolves off, right?" Owen asked.

Luke snorted. "Little late for that, but yeah, we were thorough."

Owen gave one last look toward the freighter, gently moved his nephew to the side, and throttled up the PT Boat. "Let's go find your mom."

He selected a more sedate speed to conserve their fuel reserves. As they rounded the side of the freighter, now listing hard to the tail and lifting the bow out of the water, they saw the cutter flop over and disappear below the surface. A couple lifeboats were floating away from the cutter.

Owen looked over at Luke. "Do we go after them?"

Both boats were motoring away from the freighter. Although they'd originated from the cutter, they were going in virtually opposite directions.

"How much ammo do you have left?" Luke asked, staring after the boats.

"Tobe, go check, please."

"I can already tell you there's nothing below deck, but I'll check the guns." Tobias walked from gun station to gun station, popping open the belt containers feeding each of the guns. "Maybe seventy to eighty rounds total."

Luke took a moment to think. "No. That might not do it. Also, the way they're acting, one of those boats is probably the human crew. Right now, they're probably coming out of whatever glamour the vamps had them under, and they're concentrating really hard on getting away from them. Let's slip away. You live to fight another day, Cassius."

Owen nodded and steered them away from the lifeboats and into the darkness shrouding the fleet of fishing vessels. Eventually, he looked over at Luke, catching eye contact. "By the way, what did that guy call you? Loo-keye-oos?"

"Lucius. Yeah, that was my name when we knew each other, back when I only had the name my mother gave me at birth..."

AFTER THE ALL THE boats were gathered, and Owen got the all clear from Lauren that the survivors were picked up, the flotilla put on some extra speed to gain more distance between themselves and the fleeing vampires while the PT Boat served as a rearguard. Once they felt comfortable, they slowed down and spread around the last of the extra diesel until they met up with the boats heading out to meet them with extra fuel.

While they paused in the middle of the ocean to spread around the spare fuel to the boats that needed it, Maggie, who'd been on the fuel boats sent to meet the fleet, checked in with the various crews, attending to the injured from the boat the Coast Guard helicopter had sunk, packmates who'd taken injuries on the freighter, and the rescued hostages. As Maggie attended to the injured, the fleet drained the barrels the relief boats had brought and readied to split the fleet so they could return to their various ports, avoiding Astoria and further Coast Guard involvement. Maggie's last stop was the PT Boat.

Luke, offering her a hand to help her across the boats bobbing up and down in the ocean swell, guided her safely to the deck. When her feet were stable, she squeezed Luke's hand affectionately then let it go.

"I hear you got shot in butt," Maggie said.

Luke huffed and sighed. "I didn't get shot in the butt. It just grazed the cheek."

"I'd still like to inspect it."

"It's a good-looking butt," Pablo joked. He'd rejoined Luke and Delilah on the PT Boat, jumping on board after Maggie made it across.

She blushed. "I mean the wound. I'd like to inspect the wound."

Pablo laughed as Maggie's blush deepened.

"Is the cabin available?" she asked.

Owen did a head count. "All clear. Everyone's on deck. You can use my cabin. It's first on the left."

Maggie nodded at Owen, then extended her hand out, indicating Luke should lead the way. Despite the wound being superficial, he limped a bit. Without the adrenaline of battle and being fairly sedentary on the boat chugging its way across the cold Pacific Ocean, the wound had stiffened up. His lower back and neck were sore from constantly favoring the opposite leg. Despite his best effort to hide the limp, he knew Maggie's trained eyes would suss out the nature of his injuries.

Once they shut the door to the stairs leading below decks, Maggie said, "Luke, you can quit holding back now that no one can see you."

He nodded and relaxed his muscles, allowing the limp to show. "Alright, Maggie." He no longer thought of her as the pack doctor, but as a friend.

Assuming the position, he unbuckled his belt and dropped his pants just past his butt and bent over, trying his best to keep the front covered.

"It'll probably be best if you lay out on the bed so your muscles are relaxed."

He followed her directions as she pulled a chair from under Owen's desk and slid it next to the bed.

"OK, I'm about to pull the bandage."

He braced himself but still grunted as she pulled it off. He wasn't a terribly hairy man, but he still had enough to make the bandage removal sting.

"Have you changed this bandage?"

"No, I didn't want to bother anyone with it." He turned his head and saw her furrowed brow and concerned expression.

"It looks like a couple of the butterfly bandages pulled loose. This is a bit deeper than a graze. Couldn't you find a vampire to heal you?"

"No, we were going hot and heavy after this happened. I didn't take time and there weren't many available. The team was pretty thorough putting them down for their final sleep."

"Hmm," she said as she pulled the butterfly bandages off. "I'm going to clean this again and give you a few stitches."

She bent over and rustled around in the medical kit she'd brought with her, pulling out disinfectant and the supplies she needed to stitch him up. Reaching out, she grabbed a lamp attached to the wall on an extendible arm and swung it toward Luke's butt. She flipped the switch and adjusted the aim until she had light where she wanted it. Once she was set, she sanitized her hands with disinfectant and pulled gloves on.

"This might sting," Maggie said before cleaning the wound.

It did. Luke tried to keep from clenching the muscles of his butt but didn't succeed, allowing them to relax once he got used to it.

"What's this?" Maggie mumbled. She reached up and adjusted the light again. "Hmm, this could be causing your problems. Looks like some shrapnel's stuck here."

She grabbed a set of forceps from her kit. Her hand on Luke's butt, fingers and thumb around his wound, she held it stable. He felt the twinges as she pulled out a couple pieces followed by the sting of whatever she was using to clean his wound. She pulled out another piece, then set her forceps down. A few more seconds and she had him stitched up. She coated the wound with disinfectant gel and covered it with a fresh bandage.

"There you go. Once you get home, be sure to keep it clean. Normally, for a human patient, I'd recommend getting a tetanus shot booster if it's been a while, but I'm still not one hundred percent sure how your whole deal works, medically speaking."

"I haven't had one since I was conscripted by the Brits during World War II."

"How'd they track you down? I'd figure you'd be good at avoiding governments," Maggie replied.

"Can I pull up my pants, Maggie?" Luke asked. "It's kind of chilly in here with my bum hanging out."

"Sure. But I'd recommend lying there for a bit longer. Stay off your butt as much as you can."

Luke pulled up his pants. "I'd dropped off the grid after the Great War, living in Paris mostly. I snuck out of France just before the Nazis consolidated their position. When the boat I was on was stopped by a British Destroyer, they took my information. It must have tripped something at MI6. They rounded me up, enlisted me, and sent me over to SOE."

"SOE?" Maggie asked.

"Sorry, acronyms. Governments and militaries love them. Special Operations Executive. Basically espionage and sabotage. I speak all the pertinent languages, so they kept me busy. I spent most of the war on the continent coordinating with various resistance forces and sabotaging the Nazis. After we liberated the camps and the Germans surrendered, I quit and went underground. I was done serving governments and their wars. I had no interest in becoming involved with the coming feud with the Soviets."

When Luke mentioned "camps," Maggie's right hand drifted toward her left forearm. Luke clenched his jaw, the pieces falling together. Rabinowitz was a relatively common Jewish surname in Poland. She was old enough to be on the council, and that meant she was old enough to have been alive during WWII. She'd probably spent time in Auschwitz where the forearm tattoo was common. Come to think of it, he'd never seen her in short sleeves. Maggie must have caught his eyes and the understanding in them, her gaze locked with his.

"Maggie…"

"It's OK, Luke."

She looked flushed, her eyes watery. Luke reached over and grabbed her hand, squeezing gently. He rolled over and sat on the edge of the bed, hissing as the pressure settled on his wound. He took her hand again.

"Do…do you need a hug?" Luke asked.

She nodded. He pulled her in, wrapping his arms around her. She rested her head on his shoulder and slipped her arms around his waist. Rubbing her back gently, they sat together in silence. Often focused on his own tunnel vision of trauma, the horrific snippet of Maggie's past reminded him how much some of the werewolves he'd met had lived through. Luke, his freshly stitched butt getting uncomfortable, shifted in his seat some, letting out a small grunt of discomfort.

"Your butt?" Maggie asked.

"Yeah," Luke replied.

Pushing back, Maggie gave Luke a kiss on the cheek. "Thanks, Luke. Stay off your butt as much as you can."

"I'll try."

Maggie stood up and half turned before grabbing his hand and giving it a squeeze. She walked out the door and shut it behind her. Deciding to follow the doctor's orders, Luke stretched out on his stomach, fluffed Owen's pillow, and took a nap.

# TWENTY-SIX

LIKE AFTER THE Wapato and the St. Johns Bridge incident, everyone met at the farm. The injured were attended to, but fortunately, no fatalities needed to be dealt with. Luke and the pack had gotten off lightly, considering the scale of the operation they'd just accomplished.

When Luke stepped out of Pablo's truck, Gwen blinded sided him with a fierce hug that nearly knocked him off balance, putting pressure on his injured leg. After a moment of surprise, he pulled the preteen in to return her hug.

When they realized they were the center of attention, they broke apart, blushing, uncomfortable with so many eyes on them. Sam, Delilah, and Pablo smiled broadly at their friend. Maggie's smile, though softer, also struck him. They turned to walk into the farmhouse.

"You're hurt?" Gwen asked, noticing his limp.

Pablo howled with laughter. "He got shot in the butt!"

"I did not get shot in the butt," Luke replied, exasperated. "It just grazed my butt cheek. There's a world of difference."

Gwen was trying to hide a snicker but doing a poor job of it. "In the butt?"

She broke down laughing too, her visible stress dissipating with the help of Pablo's laughter. Luke sighed and shook his head, letting everyone get their laugh in. Gwen hid her laughter behind one hand and reached out with the other to grab Luke's as they walked into the house.

After they took their shoes off and stashed them on the racks by the doors, everyone who'd been on the boats headed to their bathrooms to wash off a week's worth of not showering. The car ride back from the coast had been a fragrant journey. Luke, Maggie, Sam, and Pablo had spent much of the way back with the windows of Pablo's pickup rolled down when they got a break from the spring rain that had followed them in from the Pacific.

When Luke joined the group around the table, he found a kid's pool floaty donut sitting on the chair left for him and a group of people not even attempting to hold back snickers, even the usually stoic Holly. Luke, as seemed to be his most common gesture combination lately, sighed and shook his head. He was glad to have friends to joke with, but still...

Maggie followed Luke into the farmhouse's kitchen, swiped the donut off Luke's seat, threw it at Pablo like a Frisbee, and replaced it with a pillow. "You'd figure a nine-hundred-year-old werewolf would have more decorum," she huffed.

"Hey! I'm not that old," Pablo protested.

Luke smirked at his best friend, enjoying Maggie using the joke Pablo so often turned on him. "Thanks, Maggie."

Maggie smiled warmly at Luke and took a seat.

Delilah, like the last time they'd all met for their last major mission, leaned against the counter in the background. She'd barely spoken since they were forced to turn away from Cassius and his escape boat. Her rage at her father's murder made fresh with the escape of his murderer dampened the joviality of the earlier joking. Pieter followed Delilah in and sat next to Pablo, completing the roster of those participating in the postmortem.

"So, how'd we do?" Holly asked Luke, by way of starting the meeting.

"Overall? We hit most of our objectives. The freighter was

stopped. We destroyed a huge portion of their incoming weapons and probably killed at least a hundred if not several hundred vampires in the process," Luke replied.

"I'm hearing a lot of soft words in that statement," Holly replied.

Luke gave a half shrug. "We weren't able to confirm the sinking of the ship. It was listing heavily when we were forced to retreat with the rest of the flotilla."

Holly rested her elbows on the table, leaning closer to Luke. "Why weren't you able to stay and confirm?"

"That takes us to the less than victorious aspects of the mission. Somehow, the Coast Guard is involved. I don't know if Cassius and the Portland nest forcibly took over the Astoria Coast Guard station, if they have agents and human accomplices inside Astoria, or something worse."

"How is the Coast Guard involved?" Holly asked, her face paling at the mention of the US military's involvement.

"Cassius highjacked one of the Astoria cutters and was meeting the freighter. There's no way they could've been there unless it was pre-planned. The cutter wasn't that fast, and the freighter was a bit too far out. That's probably how they've been getting the vampires off the freighters in the first place, plucking them from freighters offshore and bringing them back to land."

"It's not going to come back on the pack, is it?" Worry flooded Holly's eyes.

"Not in any way more than we're already involved. Cassius knows I'm allied with werewolves, although he probably has no idea which pack, but the entire flotilla was running without identification. All numbers were covered and any GPS or other transponders switched off. Owen is half pirate."

"That's probably an underestimate," Holly muttered.

Luke, Pablo, Sam, and Maggie chuckled.

Sitting back, Holly ran her hand through her short, spiky hair. "Should we be expecting people in white and orange to be sniffing around?"

"It's possible," Pablo weighed in. "We did kind of sink their cutter."

"And shoot down their helicopter," Luke added.

Holly put her head in her hands. "How do you 'kind of sink' a Coast Guard cutter?"

"We kind of sunk it all the way." Pablo shrugged.

"But a couple of their lifeboats made it off. It looked like one was the crew and the other was Cassius and his fanged goons. At that point, we were running low on ammo and fuel, at least if we wanted to get home. Owen and I thought it best to move his boat back to the flotilla for defense in case the vamps had anything else planned for us or organized another response." Luke shifted uncomfortably to take some pressure off his sore butt cheek.

"Is there any way for them to recognize us?"

"Owen's boat isn't what you'd call run of the mill. I'm sure the Coasties will remember a WWII-era PT Boat. Although, I doubt any of them will make it back to shore, and if they do, they probably won't live long. The vampires will need to cover up evidence."

"That's a lot to hope on," Holly said.

"Yeah," Luke replied.

Holly sat back and ran both hands through her short, spiky hair, exhaling slowly. "I guess we knew this could happen if we got involved. I'll reach out to Lauren to see what resources they might need."

"They're a wealthier pack than we are with all their marijuana farms," Sam said bitingly.

Holly rested her hand on Sam's wrist. "True, but we're logistically more wealthy. Lauren has been a good ally to step up and put their pack and resources on the line. We'll want to keep on their good side. Besides, this keeps getting deeper and we're only one pack. We need our neighbors with us too."

"I like Owen and Lauren. They're good people," Luke weighed in.

"Yeah, the pack's lawyers work for them quite a bit. Lauren is as solid as you can find. That's why she's in charge. Owen is a lot of fun, but he's a huge troublemaker. We couldn't have a tougher ally than him. If you've made friends with him, his word carries weight with Lauren. He'll be excited you gave him an opportunity to play with his toys. He loves that boat," Sam said.

"What kind of troublemaker?" Luke asked, wondering if he needed to add another person to his mental equations of the dangers of his world.

"Oh, nothing dangerous. Just a prankster. He's the guy that'll keep you out to all hours of the night drinking then call you the next day and make fun of your hangover. That kind of stuff," Sam replied, assuaging Luke's concerns.

Nodding, Holly reached out and grasped Sam's hand before turning back to Luke. "So, what next?" she asked.

"I spoke with Owen about that on the way back to shore. They're going to keep an eye on traffic and the Coast Guard to see if there are any more drops. Also, now that they've got the scent, they'll start sweeping their communities for nests and try to track down any stray vamps."

Holly nodded, an impressed look on her face.

"I'd like to step up our patrols as well. See if we can mix newer recruits into experienced sweeper teams to get trained on the protocols and scents. Is there a possibility of bringing in any of the other Portland area packs on board?" Luke asked.

"I've been opening the dialog with the other packs. Beaverton Pack is willing to listen," Holly replied.

"As a courtesy?" Luke asked.

"No. Seriously. Now that we've settled this, I'd like to get you in front of their pack council so they can ask you any questions they might have. If I know Amalia, she's already made a few calls to some of our members who she's close with. The East Portland pack is more tentative, but I think they can be persuaded."

"And the Clackamas County pack?" Sam asked.

"They're more...uncertain," Holly responded obliquely.

Sam rolled her eyes and looked at Luke. "They're not the biggest fans of our pack. Let's just say, we pick up quite a few members from their pack who are looking for a more...open environment."

"Ah, I see," Luke replied.

"What about fucking Cassius?" Delilah asked, her poorly contained anger spilling out into the room.

Luke knew this was coming. She'd placed a lot of trust in Luke and the pack but still wasn't getting satisfaction about her personal vendetta.

"When do we put him in the ground permanently?"

"Look, Delilah, I know—"

Delilah interrupted Luke. "You don't know fucking shit. He murdered my father."

"You don't think I know the pain of burying loved ones because of vampires? I've got nearly two thousand years of it stacked up inside. Where I used to have feelings, now I have scar tissue. I've been burying people I care about longer than anyone in this room has been alive. Combined and then multiplied. You don't know the weight of that much guilt." Luke stopped himself, pulling back on the reins of his own shallowly buried anger. "And I don't want you to have to live with that kind of crushing guilt and trauma." Luke rubbed his hand over his cheek.

"I promise you this. Cassius will be my number one priority. Ending him will remove a thorn from both our sides. And it'll help us get Portland under control, or at least thin the herd considerably. Will that suffice?"

Delilah thought about it, her arms rigidly folded across her chest, her jaw clenching. She gave a single tight nod as her only sign of acceptance. Sam stood and walked over to give her friend a hug. Delilah, usually liking to maintain her tough facade, pulled the shorter woman in for a tight hug, betraying her anger and sadness with a few sniffles.

Holly called a quick break so everyone could get a breather. Pieter passed behind Luke and squeezed his shoulder before disappearing out to the house's large porch. Seizing the opportunity to take some pressure off his wound, Luke stood and leaned up against the counter so he could take the weight off the injured limb. Maggie opened a cabinet, pulled out a bottle of ibuprofen, and gave Luke a few.

Once the last person retook their seat, Holly called the meeting back to order. "Is there anything else you'll need or something the pack should be working on?"

Luke thought about it, deciding to air ideas he'd had floating in his head for a while. "I think I need to move resources from some of my storage facilities in Europe. I'll probably acquire some private warehouse space locally. And now that I think about it, some space closer to town to set up a training facility. I appreciate the use of the farm, but I'd like to leave it as a sanctuary for the pack. Every time we come up here and make noise, it makes it more likely we'll be discovered."

Holly looked thoughtfully at Luke. "I appreciate that, as does the pack. We can help you find what you're looking for in real estate. I'll have Pablo send some contacts your way of pack members who can facilitate that for you."

"I'll text you the info of our pack agents. Also, got a text from Jorge while you were showering. Your car is ready. I can drop you off on the way home," Pablo said.

"Excellent! I've missed the old beast," Luke replied, a smile returning to his face.

"Is there anything else we need to cover?" Holly asked.

"Yeah. I want to speak to Pieter about it." Luke turned to Pieter. "I'd like to see if we can open negotiations with your pack to form a closer alliance. You're the only European pack I have ties to, but I'm hoping you'll be able to work across the continent and help make some connections for us. We won't be able to stand alone with the vampires coordinating internationally. Your pack is full of good folk, and you command respect."

"What are you thinking?" Pieter asked.

"I'd like to take a team to Belgium with me. I'll want to oversee some of the resources transfer personally, plus it would be good to renew ties with your father and brother, as well as Amiata." Luke turned to Holly. "If you'd like to come, that'd be great. Pieter and I can serve as your guides on the ground."

"I'd like to, but with the upcoming special election, I need to stay here and keep an eye on local politics," Holly replied.

"Say what now?" Luke asked, shocked.

"With no news on Mayor Jorgenssen, they're holding a special election to replace him."

"Do we have any idea who's running yet?" Sam asked.

"A few of the usual no-chance candidates have already announced." Holly sat back, straightening as she looked around the table. "The only name of note is our friend Fred Bealer."

"Commissioner Smackie?" Pablo said, slapping the inside of his elbow like he was trying to raise a vein.

"Yup." Holly looked disgusted, shaking her head.

Luke's eyebrows climbed up his forehead. "Yeah, that'll need to be monitored closely. We can't have a mayor tied to the vampires, certainly not one in their control."

"I'll keep an eye on candidates and figure out who to throw our weight behind," Holly volunteered. She looked around the room. "I think that covers everything. Anyone have anything to add?"

"Are you sure we can't talk you into running, Holly?" Luke asked.

"No. I'm still not interested." Removing the option firmly from the table, Holly looked around the room, seeing nothing but shaking heads accompanied by the occasional whispered, "Nope." Only Maggie had her hand up.

"Yes, Maggie?" Holly asked.

"It's not mission related, or anything like that, but…" She hesitated for a moment, before directing her gaze toward Luke. "It's about Gwen. Now that things have settled a bit, and she's doing better, a couple pack families have offered to take her in. I wanted to bring this to you before I approached her. What are your thoughts?"

Luke's stomach dropped. "Um…" Luke hesitated, a frown spreading across his face. All his friends stared at him, their gazes kind and curious. He finally got his tongue to work again, half-heartedly asking, "I mean, what's best for Gwen?"

Maggie walked around the table and took the seat next to Luke's. She leaned toward him, resting her elbow on the table as she looked at him and took one of his hands in both hers. "I'm not asking about Gwen right now, Luke. Would you like for us to find a new home for Gwen?"

Off in the sitting room, something thudded to the ground. Luke looked into Maggie's startlingly blue eyes. He could see her empathy and concern, but also a searching he couldn't put a name to. The room shrank to just them, Maggie looking into Luke's eyes, Luke trying to manage the riot of feelings running wild through him as he tried to formulate a coherent answer.

"I...I don't think I'd like that. I don't think I'd like that at all," Luke said, his voice shaking.

The clatter of one of the end tables from the sitting room tipping over was followed by the sound of bare feet on wood floor. Luke grunted as a blur ran into the room and slammed into him, small shaking arms wrapping around him. The impact of the young were-wolf hit harder than he expected. Luke folded the crying preteen in a hug, his own tears threatening to burst forth.

"Don't make me live somewhere else, Luke, please?" Gwen stammered around her tears.

Luke looked up at Maggie. Making eye contact, he noticed her eyes were getting watery as well. She reached out and squeezed Gwen's shoulder before fixing Luke with her quiet, serious eyes.

"Luke, do you want to make the arrangement permanent?" Maggie asked.

Luke nodded. "I would."

"Gwendolyn, how about you? Do you want Luke to be your permanent guardian?"

Gwen turned toward Maggie and nodded vigorously, wiping her sniffly nose. "Yes."

Maggie smiled warmly at them. A few people around the kitchen were handing around a box of tissues. Luke's face flushed red from being the center of attention while Gwen hugged him one-armed.

Holly, sounding softer than Luke had ever heard her, cleared her throat before speaking. "I'll have Sam work with you on getting the papers drawn up so everything is legal if the state asks questions."

Luke turned toward the sound of clinking glasses as Pablo pulled down whiskey glasses from the cabinet. He sorted through a few bottles until he found the one he wanted. After filling the glasses, he handed them out.

"Last time we did this, we went with a rougher option. If we're going to celebrate, I'm breaking out something smoother. Yamazaki 18 should do the trick." Pablo raised his glass.

"Hey, Pablo, hold off a minute. We need to get something for Gwen to toast with. She's still a little young for brown liquor," Sam said, getting up to look in the fridge.

She rattled a few things around, glass clinking against glass until she called, "Ah ha!" and pulled a bottle from the back of the fridge. "We had some leftover nonalcoholic sparkling cider left from New Year's."

Pablo grabbed a champagne flute from the cupboard and set it next to Sam as she pulled the cork with a loud pop. She filled it halfway and handed it to Gwen. Now that everyone had a glass, they stood, looking toward Luke and Gwen.

Sam lifted her glass. "Luke, Gwendolyn, I want to welcome you both to our family. Everyone in this room has chosen to be part of this pack. Many of us had no other choices where we'd feel welcome. No places where we could safely be ourselves and accepted for who we are.

"Luke, you're not a werewolf, but you're one of us. You're a weird misfit who doesn't have to hide himself with us. You've become a friend and someone I rely on and trust with the safety of my family and my pack. Everyone here cares about you and accepts you.

"Gwennie, your path here wasn't an easy one, but we're all glad you're here with us now, and we'll all be here for you whenever you need us, without question. We've all chosen to be together, and we've all fought to protect our safe haven. We want this to be your safe haven, too.

"Delilah, I know this moment is about Luke and Gwen, but I can't leave you out. You've become a dear friend and someone I love like a sister. You're one of us, too, and your goals are my goals. You can always count on me to have your back."

Luke knew that meant Delilah had the resources of the pack to back Sam and her pledge to aid her friend in the quest to avenge her father. It wasn't an idle promise, and Delilah was bolstered by Sam's words, stepping forward to hug her friend. Luke smiled and nodded when he caught her eye. It was his pledge that she also had his resources to back her up as well.

"So, here's to us. To love, friendship, and the people we've chosen as our family."

"Love, friendship, and family!" everyone called out, finding glasses to touch with theirs, raising a clatter of glass on glass.

For the moment, their plans and problems were forgotten as they shared in their friendships, the humans welcomed officially into the family of the pack. Mostly, they shared in the joy of Luke and Gwen finding each other and building their own little family unit together. Luke, who'd had no one for huge parts of his long life, and Gwen, who hadn't had a safe place in the family she was born to, had found each other through the tragedy vampires had imposed on their lives.

Luke had provided the young trans girl her first safe haven and his friends had provided emotional support to both of them as they figured out how to live in a situation neither had any idea how to navigate. Even so, their arrangement wasn't typical. Luke wished he could provide a more stable home for her, but she'd chosen him over a potentially stable wolf family. He was glad she had. Until confronted with the decision, he hadn't realized how attached he'd grown to having her in his life. He'd do his best by her.

Luke pulled Gwen in for a one-armed hug, getting one in return as they stood side-by-side, quietly watching their friends laugh and chat. Sam stepped over to address them both.

"Some stuff to think about. You two will need to figure out how you want your relationship documented so you can keep your story straight. Gwen, you'll need to select a last name so we can get your paperwork finished. Luke, well... I guess I don't know. Are you using Luke Irontree as your official name?"

"No, it's more my nom de guerre, but I think I'm due for a change on the official documents. Probably about time to sell my house to myself again."

"Cool, I'll get the ball rolling on everything." She pulled Luke in for a hug, wrapping her other arm around Gwen. "I'm so happy for you two. And seriously, if either of you need anything, I'll be there for you no matter what."

"Thanks, Sam," Luke said.

When Luke let Sam go, Delilah was waiting for her turn. "Hey you two, congrats!"

She bent over and hugged Gwen. Delilah had been the first person outside of Luke to bond with the child. They still hung out regularly. Sam had joined in as her friendship with Delilah grew, both providing advice to Gwen as she finally had a safe space to explore who she was and be herself. When she stood up, she awkwardly hesitated for a moment before Luke wrapped his arms around her.

"Delilah, I'm sorry I snapped at you. That was assholish of me."

"Yeah, same on my part." Delilah exhaled sharply. "I'm just so angry, but I shouldn't take that out on my friends."

"We'll get him. I promise." Luke held Delilah's gaze and squeezed her shoulder.

Sniffing, she whipped a tear off her cheek and gave Luke a single nod. "Thank you."

# TWENTY-SEVEN

AFTER THEY FINISHED THEIR MEETING, they lounged about the farm, unwinding after the tense week and the partially successful mission. Luke found a cribbage board and taught Gwen and Delilah how to play, recruiting Sam as their fourth for team play. Gwen practically vibrated in her chair. Luke had never seen her so bubbly and happy. Her good mood was contagious, infecting Luke the most.

By deciding to not find a new home for her, Luke and Gwen had made the first move toward making their family official. Luke, happy for himself and Gwen, was also more nervous about it than anything he'd done in the last year. He was really responsible for her for the long haul. Before, it had been a temporary situation until she could be moved to a pack family. That safety valve had helped him stay calm about the situation—now he had to be a dad-type person, not just a temporary caretaker.

He had no choice but to keep at it—and remember to ask his friends for help. That's what they kept telling him to do. For now, though, Gwen turned out to be an excellent card partner, picking up the game quickly and figuring out some of the card holding strategies. It would give them something else to do together at home.

After several hours of cards, they put on their walking shoes to head down to The Birk, as it was called, for some of their famous burgers. It was a long walk from the farm, but lovely after the morning rain had cleared up. The fresh air and exercise would do everyone good after being crammed on a boat for a week, followed by the ride down from the coast.

Luke, never the most chatty of people, enjoyed the friendly give and take of the group as they walked down the gravel road to Birkenfeld. Even Holly was loosening up around him, a bit of starch coming out of her collar, as he became a more known quantity and a part of her pack.

When they arrived, they were shown to a table that had been put together for the larger group, a nice perk that came with the pack owning the roadhouse. The gang started out with a round of beers for the adults and a soda for Gwen, then ordered whichever burger looked best to them.

When the bacon cheeseburger arrived with its heaping pile of fries, Luke inhaled deeply, his mouth watering. "Mmm, this is a hell of a burger," he said after taking his first bite.

"Told ya they were good," Sam replied around a mouthful of fries.

Their burgers downed, they enjoyed another round before clearing out to make the long walk home. The trip back was louder than the trip to the bar, Pablo and Sam joking and clowning and making everyone laugh. Delilah joined in with their shenanigans. Luke and Gwen walked near the back of the group, enjoying the antics of their friends. Maggie, seeing where Luke was, drifted back to walk on Luke's other side.

Without saying anything, she reached out and took his hand in hers. Luke couldn't think of a reason to not be holding her hand, so he didn't stop it—and it felt nice to be holding an attractive woman's hand as they walked under the stars. Eventually, Pablo and Sam calmed down. When they got back to the farmhouse, Sam and Holly retired to their room. Pablo went to watch a movie in his room, and Gwen grabbed the novel she'd been reading and headed up to her room.

Luke wasn't quite ready to retire. He grabbed a whiskey bottle, a glass, and a blanket and went out to the house's large wrap-around porch to watch the moon and stars. He wrapped the blanket around his shoulders and sat, placing the bottle and glass on a small table. He looked up to the creak of the porch boards. Maggie walked toward him, a whiskey of her own in her hand.

"Mind if I sit with you, Luke?" Maggie asked.

"Not at all," he replied, shifting to give her some room. He winced slightly on his wound. "I can get up, and we can share the blanket, if you'd like."

She grabbed the corner of the blanket and pulled it aside, then picked up his arm and set it along the back of the couch. She sat down next to him, pulling her legs under her and nestling into the crook of his arm, then pulled his arm around her shoulder along with the blanket. With her head lying on his shoulder, her scent was distracting. They sat in silence, occasionally sipping from their glasses.

Seeing Maggie's glass empty, he offered to give her a refill.

"Not at the moment, but thanks. Would you mind setting my glass on the table?" She handed him her empty.

He topped up his. He nearly choked when he felt her hand on his chest, gently moving back and forth. Despite his best efforts, he was failing to keep his heart rate from picking up. It had been a long time since he'd sat this close to a woman. Confused and unsure, he had no idea what any of it meant. Younger people, and everyone was younger compared to Luke, but especially modern youth, were more physically affectionate. The pack members especially so, they often shared casual touch and hugs with their friends.

"Are you OK, Luke? You seem a bit jittery."

"Um, sorry. I don't mean to be," he replied.

"Is it me? Does this bother you? I can move if you want."

He didn't want her to move. He took a deep breath and let it out slowly. "No. I like sitting here with you." Luke tried to relax.

He continued sipping his whiskey, partially because he was enjoying the flavor and the burn but also because it distracted him from the riot of feelings Maggie's touch generated. It had been nearly fifty years since a woman had touched him in anything other than friendship.

Each day he regretted letting himself get so out of touch with living his life. His only consumption of the modern world had been through pop culture, allowing him to safely hide in a movie theater or behind a TV or computer screen. He hadn't participated in modern courtship rituals in well over a century; his last two assignations were unintended consequences of circumstances he'd found himself in.

He liked Maggie and found her attractive but had no idea what he should do or even wanted to do, and he certainly didn't want to misread the situation and fuck up a friendship because he was being stupid.

Nothing. That was often the safety default he settled on. Do nothing; enjoy the closeness. He squeezed Maggie's shoulder and relaxed a little more, taking an occasional sip.

"Luke?"

"Yes, Maggie?"

"Do you think I'm pretty?"

*"Oh shit,"* he thought. *"So much for that plan."*

"Um, yes, I think you're very pretty." That was probably safe, and it was true. She was very pretty.

Maggie adjusted herself so she sat taller, looking toward Luke. She reached over with her hand, placing it on Luke's cheek, and turned his head toward her. Luke swallowed, his mouth going dry. He was in trouble. While it had been a while since a woman had touched him affectionately in a non-platonic manner, he recognized the look in Maggie's eyes, the expression on her face—the look of desire and attraction almost universal throughout time.

"Luke?"

"Yes, Maggie?"

"I want to kiss you," Maggie replied.

He felt his heart stop as his stomach flopped. Doing nothing was a plan that had failed him miserably this time around. He decided it was a good idea to set his glass down before he dropped it.

"Don't...don't you have a partner?" he asked, a snippet of memory surfacing.

"Mhm, a romantic partner. They're ace, but I'm more demisexual or gray ace, so we've chosen to be ethically non-monogamous. If I find I'm attracted to someone, I'm allowed to pursue it."

Luke's excuses were running out, and he was being outmaneuvered. He couldn't lie to himself; he had thought about kissing the pretty doctor with the light Polish accent, but he'd always shoved those thoughts back. He didn't want to bring his disaster of a life into someone else's. His mind jolted to a halt.

Seeing he was struggling, she re-approached her question. "I would like to kiss you. Would you like to kiss me?"

Although he was sure his eyes looked a bit wild, he nodded lightly. "I would."

Maggie leaned forward, closing the distance. As he reached out to run his hands through Maggie's hair, his hand shook. Stilling it, he lowered it, feeling her silky hair gliding through his fingers. His eyes drifted closed as their lips met, sending lightening and fire coursing through him.

At first, their kiss was tentative, exploratory, but as it extended, it intensified, Maggie's tongue teasing Luke's mouth open in search of his. When they met, Luke nearly melted, overwhelmed at feeling lips against his, a sensation he'd not felt in a long time. When Maggie pulled back, Luke rested his forehead against hers, his breathing erratic.

"Are you OK?" Maggie asked.

"It's been a while since I've done that. A long while."

"Kissed someone?"

"Yeah."

"We all deserve affection in whatever way is meaningful to us," Maggie replied, adjusting her head to kiss Luke again.

This time, Luke felt more confident, his lips remembering how to kiss properly. He'd been told he was a good kisser, once upon a time; he'd had enough time to practice over the last two millennia. But something about the twentieth century had broken him. He'd left too much of himself in the trenches of Belgium and France during World

War I, not able to recover it in the century that followed or to find a way to heal it and replace it.

When their lips broke apart, Maggie snuggled into Luke even tighter. "I think I'd like that whiskey you offered."

Luke reached over and poured a finger into her glass, handing it to Maggie.

She took a sip and sighed happily. "Mmm, this is nice. I wanted something a little more aggressive and fortifying earlier, so I had some of that cheaper Bourbon Pablo always keeps around, but this is more elegant, smoother."

Luke made a noncommittal sound, not trusting himself to speak. The kisses had done nothing to clear up his confusion, mixing in dangerous new possibilities that excited and scared him. He absent-mindedly sipped his whiskey and savored the warm contact of Maggie's body next to his, wondering what would happen next and not knowing how he'd react. He had no idea how long they sat there, but when he put glass to lips and got nothing, he looked down to see an empty glass. He set it down. Once his hand was free, Maggie offered her empty glass to him.

"Another glass?" he asked.

"No, thank you." She tucked her arm back under the blanket, settling her hand on his thigh. "Luke, I'm going to make an offer, but I don't want you to feel any pressure to do anything you don't want to or aren't interested in. OK?"

He nodded.

"I'd like to invite you to come with me to my bedroom. I want to continue the discussion our lips and hands started earlier and see where it goes, or we can go snuggle under the covers together and go to sleep." She looked up at him, catching his gaze. "Would you like to go to my room with me?"

Luke licked his lip, trying to move some moisture around his mouth after it had suddenly become unreasonably dry. "Yes."

MAGGIE LAY in the crook of Luke's arm, her head on his shoulder and her arm draped across his stomach. Luke idly ran his fingers over her forearm. She tipped her head up and kissed his chin, encouraging him to move his lips closer to hers. He obliged, eager for another chance to feel Maggie's soft lips against his.

"That was fun," Maggie said, smiling up at Luke.

"I thought so."

"I'm glad you were feeling up to it again this morning."

"Me too."

Luke wasn't sure how to respond beyond simple answers. What had happened last night and this morning only added to his general confusion, but he wasn't going to complain. Maggie had been sweetly direct, guiding him along until his confidence picked up despite being so out of practice.

"Luke?"

"Yes, Maggie?"

"I'd like to hang out again, if you'd like…"

"I think I would like that."

They lay there in silence for a while longer, each of them absent-mindedly touching the other.

"Maggie?"

"Yes, Luke?"

He hesitated before continuing. "Why me?"

"What do you mean?"

"I'm kind of a mess."

"Ah. Well, you're handsome. Kind. And you probably care too much. That's why you hide from life. And I just like you."

He tipped her chin back up for another kiss. When they'd finished their kiss, he sighed.

"Why the big sigh?"

"I could lay here like this all morning, but we'd probably better get moving before people come knocking, asking why we're not ready to leave."

"This is so cozy, but you're probably right." She kissed him again before rolling out of bed. "I need a shower before we go."

Luke watched as the nude woman walked away toward her bathroom, admiring her pleasantly curvy form. She'd warned him she had some scars from before she'd been turned. Luke had plenty of his own from twenty years of fighting the empire's battles before he found his immortality. Besides, his first wife, Marpesia, had been a Sarmatian warrior and chieftain with a fine collection of scars earned in battle. Scars didn't make one ugly, only an ugly soul could make someone unattractive. They just added character, telling stories about their person.

He knew the story of every scar on his body and could guess some of the stories of Maggie's. And he knew enough about history, having lived much of it, to know the horrible stories they might tell. He felt grateful she'd trusted him enough to share her bed with him.

Peeking out of the bathroom door, she said, "I'll see you downstairs."

Luke dressed and slipped out, heading back to his room to grab a quick shower of his own. When he'd dressed in a fresh T-shirt and jeans, he headed downstairs to grab a pastry and a cup of coffee. Deciding to enjoy the nice morning, he headed out to the porch and found a seat. A few minutes later, Pablo joined him with a cup of his own. They sat in silence, enjoying the sound of birds chirping about and visiting the various feeders the pack kept filled around the farmhouse.

"So, you and the Doc, eh?" Pablo said, breaking the silence.

Luke nearly choked on his coffee. "What?"

"I know Maggie very well. I love her like a sister. I've also known her for a long time. She's a direct woman, especially on the rare occasion she's interested in someone. In your case, I told her she'd need to be extra direct."

"What?"

Pablo grinned broadly. "Dude, you got any other words in your vocabulary this morning? I know you're out of practice with modern life, and you're also you."

"You talked to her about me?" Luke asked, finally getting his brain back in gear.

"She asked me for advice. Of course, I helped her out."

Luke rolled his head back, looking at the ceiling of the porch. "Does everyone know? Was I the last to know?"

"Not everyone, but we're an open pack. I'm sure the rest of the folks here know she's interested in you. She's been very physical with you—snuggling against you the whole ride from the coast, holding your hand on the way back from The Birk last night. The people in my truck and the group who went to The Birk are the people she's closest with, the most open with. She wouldn't be this obvious in front of everyone she trusts if she wasn't into you. She's always finding an excuse to touch you. And judging by your question, you are probably the last to know. Although, I'm guessing Gwen doesn't, but she's pretty observant for a kid. Maybe not Delilah, since she didn't ride back with us, and she's been pretty in her head about not getting Cassius."

Luke sighed, shaking his head. "Is everyone laughing behind their hand at me?"

"You're too serious, buddy. We're wolves. We like to play. And no, nobody is laughing at you. We all like you. We want to see you happy and prosper. That's one of the things Holly has always made clear to new members of the pack. We're free to pursue our joys in life as long as we're not hurting anyone and everyone involved is on board. Too many of us have had to hide from society in general and our own packs because we weren't free to be who we are.

"And you may not understand this quite yet, but you're a part of this pack now. That means the same applies to you. Have some fun. Seek some joy."

Luke stared at the cup in his hands, nodding.

"Sam is right about what she said at the Howling Moon. You are my best friend, Luke. And I love you, buddy."

Luke smiled at his friend, warmth spreading through him at Pablo's words. "I love you too, Pablo. You're my first real friend in a long time, and certainly the best."

Pablo reached out and patted Luke's leg. "Good, now that we've established that. I'm going to give you some friendly advice. Maggie's a lot like you. She's a serious person. She has a touch of the melancholy to her. Although unlike Don John, she's not a plain-dealing

villain. She might be as pretty as Keanu, but in those leather pants…
And Denzel…" Pablo's eyes got far away as he thought about Keanu
Reeves's and Denzel Washington's butts in leather pants. "Anyways,
I'm digressing. Maggie… She doesn't trust easily with her friendship
or her attractions. You've earned both from her. Enjoy it."

Luke took a sip, making a face at the now cold coffee. He tossed
the remains over the edge of the porch.

"I'm going to go grab a refill. Can I get you one too?" Pablo
asked.

Luke handed him his cup and sat back, absentmindedly watching
the birds argue over spots on the feeder, Pablo's advice playing
through his mind. He did like Maggie. Now that he'd come out of
the darkest parts of his depression, he was starting to feel more alive,
and although he'd separated himself from the world, the pack had
pulled him back into the world of the living. Now that they'd
accepted him, they wanted him to prosper in whatever way that
word had meaning for Luke.

He wasn't ready for a long-term serious relationship. He didn't
think he was capable right now. Thinking back on what Maggie had
said last night, he'd have to ask her what exactly ethical non-
monogamy meant for her and her partner. He knew the words and
what the general concept was after spending too much time on the
internet and social media, but he needed to know specifically what it
meant Maggie's expectations of him were. Maggie had asked to hang
out again, which meant this probably wasn't a one-night deal; he'd
ask her for more details then. Who knew? Maybe Maggie would be
exactly what the doctor ordered. He snorted at his Pablo-worthy
joke.

When Pablo returned with a full cup, Luke sat back and blew
over the steaming cup, sipping the tasty black, caffeinated goodness.
"Pablo, thanks for the advice."

"I hope it helps. Mostly, I just want to see my friend have some
fun and find a little bit of joy out this fucked up world and situation
we're in. Maggie is a sweetheart. She'll do right by you."

Luke chuckled. Taking a deep breath and holding the fresh
spring forest air in for a moment, he let it out slowly. He'd stopped

the stem of heavy arms and vampires into Portland for now. He'd yet again spiked Cassius's wheel. He had friends and the backing of the pack. He had a little werewolf to care about who, for whatever reason, liked him and trusted him with her welfare. And he'd been invited into a beautiful woman's bed for the first time in fifty years. Today, things weren't looking too bad for Luke.

# EPILOGUE

DELILAH CAUGHT a ride back to Portland with Holly and Sam, more interested in getting back to her apartment and a date with Rosa than seeing Luke's upgraded car.

She'd see it soon enough and get to spend too much time in it roaming around looking for vamps to stake. Pablo had offered Gwen shotgun and the right to control the radio to celebrate her new status. Although, he'd winked at Luke when he'd set it up.

That left Maggie and Luke alone in the back seat of the pickup. As soon as they were settled in and moving, she shifted her spot to the middle of the seat, buckling in next to Luke who sat in the passenger side seat behind Gwen. He felt incredibly awkward with the display of affection, but Maggie knew the entire equation and had chosen to use the time to snuggle in close with Luke. Following Pablo's advice and putting his trust in Maggie, he relaxed into it, holding her hand and enjoying the casual closeness. He periodically caught Pablo smiling at him.

Luke was disappointed when they reached Jorge's shop, and he had to let go of Maggie. He hadn't realized how touch-starved he was, how nice it felt having Maggie's soft hand touching him. Fortunately, he had his souped-up Volvo wagon to distract him as he stretched out, trying to loosen the muscles he'd been using to shift the weight off his healing butt cheek.

The outward appearance was identical to when he'd left it, except for a few repaired dents and the complete car wash Jorge had given it. So far, so good. Seeing Pablo's pickup parking across the street, Jorge stepped out of the garage and into the lot, waving at his uncle and his friends.

"Tio Pablo, how you doing? Luke, good to see you. Doc, always a pleasure."

He walked over to Gwen who was hanging beside and a little behind Luke, keeping a wary eye on the stranger. Squatting down so he was closer to Gwen's height, he extended his fist for a knuckle bump. Surprisingly, Gwen reciprocated with a grin.

Jorge hitched a lop-sided smile on his face. "Hey, little mama, I'm Jorge, Pablo's nephew."

"Hi! I'm Gwen."

"Welcome to my shop. You want to go check out Luke's car with us?"

Gwen nodded enthusiastically. Jorge stood up and waved them after him, pulling out a set of keys from his pocket.

"Hang back a few feet while I open it up." He popped the hood and opened all the doors. "OK, let's start at the front. We've got a new-to-you engine that'll hit all your parameters. It'll get you a lot more power and speed and oddly enough, it's more fuel efficient than the old 4-cylinder hauling around this tank. It's also sounds pretty close to the original as well." Jorge walked to the passenger doors.

"I've stripped every bit of excess weight I can without affecting the structure or strength of the car. I also put in some newer speakers to go with the nice radio you had." Sitting in the passenger side, he reached under the open cubby on the dash console and a small panel flipped down. "I installed some... Let's just say 'components that might not be strictly speaking legal in this or many other countries' that'll confuse any official types stopping speeders. I take no responsibility for the efficacy. You should drive as fast as you can afford to."

Gwen giggled at Jorge; he turned and winked at her.

"Next, I've converted these door compartments so they look solid, but you can hide whatever you'd like in them. That's up to y'all. Same for the passenger seats in the back."

He stepped out and walked toward the rear. "I tinted the back windows to give you a touch more privacy and to distract from the dimension changes I had to make to get your compartment installed."

Pablo leaned in closer to the back windows. "Jorge, why all the bubbles in the tint?"

Jorge shrugged. "I figured anyone with a cheap DIY tint wouldn't have anything worth hiding in the back. If you want, we can put in a proper job. Just figured I'd offer some additional psychological urban camo."

"We'll see how it does, but I like your thinking," Luke said.

Jorge popped the back hatch open. The modification work become instantly clear as the rear compartment was no longer level with the bumper but raised up.

"OK, here's the big payout," Jorge said, doing his best game show host. "Hit this button right here..."

The bumper lowered, and a door folded down, revealing a tray that extended out about six inches. Jorge grabbed the handle and pulled. The tray slid out effortlessly. Reaching underneath, he hit another button, and a leg with a small wheel at the end folded down onto the ground.

Maggie rubbed Luke's back, making an impressed noise as she followed along with the car report.

"I put the leg on there to provide some reinforcement. If you're in a hurry, the tray will hold up. I just like some redundancies for long term wear and tear. It's designed for a quick fold up, so if you need to hustle, it'll be out of your way quick."

He demonstrated.

"That's really cool," Gwen said.

"Thanks, little mama," Jorge said before turning back to the adults. "The lid raises on hydraulic pistons." He hit another button, and the top popped up. "The lid also folds on these hinges if you want a bit more headroom." He flipped the lid back on its hinge and then another time. "I've set up compartment space for all your gear, plus some extra compartments. I figured a few long thinner ones might come in handy. Ya know, if you need to bring more than antiques with you."

Gwen snickered.

"Hush, you," Luke chided, smiling at her. "This looks amazing. I can't wait to take it for a spin."

"So, about the bill…" Jorge said.

"Send the invoice to the pack accountants. They can check in with me if they need to," Pablo interjected.

"Sounds good! Oh, Mama and Tony got bored with y'all out of town, so they had a Tamale making party. I have some in the garage if you want any."

Luke grinned broadly. There were few better things than a well-made tamale. Jorge went in and grabbed several tinfoil packets for everyone. "Do you like tamales, Gwen?"

She shrugged. "Never had them."

"Well, you're in for a treat. Mama makes the best tamales you'll ever have. Hopefully we'll see you at the next feast we do."

"OK," Gwen replied.

She smiled and bounced lightly on the balls of her feet. Jorge's casual good nature coaxing her out of her shell and making her comfortable enough to step out from behind Luke.

"I better get back to the shop. I got a lot of work today, and we're a bit short handed. Glad you like the work, Luke. You'll have to give me an official review after you put it to use." Jorge waved to Luke and his friends.

"Will do, Jorge. And thanks again. It looks great."

"Love to Tio Tony!" Jorge said to Pablo.

"Same to your mama!" Pablo replied.

"It was good to see you, Doc!"

"You too, Jorge."

He disappeared back into the shop. Maggie walked over to Luke and Gwen, hugging Gwen first, then Luke, lingering longer and more intimately before kissing his cheek.

"I'll see you both soon. I should get home." She turned to Pablo. "Mind dropping me at my house on your way home?"

"Sure thing, Doc," Pablo said, then called over his shoulder to Luke and Gwen, "See ya later, alligators!"

"In a while, crocodile!" Gwen called back.

Luke and Gwen walked back to the Volvo, and Luke shut everything down before getting behind the wheel. Gwen buckled into the front seat.

Luke turned his head toward Gwen. "Want to take the beast for a drive? How does lunch in Hood River sound?"

"Punch it, Chewie!"

"Hey, I'm the pilot here. That makes you Chewie. But I'll let it slide this time," Luke replied to the smiling kid as he backed out onto Fessenden.

Luke let Gwen pick the music, since she was still exploring what she liked. He provided suggestions periodically. Some she liked, and some she didn't, but it was a fun way to pass the time and continue their bonding on the hour-long drive to Hood River. He figured lunch at Pfriem with its view of the Columbia River and the Washington side of the gorge would be a fun choice, then they could take a walk around the small park on the Columbia before heading back to town.

Luke ran the speed up gradually, testing the engine and all the handling upgrades Jorge had made. The Volvo wagon had never handled better. He'd have to add a tip to the bill for the quality of Jorge's work. He'd find another time to really test out the engine, but he had a good idea of the car's new capabilities.

After lunch, they strolled along the edge of the Columbia, getting blown about by the stiff winds the Columbia Gorge was famous for, watching the wind surfers taking advantage of the lack of rain and surplus of wind. Luke was about to suggest a drive up through the orchards and a closer look at Mt Hood when he saw clouds darkening the western sky. Some more serious weather was rolling in off the Pacific, changing his mind. They'd make another trip out this way again later in the spring when they'd have safer weather.

When they pulled back onto I-84, Gwen paused the music. "So... Is Doctor Maggie a good kisser?"

Luke choked on the sparkling water he was drinking. Did

everyone wait until he had a mouthful of liquid to bust out the shockers? Once he'd gathered himself and stopped choking, he took a deep breath and a moment to ready an answer. "What do you mean?"

"I woke up and came downstairs and saw you on the porch last night."

"Oh." Luke's stomach dropped, shifting off his weight to take some pressure off his sore butt cheek. "About that…"

Gwen interrupted him. "I'm not a baby. I like Doctor Maggie, and you could use some good smooches."

"I could?" He looked at her out the corner of her eye, his eyebrow raised.

"Yeah."

He was saved from further exploring Gwen's opinions on his lack of a dating life by his phone exploding in vibrations. It sounded like multiple calls and texts coming in at once as the phone bounced around the little shelf on the center console.

"Well, hell. Wonder what that's about." He picked up the phone and opened it, handing it to Gwen. He figured it would be safe. He only texted with a few people, mostly innocuous stuff like meeting times and locations. "Check who's calling, then read me any texts."

"Um, looks like Pablo, Sam, and Delilah have all tried to call you. A couple voice mails are showing. All the texts look like basically the same message," Gwen replied.

"Pick one and read it to me, please."

"From Pablo, 'Luke, I think we may have a break in Cassius's location. Someone from one of the tracker teams thinks they saw him go into a house. They've been keeping an eye on it, and it doesn't look like he's come out yet. Delilah wants to go in tonight.'"

"Fuck. Text them that we're on the way back, about an hour out. Tell him to have everyone meet at my house in ninety minutes." Luke edged the gas pedal down, speeding back to Portland.

**To be continued in Dark Fangs Descending…**

**Keep reading for a brief excerpt.**

# LEAVE A REVIEW

Reviews are the lifeblood of every indie author. Even a simple star rating means the world to us. If you enjoyed this book, please leave an honest review at Goodreads, BookBub, or your preferred online book retailer.

Would you like to join other readers who enjoyed this book? Join my Facebook Reader Group!

facebook.com/groups/CThomasLafolletteReaderGroup

Thank you!

C. Thomas Lafollette

# LUKE IRONTREE WILL RETURN IN

## DARK FANGS DESCENDING

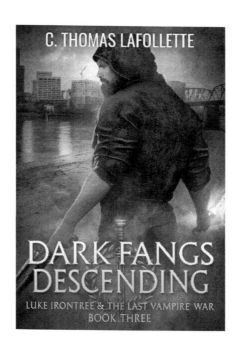

## DARK FANGS DESCENDING: BOOK THREE

NOTE: This is an unproofed sample.

### Chapter One

Luke concentrated on the road for a moment, not letting this thoughts wander to the news Gwen had just read to him. After a nice lunch with his ward, he was looking forward to some time at home so he could rest and relax. He'd hoped for a bit of respite after the weeks of near constant action and fighting—time to reset mentally and prepare for the next stage of their campaign against Cassius and his horde of vampires. Instead, annoyance and anxiety warred within him as he tried to focus on driving instead of planning his next campaign.

Luke looked into the rear view mirror at the preteen girl in the back seat of his old, black 1989 Volvo 240DL wagon. "Read the message to me again, please."

"'I think we found Cassius.'"

"Anything else?" Luke asked.

"Not on this message." She scrolled through the other messages that had come in at the same time as the other one. "Want me to read this one from Sam?"

"Yeah, pick whichever one has the most information."

"'One of people from the tracking teams thinks they saw Cassius last night. They've been staking out the area and don't think he's left yet. He wants to know what to do now that we're all back in town. What do you think?'" Gwen read.

Luke looked at the radio to see what time it was. It wasn't too long until dark, and they still had to stop and pick up Alfred from the pet hotel. They were about forty-five minutes from his house.

"Gwen, can you text Sam back? Tell her to gather Pablo, Delilah, and Pieter at my house in ninety minutes. See if they can get some extra shotgun shells."

"OK." Gwen typed the message and sent it. "She says, 'Okie dokie.'"

"Alright, let's go pick up Alfred then." Luke sighed.

"How are you doing, Luke?"

"Fine, I guess. I was just hoping for some time to rest. Well, maybe later. I need some music, I think. Mind picking something?" The kid was entirely too perceptive and probably had guess he wasn't actually fine as he tried to compartmentalize his feelings until he had time and space to examine them.

"Can do." She set Luke's phone on the seat beside her and took out her phone.

He wasn't paying attention to whatever Gwen had picked until the eerie vibe, heavy tones, and aggressive female vocals pulled him back into the moment. "This is good, what is it?"

Gwen looked at her screen. "It's called 'Like Blood.'"

"What's the band?"

"Kitchen Witch."

"I like it. Where'd you find them?"

"Um, they were on a playlist I was checking out, and I liked them so I saved them to my list."

The song ended, advancing to the next.

"Can you play that again? I wasn't paying attention for the first part."

Gwen complied. Soon, the witchy sounds of the song had them both bobbing their heads as they cruised down I-84. When the song ended, Luke had her find the album to listen to, the metal band matching his mood. The album lasted them until pulled off the freeway to pick up Alfred at the pet hotel. Gwen, enjoying the band as much as Luke, put on another of their EPs.

When they stopped at the hotel, Alfred was sitting on the counter like he owned the place. The person behind the counter stood up when they walked through the door. Alfred meowed when he saw them, hopping down to greet Gwen.

"I'm here to pick up this guy." Luke bent over and scratched Alfie behind the ears as he purred.

"Sorry, we had him out. Everyone here loves him so much. He's kind of the boss around here," the woman replied.

Luke chuckled. "That sounds like Alfie. Can you please grab his carrier?"

"Sure thing." The clerk got up and walked into the back room, reemerging a minute later with a large pet carrier.

She handed it to Luke. Setting it on the ground tipped up on its back so the opening faced up, Luke scooped up Alfred, grabbing his back legs and tail in one hand, and dropped him into the carrier butt first, closing the door as the cat's head disappeared inside. When he stood back up, the clerk had his paperwork ready.

"Looks like you're all paid up. We'll see you next time!"

Luke nodded. "Thanks!"

Gwen held the door for Luke as he exited.

"Bye, Alfred," the attendant called just before the door shut behind them.

#

When Luke and Gwen got home, Sam, Delilah, and Pablo were already parked out front, lined down the street, waiting. As soon as Luke pulled into the driveway, they got out of their vehicles and stood by the door. A smile tugged at the corner of his lips at the sight of his friends, even though he'd seen them only hours earlier. It had been too long since he'd had people in his life that he cared about this much. That was a different time and place.

Luke, finding his house key, said, "Hmm, I should probably get a few spare key made for you all so you don't have to wait outside. Where's Pieter?"

"We'll pick him up on the way from the pack guest house." Pablo patted Luke on the back. "How was the drive in your fancy car?"

"Excellent! I can't wait to see what it can really do. So far it responds nicely."

After the door closed, Luke set down Alfie's carrier and let the giant orange tabby out. The team followed Luke into the living room and grabbed a seat.

"I need to send a quick message." Luke pulled out his phone. *Hey, Maggie. I hate to impose on you, but can you watch Gwen tonight? We may have found Cassius, and everyone wants to take the shot.*

He walked into the kitchen to grab a sparkling water for Gwen and himself; no one else wanted anything. When his phone vibrated in his pocket, he pulled it out.

*Sure. Mind if she stays here though?*

Luke found Gwen sitting in a chair along the wall. "Gwen, I'm going to have Maggie watch you tonight, do you mind if I drop you off there?"

Gwen crossed her arms. "I guess so. Can't she come here?"

"I think she would like to spend some time with her partner. I'm sure they're very nice." He looked down as his phone vibrated again.

*There are fresh baked chocolate chip cookies.*

"Maggie says there are fresh cookies." Luke tipped his head to the side and raised his eyebrows.

Gwen looked uncertain. She liked Maggie, but had never met her partner and was still wary of werewolves other than the few she'd accepted. Of course, Luke didn't even know if Maggie's partner was a wolf. He'd been told there were a lot of human members in the pack, partners and other family members.

Gwen narrowed her eyes. "Well, if there are cookies…"

*I'll drop her off shortly, but Gwen has made it clear this is conditional on the cookies. I think she's nervous about meeting someone new.*

*I'm sure she'll love my partner. They're very sweet and make the best cookies. We'll make her dinner and watch a movie or two,* Maggie texted back.

*Thanks. What's your address?*

"Hey, Luke, what's got you smiling like that?" Delilah asked.

"What? I'm just making arrangements." He hadn't realized he was smiling.

When he looked around the room, Gwen was snickering but trying to hide it. Sam looked as serene as ever while Pablo had both of his lips pulled in between his teeth as he forced himself to keep something in, probably laughter or jokes knowing Pablo.

Luke chose to ignore the question for the moment. "Any updates since the first flurry of messages?"

Sam raised her hand. "I sent out another of one of our sweepers to relieve Joe; he's been there since last night. So far no changes. No vehicles have pulled up and no one has left, vampire or thrall. I did have a thought, though. Or rather a question. Is it really Cassius?"

"What do you mean?" Luke asked, narrowing his eyes.

"When we left him, he was motoring away in the Coast Guard life boat."

"Well, they're not fast, but if he headed straight for Astoria, he probably could have beat us in. We were going pretty slow to conserve fuel and had to go further south. They had a straight line back into the Columbia. Also, we spent time out at the farm." Delilah looked like she was about to say something before Luke continued, "Besides, it's too good of an opportunity to pass up. At worst, we'll root out another nest. But, if it is him, this is the break we need. I'm not saying killing Cassius is going to solve all our vampire problems, but it'll buy us some breathing room."

Luke took a drink from the can of sparkling water. "There's definitely something bigger going on. We got hints of that last fall on the St. Johns Bridge. That bearded man who took Cassius's body is still out there and probably calling the shots. And now we have to worry about Commissioner Bealer and his connection to the vampires and the upcoming mayoral race."

"Could it be a trap?" Pablo shifted nervously. "I'm not in the mood to get blown up again."

"We'll have to be wary of that," Luke said. "But if I sense vampires there, then it's unlikely to be explosives. We should see if there's anyone else available to back us up in case they're got a gang of vamps ready to stomp us.

"All good points," Pablo conceded. "What's the plan?"

"Put out the word for volunteers. I don't want to force anyone else into duty after everything we've been through the last several weeks. We'll even take some non-trained people from the sign up list. All they'll need to do is sit back and keep an eye on various escape routes, nothing dangerous."

"Right, can I borrow your laptop so I can access my lists easier?" Sam asked, her tone shifting to "business Sam."

Luke looked at Gwen. "Could you grab my laptop out of the office, please? And when you're done, you'll probably want a fresh change of clothes and your overnight bag."

Gwen nodded and walked toward the office. While Gwen

fetched the computer, Luke cast a quick glance toward Delilah. Her face was a riot of emotions as she tried to force her face into a calm, cool expression, failing repeatedly as anger and worry fought for dominance when she lost control.

Pablo stood up and went to the kitchen, opening the fridge, returning with a bottle of beer. "Figured if we're going to be planning for a bit, I've got time for one." He took a sip before continuing, "I put the word out to have everyone drop their guns and excess shells at the pack guest house with Pieter. I'm not sure who all is back in town yet. Some people took the opportunity to take some time off at the coast since everyone was already there."

Luke nodded, his anxiety rising. He'd settle in when the got closer to action, as he always did, but right now, the what ifs were making their presence known. "That's good. We have enough M12s since we all threw ours in your pickup, but we'll need more shells. Our supply was looking pretty thin when we loaded up."

Pablo, shifting in his seat, pulled out his phone. "Well, Archie wants to know if he can help out."

"Yeah, tell him we could use him. I'd like more people when we go in. Have him meet us at the pack guest house." Luke dropped into an arm chair.

Delilah cleared her throat. "So, we just gonna carry shotguns down a street out in the open?"

Sam, looking up from Luke's laptop with a furrowed brow, added, "Yeah, that might not be the best idea. The whole city is hyper vigilant after two buildings blew up downtown. We'd have the police called on us super fast."

"They're already in the duffel bags we used to haul them up to the freighter. It's just luggage, so we'll look natural enough," Pablo said, shrugging before taking another drink of beer.

"I guess I didn't think of that," Delilah replied, crossing her legs, then uncrossing them and adjusting in her seat.

They sat quietly, the nervous energy in the room palpable, while Sam worked her text and email chains.

Closing Luke's laptop, Sam stood up. "OK. That's done, we'll see who can help. I'm going to use the restroom."

"Alright, when you're done there, I want to head over to the pack guest house so we can get prepped, plus I need to drop Gwen off at Maggie's," Luke said.

Satisfied they'd accomplished everything they could at Luke's, Luke, Gwen, and Sam—volunteering to direct him to Maggie's house—got into Luke's Volvo while Delilah went with Pablo. When they parked on the street outside Maggie's bungalow-style house, Pablo parked behind him.

Luke knew Gwen was nervous about meeting someone new, but now that it was time to meet Maggie's partner, his own nerves kicked in. It wasn't the first time he'd been involved with someone involved with someone else, nor was it the first time he'd met the other person, but that was a long time ago and a lot had changed in the world, not least of which included Luke. Trust Maggie. That had become his motto the last couple of days in regards to all that had changed.

He hadn't expected to meet Maggie's partner this soon in...whatever it was they had. It was too early to call it anything other than an attractive woman woman he liked had invited him to her bed and that she wanted to see him again in an intimate manner. Oh well, it was too late to do anything about it now.

He pushed the doorbell. A few moments later, a short person, maybe five-two, of south Asian heritage with dark brown skin opened the door. They had one of the sides and the back of their head shaved with the hair on top long and swept to the side, landing at the top of their shoulder.

"Ah, hello. You must be Luke and Gwen. Come in, Magdalena will be down in a moment," they said through a mild London accent. "I'm Zel, by the way."

Luke extended his hand, and Zel took it, shaking it. "It's nice to meet you, Zel. Thanks for letting me impose on you, but it's kind of an emergency."

Zel smiled warmly. "No worries. I've been wanting to meet you and Gwen. We'll take good care of her. I've made up the spare bedroom for her, plus I have warm cookies in the kitchen."

Gwen perked up at the word cookies, sniffing deeper looking for the telltale cookie smell. She was standing a little behind Luke and to the side, the place she usually stood when she was nervous—close to Luke for protection but curious enough to not hide entirely behind him.

Luke's gaze drifted up to the stairs when he heard footsteps coming down. His face split into a smile when Maggie came into view. The blond Polish doctor had her hair pulled back in a ponytail. The black yoga pants she wore highlighted her curvy hips. She rounded out her comfy look with a baggy sweatshirt. When she saw Gwen and Luke, she smiled and walked over, hugging Gwen then Luke.

"Come on, Gwen. Let's go see about those cookies." Zel gestured toward the back of the house with their head. "Luke, it was very nice to meet you. Good luck tonight."

"Thanks, Zel. It was good meeting you too." Luke smiled and nodded at Maggie's partner. He hugged Gwen then guided her after Zel.

When they disappeared through the door leading to what Luke assumed was the kitchen, he was left alone with Maggie. Not sure what to do, he put his hands in his jean pockets. "You have a very nice home, Maggie."

"Thanks." She stepped forward and pulled Luke into a more intimate hug.

He responded stiffly until her warmth and pleasant scent won over his nervousness and he loosened up, sinking into her arms.

Maggie pulled back, holding him at arm's length. "A little nervous?"

He chuckled. "Yeah. This is all…new."

She smiled at him and rubbed his arm. "Can I get you anything?"

"No, I should get going. We're meeting up with Pieter before heading out and still need to check that all the shotguns are ready."

"OK, I'll walk you out." She held the door for him and followed him out onto her porch. "Luke?"

"Yes?"

Maggie stepped into him, wrapping her arms around him and looking up at him. He looked deep into her blue eyes, the world around them disappearing and narrowing to just them. When she tipped her lips up toward him, he responded. The gentle and lingering kiss caused his heart rate to spike as warmth spread over his body. When they parted, she ran her hand along his cheek.

"Good luck, Luke."

"Thank you, Maggie."

She let him go with a final squeeze of his hand. He watched Maggie walk back into her house and shut the door before turning around. When he saw three sets of eyes staring back at him from his car and Pablo's truck, he froze, nearly missing his step. He caught himself, stumbling down the steps to the sidewalk. Pablo grinned from ear to ear. Sam looked amused. He wasn't sure about the look on Delilah's face. He sighed. At least he'd have a few minutes to get himself together before Delilah interrogated him. On the positive side, it distracted him from his thoughts about the upcoming mission.

When he got back into his Volvo, Sam looked over and patted his knee. "Good for you two. I knew she was interested in you. I'm glad she did something about it."

"Um, thanks. How do you know it wasn't me who did something?"

Sam stared him, one eyebrow rising. "Luke. Come on. It's you."

Luke sighed, shaking his head as he put the car in drive and pulled out onto the street. "You're right."

"She wasn't terribly subtle about it, at least around the people who know her best."

Once they got to the guest house, Pablo let them in, punching in the code to the lock. Delilah kept flicking her eyes toward Luke, curiosity mixing in with the other array of emotions that had been playing across her face all evening.

As soon as they closed the door, she grabbed the chair next to his as they pulled off their shoes. "Soooo, Luke." She drew out the syllables of his name as well. "What's going on with you and Maggie?"

"Um, I'm not sure." He knew the answer sounded pathetic as soon as it left his mouth, but it was mostly true. It had been just twenty four hours.

"That kiss looked pretty serious for 'not sure.'"

Pablo laughed nearby.

"You hush, Pablo," Luke said, causing Pablo to laugh harder.

"Are you two seeing each other?" Delilah leaned away from him so she could properly stare at him.

"I don't know, I guess?" Luke, already discombobulated, was growing increasingly uncomfortable under Delilah's scrutiny.

"When did this happen?" Delilah asked.

"At the farm," Luke mumbled, looking down at the floor.

Delilah's eyebrows shot up. "That was yesterday. I was there."

"But you weren't paying attention," Pablo chimed in.

"Hush, wolfboy!" Delilah extended her hand toward Pablo and brought her fingers to her thumb in the "close your lips" gesture.

Luke, pulling off his second boot and setting it down, stood up. "Delilah. It's new and confusing and that's probably about all the answer I have for you." He walked into the other room, leaning up against the wall out of eyesight but still within earshot.

"I didn't mean to upset him," Delilah said to no one specific.

"I don't think you really upset him," Sam said, her voice calm and filled with kind understanding. "I think he's sincere when he says he doesn't know and that it's confusing for him."

Delilah sighed. "Yeah, I shouldn't have grilled him so hard. Well, I'm glad someone took pity on him."

Luke's stomach dropped, the comment cutting him deeper than he thought it would have.

"Hey," Pablo said, sounding indigent.

"Pablo." Sam put her hand on Pablo's arm to forestall him. "Delilah, that was uncharitable of you. Luke is a sweet man and handsome. It's perfectly understandable that Maggie would find him attractive and want to do something about it."

Delilah sighed, straightening her back and rolling her head round to loosen up her neck. "You're right. That was not cool. I'm just so fucking keyed up about tonight. I let my anxiety get the better of me." She turned her head toward the doorway Luke had walked through. "Luke?"

"Yeah?" It felt weird to hear them talking about him so openly, but the pack was more open than he was. He didn't dislike it. It felt good to be cared about, even if it was awkward for him.

"I'm sorry. That was rude," Delilah said.

He popped his head back through the door. "That's OK. It's all...new."

"Speaking of kissing pretty werewolves, Rosa OK with canceling your date after not seeing you for weeks?" Sam asked.

Delilah's face slipped into a neutral expression. "Yeah. She understands."

Sam nodded. Delilah finished pulling her boots off and followed Luke through the door to the back end of the house. When she saw him leaning against a wall, she smiled softly, her expression losing some of its hard edges. She offered a hug.

Stepping away from the wall, Luke hugged her. He needed to get his emotions under control before they went into action, but he was finding it hard to manage with so much happening. Dating and having friends who cared about his well-being were all new and added on top of their impending confrontation with his ancient and former friend Cassius, created a maelstrom of feelings Luke was struggling to manage.

Delilah sighed, shaking her head. "Luke. I'm sorry." She swallowed and looked down. "I'm just... I'm so fucking angry all the time." She looked up and into Luke's eyes, a note of pleading in her dark brown eyes. "All I can think about is killing that piece of shit." Breathing deeply, she shifted on her feet anxiously. "I shouldn't take it out on my friends."

Luke nodded wobbly. "I know, Delilah. I know. Cassius is like a piece of unfinished business niggling at the front of my mind incessantly." He ran a hand through his hair. "Gods, I wish he'd stayed dead. At least then he was a memory of a friend, not a monster who orchestrates the killing of innocents. I need to put him down just as much as you. We'll do this."

Delilah clenched her jaw and exhaled sharply through her nostrils. "We'll do this."

Squeezing her shoulder, he turned to face Sam and Pablo. "Ready to go find Pieter?"

They found Pieter, the son of Belgium's packleader, in the basement, hunched over a table full of shotguns. The tall, trim man was dressed down in a pair of jeans and a tight fitting black t-shirt. He was inspecting them all, ensuring everything was clean and in working order, a pile of ammo boxes stacked to one side. Sam and Pablo joined them all a minute later.

"How's everything looking, Pieter?" Luke asked.

"Pretty good. We're only down one shotgun. We'll need to get some parts for it. How many will we need tonight?"

"Just the hit team will need them. So us five and one for Archie." Luke picked up a gun, inspecting it.

Pieter looked up from the shotgun he was cleaning. "Six people enough?"

"Yeah, too many in the tight confines of a house would be almost more dangerous than too few. Plus, we don't have many trained assets available right now. People are taking time off after the freighter. We weren't expecting to go back into action immediately. We've got some volunteers to stake out escape routes for non-engagement and following, but the six of us will have to do."

Pieter held his gaze for a moment then nodded, returning to his work on the shotgun. Luke's team was confident in their leader, but he was still unsure of what waited for them. He hoped the severe blow they'd dealt Cassius on the freighter would keep him from preparing a response this quickly. Once they got there, they'd make a final check in with the packmembers watching the house before making a final decision.

**Get Dark Fangs Descending Now!**
**Available May 17, 2022**

# NEWSLETTER

The Centurion Immortal is a Luke Irontree prequel novella and is exclusive to the Dispatches from C. Thomas Lafollette newsletter. Please sign up for your free copy and you'll also receive a twice-monthly newsletter with news, book updates, recipes, drinks tips, and other fun stuff. Your email will never be given out, rented, or sold.

CThomasLafollette.com/newsletter/

# ACKNOWLEDGMENTS

I'd like to thank all the people who made this book possible.

Suzanne, your editorial eye has made this book and series infinitely better. Your belief in my vision for these characters has made this a kick ass team effort.

Ravven, your covers are amazing and really capture the essence of Luke and his world.

Amy, you're my alpha reader and my line editor. These books wouldn't be possible without you.

Doochie, you've been my earliest reader and a great hype man as well as a wonderful friend.

To my critique group, you've only gotten to see the first few chapters late in the process, but you've had a truly positive impact on making the opening chapters so much better. I look forward to sharing the rest of this series with you as we go.

# ABOUT THE AUTHOR

C. Thomas Lafollette is a writer of Urban Fantasy and Historical Fantasy and is the author of the forthcoming Luke Irontree novels. He earned a degree in Ancient History with a specialization in Classics at The College of Idaho. He's read poetry on stage with Yevgeny Yevtushenko* and dined with the Belgian Prime Minister**. C. Thomas has lived in Portland, Oregon for over Twenty years. He lives with his wife, fellow author Amy Cissell, his stepdaughter, and his three jerkface cats. He and Amy also run their own freelance editing business - Cissell Ink

*Yevtushenko was friends with a professor at C. Thomas's college. He was studying Russian at the time and Yevtushenko decided he wanted the Russian students to read with him on stage at his performance.

**This was purely coincidental. C. Thomas's host took him to dinner at a restaurant in Mons, which was Elio De Rupo's favorite spot. He'd had a pie thrown at him earlier that day and was having dinner with some friends. C. Thomas is still not sure what kind of pie it was though.

twitter.com/CTLafollette

facebook.com/CThomasLafollette

tiktok.com/@cthomaslafollette

instagram.com/CThomasLafollette

bookbub.com/authors/c-thomas-lafollette

amazon.com/C-Thomas-Lafollette/e/B09JMTR7W7

goodreads.com/cthomaslafollette

# ALSO BY C. THOMAS LAFOLLETTE

**Luke Irontree & The Last Vampire War**

Book 0 - The Centurion Immortal

Book 1 - Dark Fangs Rising - March 22, 2022

Book 2 - Dark Fangs Raging - April 19, 2022

Book 3 - Dark Fangs Descending* - May 17, 2022

Book 4 - Blood Empire Reborn* - July 12, 2022

Book 5 - Blood Empire Avenged* - August 9, 2022

Book 6 - Blood Empire Burning* - September 6, 2022

Book 7 - Blood Empire Collapsing* - October 4, 2022

Book 8 - Ancient Sword Falling* - November 29, 2022

Book 9 - Ancient Sword Unyielding* - December 27, 2022

Book 10 - Ancient Sword Shattering* - February 7, 2023

**The Luke Irontree Historical Adventures**

Rise of the Centurio Immortalis - April 5, 2022

Fall of the Centurio Immortalis* - May 31, 2022

The Moonlight Centurion* - November 1, 2022

The Highway Centurion* - January 24, 2023

*Forthcoming

Made in the USA
Columbia, SC
20 October 2023

24742173R00209